Cuddling
a dreamspinner press anthology

Published by
Dreamspinner Press
5032 Capital Circle SW
Ste 2, PMB# 279
Tallahassee, FL 32305-7886 USA
http://www.dreamspinnerpress.com/

This is a work of fiction. Names, characters, places and incidents either are the product of the authors' imagination or are used fictitiously, and any resemblance to actual persons, living or dead, business establishments, events or locales is entirely coincidental.

Edited by Anne Regan

Reboot Copyright © 2013 by S. H. Allan
Happy Holidays Copyright © 2013 by Anna Butler
Remember When Copyright © 2013 by River Clair
The Responsible One Copyright © 2013 by Eva Clancy
The Thing I Love Best About Mitch Copyright © 2013 by Dawn Douglas
Like an Old Sweater Copyright © 2013 by Elizabella Gold
Dream Lover Copyright © 2013 by Audrey Jeung
Change of Heart Copyright © 2013 by Rhidian Brenig Jones
Cupcakes for Two Copyright © 2013 by K. Lynn
Home on the Range Copyright © 2013 by Anna Martin
The Cat's Out of the Bag Copyright © 2013 by Rowan McAllister
Quarter Moon Over a Ten-Cent Town Copyright © 2013 by Stephen Osborne
The Making of a Family Copyright © 2013 by Caitlin Ricci
Looking Back Copyright © 2013 by Rob Rosen
How to Date Your Husband Copyright © 2013 by AC Valentine
At First Sound Copyright © 2013 by G.S. Wiley

Cover Art by Michael Breyette
http://www.breyette.com

Cover content is being used for illustrative purposes only
and any person depicted on the cover is a model.

All rights reserved. No part of this book may be reproduced or transmitted in any form or by any means, electronic or mechanical, including photocopying, recording, or by any information storage and retrieval system without the written permission of the Publisher, except where permitted by law. To request permission and all other inquiries, contact Dreamspinner Press at: 5032 Capital Circle SW Ste 2, PMB# 279 Tallahassee, FL 32305-7886 USA
http://www.dreamspinnerpress.com/

ISBN: 978-1-62380-651-4

Printed in the United States of America
First Edition
August 2013

eBook edition available
eBook ISBN: 978-1-62380-652-1

Table of Contents

Cupcakes for Two by K. Lynn 5
At First Sound by G.S. Wiley 16
Dream Lover by Nico Jaye 39
Happy Holidays by Anna Butler 59
The Responsible One by Eva Clancy 76
Home on the Range by Anna Martin..102
The Cat's Out of the Bag by Rowan McAllister 118
Like an Old Sweater by Elizabella Gold 138
Change of Heart by Rhidian Brenig Jones 161
The Thing I Love Best About Mitch by Dawn Douglas 183
Looking Back by Rob Rosen...196
Quarter Moon Over a Ten-Cent Town by Stephen Osborne.................206
Reboot by S. H. Allan..228
The Making of a Family by Caitlin Ricci...254
Remember When by River Clair 266
How to Date Your Husband by AC Valentine 284

Cupcakes for Two

K. Lynn

"Yes, Mom, I made it just like you told me to," Jacob said, cradling the phone against his shoulder as he stirred the mashed potatoes. "They taste fine."

"I'm just making sure," his mother said. "Just because you've been at college for four years doesn't mean I can't still teach you some things."

"They taste just like yours," Jacob said, but when his mother's huff came across the line, he revised his statement. "Okay, well, not exactly like yours, but close enough." Jacob heard rattling at the door, signaling the return of his boyfriend. He replaced the lid on the pot so the mashed potatoes would stay warm. "I've got to go. Matt's home."

"Okay, sweetheart. You two have fun tonight, and call me when you can."

"Love you," he said before hanging up the phone.

"Cheating on me already?" Matt asked, a smile on his face as he set the pastry box down on the counter. "I've only been gone three hours."

"Gotta be fast if you want to keep me," Jacob teased back, leaning over to give Matt a kiss. "How was your exam?"

Matt sighed, leaning his hip against the counter. "I've changed my mind. I don't want to be an engineer anymore."

Jacob gave a short laugh. "I think it's a little too late for that, considering we're in our senior year." His boyfriend groaned at the reminder. "Anyway, what would you do instead?"

"I don't know. Maybe I can be your kept boy," Matt said. "Make sure the house is neat and tidy when you come home from a hard day's work."

"Hate to break it to you, but I doubt a teacher's salary is going to keep us going for long. Besides, I bet you did fine."

"Dr. Baldwin has it in for our whole class. I'd be surprised if anyone passed."

"Then he'll grade on a curve," Jacob said, adjusting the temperature of the oven. "Don't even worry about it anymore tonight."

"Yeah, I guess," Matt said, though he didn't sound convinced.

"What'd you bring us?" Jacob asked, starting toward the pastry box, but Matt blocked his way.

"Uh-uh, no peeking. It's a surprise for after dinner." He picked up the box, holding it above Jacob's head as he moved around him and over to the high cabinet in the corner. It was the only one Jacob couldn't reach without Matt's help.

"Seriously?"

"Hey, not my fault you're a shortie," Matt said.

Jacob crossed his arms over his chest. "Keep on. See how you like it when I lock you out of the apartment next time you go for a run. I bet you won't be laughing then."

"Aw," Matt said, closing the gap between them. "Don't be like that. Besides, what's an anniversary without some surprises thrown in?"

"Boring? When has that ever described our lives?"

Nearing the stove, Matt sniffed the air. His eyes lit up, and a smile crossed his face as the tasty smell reached him. "Is that Mama Nelson's mashed potatoes?"

Jacob nodded, lifting the lid so Matt could have a good look. "That's who was on the phone. She wanted to make sure I did it right," he said, replacing the lid again.

"That's because I'm her favorite," Matt teased. "Though she still won't give me the recipe."

"I already told you, it's a secret. The only way you're getting it is if you marry into the family."

Matt seemed to pause at that, his face going blank for a second, but then the happy appearance once again returned. "What else are you making?" He cracked open the oven door to take a peek, slamming it shut again so the heat wouldn't escape. Matt looked over to Jacob, his eyes widening. "Seasoned steak?"

"And green beans, keeping warm in the microwave," Jacob said, taking the dish out to sit on the stovetop.

"It's like you love me or something," Matt said, pressing himself against Jacob's back and sliding his arms around Jacob's stomach to give him a squeeze.

"Or something," Jacob teased, patting Matt's hands. "Can you go pour us some wine? I'll get the plates fixed."

"Sure," Matt said, giving one last squeeze before releasing his hold on Jacob. He moved over to their wine rack, taking a moment to look through the choices before grabbing a bottle. "Your mom have any news from the home front?"

"She said that Cassie's going to give her a heart attack before the year's out," Jacob said, grabbing two plates out of the cabinet. "Mom refuses to go driving with her anymore. She's started making Dad do it."

"Your sister still hasn't learned the use of her brakes, I'm guessing."

"Not yet," Jacob laughed. "Though she kind of reminds me of you when we were learning to drive."

"I beg your pardon," Matt said, sounding offended as he clutched the bottle of wine against his chest. "I was a perfect driver, and you know it."

"So it was someone else who drove his truck into the ditch three times before he got his license?"

"That damn ditch had it out for me," Matt grumbled, getting two wineglasses out of the cabinet beside Jacob.

"Yes, such an evil thing," Jacob teased, giving Matt a wink as he hip-checked his boyfriend. "Oh, and your mom wants us to call her soon because"—he changed his voice, trying to give a perfect imitation of Matt's mother—"just because you're in college doesn't mean I shouldn't get a call more than once a week." Jacob cleared his throat, returning his voice back to its natural register. "My mom agrees with her."

"Of course she does. They've always been in cahoots." Matt laughed as he exited the kitchen and headed toward the table to fill their wineglasses.

"Speaking of being in cahoots," Jacob said, following after him with now full plates, "Vivian and Derek caught up with me after class today."

"Oh yeah?" Matt asked, trading Jacob's wineglass for a plate before he went to sit down. "What'd they want?"

"Besides to harass me about the fact we haven't hung out with them in over a week?" Jacob asked, grinning as he took his own seat. "Just wanted to make sure we were still coming up to the cabin with them after exams were over. They promised to give us the big bedroom this time."

"Good. The bunk beds last year were not funny at all."

"Aw, come on," Jacob teased. "It was like Camp Dixon all over again. Sneaking into each other's beds and trying not to get caught."

Matt raised an eyebrow at him. "Yeah, but we were doing a whole lot more than reading comic books under the sheets at Derek's cabin."

"That we were." Jacob laughed, taking a sip of his wine before cutting into his steak. "I'm more than ready to get away for a few days."

"College life not all it's lived up to be, huh?" Matt asked, sounding sympathetic.

"Less late-night parties, more late-night lesson plans. And it's just the beginning." Jacob sighed. "I think that's why Vivian and Derek were so insistent that we tag along. It'll be the last time we get to spend any real time together. After we get back, it's final projects and getting ready for graduation, then they're heading out not long after."

"I can't believe they're moving across the country," Matt said, a frown crossing his face as he took a bite of green beans, swallowing before he continued. "I mean, it's awesome that he got the job with Hanson's, but we're never going to get to see them."

"Just gotta make the time. We can fly out there sometime, or they can come visit when they're home to visit their folks."

"Yeah, I guess," Matt said, though he didn't sound convinced. "I just hate feeling like we're counting down to the end. Last visit to the cabin, last end-of-midterms party, last time for a lot of things."

"Hey," Jacob said, reaching out to squeeze Matt's hand. "Nobody should be that sad eating my mom's potatoes."

Matt huffed a quick laugh, the corner of his mouth going up. "True. She'd beat me if she knew I wasn't fully appreciating your fine culinary skills."

"Exactly," Jacob said, releasing his hold to return to his own meal. "Lavish me with the praise I deserve."

"Like I don't do that already," Matt teased, taking a bite of his steak. He moaned in pleasure. "Seriously, why don't you make this more often?"

"Because it wouldn't be a special treat if I cooked it every week," Jacob said, giving him a soft smile. "But tonight deserved to be special."

"Five years together," Matt said, looking lost in thought.

"Or fifteen to be technical, though you were oblivious to my natural charms for a while there."

"We went from Hot Wheels to hormones. It was a little bit of a jumbled mess."

"Didn't help that I was falling in love with my best friend either," Jacob said, sounding sad. "Not that you knew it."

"Yeah, well, I was always a little bit blind to what was right in front of me," Matt said, giving Jacob a comforting smile. "But eventually I figured it out and figured myself out too."

"That's what matters."

Matt's expression sobered a little. "Do you realize that August will be the first time I'm going to be in school without you?"

"Well, you're the one who wanted to go to grad school. I can't help it if I'm ready for the real world and you still want to hide out in the library," Jacob teased. "Then again, I always was the mature one."

"Right," Matt scoffed. "I'll remember that when you come home crying your first day because the kids decided to attack you."

"Don't jinx it. I already have nightmares of a minimutiny."

"It's going to be weird not getting to see each other during the day. No more lunchtimes together."

"Can't steal my peanut-butter-and-jelly sandwiches anymore." Jacob winked at him. "But it'll be okay. We're just gonna have to make the time we have together count. I even promise to help you with your homework if you're a good boy."

"I'm always a good boy. My momma says so."

"Hate to break it to you, but sometimes she lies."

"Those are fighting words," Matt said, pretending he was taking offense. "Why do I love you again?"

"Because I'm the only guy who would put up with you," Jacob joked back. "And I can cook."

"Hmm, true," Matt said, seeming to take that under consideration. "Okay, I guess you can be forgiven."

"You're too kind," Jacob said, taking the last swallow of his wine. He nodded to Matt's plate, now empty of most of his meal. "How'd you like your dinner?"

Matt seemed to come out of a daze, looking at his plate as if he was seeing it for the first time. "Oh," he said, his face coloring a bit. "I guess I liked it a lot." Matt glanced at Jacob's plate as well, which was also cleared of food. "Thanks."

"You're welcome." Jacob leaned forward, grabbing the bottle of wine to refill his glass. "So, you gonna let me see what you've got hiding in the cabinet now?"

"Ah!" Matt jumped from his seat, grabbing his plate along with Jacob's. "Yeah, just a minute. Don't move."

Jacob wrinkled his forehead in confusion as he watched his boyfriend rush through the kitchen door. He tended to joke that Matt was addicted to sugar, but this was a bit weird even for him. "What's up with you tonight?" Jacob called out when he heard some shuffling in the kitchen. When no answer came and then there was just silence, Jacob began to worry. "You okay in there?"

It took a few seconds, but Matt finally appeared in the doorway, holding the pastry box close to his chest. "Yeah, fine, nothing to worry about with me." The nervousness in his voice contradicted his words.

"Really? Because you're acting like I dosed your food or something." He reached out a hand toward the box Matt had set on the table. "Or maybe you're just wanting to get wasted on sugar, huh?"

Matt grabbed for the box, pulling it close to him and out of Jacob's reach. "Wait, not yet."

Jacob leaned back in his chair, his confusion increasing. "Okay, seriously, what's going on?"

"Give me a minute," Matt said, taking in a deep breath, then another, as if he was trying to steady his nerves. His eyes were focused on the box instead of Jacob as he started talking. "You remember the first time we met?"

Jacob had no idea where Matt was going with this, but he answered anyway. "Uh, yeah? It was lunchtime, and your table was the only one with an empty seat."

Matt looked up at him then, a smile slowly edging onto his face. "You were the new kid in second grade, and everyone was curious about you."

"And I was scared to death because no one would really talk to me," Jacob said, remembering that day fondly. "They'd keep looking at me and then turning away to whisper. It was a lot for a seven-year-old to handle."

"But I never had that problem."

Jacob laughed. "No, you looked right at me and said, 'You talk funny, but I think we should be friends. Want a cupcake?'"

"And we were best friends ever since," Matt said, his voice faltering a little. "Thank goodness Momma packed me a second dessert that day."

Jacob scoffed at that. "Are you saying you wouldn't have been my friend if you didn't have an extra?"

"Hey, you know how much I loved the cupcakes from Walton's," Matt said, his tone teasing. "I'm just saying it made the choice easier."

"I do know. You were the only kid I knew who refused to have a birthday cake but insisted on birthday cupcakes every year."

"And I was devastated when Walton's closed up shop," Matt said, pressing his fingers tighter on the edges of the pastry box. "Your parents let you stay over all weekend to keep me distracted."

"They loved you like you were their own kid," Jacob said, giving an encouraging smile to his boyfriend. "They still do."

"It's always been that way with the two of us, huh? I got a best friend and an extended family to go along with it."

"Exactly. And it didn't matter whose house we ended up at, we knew we'd be welcome."

"Our moms in the kitchen baking shared Sunday dinner," Matt said, recalling their youths, "and our dads out playing touch football with us until they called us in."

"Best friends forever," Jacob said, nodding.

"I was so scared that it would all go wrong when my feelings changed. Almost lost you before all that anyway."

"Hey." Jacob leaned forward, wanting to reach out and grab Matt's hand for reassurance, but the other man wouldn't let go of the box he was holding. "You think I wasn't scared too? I fell in love with my best friend and couldn't tell him. It tore me up inside. That's why I tried to keep it a secret."

"Didn't really work out that well," Matt said, giving a slight grin, though his eyes looked sad. "We pulled away from each other, and I got angry. You could have said a million things that night, walked out of my life forever, but instead you kissed me."

Jacob laughed. "I'd never seen you speechless before. If I knew that was the way to shut you up, maybe I would have done it sooner."

"Yeah, you always did play dirty," Matt said, seeming happier than before. He took a deep breath, looking down at the pastry box. "Maybe it's time I evened the score a little."

Jacob wrinkled his forehead in confusion. "What?"

"So, Walton's isn't around anymore, but that bakery on Vine makes pretty good desserts." Matt pushed the box toward Jacob. "Happy anniversary."

Jacob felt a rush of joy, thinking of how much of a sap his boyfriend was. "Really? You got us cupcakes to celebrate?" he asked, running his finger around the edge of the box.

Flipping open the lid, he saw that there were two huge cupcakes inside, both decorated with layers of blue frosting reminiscent of the ones Matt had shared all those years ago. But the designs weren't what caught his eye. Sitting atop the mound of sugary blue was a gold band, one on each cupcake, like they were just another decoration the bakery added.

"What…?" Jacob began, unable to find the words. He looked up, expecting to see Matt across the table from him, but instead his boyfriend was now kneeling beside Jacob's chair. His eyes widened at the sight.

"You've been my best friend for fifteen years," Matt began, his voice a bit shaky as he looked up at Jacob. "We've grown up and faced every one of life's challenges together."

"And been stronger because of it," Jacob said, his own voice unsteady as he tried to control his emotions.

"Every first I had was shared with you." Matt gave a soft smile. "My first school dance was spent hiding in the corner with you, making fun of all the girls in their ugly pink dresses."

Jacob let out a laugh at the memory as Matt continued.

"My first football game, you were in the stands cheering the loudest."

"I think your mom was drowning me out, actually," Jacob said, feeling like he was on the edge of falling apart, though he didn't know if it was from joy or anticipation.

"And the first time I fell in love, real love, I was looking at you," Matt said, taking Jacob's hands in his own. "Every day I get that same rush of happiness I had back then, sharing my life with the one person who knows me inside and out."

Jacob was silent as Matt released his hold, pushing himself up straighter on his knees to reach the pastry box and pull it toward the edge of the table. He reached inside, grabbing one of the gold bands and pulling it out. There was still a streak of blue icing staining the underside of the metal, but Jacob couldn't find his voice to point that out.

"I can't see my life without you in it, and I don't want to," Matt said, lifting Jacob's left hand as he offered the ring in his right. "I love you, and I would be honored if you would be my husband. Jacob Thomas Nelson, will you marry me?"

Jacob sat frozen, looking from the ring to Matt's face and then back again. As the seconds ticked by, Matt started looking unsure, but soon Jacob broke out of his self-imposed silence to answer with a loud, "Yes, of course!"

Matt starting laughing, his hold on Jacob's hand shaking as he pushed the ring onto its rightful place. Once the gold band was on Jacob's finger, his hands went to the sides of Matt's face, pulling him closer so they could kiss. Jacob wasn't going to hold off his tears any longer, feeling they were well deserved at this point.

"I love you, I love you," he kept repeating as he touched Matt's lips with his own.

"Me too," Matt said, his voice rough, as if he was trying to control his emotions as well.

Jacob pressed their foreheads together, the sound of their breathing the only noise between them for the moment. He concentrated on that, gathering his own thoughts before he was ready to speak again.

"My turn," he said, pulling back. The blue icing from his ring had marked his boyfriend's cheek. No, his fiancé, he corrected himself.

Matt looked up at him, confusion evident in his eyes, but that soon cleared up as Jacob reached for the other gold band. He rubbed the metal against his pants leg, trying to clean off the sticky blue that marked it. Once Jacob deemed it okay, he reached for Matt's left hand.

"My life changed when I met you, and it's been changing ever since. It's been difficult at times, but everything we've done and everything we've experienced has led us here." Jacob took a deep breath, making sure he could get the words out without faltering. "Matthew Edward Brooks, I will love you until my dying day. Will you marry me?"

"Of course I will," Matt said, his tone matching the utter joy evident on his face.

Jacob slid the gold band onto Matt's finger, then joined their hands together so their rings were touching. Forever and a day, that's how long he would spend with this man. Best friends to boyfriends and now to husbands, all because of cupcakes. Jacob thought it was the perfect beginning to their story.

In her youth, K. LYNN could be found in the local library, devouring books that covered everything from WWII to Dr. McCoy's latest adventures aboard the Enterprise, with some X-Men thrown in for good measure. She also created elaborate adventures that more than once made it to the page. Ink-filled papers gave way to overflowing computer memory as the years went on, but the stories never ceased.

While in college, K. Lynn increased her involvement in LGBT issues and writing within the LGBT genre. She has become a long-time fan of the authors who seek to explore the commonality that exists within all sexualities and genders. Most of K. Lynn's work features LGBT characters, many of whom are in established relationships and show how love perseveres through every trial and tribulation that life holds.

K. Lynn has degrees and certificates from UNC-Chapel Hill in the areas of American History, Religion, Creative Writing, Public Health, and Journalism. She is a member of Mensa and has an extensive writing and editing background. When K. Lynn is not writing short stories, she is working on her novels.

Find K. Lynn online at http://WriterKLynn.com, on Twitter @WriterKLynn, or drop her a line at writerklynn@gmail.com.

At First Sound

G.S. Wiley

"OH, MR. KENDRICK. I don't know how I can ever thank you for saving my father's ranch." Ada Mae Scruggs clutched a white-gloved hand to her breast. Her accent was a strange amalgam of British and Bostonian, made all the more surprising by the fact they were in the Arizona desert. Through the living room window, a saguaro cactus was visible, and a cow's skull hung above the fireplace.

"Knowing you're safe is all the thanks I need," cattle wrangler Bud Kendrick replied, his voice tinged with the barest hint of manly emotion.

"Oh, Mr. Kendrick."

"Oh, Miss Scruggs." They came together, their lips pressed firmly and chastely against one another. Bud took Ada Mae in his arms, making sure not to turn either of their faces toward the wall. Ada Mae moved, just a little, and the top of her stiff, high bonnet pushed Bud's cowboy hat off the back of his head.

Bud heard it fall to the floor behind him. He held the kiss gamely, hanging on until a voice said, "Cut," and Ada Mae pushed him away like he was carrying fleas.

The camera, encased in its huge soundproof box, ground to a halt. Bud—Bobby Carling—stepped back and retrieved his hat. "Again?" Ada Mae Scruggs, now speaking in the dulcet Brooklyn tones of America's scrappiest sweetheart, Daisy O'Reilly, flung down her bonnet in despair. Rather, she tried to, but the ribbon caught around her throat, leaving her with the bonnet hanging haphazardly down her back. "Mr. Cukor would have had this in the can seven takes ago."

"Perhaps he would have, Miss O'Reilly." The director, Mr. Gish, refrained from sighing. Bobby recognized that as a significant accomplishment. He couldn't have managed it. "Why don't we leave it there for today? We'll take it up again in the morning." Daisy stormed off scrappily, the bonnet still around her neck. Bobby smiled at Mr. Gish, who pushed up his little round glasses, a look of long-suffering in his myopic, moleish eyes.

"Well done, Mr. Carling, as usual."

"Thank you, Mr. Gish." Bobby meant it. He glanced off set. Daisy was arguing with her dresser, a portly German woman she treated like an old-fashioned maid. Or a slave. "Miss O'Reilly certainly is—"

"Scrappy?" Mr. Gish put in.

"That would be one word for it." The others couldn't be uttered in polite company. Bobby wasn't even going to utter them around the crew, who could surely have handled them.

"There's an interviewer here for you, Bobby." The second assistant director, a gangly young man with an Adam's apple the size of a cantaloupe, came up beside Mr. Gish. "From *Movie Photo Digest*."

"Of course." Bobby couldn't keep these magazines straight. He didn't know his *Movie Mirror* from his *Photoplay Pictorial*, but his agent told him they were good for business. He couldn't doubt it, even if it did give him a strange, awkward feeling in his stomach when they sent him the issues and he saw his own face beside the likes of Clark Gable and Claudette Colbert. "I'll get my makeup off first. Would you tell him to give me ten minutes?"

"It's a her," the second assistant director corrected, leering. "And a heck of a her, if you ask me."

Bobby had been at the studio longer than Daisy O'Reilly, but his dressing room was smaller. He could have made a fuss about that—it was the sort of thing his agent was always telling him he ought to make a fuss about—but Bobby couldn't bring himself to care. It had all he needed. There was a sofa for lying down on breaks, a comfortable chair for guests, and a dressing table. Two posters from earlier studio productions, neither of which had featured Bobby, hung on the walls, put there by the studio. The only personal touch was a photograph of Bobby's Saint Bernard, Freya, stuck into the frame of the mirror.

Bobby wiped off the thick layers of makeup using a cloth and a bowl of warm water. He ran a comb through his hair, in case the lady from *Movie Picture Screen* or whatever it was called wanted to take a photograph.

Bobby knew he was very handsome. He wasn't naive. He knew that was why he'd been popular in school, even though he was smart and loved books; he knew that was why his agent, Joseph Goldstein, had noticed him at the beachside soda fountain where Bobby once worked as a waiter. He knew it was why he had a mansion in the Hollywood Hills, with a swimming pool and a movie screen and three brand-new cars, when other men his age were picking oranges for starvation wages or standing on the breadline. Still, he didn't feel any pride in his looks. They weren't an accomplishment; they were an accident of birth.

"A gift," Bobby's best friend Soren called it, one afternoon when they were lying out by the swimming pool. "Like being very intelligent, or being very good at baseball, ya? You should be feeling happy about it." Bobby tried to, but there was no escaping the little voice, forever lurking in the back of Bobby's mind, that asked *What will you do when your looks fade?*

When Bobby was ready, he opened the dressing room door. A knot of people had gathered in the hallway, all men. Bobby squeezed past gaffers and best boys, set dressers and carpenters and a few of the minor actors, until he came face-to-face with the woman at the center of it all.

She was young—younger than Bobby, who was twenty-six—with a Betty Boop figure and bright-red lips, wearing a white cloche hat and matching shoes. When she looked up at Bobby, she batted thick, long eyelashes. Bobby knew at once why every man in the studio had chosen this moment to congregate in the hallway.

"Mr. Carling?" At once, Bobby felt the jealousy of every man there as if it were a palpable thing, weighing on his shoulders. "I'm Jeanette Theodore. From *Movie Photo Digest*."

"Of course." Bobby gave her his most charming smile. She held out a hand covered in a white lace glove. Bobby took it. His first instinct was to shake it, like he'd shake a man's hand, but that didn't seem appropriate somehow. A more courtly man, a man like Soren, would kiss it, so that was what Bobby did. He planted the lightest of pecks on the back of Miss Theodore's glove. "Will you come inside?"

"You'll need a chaperone, won't you?" Bobby looked up and saw Charlie Gregson. He'd worked on several films with Bobby, always as a background actor. Bobby didn't know him particularly well, but on occasion they shared a cigarette between takes or an early-morning coffee on set.

"I'll leave the door open." Bobby made his tone just a touch roguish. Miss Theodore laughed and followed him into the dressing room.

Miss Theodore's gaze landed on the photo of Freya first. Bobby supposed that was natural. There wasn't much else of interest in the room. "Oh, how sweet. Is it yours?"

"Yes," Bobby said. That was the simple answer. The more complicated, and truthful, answer was that she was Soren's dog, but Bobby lived with her.

Soren had encountered the word *stepmother* recently, probably listening to *Painted Dreams* or some other serial with Lupe, and he'd been intrigued by it. "You are Freya's stepmother, ya?" he'd said to Bobby as they lay in bed one lazy Sunday morning, Freya snoring on the floor beside them.

"Maybe stepfather." Bobby conceded. That sounded a bit better.

"What's the dog's name?" Miss Theodore took a seat on the chair. Bobby sat on the sofa across from her. She pulled a pen and a notepad from the leather bag over her shoulder.

"Freya." He spelled it out, and Miss Theodore wrote it down.

"That's just the sort of thing our readers love. Little details about a star's life." She smiled. Her teeth were perfect, even and white. Bobby would have asked her if she'd ever thought of becoming an actress, but he didn't know how to phrase it without sounding like every lecherous Joe in Hollywood.

Instead, he said, "What kind of details?"

Miss Theodore rested the end of her pen against her Cupid's-bow lips. "What do you like to do, when you're away from the set?"

Several answers sprung to mind. All of them were inadvisable, and most of them would end his career. "I love going to parties." He lied. "I've got a lot of friends, and they throw some real juicy parties."

"Is that so?" Miss Theodore's smile grew. "Can you give us any names?"

"Barbara Stanwyck." She had so many parties, not even she would know whether he went or not.

The interview went on. Miss Theodore asked the usual questions, about Bobby's childhood in Orange Tree, California, and about being discovered at the Coconut Shack. They talked about his past films and those he had upcoming, and then Miss Theodore asked The Question, the one Bobby hated but which they all got to eventually. "I hope you won't think this too personal," she began, and Bobby knew immediately that he would, "but our female readers would love to know if you've got a special lady."

He didn't. Bobby had a special gentleman. They lived together, they loved each other, they shared a dog, and he would never be able to breathe a word of that to anyone. Instead, he told Miss Theodore what he told everyone who asked the question: "I'm always hoping I'll meet my kitten one day."

Miss Theodore finished writing and began to pack up her things. "Are you doing any photographs?" Bobby asked.

"Our photographer will be at your house tomorrow." She looked up. Bobby's alarm must have shown on his face, because she went on. "We arranged it with your agent. I would have done the interview then too, but I'm meeting Clark Gable." A dreamy look came to her eyes. Bobby couldn't blame her.

"Of course. That's fine." Bobby stood to see her out. She hesitated for a moment at the dressing-room door.

"You'll probably think I'm a dumb Dora." She looked Bobby in the eye. "But if you like good music, there's a keen juke joint on Hollywood Boulevard. Max's Place. I go there all the time." Her meaning was unmistakable.

Bobby's cheeks grew warm. "That's nifty."

"Maybe I'll see you there one night."

"Maybe." *Never.* Miss Theodore left. Bobby waited a minute or two, so he wouldn't have to run into her again, and did the same. As he passed Daisy O'Reilly's dressing room, he heard her shriek, "And tell my goddamn agent this is the last picture I'm working for anyone less than Curtiz, or he can look for a new goddamn job!" There was a crash of something heavy hitting a wall. Bobby flinched, thanked God yet again he wasn't her agent or her director or her maid, and walked on.

Growing up in Orange Tree, California, in a tiny house with two bedrooms and five siblings, Bobby had dreamed of owning a mansion. He'd never expected his dream to actually come true, but there was no other word to describe his home. It had been built especially for him, carved into the Hollywood Hills. Bobby liked that. He liked the idea that in a hundred years, or fifty, or whenever everyone had forgotten about him and all his films had turned to dust, he would still have left his mark in some way.

Bobby parked his bright-blue Cadillac Twelve inside the heavy iron gates. Rather than go inside, he went around to the back of the house, passing through the grove of orange trees until he came to the swimming pool. He knew that was where Soren would be.

Even after sixteen years in California, Soren was still amazed by the weather. "You are not understanding, darling Bobby," he'd explained once, and Bobby's heart had swelled at the endearment. "In Sweden, it is always cold. Even when it is warm, it is cold. Why are you thinking Garbo is so icy?"

Bobby had laughed. *Fine words for someone who spent his career pretending to be Italian*, he almost said, but didn't. It hadn't been Soren's choice to perform as Silvestro Sardini, and that decision, among other things, was what had eventually doomed his career.

Sure enough, as Bobby rounded the corner, he saw Soren in the swimming pool, his body hidden just beneath the shimmering surface. He emerged with a splash, his dark hair gleaming in the sun. He pushed it back, out of his face, and swam over to the ladder. "Oh, Freya," he said in a loud, theatrical voice. His accent was very strong, even after all this time. That was another large part of what had finished him in show business, before he was even thirty-five years old. "I am thinking someone is watching me." Freya thumped her tail lethargically from her position beneath a palm tree, her huge head resting on her paws. "I am hoping this person has no ill intentions." Still not looking at Bobby, he pulled himself out of the pool, the water streaming down his body. His formfitting black bathing suit clung to his body, from the straps on his shoulders all the way down to the hem, halfway down his muscular thighs.

Soren was thirty-seven years old now, and in Bobby's opinion, he was as earthshakingly handsome as when he'd filmed his first picture at twenty-one. That film was called *The Italian Gentleman*, and Bobby had seen it, dragged to the cinema in Orange Tree as a reluctant chaperone to his older sister Gertie and her boyfriend. Soren had walked onto the screen, and at that instant, that precise moment in time, Bobby knew he wasn't like other boys and never would be. He also knew he wanted to be an actor. He never thought he would meet "Silvestro Sardini" in person, let alone fall in love with the man behind the stage name. Let alone have that man fall in love with him.

Soren bent and took a towel from the deck chair. He ran it over his body, then threw it backward, in Bobby's direction. Bobby emerged from between the trees and said, "You shouldn't go swimming on your own. What if you got a cramp?"

"Then Freya would be heroically jumping in to rescue me. Isn't that right, Freya?" Freya yawned. Soren turned, beaming at Bobby so brightly, Bobby wanted nothing more than to kiss him, right then and there.

But it was dangerous. They were in their own backyard, sheltered by trees and hills, but they still weren't entirely safe. Some yellow journalist had hired a plane to fly over Pickfair, Bobby had heard, and snap pictures of Douglas Fairbanks and Mary Pickford unawares. It was disgusting, a flagrant breach of privacy. Bobby wasn't Douglas Fairbanks or Mary Pickford, but he still couldn't risk it.

Instead, Bobby went over and slid open the glass door. Soren followed him into the conservatory, and there, amid the plants, Bobby embraced his wet lover.

Soren hugged back, then planted a kiss on Bobby's cheek. "How was the interview?"

"Eggs in coffee."

"Good." Soren smiled. "You are hungry? Lupe is leaving us beans and rice for dinner. I am telling her, 'Lupe, this food is very good, but is always giving me the....'" He made a noise that could only denote flatulence in any language. "So Lupe is saying, 'Then maybe Mr. Carling is staying away from your backside tonight, ya?'"

"Soren!" Bobby blushed, his face heating all the way up to his ears.

Soren laughed uproariously, as if this were the best joke he'd heard in years. He looked at Bobby and stopped, although the grin remained on his face. "It is only a joke, Bobby. Lupe is my friend." Bobby understood that, but she was also their maid. And if anything ever went wrong, if they ever needed to part ways for any reason, then she knew a great deal more about them than was safe. "She is telling me she is wishing her husband was as romantic as you. Or her son. Marco is having the troubles with his wife again." Soren shook his head sadly. "But do not be worrying, Bobby."

Bobby did worry. Not about Lupe's son's marriage, obviously, but about them, about him and Soren. He always worried, because they had so much to lose. Soren had already lost it, for other reasons, but he didn't seem at all concerned about what could happen. "I am getting dressed," he said, carefree as always. "Then I am having dinner. With you, I am hoping?"

Bobby nodded. Soren disappeared through the conservatory door into the house. Bobby followed, going over to the sideboard in the living room and pouring himself a large, stiff predinner drink.

A piano sat in the corner of the room. It was Soren's, but photographs of Bobby's family were arranged in silver frames on the top. Behind that, on the wall, hung framed posters of Soren's films, *The Countess* and *Road to Rome* and *The Italian Gentleman*, where it had all begun.

Soren's story was far from unique. Bobby knew that, but it still broke his heart every time he thought of it. Soren was a handsome man and a great actor, able to convey worlds of emotion with one look or one gesture. He did more with his face than most actors Bobby knew could do with their whole bodies, including their voices, but people wanted to hear actors speak, and that was what killed Soren's career. He couldn't speak, not in the way the studios wanted. "I am not sounding American" was how Soren explained it. "Or even Italian, and I am not looking Swedish. So, it is good-bye, Soren." He didn't seem particularly upset about it. When Bobby asked him why he wasn't furious, why he hadn't broken down completely over this injustice, he just smiled. "I am having you, ya? So maybe, that is all I need. Maybe I can be your...." He hesitated, like he always did when approaching a new word. "Your mistress. That is what Lupe is teaching me."

"Lupe needs some English lessons herself," Bobby replied, but he was touched all the same. He could be everything for Soren, if that was what Soren wanted. It just wasn't fair he had no other choice.

When Soren came back downstairs, he was dressed in a crisp white shirt and neatly pressed trousers. Despite her sense of humor, Lupe was an excellent housekeeper, there was no denying it. She was a good cook as well. Soren reheated her beans and rice on the stove, and Bobby said, "Maybe we could drive up the coast this weekend." Bobby was well-known, but he wasn't Clark Gable. There were still fishing villages where no one recognized him, places they could rent a room in a run-down hotel and mess up both beds before they left, so everyone could pretend they'd both been slept in.

"Or maybe," Soren replied, stirring the pot, "we are going to Orange Tree and seeing your family."

"We can't do that."

"You are always saying this, but I am never understanding why."

Irritation flashed through Bobby. "What do you expect me to do? I can't introduce you as my...." He didn't even know what word to use. "Mistress," he finished with a smile. He hoped that would defuse things a little. Soren smiled back, but the fuse was still there.

"You are introducing me as your friend, of course. That is what we are always saying."

"They would see through me." He couldn't fool his mother. He never could. One day, when he was fifteen years old, she'd come into the bedroom he'd shared with his two brothers. Bobby had been on the bed, reading a book. Dickens, probably, or Nathaniel Hawthorne. He'd been that kind of boy. For the longest time, his mother stood at the door; then she'd come forward and hugged him tightly.

"I will always love you," she said, alarmingly. "No matter what." Then she was gone. Bobby had bought her a new house when he became famous. The second biggest in Orange Tree, after the mayor's. He'd bought houses for all his brothers and sisters too, and cars, and toys for their children, but he couldn't go visit them. Not with Soren, and he didn't want to be parted from Soren, not even for a day.

"You are embarrassed." Soren reached for the plates. He ladled out the beans and rice, adding a golden-brown tortilla to each plate. Lupe must have baked them as well. They certainly hadn't been there in the morning. "Because I am an old man." The smile on his lips told Bobby he was teasing, but he replied anyway.

"You're not an old man."

"I am." He brought the dishes over to the table. There was a formal dining room, with a long table and a candelabra, but they rarely used it. Most of the time, they ate here, in the kitchen. Bobby sat in his usual place, in a brown wooden chair facing the window. He looked out over the green hills dotted with palm trees. They were far enough from their neighbors that there wasn't a single other house in sight. "Thirty-seven years old." Soren sighed dramatically. "Old enough to be your father."

"Not unless you were extremely precocious."

"I am a cradle taker."

"Cradle robber."

"See?" Soren grinned triumphantly. "You agree."

"You're ridiculous." Bobby picked up his fork.

"And you love me."

"Yes." *Always.* Soren went back and picked up a bottle of wine. He filled two glasses and brought them over to the table. He sat down across from Bobby, raising his glass.

"*Jag älskar dig också,*" he said, as if he were proposing a toast. Bobby knew better than that. After nearly two years, it was one of the few Swedish phrases he'd picked up. *I love you too.* Bobby took a sip of wine and reached for his fork.

After dinner, they went into the living room. Freya came in from outside, wedging herself beneath the piano as Soren sat playing. It was a new tune, something jazzy, and Bobby found himself tapping along with his foot as he sat on the sofa, looking over a new script.

"That's really good." Bobby said. "What is it?"

"'You Do Something to Me'. I am getting it yesterday."

"And you already know it?"

Soren shrugged. "It is not a difficult piece." For Bobby, it would have been. For Bobby, it would have been impossible. All of Soren's sheet music was incomprehensible to him, nothing but dots and lines covering a page in seemingly random patterns. Soren was a wonderful pianist, though. It was what he had trained for, he said, until "I am getting the sore feet"—"Itchy feet," Bobby corrected—"itchy feet and am coming to America."

Bobby closed his eyes, letting Soren's music wash over him. The new script was nothing special. It was another cowboy picture, this one about a Texas ranch hand in love with the ranch owner's daughter. The standout scene was going to be a twenty-minute cattle stampede. Bobby, of course, wouldn't be filming that. He wouldn't even be on set. It would all be done by stuntmen. The picture would make a fortune, Joseph Goldstein promised, and Bobby would be more popular than ever.

Bobby wasn't a fool. He knew what he was and what he wasn't, but still, it would have been nice to do something different for a change. A serious drama, or even a screwball comedy.

Soren stopped the jazzy tune and went into something more classical. A minute or two in, Bobby recognized the song and smiled. Beethoven's Piano Sonata No. 8, the only song—apart from "Ain't Misbehavin'" and "It Had To Be You"—he ever recognized. Soren had been playing it when they met.

It was at a studio party at some big producer's house. Bobby couldn't even remember who'd hosted it. He'd just been signed on by the studio. He was excited and nervous and desperate to make a good impression. The younger actors and actresses, the ones of his age, were all outside, flirting and drinking and threatening to throw one another in the swimming pool. Bobby stood around gamely for a while, but he got bored. He ventured into the house. He heard music coming from another room, and following the sound, he found a man playing the piano in the living room with a knot of middle-aged ladies gathered around him.

The man was very good, Bobby could tell right away, and he was handsome. His hair was black, slicked back with pomade, and he wore a beautiful black suit. As Bobby moved closer, he caught a glimpse of Soren's face and realized at once who he was.

Bobby felt both sick and elated. This man was why he was here, he was why he'd come to Hollywood rather than staying in Orange Tree, working at the filling station with his brothers and married to the girl next door. Silvestro Sardini was, in fact, the very reason Bobby first realized why he was so vehemently against the idea of the girl next door. Bobby wanted desperately to meet him, but at the same time, he longed to run away.

As a compromise, he stood there, frozen in place, until the music stopped. Silvestro Sardini threw up his hands theatrically and laughed. "That was wonderful, Mr. Sardini," one of the women said. She was around Bobby's mother's age, buxom and broad with a diamond pince-nez. Mr. Sardini smiled at her and said, "You are being very kind, Mrs. Hoffstetter, but I am telling you, it is nothing."

"You are too modest." Beneath a veneer of icy politeness, Mrs. Hoffstetter sounded personally insulted. Mr. Sardini began to play again, a more modern tune Bobby recognized as a Charleston. Mr. Hoffstetter, a tubby bald man Bobby had often seen around the studio, came in. He said something to his wife and took her elbow. They moved off, out into the garden, and Mrs. Hoffstetter's coterie of ladies-in-waiting followed. By the time Mr. Sardini finished the song, Bobby was the only one still there, clutching his drink in his hand, his heart hammering.

Again, Mr. Sardini finished with a flourish. For a long moment, he sat without turning around. Bobby was in agony. He didn't know whether he should slip away or speak up. It was Mr. Sardini, finally, who made the decision for him. "I am feeling," he said in that unusual accent, "that somebody is watching me."

"I'm sorry," Bobby blurted out.

Mr. Sardini glanced over his shoulder. "You are not needing to apologize. Please, come and sit with me." He indicated the piano bench. Bobby wanted nothing more; at the same time, there was nothing he desired less. After an awkward pause, he went. He sat backward, his legs facing the other direction from Mr. Sardini's.

"I really like your pictures, Mr. Sardini." It sounded stupid, the gushing of a mindless fan, but he had to say something.

Mr. Sardini beamed, as if he found it a true compliment. "Thank you. Then you are knowing that Mr. Sardini has not made a picture for quite some time." Three years. A lifetime in Hollywood. "And now, I am calling myself by my real name again." Nearly everyone took stage names. Bobby wasn't surprised to learn Sardini was one, although he was surprised when the man continued, "Soren Sjovold." Bobby blinked. He had never heard those sounds from anyone's mouth. "It is Swedish."

"You don't look…," Bobby began, then stopped himself.

"It is true." Mr. Sjovold sighed dramatically. "I am not having the beauty of a Garbo, but not everyone in Sweden is so fortunate."

That wasn't what Bobby had meant, not at all. He felt himself floundering. "Whereabouts in Sweden are you from?" he asked, reaching desperately for some inoffensive question. Mr. Sjovold blinked, and Bobby wondered if maybe it wasn't that inoffensive after all.

"No one is ever asking me this before. You are knowing Sweden?"

"No." Bobby barely had any concept of where it was.

Mr. Sjovold smiled. It was different than before, bigger, and seemingly more genuine. Bobby felt a bloom of warmth begin in his chest and spread outward, filling his body. "I am from Göteborg. In the west. It is a very beautiful city. I am missing it sometimes. But I am not missing the weather." He nudged Bobby slightly, his shoulder bumping Bobby's. Bobby took a sip from his wineglass, forgotten in his hand. He needed fortification. "Where are you coming from?"

"Orange Tree."

"It is sounding very beautiful."

"Not really." It was a small town, like a thousand other small towns in California.

"You are an actor?"

Bobby nodded. "I've made two pictures. They aren't out yet."

"I am looking very forward to seeing them." Mr. Sjovold's smile grew. Bobby hadn't thought it possible. "But I am needing to know your name, so I am not missing them."

He hadn't even introduced himself. Bobby wanted to crawl under a rock, or under the thick Persian carpet on the floor. "Sorry. I'm Bobby Carling."

"I am being pleased to meet you, Mr. Carling."

"Bobby, please."

"And you are calling me Soren. You are liking my music?"

I am liking you, Bobby thought. "Yes. You play very beautifully."

"Then I am playing something very beautiful for a very beautiful young man." Soren's expression didn't change, but Bobby could see the question in his eyes. It was flawlessly done, without a trace of the awkwardness and embarrassment and potential for disaster that usually accompanied that always dangerous, unspoken question.

"That sounds wonderful," Bobby said, feeling like the luckiest man in the world.

Two years later, he still felt that way. He tossed the boring ranch hand script aside and stretched his arms over his head. It was dark outside; he looked at the window, but all he could see was the room, reflected back at him. Freya stood up and padded off toward the kitchen. Still playing, Soren said, "You are having the melancholy, my love."

"No, I'm fine."

Soren stopped and turned around. "There are many things you can be hiding from me, darling Bobby, but not the melancholy. You are forgetting I am Swedish."

"All right." Bobby sighed. "I'm just a bit…." He didn't even know the word for it. Bored? That sounded stupidly ungrateful. He had everything he'd ever wanted, much more than he deserved. There were thousands, millions, of people who'd give their eyeteeth to be in his place.

Soren came over to the sofa. Bobby lifted his feet, and Soren sat down and pulled Bobby's feet into his lap. "You are a bit…."

"I don't know." Bobby rubbed his eyes with the heels of his hands. "I'm just tired, I guess, of playing the same thing over and over again." Including those two pictures he'd done before he met Soren and the one he was filming now, Bobby had starred in nine pictures. In every one, he was a cowboy or a soldier or, on one occasion, a pet shop salesman in love with some beautiful woman far above his station. The first time he picked up his scripts, he could predict the outcome from the very first page. He was always right. "I'd like to do something different." But he'd never be given the opportunity. He had his role to play, offscreen as well as on, and the studio would never allow him to step out of line.

"You are feeling trapped."

"Yes." Of course Soren would have the word for it, where Bobby failed.

"I am knowing something about this feeling."

"Of course you would. I don't mean to—"

Soren reached out and laid a finger across Bobby's lips. "I am feeling trapped for years. 'You look like an Italian', they are saying to me, 'so you are acting like an Italian'. Always, always, always. And then"—he shrugged—"they are saying to me, 'You are not sounding like an Italian. Or like an American. So we are finished with you.' They are putting me in the trap; they are opening the trap. But you know who is having the last chuckle?"

"The last laugh," Bobby corrected absently.

"Yes. It is me. Because while I am in the trap, I am having the fun sometimes, but also I am making more money than I am ever seeing in my life. And when they are letting me out of the trap, I am still having this money." That was true. Soren had been wise with his money, as Bobby was trying to be. The last thing he wanted was to end up back in Orange Tree, after all. "And I am finding you." Soren took Bobby's hand in his, squeezing it. "And I am having a life I never would have been living if not for my time in the trap."

"So you think I should just use them for as long as they'll have me." It wasn't a bad idea. It had worked for Soren, clearly. He'd never seemed upset about what had happened to him, not once. But Soren was very different than Bobby in a lot of ways.

Soren brought Bobby's hand to his lips and kissed it gently. It was how they'd parted, that first night at the big studio party. Outside in the dark, hidden behind an orange tree, Soren had kissed Bobby's hand. Bobby, emboldened by that and the wine and the hours of conversation they'd had, grabbed the lapels of Soren's dinner jacket and kissed his lips. The guilt and humiliation began even before Bobby withdrew his tongue from Soren's mouth. They might have had this forbidden thing in common, but clearly Soren was a gentleman, and Bobby was an animal. It was embarrassing; it was inexcusable. Bobby pulled back, ready to apologize, only to see Soren smiling.

"I am coming to your house tomorrow night," he whispered. "Ya?"

"Ya—I mean, yes." Bobby had never been so nervous for a date. *He's just a man*, Bobby told himself over and over. He changed outfits four times. He made sure Lupe had the place spotlessly clean. When Soren finally arrived, bottle of wine in hand, Bobby was ready to throw up. Instead, he said, "Welcome, Soren," and Soren said, "Where is the bedroom?" Now, together in the home they'd shared almost since that night, Soren let go of Bobby's hand and stood up. "Get up." Bobby hesitated. He was supposed to read over the ranch hand script, and he'd been putting it off. "Come on," Soren insisted. He nudged Bobby with his foot. When Bobby still didn't move, he took both hands and hauled Bobby to his feet. "I am having a surprise for you."

"A surprise?"

"I am thinking I am waiting until Monday, but now I am thinking you are needing it now."

"Why Monday?"

"It will be two years since we are meeting," Soren said, as if Bobby should have known that. He had known that. He just hadn't realized it was this Monday.

Soren took his hand, interlacing their fingers, and urged Bobby through the living room to the stairs. They went down, past the billiard room to the lowest level of the house, barring the basement: the cinema.

It wasn't exactly a cinema, but a projection screen with two large red velvet sofas set up facing it, side by side. A projector sat in the back of the room. Bobby glanced over and saw it was threaded with a reel of film. "Who did that?" It was tricky. Bobby could do it, but it always took many tries and a lot of cursing.

"Lupe."

"*Lupe?*"

"She is telling me she is running the projector sometimes in her village in Mexico." Of course she was, Bobby thought. He'd known Lupe for an entire year before he'd met Soren, but she was Soren's friend. He knew far more about her than Bobby ever would.

"What film is it?"

"Just sit and watch."

Bobby sat. Soren stood beside the projector for a long moment, considering; then he set it into motion. It flickered to life, and he turned off the lights before joining Bobby on the sofa. "I am sorry I am not being able to play the piano along with it," Soren said as the countdown disappeared from the screen. "We are just having to use our imagination."

Bobby didn't need much of one. The title card appeared, letting everyone know this was "Mary Hopewell and Silvestro Sardini in: *The Italian Gentleman*." The card lingered for a moment. Soren put an arm around Bobby, and the title card was replaced by a wealthy woman in an enormous dress, making herself up in a mirror.

The woman dropped a powder puff as a young girl ran in, waving a piece of paper. "Mama," the next title card read. "Mama! We have a telegram from Italy."

The girl's mother reacted, grabbing the paper from her hand. Her eyebrows went up, and her painted mouth opened wide. "Oh. Oh. It is from my cousin, Signora Fortunata. She is coming to visit with her brother-in-law, the Duke of Codibardi." Another title card. "She says he is looking for a wife." The woman and the girl grasped arms and jumped about maniacally.

"She is being a devil to work with," Soren murmured.

"Signora Fortunata?"

"No, her." He nodded at the screen. The mother had picked up her powder puff and was bashing it against her daughter's face. "Mary Hopewell. She is always calling me a 'dirty wop' even when I am telling her I am Swedish. The girl is very nice, though. Irene Allen. I am thinking she is still making pictures."

Bobby rested his head on Soren's shoulder. It was surreal. The more he watched of the picture, the more he remembered sitting in the Orange Tree Odeon, refusing to look at his sister Gertie and her boyfriend kissing beside him. He'd been bored silly—there was very little in the picture to appeal to a ten-year-old boy—until Silvestro Sardini came on-screen.

Then, as now, Soren's presence was immediate. There were other actors in the scene, Mary Hopewell and her cousin and the Duke of Codibardi's retinue, but next to him, they were all invisible. Soren was handsome, with swept-back dark hair and broad shoulders, but he was also beautiful, his lips painted dark in the way actors were made up in those movies, his skin ghostly pale. Similar to how Soren looked normally, Bobby thought, but more so, made larger than life for the movies, like everything was. The duke kissed Mary Hopewell's hand.

"Greetings, madame," the title card read. "I am very pleased to be in America."

Mary Hopewell fanned herself, as if she were about to faint. Bobby could sympathize.

Seeing the Duke of Codibardi, or Silvestro Sardini, or Soren Sjovold, for the first time had changed Bobby's life. He'd always been aware there was something different about him, something not quite the same as the other boys, but he'd never been able to place exactly what it was. He liked baseball; he liked swimming in the watering hole; he liked getting dirty and catching frogs and keeping lightning bugs in jars. He also liked men. He liked this man.

Bobby had no idea what that meant, or what it might encompass. It was years before he learned the answers to those questions. At the time, all he could do was sit in the dark, staring at Silvestro Sardini and wondering what it might be like to meet him, to know him, to be his friend. Fourteen years later, he got his wish.

Bobby looked over. Light from the screen flickered across Soren's face. He grimaced without taking his eyes off the movie. "I am having no—what is the word?"

"Trouble watching yourself?"

Soren smiled, but then he shook his head. "I am not being of the subtle. I am doing everything like I am acting for the blind people. I am getting better in my other pictures, I am promising you." Bobby knew that. He'd seen them all and loved them. At the moment, however, he wasn't interested in watching another moment of *The Italian Gentleman*. There was something much more important he wanted to do.

Bobby began slowly, leaning over and planting a kiss on the side of Soren's face. Soren smiled but didn't take his eyes off the screen. Bobby glanced up. Silvestro Sardini had taken Mary Hopewell's hand, kissing up her arm while Miss Hopewell leaned back, her other hand on her heaving bosom. Bobby took Soren's hand in his, planting kisses first on his fingers, then on the back of his hand. He unfastened Soren's shirt cuff and moved upward, kissing Soren's wrist and along his forearm, lightly dusted with dark hairs. On-screen, the title card read, "I have never seen a more perfect specimen of womanhood."

"You're the handsomest man I've ever met," Bobby said. This sort of thing didn't come naturally to him. Bedroom talk, dirty talk, love talk had all seemed hopelessly embarrassing at first. He hadn't thought himself capable of it. With Soren, though, the words came naturally. It was easy to tell Soren he was attractive, or that he was wonderful, or even that Bobby longed to feel his cock inside him. All these things were true; when they were alone, there was no reason to hide them.

"Hmm," Soren replied, still facing forward. A smile played on his lips. "I am not thinking this is a very original script, Bobby."

Bobby laughed. Soren was always good; when he was playful, it was even better. "I love it when you fuck me," he went on. Mary

Hopewell fell into a swoon. Silvestro Sardini caught her, wafting a handkerchief over her face as her daughter ran up with smelling salts. "I love that best of all. I love it when I can feel you afterward, when I sit down on set the next day and remember what we were doing." Soren swallowed, but still, he didn't turn around. "I wish I could tell everyone about it," Bobby went on. "I wish everyone could know. But if they did, all of them would want you. I wouldn't be able to get near you, and that would kill me, because I love you so much."

"Scandal!" said the title card. "The Duke of Codibardi has fallen in love with Violet's mother!"

Now Soren turned, pressing his mouth against Bobby's and yanking Bobby into his arms.

The projector flickered on, the movie forgotten, as Soren took over, pushing Bobby back onto the sofa without breaking their kiss. His tongue brushed against Bobby's, battling deliciously. Bobby reached for Soren's buttons, but Soren caught his wrists, moving them above Bobby's head. He lay on top of Bobby, his arousal evident. Bobby shifted, pressing his growing erection against Soren's, and Soren groaned in response. "Let me get my pants down," Bobby murmured.

"No," Soren said, ridiculously, but he let go of Bobby's wrists. "This is being your present, yes?"

"I don't need a...." Soren shook his head. "Okay." Bobby kept his hands over his head, resting on the arm of the sofa. Bypassing his shirt entirely, Soren went directly for Bobby's pants. Bobby bit his lip to keep from coming the instant Soren's hand brushed over his cock. He restrained himself, thankfully, and Soren pushed down his pants and his undershorts, moving them to his knees. Bobby surged upward, hoping Soren would take the hint. Instead, Soren held down his hips and came up for another kiss on the mouth.

Bobby groaned into Soren's mouth, his eyes squeezed shut. He felt a hand in his hair and then on his cheek, stroking with a gentleness Bobby often appreciated, but not when his cock was exposed to the air and straining for attention. "Soren," he gasped.

"You are not having the patience, my darling." There was a laugh in his voice.

"No." Pointless to deny it. The evidence was right there, leaking onto the front of Soren's pants.

Soren sighed, a man with many difficulties, and slid back down. He kissed Bobby's thigh, then his hip, and then he pressed his lips to the head of Bobby's cock.

There had been other men before Soren. Not many, and never more than once each. None of them had meant anything. Not the way Soren meant something. When he at last took Bobby's cock into his mouth, Bobby had to stifle a sob, borne not only out of pure, unadulterated lust, but also out of love. He felt so much love for Soren, now and always, that sometimes Bobby worried it was too much. It was wrong, a little voice said, to put so much onto one man, to tie up his hopes and his future with one other person. *What if he leaves you?* the voice said. *What then?*

Soren's mouth came off his cock, leaving Bobby at once cold and bereft. "You are opening your eyes, my darling," Soren said. "And you are looking at the movie."

Bobby obeyed, turning his head to face the screen. Soren, twenty-one years old and phenomenally gorgeous, was there in all his glory, staring at the camera. Staring at Bobby. It wasn't what Bobby wanted to see. He looked down, instead, at the real Soren crouched over him, a smile on his face. He watched that Soren, the thirty-seven-year-old one, the one who'd lost his career for no good reason. The one who'd suffered the whims of Hollywood and was still happy. The one who loved Bobby the way Bobby loved him and was never shy about saying it. That man took Bobby's cock in hand, the barest of touches, and Bobby came.

Soren lay down on top of him, carefully avoiding his sensitive, spent cock. Bobby brought up his arms and hugged him, holding him tightly. "*Du är underbar. Du är den viktigaste personen i mitt liv.*" Bedroom Swedish, Bobby called it. Or, in this case, sofa Swedish. Assorted compliments he couldn't understand, exactly, but it didn't matter. He got the idea. That was all he needed. Soren pulled back, far enough that he could look Bobby in the eye. The movie played on, the lights flickering over Soren's face. "But you are still being melancholy?"

"No." Bobby shook his head and said, again, more firmly, "No, I'm not. Truly." He smiled. Soren smiled back and kissed him, a peck on the lips. Soren shifted a little, and Bobby was immediately reminded that Soren needed tending to.

"Fuck me," he said without preamble. That always excited Soren; sure enough, Bobby saw him blush, even in the dim light.

"Here?"

"Or in bed, if you want." Bobby slid a hand down between them, running it the length of Soren's body until he arrived at his cock. "But do you want to travel?"

"No." Soren sat up suddenly. He began work on his own shirt, quicker than Bobby had ever seen him undress. Bobby did the same, tossing his clothes onto the floor until he was naked on his back. When Soren was naked, he reached over, fumbling beneath the sofa for a moment. When he came up again, he had a little jar of Vaseline in his hand.

The implications of this made Bobby's eyes widen. "You put that there?"

Soren shrugged, but he didn't meet Bobby's gaze. "I am thinking that maybe, for our anniversary…."

"You'd better be careful Freya doesn't get it." She'd embarrassed them before that way. She'd got into Soren's bedside drawer and left a trail of goop across the bedroom carpet and halfway down the hall, culminating in a jar with a chewed lid abandoned outside the door to the guest bedroom. Lupe had had a terrible mess to clean up.

"I am telling her you are getting the very chapped hands," Soren had explained to Bobby later. "She is laughing. Very much." Bobby had nearly died of embarrassment.

Now, embarrassment was the least of his concerns. He shifted, getting comfortable on the soft velvet of the sofa as Soren took a scoop of Vaseline from the jar. He kissed Bobby on the calf and moved his legs up.

The pain never lasted long with Soren. It never had, even in the early days. Part of Bobby saw that as unlikely, a romanticized rose-colored memory, but Soren knew what he was doing. He'd had others before as well. Bobby had never asked for numbers or names or situations. He didn't want to know.

"And what is it mattering anyway," Soren said once, pressed against Bobby as they lay in bed, "when all my eyes are for you now?"

It didn't matter. What mattered was this closeness, the way Soren moved inside him, the way sweat stuck Soren's normally perfect hair to his forehead, as if he'd just stepped out of the pool. Soren talked, a stream of bedroom Swedish tapering into wordless groans. Bobby tightened his legs around Soren's body. Soren leaned forward, clumsily kissing Bobby's cheek and then the corner of his mouth. His thrusts grew harder, his hands digging into Bobby's shoulders so tightly, Bobby was glad he didn't have any bathing suit scenes in this new picture. Soren buried his face in Bobby's neck and surged forward once more. Bobby wound his arms around Soren's back, holding him tightly as he came.

They lay together for a long moment afterward, Soren's head resting on his chest as their breathing slowed to normal. Bobby turned a little, his nose buried in Soren's hair, and saw a title card on the screen in front of him. "Happiness at last. The Duke and his Bride return to Italy." Soren stood on a boat in some studio backlot somewhere, his arm around Irene Allen in a wedding dress. Irene Allen threw a bouquet off the side of the boat, and Soren peeled himself off Bobby.

Bobby sat up, his back sweaty from lying on the velvet. He felt sore, in the best of ways, and he kissed Soren once more on the cheek, just because he could.

Then he remembered. "Oh."

"What?" Soren glanced over, alarmed. He'd bent over and picked up his pants, fumbling through his pockets for his cigarettes. He brought them out. "What is the matter?"

"I just remembered, a photographer is coming to the house tomorrow. You'll have to skedaddle. Sorry."

Soren lit two cigarettes and handed one to Bobby. "There is no needing for sorry. I will take Freya to the beach. She is loving to chase the crabs." Soren took a drag on his cigarette. "I am not knowing what she will do if she is ever catching one."

Bobby smiled. He reached out, resting a hand on Soren's bare, sweat-slicked thigh as the film stopped, the reels spinning to a halt behind them. "*Jag älskar dig.*" Bobby spoke Swedish about as well as anyone else from Orange Tree, but he'd learned that phrase, and he knew Soren loved to hear it in any language. *I love you.* He meant it. He meant it more every day. "Happy anniversary."

"Happy anniversary, my darling." Soren took Bobby's hand. He kissed it, then returned it to his thigh and left it there, their fingers intertwined on his pale skin.

G.S. WILEY is a writer, reader, sometime painter, and semi-avid scrapbooker who lives in Canada.

Visit G.S.'s web site at http://www.gswiley.com.

Dream Lover

Nico Jaye

*S*ORRY, *baby, deal closing tonight. Stuck on calls w Tokyo office & will be back late. Don't wait up. Love you. XOXO.*

Chris texted a quick reply, then tucked his cell phone away. He glanced at the little clock in the corner of his computer screen and sighed.

11:38 p.m.

With a shake of his head, Chris turned his attention back toward revising the article on at-home *sous-vide* gadgetry he needed to finish this weekend so he could send it to his editor by Monday. He was a little proud that he was actually a couple of days ahead of schedule this time. As he typed out the closing paragraph, Chris contemplated the text he'd just received.

After six years, he shouldn't be surprised that Brady's law firm would have him working late on his own birthday, but really, sometimes it was just too much. Over the years, Chris had come to expect the late nights and unpredictable schedule. He understood that innumerable pressures came with being an attorney at a top firm, and he was as supportive as he could be of Brady's profession. Brady's job might get in the way sometimes, but in the end, Chris knew Brady was worth it.

And after all these years, Brady was still worth it.

When Chris had been chosen to lead the law firm's food tour that summer six years ago, he'd never imagined he would meet someone like Brady among the group of suits who were participating that evening.

Jones, Hardaway & Lewis—more commonly known as JHL in law circles, which Chris sometimes secretly and in his innermost thoughts said quickly so it rhymed with "jail"—had been looking for something fresh and outside the box for its summer associates program. The recruiting manager had approached Chris, whose food blog was just getting some serious word-of-mouth props among the foodie circles, and asked him if he could lead a food tour through some of Los Angeles's lesser-known eats. Chris had never done one before, but as a freelance writer who'd just left his job with one of the local gay zines, he was his own man and up for pretty much anything that sounded interesting. Besides, the fee they proposed paying him for the tour was enough to cover two months' rent.

That fateful day, Chris arrived early at JHL's downtown LA office and was ushered into a conference room that overlooked the city from its twenty-third-floor vantage point. Earlier that week, he'd prepared the itinerary and sent it along to the firm in order for them to charter a shuttle for the locations at which they'd stop for the tour. According to the recruiting manager, Marie, there would be twelve summer associates and a handful of lawyers who would participate that evening. Marie had been vague as to how many attorneys would come along because, as she noted matter-of-factly, their work schedules were so hard to predict.

Over the course of the next hour, Marie introduced him to the dozen summer associates, who mostly appeared to be in their early to midtwenties, and the four lawyers—two older men in their late thirties or early forties and two polished young women in their late twenties—who would join the tour. They were getting ready to go and would already be starting about fifteen minutes late, anyway, when Brady hurried into the room.

"Oh, fantastic. I'm glad I caught you guys before you left."

Chris's eyes went wide upon seeing the new arrival.

Maybe Christian Bale is method acting a corporate law role soon? That explains his presence right now....

The dark-haired heartbreaker greeted Marie, the lawyers, and the summer associates with a charming grin, introducing himself to a couple of the summers whom he apparently had not met before. He then turned to Chris with a curious smile quirking his lips. Marie introduced him as "Brady Tannen" and explained he was a fourth-year associate at the firm.

Brady shook his hand with a heart-stopping smile on his lips, and Chris tried not to stutter as he said, "Chris Wexler."

When Brady turned back to chat with the summer associates, Chris took a moment to collect himself. He just... well, it's just that he didn't think lawyers came in that kind of a package.

At least, not any who weren't appearing regularly on CBS's primetime lineup every week, that is.

Brady was dark-haired and classically good-looking, and his broad shoulders and trim-waisted frame turned the dark tailored slacks and slim-fitting cobalt-blue button-down of his business casual uniform into something impossibly sexy. He sported a five o'clock shadow that didn't look scruffy at all on the square jawline of his handsome face. No, instead it gave him a rugged, rakish air, and he looked like he should have stepped out of a men's cologne ad with the seas of Tuscany sparkling in the background.

He seemed of a height with Chris's six feet one—give or take an inch—but while Chris always felt gangly and awkward at this size, Brady wore it with a graceful athleticism and confident authority that just drew the eye. Brady appeared to be in his late twenties or early thirties—in other words, Chris's libido piped up, the perfect age to complement Chris's own twenty-eight years.

Chris shook his head at himself and brought his focus back to the task at hand: to guide this buttoned-up professional crowd on a night of fun food adventure through the urban jungle of Los Angeles. After launching into his prepared introduction to the tour, he passed the rest of the evening trying not to spend a disproportionate amount of time noticing Brady's thickly lashed coffee-dark eyes or his rich laughter as he socialized with the crowd.

Chris thought he'd done a pretty good job of it until the end of the night.

The evening was winding down, and they had completed their final food tasting at a Korean barbecue stop in Koreatown. Enthusiastic summer associates and slightly more subdued, but smiling, already-lawyers alike were hopping into cabs and car service sedans on their way home. Chris had just finished speaking with Marie and was scrolling through his cell phone's missed calls when a voice interrupted him.

"You were great tonight."

Chris looked up and gazed into warm espresso-colored eyes. His heart beat a little faster, and Chris blushed as he slipped his phone back into his pocket. "Thanks. It was my first tour."

Brady's eyes twinkled. "Well, you're a natural." He looked to the side for a moment and then met Chris's gaze, his lips curving in a slow smile. "Look, I'm not sure if I'm reading you wrong or anything, and if I am, then I hope you won't mind. But I was wondering if maybe you wanted to go grab a bite sometime?"

Chris's eyes widened. He cleared his throat and spoke without thinking. "With you?" he asked, then instantly regretted how obtuse it sounded.

Brady chuckled and ran a hand through his thick dark hair. "Yeah, with me, I mean. But not on a tour. You know, on a date," Brady added with a grin and an endearing tilt of his head.

Chris answered him with a grin of his own even as his heart continued to beat in double time. "Sure. I mean, yes. I'd love to."

Brady had then pulled out his business card to scribble his cell phone number on the back. He'd taken down Chris's number at the same time too, and they'd had their first date that weekend.

Chris smiled as he remembered those early days. The maneuvering of schedules and shuffling of meeting times had taken some getting used to, but he'd had a hunch Brady would be worth it.

And he was.

Getting to know Brady had been thrilling and exhilarating, and Chris had been impressed by his ambition and talent. His heart had melted when he'd learned Brady volunteered at a local rescue shelter because, even though Brady thought it would be unfair to have a pet with his hectic lifestyle, he still couldn't resist the opportunity to interact and play with them. And Brady hadn't batted an eyelash when Chris had shyly discussed his writing goals and his life as a freelancer, even though that unpredictable lifestyle was clearly so different from Brady's own extremely regimented path.

In truth, they'd had some ups and downs over the years, but Chris loved Brady, ridiculous schedule, animal lover, chaotic work life, fantastically supportive partner, and all.

Chris looked at his computer screen and covered up a yawn. After doing a quick read-through of what he'd written, he e-mailed his article to his editor and shut down his laptop. Chris set his computer aside and stood to switch the lights off. Stretching his arms over his head, he made his way into the kitchen.

In the dim light of the hood lamp he'd left on earlier, Chris caught sight of the carrot cake frosted with cream cheese he'd baked earlier that evening and left sitting on the kitchen counter. He couldn't help the small flicker of disappointment that shot through him. He'd made the cake because it was Brady's favorite, and he'd hoped they'd be able to share it when it was still fresh out of the oven, right before they shared an evening of a more... intimate nature.

Chris suppressed a small sigh.

He'd hoped that, after Brady had made partner at JHL two years ago, this type of unpredictability would be less frequent, but instead, it seemed like everybody wanted Brady on their deals. It appeared he was being groomed to take over a number of the firm's large clients once the senior partners on those accounts retired, and Brady was just as busy as a junior partner as he had been as an associate.

Swallowing his disappointment, Chris rummaged through the lower cabinet for the dome lid to the cake dish. He sealed it onto the base and opened the fridge door to slide it onto the bottom shelf. As he shut the door and made his way upstairs to prepare for bed, Chris was matter-of-fact about the evening's turn of events.

This type of last-minute urgency wasn't new, and it certainly wouldn't be the first time their plans had been thrown a curveball. The fact that it was on Brady's birthday, though, was a tad annoying.

There had been plenty of opportunities in the past for Chris to reflect on whether the unpredictable nature of Brady's work was enough for Chris to think that spending his life with Brady wasn't worth it. And quite honestly, in those early days, it had been a bit touch and go. In the end, though, Chris had decided he was in it for the long run because the happiness and joy he gained from loving Brady and spending time with him far outweighed the disappointment he might feel at these last-minute inconveniences. Besides, Chris knew how much Brady excelled in high-pressure environments, and he wouldn't want to deny him these opportunities to shine.

After washing up, Chris headed into their bedroom. He peeled off his socks and stripped off his T-shirt and flannel lounge pants, then flipped up the corner of the light bedspread. As he sat on the edge of the bed in his blue-and-white-striped boxers, he slowly rubbed in some hand cream. Finally, he switched off the bedside lamp and climbed into their king-size sleigh bed.

He understood that Brady's job was hectic. The time they spent together, though, was always wonderful and, if possible, somehow made him fall more and more in love with Brady every time.

Chris reached for Brady's pillow and hugged it to himself as he closed his eyes.

He just sometimes, in the tiniest corner of his heart, wished those times he did see Brady were a little more frequent and predictable.

CHRIS was standing in the middle of what looked like a cornfield in his native Iowa. He ran his hands over the swaying stalks of lush golden-green. The wind sifted through his hair—it was longer, like he'd worn it in college—and he brushed a strand of light brown behind his ear. He was looking for someone. Chris moved forward between the high stalks.

He was looking for Brady.

A rustling sounded to his right. He turned toward it and only saw the golden-green of corn stalks.

Chris rolled onto his side, and, through a residual haze of cornfields, summer breezes, and earthy hay scents, he registered a rustling sound in the dark room.

He tensed for a moment but then recognized this type of rustling wasn't foreign to him. Without opening his eyes, Chris murmured sleepily into his pillow. "Brady?"

The rustling stopped. Then a familiar voice whispered into the dark. "It's just me."

Chris relaxed and resumed cradling his pillow. He murmured a "welcome home" as he dozed in a half slumber.

Brady's voice drifted through Chris's semiconscious mind. "Thanks, baby. Go back to sleep."

"Mmm-hmm," Chris mumbled in agreement.

Chris couldn't say how long he drifted in and out of sleep, but he heard Brady rustling around in the background a bit longer. He fell asleep again before he had a chance to ask Brady what he was doing.

A bird was whistling in the background as a light breeze drifted through the cornfield, filtering through the tall, solid stalks. He was closer and closer to Brady. Chris could hear him just around the corner. If he could just find him....

"Mmmmm." Chris grumbled in protest when he felt a gentle tugging on his Brady-pillow. He hugged it closer to his body, but he finally let go of it, as he always did, when he felt the weight of Brady's body settle into place next to his.

Chris snuggled up against the soft cotton of Brady's T-shirt and breathed in the clean scent of detergent mixed with Brady's light aftershave. He eased into Brady's warmth and sighed peacefully when he felt Brady's arm curl around him. Chris moved one of his hands up to rest it on Brady's firm chest. Chris's lips tried to form the words "Happy birthday" before he drifted back into the land of dreams.

Brady hugged him gently to his side, and Chris's half-conscious state registered that Brady's voice was warm with amusement. "Thanks, baby. I love you."

"Love you too." Chris was pretty sure he managed to murmur the words before he returned to those cornfields of Iowa, wandering through acres of golden-green rows, always closer and closer to reaching Brady.

"CHRIS."

Chris thought he heard his name, but that couldn't be possible. It was Saturday morning, and he usually woke up to a kiss from Brady. It was a habit they had formed when they'd first started living together, and honestly, call him a sentimental fool, but he just loved it.

Chris felt Brady's lips touch his, and he smiled against them. "Mmmm, this is more like it," Chris whispered before returning Brady's kiss. He opened his eyes lazily and saw that Brady was crouched by the side of the bed—in other words, not in it—and, to Chris's sleepy brain, appeared to be dressed and shaved already.

Chris's eyes shot open. "What's going on?"

Brady smiled warmly and rubbed Chris's shoulder with a soft hand. "Good morning," he said, leaning in for a quick kiss. Chris returned it on automatic and then shifted to sit upright. Brady's lips curved up in a half smile. "C'mon, baby, time to get up. You can sleep on the plane."

Chris reached up with his hands and tried to rub the sleep out of his eyes. "Plane?"

Brady's smile widened into a grin. "We've gotta head to the airport. Our flight's at eight."

Chris dropped his hands, and he was positive his jaw dropped as well. "Flight? What?" He was pretty sure someone had pushed a button on his brain, because he couldn't seem to do anything other than repeat Brady's words. Chris blinked blearily and looked around. Near the bedroom door stood their two carry-ons. Brows lifted, Chris slowly turned toward Brady.

Brady sat on the edge of the bed and took Chris's hands in his. "Flight," he confirmed, his eyes bright and the corner of his lip quirking up in a mischievous smile. "We're going up to Napa for a long weekend in wine country." He began playing with Chris's fingers, smoothing over them and interlacing them with his own. Brady's dark lashes swept down to cover his eyes, and when he looked up again, his rich brown gaze was warm with affection. "I know how much you love that Trinity Estates Private Reserve Cabernet, so I planned this trip a while ago. As a surprise. I was at the office late to close that deal so that work wouldn't interfere, and I even took vacation days through Wednesday so that we could do a few different vineyard tours." Brady smiled and brought Chris's hand to his lips for a quick kiss. "I packed last night so we could sleep later and still be ready to go. I... well, I just want us to spend some time together. Just you and me. But first," Brady added with a touch of humor, "you might need to get out of bed."

Chris's eyes widened as his brain worked to process the information. "Really? Napa? For me?"

Brady smiled softly. He leaned forward and pressed a lingering kiss to Chris's lips. "Really. For us."

Chris melted. The rustling in the middle of the night... the missed birthday... the late-nights working... all so they could go on this trip together. It all clicked.

Chris pulled Brady in and kissed him hard. "You're the best. You know that, right?"

Brady grinned. "And you're a sleepyhead," he said affectionately.

"I'm awake, I swear." Chris stretched his arms over his head and nearly cracked his jaw on a wide yawn. He caught sight of the clock. Six o'clock. Right. He shook his head briskly.

Chris gave Brady a playful shove to move him off the bed, then tossed back the covers with a grin on his face. "Now stand aside, lover, because I'm getting dressed. We've got a plane to catch."

CHRIS shut his eyes and stood under the shower spray to finish rinsing off his shampoo. He wiped the water from his eyes and grabbed the showerhead handle for one last rinse after his—*ahem*—thorough postflight shower. After shutting off the water, he pushed open the glass door and stepped into the large and brightly lit private bathroom. As he toweled himself dry and combed his hair, he reflected on the events of the morning that had brought them to this place.

After breakfast and a quick dash to the airport, the flight earlier that day had been smooth, and they'd picked up a rental car at SFO for the trek out to wine country. As they drove along the winding roads that spring morning, the geraniums and poppies on the sides of the road bobbed their heads cheerfully in greeting. When Brady pulled up to the Astor Manor Inn shortly before eleven o'clock, Chris thought they'd fallen into a storybook fantasy. The solid three-story whitewashed façade of the bed-and-breakfast was warm and inviting with the morning sun reflecting brightly off its paneled windows. Two Corinthian columns on each side of the double-wide burgundy door stood tall and proud. Ivy and vines trailed up at the edges of the first two stories and tickled the third-floor balcony that faced the wide circular drive.

In one word, it was magical.

Once they parked the silver Audi, they checked in with the B and B host, who sent them upstairs to their suite with a bottle of wine. Their third-floor room was bright and airy and featured a color theme that blended well with the natural greenery that surrounded the area. The suite had generous proportions, with a short foyer leading to a sitting area that featured a beautiful antique chaise lounge and a plush sofa in a lovely seafoam green. A large fruit and cheese basket sat in the center of the low coffee table. On the far side of the sitting area and near the balcony was a king-size four-poster bed covered with an embroidered cream-colored quilt. French doors with airy white drapes opened onto a balcony with two sitting chairs, a table, and a padded wicker rocking bench for two. Their corner room was west facing, and tall shrubs provided privacy from the neighboring rooms on either side.

Chris felt a warm burst of love race through him. This retreat was beautiful and peaceful, and Brady had chosen it just for them.

A smile played on Chris's lips as he checked his reflection in the gilt-framed mirror. He had slicked back his hair, and his hazel eyes finally—finally—looked wide-awake. He pulled on one of the thick white robes before he brushed his teeth and shaved.

When Brady had come out of his shower, he'd mentioned checking the times for vineyard tours nearby. A wicked smile spread across Chris's face as he reached for his shaving kit.

Even though he was excited to explore the area, Chris was pretty sure the vineyards could wait.

A few minutes later, Chris slid open the bathroom's dark wood panel and padded barefoot toward the open balcony doors. He paused in the doorway to admire the view. Brady sat in one of the chairs in dark jeans and a gray polo, and his caramel-brown loafers matched the woven belt that was looped around his waist. Brady looked up and set aside his BlackBerry.

Brady's smile was teasing as he caught sight of Chris's robe. He lifted his brows. "I thought we were heading out. Going back to bed, Sleeping Beauty?"

Chris darted a glance around before focusing on Brady. Chris's lids dropped to half-mast. "Maybe," he murmured. "But not to sleep." His words trailed off as he let his robe fall open.

Chris watched Brady closely. Brady's eyes went wide, and Chris could pinpoint the exact moment Brady saw it.

The silver cock ring was just snug enough around the base of Chris's cock to be pleasurable on the erection he had stroked for himself in the bathroom. However, Chris didn't wear it just for his own enjoyment. Honestly, while the metal ring heightened sensation at his climax, he could take it or leave it in the end. No, Chris wore it because he knew Brady loved it.

Loved it when it was wrapped around Chris's cock, that is.

Brady drew in a shaky breath as he stood. Brady's gaze landed on Chris's cock once more before those intense dark eyes lifted to meet Chris's own. Brady's voice was a hoarse rasp. "I wanna fuck you so bad right now."

The corner of Chris's lips curled up as he reached for Brady's hand. Chris walked backward, guiding them through the French doors. "Well, what's stopping you, handsome?" he asked with a provocative smile and a gleam in his eyes.

Brady growled, and suddenly, Chris's senses were filled with him.

Brady's hands came up to push the robe off Chris's shoulders. Then one hand gripped Chris's shoulder to maneuver him backward against the bed while the other moved to take a possessive grip on Chris's cock. Brady covered his mouth with hungry lips, and Chris eagerly tangled his tongue with Brady's own while that hand on his cock stroked him firmly from base to tip. Brady pushed him onto the bed, and Chris's breath came in gasps as he settled onto his back on the soft surface of the quilt, displaying himself—and the silver cock ring—for Brady.

Brady took a step back. He stood by the bed and pinned Chris with a heated look. His tongue came out to wet his lips before he spoke in a low, intimate voice. "I like you like that." Brady pulled his shirt over his head, revealing his sculpted torso and the defined musculature of his broad chest. He stepped out of his shoes and reached for his belt. "Ready for me." Brady popped the buttons on his jeans and slid them, along with his burgundy boxers, down his long tanned legs. His cock sprang out, already hard and thick with desire. "Ready for us." Brady gripped his cock and gave it a long stroke.

Chris's breath caught in his throat as Brady climbed onto the bed. Chris let out a needy moan as he reached for Brady, eager to be skin to skin.

He wanted Brady. Now.

Brady leaned over Chris and covered him with his body, his firm muscles warm and enticingly familiar. Chris wrapped his arms around Brady, pressing him close. Chris sighed contentedly. It felt wonderful to have him close. Brady rested on his elbows as his hands came up to tunnel through Chris's honey-brown hair. "Did you bring that ring here for me?" Brady asked affectionately.

Chris nodded, a soft smile playing on his face.

Brady's gaze dipped to Chris's lips before lifting to meet his eyes. His voice was warm and matched the smile on his face. "I love you so much, you know?"

Chris nodded again. "Show me," he whispered, arching his back and rolling his hips up to press his aching erection against Brady's.

Brady's eyes squeezed shut upon the sensual contact, and Chris leaned up to kiss his soft lips. When Brady's eyes opened again, his gaze was heated. Wicked with intent. "You're gonna feel me for days."

Chris's breath caught on that promise, and his lids fluttered shut as Brady began kissing his way down his chest. Chris groaned as he felt Brady's mouth on his nipples, first licking them with soft rasps of his tongue, then sucking on them. Chris glanced down and saw Brady's rapt gaze on him. Brady smiled around the stiffened peak in his mouth, then bit it gently.

Chris felt the pleasure-pain of it like there was a wired connection that went directly to his cock.

"Fuck, I love that. Love it."

Brady lifted his head and smiled. "I know." Brady continued his path southward, and Chris shivered as he felt Brady's breath against his belly and then, suddenly, on his cock.

Chris angled his head so he could watch Brady. Brady wrapped his hand around the base of Chris's cock, fingering the silver cock ring lightly. Brady's lids grew heavy as he leaned closer, his tongue leading the way until it touched the head of Chris's cock.

Chris groaned, and his hips jerked up as Brady's lips parted to take the shining head of Chris's cock into his mouth. "Fuuuuuuuuuuck." Chris reached for Brady, and his fingers tangled in Brady's dark hair.

Brady murmured around his mouthful, causing an amazing buzzing sensation to run from the tip of Chris's cock straight through his veins. Brady's wide palm encircled the base of Chris's cock, and he gave it a soft stroke as his warm, slick mouth worked the head.

Brady released Chris's cock with a gentle *pop*, then licked it underneath from base to tip. He made eye contact with Chris, whose breath came in gasps. "You like that, baby?" Brady asked, a gleam in his eye.

Chris swallowed and choked out, "You know I do."

Brady smiled knowingly. "Good."

Chris's cock was throbbing, and when Brady just sat there watching him, Chris reached with one hand to palm it, to stroke it—to do something to alleviate this ache. Brady intercepted Chris's hand, gently grasping his wrist. "Nuh-uh," Brady said with a playful scold. "That's my job."

Chris groaned and shut his eyes. "Then fucking fuck me, dammit!" Once Brady released his wrist, Chris moved to grasp the bedspread, following along with Brady's tacit no-touch instructions. Chris shifted his hips on the bed, his cock pounding in time with his heartbeat and his ass just begging for Brady's eight achingly and wondrously familiar inches to fill it.

Brady's voice was gently teasing. "You want me to fuck you?" Brady's hand skimmed over Chris's cock and down over his balls. He massaged them gently.

Chris lifted his head and met Brady's dark gaze. Chris nodded, sure his wide eyes were sending a silent cry for mercy. In case that wasn't enough, he voiced his plea. "Please."

Brady's lips twisted in a contemplative moue. "Hrmmm… where do you want me to fuck you, baby?"

Chris flopped back and huffed out a frustrated breath. God, Brady was so sexy when he did this, but holy fuck, Chris wanted Brady inside him.

Now.

Chris shut his eyes and prayed for patience, even while his body was drawn tight and his cock was begging for release. "Fuck my ass. Please, Brady. Just fuck me," he whispered hoarsely.

Chris felt Brady shift on the bed. Finally, Brady's hands slid under his rounded cheeks and lifted him, and Chris almost sang Hallelujah that his ass was finally—

Oh God.

A soft hot tongue began tracing the edges of Chris's entrance. The moisture from Brady's tongue left Chris's skin sensitive to the cooler air when Brady pulled back.

"You mean right there?" Brady's voice was husky as he posed the question.

He clearly didn't expect an answer, because Chris soon felt that tongue on his hole once more. Probing, pushing gently until the pointed tip found purchase. Chris couldn't stop muttering "Oh God, oh God, oh God" under his breath as he felt that firm slick muscle push deep into his ass.

Chris whimpered, and his breathing grew harsh and erratic. He squeezed his eyes tighter and tried to take a calming breath. He bit his lip but couldn't hold back a ragged moan. The silver cock ring was tight around his shaft, and he was grateful for what little preventative measures it was providing, because as amazing as Brady's tongue felt, Chris didn't want to come yet.

He wanted to come with Brady inside him.

Finally, Brady pulled back. Chris sighed as he felt Brady push a finger into his warm, wet hole. Chris looked up and saw Brady sitting back on his heels near the foot of the bed. One of Brady's hands was stroking his own cock, and the other was between Chris's legs as that finger—*correction, fingers*—pressed deep into Chris, spreading him.

Brady met Chris's gaze as he removed his fingers, and those dark eyes were focused. Intense. "You ready, baby?"

Chris nodded enthusiastically and, in a moment of lucidity, looked to the side at the nightstand where he'd placed the lube he'd packed in his shaving kit. He released his hold on the bedspread to reach out and grab the bottle of clear liquid. Chris tossed it toward the foot of the bed. "Give it to me, Brady. Make me feel it."

Brady's eyes went wide at the provocative words. The corner of Brady's lip curled up as he flipped the cap open with a soft *snick*. Chris bit his lip while he watched Brady coat his thick cock generously with the liquid. Brady stroked his hand down his shaft a couple of times, then reached forward to insert those lubed fingers into Chris's opening.

Chris grunted and spread his legs wide as Brady's fingers penetrated him once more. They felt good, but they still weren't Brady's cock. "Don't fuck around. Just fuck me, Brady. Do it."

Brady's eyes were dark with passion as he slipped his fingers out of Chris's ass. Chris felt the thick head of Brady's cock as it lined up with his entrance. Their gazes met, and their lips parted on a silent, synchronized gasp when Brady pushed inside. Chris took deep breaths as

Brady pulled back and pushed in and pulled back and pushed in again until he was at last seated fully.

They were finally one, and Chris could feel him all the way to his Brady-loving heart.

Brady leaned forward to cover Chris's torso, and his chest was flush with Chris's as he kissed Chris deeply. Brady continued his rhythmic strokes as he lifted his head, his firm lower abs skimming over Chris's erect cock. Brady's gaze was wide and lust-blown when he looked into Chris's hazel eyes. Brady's lips curved in a sinful smile. "You like that, baby?"

Chris panted with each strong, penetrating stroke. "Fuck yeah."

Brady shifted his hips, changing the angle, and managed to nail Chris's prostate.

Chris somehow gasped and cried out simultaneously. Brady… Brady was going to make him come.

Soon.

Like now.

"Brady… Brady…." Chris breathed out his name and hoped it was enough for Brady to know.

"I know, baby." Brady kept that angle and continued to stroke in and out in those high, probing thrusts. "Come for me, Chris. Come for me."

Chris's eyes went wide. He felt the climax building in the depths of his soul, and he cried out suddenly as his cock erupted with it.

The sensations were electrifying as they traveled through his veins and zeroed in on his cock. He called out Brady's name once more and watched through a passion-filled haze as Brady moved his hips and began to penetrate him with longer, deeper strokes. Finally, Brady's dark eyes met his, and Brady let out a strangled cry.

"Chris! Oh God, baby, yes!"

Brady dipped his head and claimed Chris's lips in a deep, devouring kiss. Chris felt Brady's cock jerk inside him, and he was filled with liquid heat. Chris lost track of time as he savored their heat, their passion, their unity.

They were breathing harshly as their lips parted and their gazes held. Chris hugged Brady close, relishing the togetherness of their coupling.

Brady… God, Chris didn't know how, but Brady always knew exactly how to give Chris what he wanted.

Brady rested his head on Chris's shoulder for a moment, then nuzzled against Chris's neck, brushing soft kisses to the tender spot behind Chris's ear. "Well, I liked your little surprise."

Chris smiled languidly. "I could tell." He turned to press a kiss to Brady's lips.

"God, I love you." Brady's kiss in return was long and slow. "Maybe we'll put the vineyard tour on hold for today," Brady said with a sated—and sleepy—smile on his lips.

Chris nodded and returned the look with affection. "Love you too," he murmured.

And even though he knew he needed to take the cock ring off and he knew they needed to get cleaned up, for just that instant, lying there in bed, Chris took the opportunity to cherish the moments that had brought him to be exactly where he was: close, connected, and sheltered from the outside world with Brady.

CHRIS took a sip of his Trinity Estates Private Reserve Cabernet—*damn, this stuff is good*—and set his glass down on the floor next to the balcony's rocking bench. He glanced at Brady, who smiled and settled his arm around Chris. Chris rested his head against Brady's shoulder and took a deep breath of the clean valley air. While they spent their last evening here watching the sun set over the rolling hills of a neighboring vineyard, Chris smiled to himself as he remembered the last few days.

After they—*ahem*—recovered enough to wake up from their Saturday morning activities, they had lunch and spent a leisurely afternoon checking out the B and B's grounds and figuring out the tours they would go on the next day. Of course, they made it to the Trinity Estates Winery & Vineyards that weekend as planned, but they also managed to catch a valley-wide tastings tour that included six other local wineries over the next two days.

And, through it all, they were together.

Granted, Brady brought his BlackBerry with him and checked it periodically, but Chris was grateful Brady didn't have to field any calls during their time here. And, to be honest, Brady wasn't even checking his BlackBerry around the clock as he sometimes did on vacations.

All in all, Chris was pleased with this trip, and he wished it could be like this always.

Chris rubbed his cheek against the soft cotton of Brady's blue henley shirt. The sun touched the horizon and began to disappear behind the vineyard's sloping hill.

Brady hugged Chris close. "You doing okay?"

Chris looked up and met Brady's gaze. Chris's lips curved up at the warmth he read there, and Brady's eyes crinkled at the corners as he returned the smile. "I'm doing wonderfully." Chris settled back against Brady's shoulder and sighed. "It's so peaceful here. I wish it could be like this at home."

Silence reigned, and the noises made by nearby wildlife were the only sounds for a moment.

Brady cleared his throat. "Well, I've been thinking...." Brady's words trailed off.

Chris glanced up and lifted his brows. This was new; he wasn't used to hesitation from Brady. Chris sat up straighter. "About?"

Brady's eyes were serious as they met Chris's gaze. "About a lot of things." Brady cleared his throat again. "But mainly about us. And how I'm not there for you enough."

Chris's brows shot up. "But you are. You're wonderful."

Brady shook his head, and he wore a smile that didn't quite reach his eyes. "I don't deserve someone as sweet as you. Really, Chris. I know I work too damn hard. I'm always late for stuff, and I hate that I keep you waiting." The halfhearted smile disappeared from Brady's lips. "I saw that cake in the fridge on Friday night. Baby, it was so sweet of you to make it. I know you were thinking of me, and I know it must've been awful when I wasn't there. It had to have been." Brady's brow creased in a frown. "I don't like that the firm's doing that to us."

Chris spoke quickly. "It's okay, really. I know your job's important. I know that, sweetie." Chris reached for Brady's hand and smoothed his fingers over the back of it.

He was soothing Brady, but inside, his mind was reeling.

Chris hadn't known that Brady felt this way about his life at JHL. And Chris thought he'd done a decent job of masking the hostility he sometimes felt toward the firm that often took Brady away from him for long hours of the day and night. Chris thought he'd hidden it well, but perhaps Brady had picked up on that resentment.

Perhaps Brady felt some of his own....

Brady met Chris's gaze, and his eyes were clear with purpose. "It's not okay. I'm not okay with it, and I'm going to try harder, I swear. The job and the clients are important, but not as important as you. You're the most important thing in my life. I want you to know that." Brady searched Chris's gaze. "I need you to know that."

A small smile curved Chris's lips. He knew it, but it was nice to hear it sometimes. Really nice.

Brady returned it with a slow smile of his own. Brady looked down at their hands and clasped Chris's hands between his palms. He cleared his throat and suddenly looked nervous. "And I...." He took a deep breath, then lifted his gaze to meet Chris's. "I want to talk to you—not now, but soon—about what I'm doing with my career. I've put a lot of thought into it, and I was thinking of branching off from the firm. Leaving them and going solo. You know, trying it out on my own." Brady's voice rose with enthusiasm, yet still held a note of nervousness.

Chris's eyes widened, and he nodded encouragingly.

Brady's gaze was earnest as he continued. "I just mean... building my own practice will be a lot of responsibility. I know it'll be a lot of hard work and long hours to establish my name with my own shop, but I'm hoping it'll also eventually mean more flexibility. So that the time I have is my own, not the firm's." Brady's lips quirked up in a tiny smile. "I don't know—maybe we could even get a dog."

Chris's heart raced at the prospect of Brady's independence from law firm life, which he'd never even considered possible. "That sounds nice," Chris said slowly, his lips curving into a smile as he met Brady's gaze with a hopeful look. "All of it."

Brady's expression softened, and he leaned forward to press a gentle kiss to Chris's lips. "I think so too. It'll be nice to have time that's my own. Because I know how I want to spend that time."

Chris leaned into Brady with a contented sigh. "Oh yeah? How's that?" Chris asked, his heart feeling inexplicably lighter.

Brady turned his head, and his breath tickled the hairs that fell by Chris's ear. "With you," Brady murmured. Brady reached into his pocket and presented Chris with a small box covered in black velvet. "As husband and husband."

Chris's breath caught in his throat as he met Brady's eyes. The love he saw there was vast and unwavering. It instilled in him a belief that, no matter what the future held for them, they would always be that much stronger because they would be facing it together.

Chris accepted the jeweler's box and lifted the hinged lid. Nestled in a bed of black satin were two platinum bands. They were solid and strong, just like their love for each other.

Swallowing past a lump of emotion, Chris closed the lid and looked up. "I'd love that, Brady." Brady's answering smile was breathtaking.

Chris reached up to frame Brady's well-loved and familiar face and looked into his smiling gaze. By the sun's setting rays on that beautiful spring evening, they shared a kiss that sealed their promise today, their future tomorrow, and their love for years and years to come.

THAT night, Chris dreamed.

The stalks of corn weren't as high as they usually were in the peak of summer. Rather, they were up to his waist and still young, and Brady was clearly visible in the middle of the field. Chris walked straight toward him.

And Brady? He stayed right there.

When Chris reached the center, Brady smiled and opened his arms wide. Chris savored Brady's warmth as they embraced.

It felt like coming home.

NICO JAYE thinks reading is awesome and loves that she can hang out night after night with crinoline-wearing debutantes, brawny firemen in suspenders, and werewolf shifters with Scottish brogues. After spending time doing stuff (yes, very mysterious stuff!) in Los Angeles, Chicago, and New York, she now lives in her native San Francisco. An overall feline enthusiast, she may or may not have a cat named "Nico" from whom she borrowed this pen name. She can be found online chitchatting about cats, popcorn for dinner, spontaneous trips to Iceland, and boys who like boys at any of the following:

Website: http://www.nicojaye.com

Twitter: @nicojaye

Goodreads: http://www.goodreads.com/nicojaye

Tumblr: http://nicojaye.tumblr.com

E-mail: nicojaye@gmail.com

If you'd like to read more by Nico Jaye, then please feel free to check out her website for online freebies and additional info about other publications. Happy reading!

Happy Holidays

Anna Butler

"Do you know what day this is?"

John Hogarth started, taken by surprise by his partner's sudden and stealthy appearance in the dimly lit storeroom. He suppressed a quiet little shriek, and only the convulsive tightening of his grip stopped him from dropping his clipboard. How in hell did Kit Lewis do that? He was perpetually creeping up on John when John was least expecting it.

Kit leaned up against the doorframe. The light of the hallway behind him edged down the side of his cheek as he turned his head, sliding across his nose and jaw to illuminate the mouth that only that morning had kissed John into jelly-kneed submission. Nice images, both Kit limned by light and the memory of the fun in the shower they'd had earlier. Both were guaranteed to appeal to the artist in John.

John swallowed and loosened his grip on the clipboard. His fingers were aching. "What?"

"Do you know what day this is?"

Heart hammering, John considered the question. He looked it in the face, noting its innocent and inoffensive expression, and thought about it. He walked round behind it, considering it from all angles, carefully scanning every surface, eyes narrowed in concentration, looking for even the slightest, microscopic sign of trouble. And then he picked it up and shook it vigorously to see what sort of scam and trap could possibly fall out of it.

Nothing. It seemed harmless enough. But then, he'd been caught by Kit's seemingly harmless questions before. More than once and far too often.

"Er… Tuesday?"

"Well, of course it's Tuesday!" The *you idiot!* was unspoken, but so loud it was deafening. "But what else?"

John shook his head. He dropped the clipboard onto a shelf and straightened, stretching his back.

"You got me there," he admitted.

"That's very bad of you, John. It's not very enlightened, this ignorance about the world. I always thought you were a liberal kind of guy."

John stuck his hands into his jeans pockets. "Fully paid up and card-carrying member. I'm as liberal as they come."

"Caring. Sharing. With a social conscience."

"But of course. I support human rights. I support the idea of helping those less fortunate than me. I'd rather my tax dollars went on job creation than nuclear weapons. I support my local mom-and-pop coffee shop over heartless global megacorporations. I'd rescue a kitten in distress if I knew where to find one—"

"But you don't know what day this is." Kit's mouth curved upward into the familiar lopsided grin. "I'm disappointed with you. Any true humanitarian would be working to increase understanding of different cultures and our city's minorities. They'd reach out to others, encourage everyone to join in each other's celebrations and share their cultural heritage."

John sighed. It hadn't been a harmless question after all. "All right," he said with the deep fatalism that came from too many years as Kit's favorite fall guy. "Enlighten my ignorance. What day is it, and what does that have to do with my liberalness or the lack thereof?"

"It's Health and Sports Day in Japan," said Kit, and smiled.

"Health and Sports Day."

"Yeah."

"In Japan."

"That's what I said."

"Kit, last time I looked, your family was of Scottish descent and mine was so English they didn't have blood in their veins, they had tea. We're both Caucasian. We've never even been to Japan on vacation. You hate sushi."

"We should go. Anyhow, the recruitment agency just sent us details of a likely candidate for junior graphics designer. Miko Takahashi. She's Japanese. She sent me a link to her online portfolio."

"Looking good?"

"Very good. She's only a year out of school, but she's done some good work, and we can train her up. I'll send you the link. I've arranged to do a phone interview tomorrow, and if that's good, I'll bring her in to meet everyone and maybe she can start Monday."

"Great. There's more work than we can handle right now. Which is why I'm the one in here checking how much PVC mesh substrate we have for the banners Williams Consulting wants to hang in their atrium."

Kit's grin widened. "I know we're busy. Great, isn't it? Better than when we started out, when one job a month if we were lucky was all we had between us and financial ruin. Thing is, since we took on our own printing shop and expanded the studio, we're getting to be quite the mixed team here. I kind of like it. So I vote we start celebrating everyone's holidays."

"We'd never get any work done!"

Kit rolled his eyes. "I didn't say we should have the day off. Just that we should celebrate the holidays."

Another jolt of suspicion screamed at John to be careful. To be very, very careful. "If this celebration involves me paying for all the drinks in the bar tonight, or sponsoring your next Vegas trip, or—"

"My, aren't we the suspicious one! Nothing like that. It's more fun than that."

"Uh-huh," said John, unconvinced.

"What do you think about when someone says Health and Sports to you?"

John crushed down the memories of humiliating field days at school where his straight As hadn't done much to stop him from coming last in the 400-yards relay every year. He hadn't shone at sports.

"Running," he offered, and from Kit's wry grin, the double meaning hadn't escaped his clever partner in crime.

"Good!" Kit applauded. "Very good! We're getting there. Close, anyway, and here's a clue. Try thinking about physical activity and exercise."

Waggling eyebrows were a clue? Who knew?

"Physical activity and exercise," said John, playing for time.

"Will you stop repeating everything I say? It's beginning to get to me. Physical activity." Kit smiled and reached to turn the key in the lock. "Physical. Activity."

"Ah," said John, understanding at last. He grinned. "Well, now. Physical. Activity."

"And exercise." This time Kit didn't complain about his words being repeated, right down to the significant pauses between them. "Slow but sure, that's my boy John."

"Oh, I dunno. I don't think I have the time. There's so much to do, and problem is, I have this business partner. He's very driven. Demanding."

"I checked. He's okay with a little physical activity, and you bet he's going to be demanding."

Kit pushed back against the doorframe to give himself some momentum and moved forward. He was beside John so fast his feet blurred. John, backed up against the wall, had nowhere to go. Kit blocked him in, pressed up against him, warm and close. Kit's expression was the one he wore when they had a tricky design to pull together, like the concepts they'd done for the Met's last exhibition. It was his focused and intent expression. John liked having Kit focus on him like that, watching Kit's gray eyes sharpen and brighten, seeing the little frown between the eyes smooth out as whatever the issue was fell victim to Kit's invention and creativity. John had fallen victim himself there, once or twice, over the last fifteen years.

"I wish we were home." Kit lifted his hand and rested it against the side of John's face. "I could show you properly there." He winked. "Some real one-on-one physical activity. Until then…."

His voice trailed off. He brushed his mouth against John's, so gently John had to strain to feel it, had to press right back with his lips. He pulled John in close, tugging until John leaned in and pressed the side of his face against Kit's. He could feel Kit's warm breath on his ear.

They stood quiet and entwined for a long time, just holding on. Until, that is, their studio manager banged on the door, yelling about the Williams account. Even then, it was several minutes before either of them felt inclined to move, and it was only to close up early and head on home.

They both felt the need for some exercise.

"Do you know what day this is?"

John jumped, startled. All right, he wasn't supposed to be working this hard over the weekend—at all, really, as that was one of the things he and Kit had promised each other, that they'd leave the business behind on weekends and damn the deadlines—but the following week was going to be damn awful with two client presentations and a reception to organize. If he didn't get a little ahead, he'd spend all day Monday running to catch up.

"Huh?" He got his heart rate back under control and stared.

"I said, do you know what day this is?"

John considered the question. He looked it in the face, noting its innocent and inoffensive expression, and thought about it. He walked round behind it, considering it from all angles, carefully scanning every surface—hey! Wait a minute.

Last time Kit asked this question, it led to some very enjoyable physical activity and exercise. It couldn't possibly be Health and Sports Day in Japan again, but it was all too probable Kit had something up his sleeve....

"Er... Saturday," said John, tentatively.

"Of course it's Saturday!" Kit shouldered John out from in front of the Mac and held out an imperious hand. "Come on."

John sighed and got up. He was too well-conditioned, he realized, to put up much resistance when Kit crooked a finger. "You should be the one doing the presentation to Michael Bowyer next week, anyway. You're better at schmoozing the clients than I am."

"Equal partners, remember? You're the creative director, and it'll be your work you're showing off."

"I can't believe you suckered me into doing this. I need my head examined. You really are better at this than me, Kit."

"You can do it. I hook 'em, you land 'em."

"I hate fishing." But John was grinning as Kit linked their hands together and tugged him out of the study and into the living room. Kit had the sound system remote in his hand and used it as they stepped over the threshold. He'd pulled out all the stops while John had been working on that damn presentation. Dinner, dim lights, Lou Reed on the sound system. John let his grin widen. Lou Reed. Right.

"Romantic," he said, and half turned to meet Kit's kiss.

Kit licked his way into the kiss, parting John's mouth with his tongue, and licked his way out again, leaving John aching for more. "As you said, it's Saturday. Date night." He tilted his head to one side. "Do you know what day this is?"

John nodded to the iPod deck. "A perfect day, by the sound of it."

"It will be," promised Kit, "but it's also Cry of Liberation Day in Mexico."

John made a helpless gesture with his free hand. "Cry of Liberation Day."

"Yup."

"In Mexico."

"We aren't going through that repeating-every-word-I-say thing again, are we?" asked Kit uneasily.

"You're making it up. No one could have a holiday called Cry of Liberation Day."

"They do in Mexico. Well, it's Cry of Dolores, really, but I don't want to get us confused by bringing girls into it. It was something to do with a revolution. Don't ask me what or which revolution. Mexico's had a few."

"And how do you propose to celebrate that?" John glanced at Kit's preparations. "With takeout General Tso? That's the best you can come up with to celebrate the Cry of Dolores? Couldn't you at least have got tamales?"

"I like General Tso," said Kit, and grinned. He tugged at John's hand, getting him over to the long sectional couch and pushing him back onto it. "Cry of Dolores, Johnny. You're the noisy one. I'm going to liberate you outta those jeans, and if I don't have you crying out loud with delight, then my name isn't Kit Lewis."

John smiled. "I love a challenge. I don't cry out loud, for God's sake!"

"That a bet?" asked Kit.

"It is. What is your name, anyway?"

It only took a mere half hour to prove it was Kit Lewis, of course. The man won his bet. As always. John didn't mind. He didn't even protest at the time it took. He liked slow and deep.

Good thing they had a microwave, or they'd have had to eat the General Tso cold.

"DO YOU know what day this is?" Kit rolled over in bed, ignoring the Sunday paper he crushed on the way. He rolled right over the arts section without so much as a by-your-leave and certainly without remorse.

He was naked and so very beautiful, even with his brown hair on end and mouth still sticky from the syrupy pancakes they'd had for breakfast. John decided he could live without remorse. He had more of a struggle about living without licking the sticky syrup away. That was more of a moral dilemma.

John's reading spectacles slid down his nose as he folded the business section carefully—the article on Bowyer Industries was desperately uninteresting, but he kept on going for the sake of their little company. Bowyer's would be the biggest contract they'd ever landed.

Kit glanced at the paper and grimaced. "Your sense of duty is overdeveloped. You have the presentation done, and you're good, John. You're always good. Bowyer will take one look at your designs, and he'll want to marry them and have a dozen children with them. You'll sweep him off his feet."

"I'm glad you're so confident."

"In you? Always." Kit's hand closed over John's. With his other hand, he reached up and carefully took away the spectacles and writhed over John for a second to put them on the nightstand. Which was exciting and led to several minutes of distraction, in which John reinforced his decision that remorse wasn't necessary, and he could get to like kissing sweet, sticky mouths.

Kit pulled back, stretching out his long, still-lean body. "You didn't answer me. Do you know what day this is?"

John considered the question. He looked it in the face, noting its innocent and inoffensive expression, and thought about it. He walked round behind it…. Mmn. There was a pattern here, he was sure of it.

A pattern that had so far ended in cuddling, exercise, and a really stellar date night. And indigestion. General Tso was best eaten fresh.

He let the smile start. The indigestion had faded, thanks to a benevolent deity and whoever invented Pepto-Bismol. "Sunday?"

Kit blew out a noisy sigh, blowing strands of hair away from his eyes. "Yeah, it's Sunday. You know, for the best artistic designer in New York, you have no imagination. At all. Today is a very special day."

"Okay," said John. He waited.

"It's the Day of the Union of Eastern Romalia with the Bulga. In Bulgaria."

"Day of the Union of Eastern Romalia with the Bulga."

"Yeah."

"In Bulgaria."

"John!" warned Kit.

"You're talking about the assimilation of one bit of country by another, right? And you intend to celebrate this how, exactly?"

"Think of it as metaphorical." Another writhe across John to reach the nightstand had Kit rubbing himself up against John like a cat, and John's breath coming short. Very short. Kit grabbed the tube of lubricant. "I thought union might be in order here. You like being assimilated."

John looked down at the tube, then up at Kit. He licked his lips. He could still taste the syrup. "Only the one union?"

"Oh my, no. I've a few future reunions in mind, as it happens. We have all day."

John smiled and slid down the bed. "Do you want to be Eastern Romalia or the Bulga?" he asked.

Kit indicated his groin. "What do you think, Romy?"

"I don't know why I asked." John wriggled to get himself lined up with Kit, nose to nose.

Kit's response was to push at John's shoulder until John rolled onto his back, compliant and lazy and grinning. Kit sat up and looked John over a couple of times, gaze sweeping from head to foot to head again. It was so intense, John thought he should be able to feel it, like a ghost touch as it passed over him. It made him shiver. In a good way, but still a shiver.

Kit slithered over him, skin to skin, to give him a kiss that threatened to take John's soul out through his lips and left him complaining when Kit shifted away to straddle John's legs. Only then did Kit touch him properly, and only with his fingertips. He stroked careful little shapes over the outsides of John's thighs, keeping everything symmetrical so John's hips were cocooned between Kit's hands. Kit's fingertips moved up and across John's thighs, skirting his balls and dick, and, as John parted his legs, kept up those precise little shapes as they moved round onto John's inner thighs, up to the crease at the very top, and slowly, very slowly and featherlight, down to John's knees.

The light touch was maddening. John wanted more, wanted harder, wanted to know what in hell it was Kit was drawing on his skin. Most of all, he wanted more and harder. Kit's fingertips touched and smoothed while John twisted, arching his back and whining out a complaining "Kit!"

Kit moved quickly up to straddle the tops of John's thighs and swooped down to smother the next whining complaint in John's throat, stopping John's mouth with his own. They were pressed chest to chest. John's nipples peaked at the contact, rubbing against Kit's chest, and heat pooled down between his legs. His hips heaved, and he let his mouth curve into a smile under Kit's, letting Kit know how much he liked this. He lifted his hips and rotated them to rub his dick up against the sensitive area between Kit's thighs. It was Kit's turn to do a little whining.

John chuckled, tilting back his head to let Kit lick his throat in long sweeps of his tongue up over John's chin. Another deep and dirty kiss. Very deep. Very dirty. John liked that. So Kit did it again. And again, before working his way back down John's throat, using lips and tongue to feel and taste the skin before licking down John's breastbone with broad, wet strokes. Kit was bent at an angle, bowing his back and shifting his ass down over John's legs, his fingers painting invisible shapes…. Hearts. They were little hearts. Kit's fingers painted invisible hearts over John's skin as he went.

"Kit," said John, again, as Kit knelt between his legs.

He lifted his legs up onto Kit's shoulders, crossing his ankles to anchor himself. Kit, smiling, turned his head from side to side, kissing each knee. Sweet. As sweet as the hearts. Careful not to dislodge John, Kit leaned forward again, brushing his lips down the inside of John's left leg from knee to thigh, stooping to get his tongue sweeping over the base of John's balls. Kit hummed something in the back of his throat as he mouthed at them. One hand still traced little hearts on John's skin, while the other worked into his ass, stretching him open.

This time, when John whined, he couldn't even manage Kit's name. Kit laughed. Somehow, Kit had found time to lube up his own dick. Happened every time they made love, and John could never work out how Kit did it, because Kit's hands still appeared to be busy on his skin and getting him ready. John couldn't recall an instant when he couldn't feel the touch of both. But somehow Kit did it.

After fifteen years together, John's body opened easily for Kit, used to him. It welcomed him. John let out a long shuddery moan, and Kit surged in, gasping. Kit's hand was slick with lube. He closed it around John's dick, fisting it to the same rhythm his own found inside John's body. Their breath came hard and fast.

John pushed back against the dick in his ass, contracting the muscles when Kit surged forward and making the Kit-shaped channel in him tighter, relaxing when Kit pulled back. His legs slipped down to hook around Kit's waist, giving him more purchase on every thrust Kit made—tightening and relaxing, tightening and relaxing. Kit wasn't just rubbing up against John's prostate then, but banging on it, every blow sending lightning sizzling through John's veins. He couldn't think anymore. Lightning and fire were all he was, heat and the sweet sort-of pain that had him yelling, and Kit yelling, and had Kit's hips juddering as he slammed in one last time. Kit tightened his hand on John's dick until John spurted over his fingers at the same time Kit's dick spasmed.

Kit's mouth was on his. Kit's voice murmured against his lips. Kit loved him. Again and again, over and over, that was what Kit whispered as he kissed John's lips and put little feather kisses along the line of

John's jaw, and slowly their heart rates slowed and John could breathe again.

They were chest to chest again, Kit still firmly lodged inside. John took his first real breath for several minutes, getting enough air into his lungs to speak. He carded his fingers through Kit's hair.

"Do you reckon they have this much fun in Bulgaria?"

Kit grinned. "No way in hell. They only have the one union. Give me time to get my breath back, and we'll have our first reunion. First of many."

Once it would have taken only minutes for them to be ready for another bout, John observed. "We're getting older. These days, we're taking longer."

"I sent for Viagra online, did I tell you?"

John snorted and shifted his ass, loving the burn and the fullness from Kit's dick in there. "As if. I'm not going to be outdone by you, Kit Lewis. Ready to be assimilated again whenever you are."

Kit grinned. "Resistance is futile," he said. And pounced.

[09:55:07] Kit.Lewis1: *Do you know what day this is?*

John pulled down the laptop lid, hiding the IM message that had just flashed on his screen. He didn't close the laptop down completely. He couldn't. In thirty minutes he'd need the presentation notes he'd labored over for the last couple of days. The little icon in the taskbar winked at him, defying his efforts to ignore it.

Michael Bowyer, CEO of Bowyer Industries, was still talking. The man had an economic vision to impart, it appeared, and was deaf and blind to everything else. The members of the BI board hung on his every word, staring at him like they were witnessing the Second Coming, or something.

Sycophants. Sycophants in sharp Tom Ford suits and handmade shoes.

John shifted uncomfortably. He'd made a gesture toward convention by wearing a suit jacket with his best, most designery jeans. Compared to this lot, he looked dangerously Bohemian. One or two glanced his way and smiled, the way sharks smiled while they eyed up lunch, before turning those intent gazes onto Bowyer again. They were all like puppies, waiting for the alpha dog's permission to attack.

John inched open the laptop lid. The icon flashed at him cheerily.

[10:01:24] Kit.Lewis1: *I know you're there. Do you know what day this is?*

Bowyer droned on. "And before we go any further, I'd better introduce John Hogarth, of Hogarth Lewis, our new design and branding contractors...."

[10:03:01] John Hogarth5: *Working here!*

He sat through the introductions, committing the names to memory.

[10:03:32] Kit.Lewis1: *It'll be a breeze.*

"I invited John to listen to our meeting today so he could get a real feel for our mission and values. John and his team at Hogarth Lewis will be working on the full expression of our new brand—I think that's what you call it, John? The brand expression?"

"Yes, Mike. Everything from your e-mail signatures to stationery, from every possible public relations and publicity tool to your website. And, of course, your internal communications too. We have plans for your company intranet and how to brand all staff communications." John tapped the laptop. "I have examples here."

They would get on to the detail in a moment or two, apparently, although Mike Bowyer said clearly that he'd seen the designs and loved them. Despite Kit's prediction, he didn't express any matrimonial intentions toward them or their creator, but he liked them. One or two of the suits looked disappointed. They'd been balked of their prey with that public endorsement and wouldn't dare treat John like so much chum in the water waiting to be eaten. In the meantime, Bowyer had more wisdom to impart on his company's vision and mission. Feeling safer, John opened the laptop lid a little farther.

[10:07:51] Kit.Lewis1: *C'mon, John. Do you know what day this is?*

John didn't jump this time. He considered Kit's question and looked it in the face, noting its innocent and inoffensive expression and answering it with an innocent and inoffensive expression of his own.

[10:08:17] John.Hogarth5: *It's Thursday.*

[10:08:46] John Hogarth5: *This is where I start getting out of my clothes, right?*

[10:09:15] **Kit.Lewis1:** *In a meeting with a *client*?*

[10:10:05] **Kit.Lewis1:** *Do you think that'll seal the deal with Bowyer? Not my type. And I don't like sharing.*

[10:10:31] **Kit.Lewis1**: *I mean, I was just asking what day this is.*

John let his mouth tighten and looked away from the screen. Bowyer had moved on to a review of the general economic situation, analyzing global economic trends solely in relation to how they affected Bowyer Industries' bottom line.

[10:12:43] **Kit.Lewis1:** *John?*

[10:15:13] **Kit.Lewis1:** *Okay. I lied. It is a special day.*

[10:15:56] **Kit.Lewis1:** *It's Motherhood and Beauty Day in Armenia."*

John hoped he looked like he was taking notes while apparently listening to Bowyer as intently as any BI employee. He smiled and nodded whenever Bowyer glanced at him.

[10:16:48] **John.Hogarth5:** *Motherhood and Beauty Day.*

[10:17:11] **Kit.Lewis1:** *You've got it.*

[10:17:50] **John.Hogarth5:** *In Armenia.*

[10:18:39] **Kit.Lewis1:** *Stop that!*

[10:20:14] **John.Hogarth5:** *No. I don't see how you can celebrate that one.*

"I'll ask John to take us through the designs in a moment, but first I wanted to add a word or two about my expectations of—"

[10:22:02] **Kit.Lewis1:** *We'll strike a blow for men's liberation and pretend it's Manhood and Beauty Day. We're both men.*

[10:22:47] **Kit.Lewis1:** *And I'm beautiful.*

[10:23:24] **John.Hogarth5:** *You're on your own, Kit. Signing out.*

[10:25:18] **Kit.Lewis1:** *Hey!*

[10:26:06] **Kit.Lewis1:** *Just kidding.*

[10:30:31] **Kit.Lewis1:** *John?*

[10:31:19] **Kit.Lewis1:** *If you don't like that one, we could celebrate another one. How about the Landing Day of the Thirty-Three Orientales in Uruguay?*

[10:33:24] **John.Hogarth5:** *Landing Day of the Thirty-Three Orientales.*

[10:35:08] Kit.Lewis1: *Sigh. Yes.*
[10:35:49] John.Hogarth5: *In Uruguay.*
[10:37:12] Kit.Lewis1: *I'm going to kill you.*

"And now over to John." Mike Bowyer nodded in John's direction.

John sighed, flicked out of IM and into his presentation notes. The IM icon flashed at him, but he had a job to do.

Anyway, he knew his Kit. He wasn't really in danger of death, although injury was another matter. The least he could expect would be that Kit would make pretty damn certain both of them walked around pretty carefully for a couple of days.

He pointed the laser at the projector and launched into the presentation, and all the time he was smiling so much his audience of suits probably thought he was a typical artist, out of his head on something trippy composed of illegal chemicals.

But then, none of them was going home that night to celebrate the Landing of the Thirty-Three Orientales with Kit Lewis.

Poor suckers.

"Do you know what day this is?" Kit was lounging on the sofa, smiling.

John considered his answer. "It's the Day of the Autonomous Community in Spain."

Kit's jaw dropped. "The Day of the Autonomous Community?"

"Yes."

"In Spain."

"That's the one."

Kit frowned. "Which autonomous community? La Rioja? Castile?"

"Dunno. Does it matter?"

"Oh," said Kit. "No. Guess not. I didn't mean that one anyway."

John joined him on the sofa. "Ah, then you have to be referring to Upswing of the Revolution Day in the Congo."

"Upswing of the Revolution Day."

"Yup."

"In the Congo."

John had a sudden realization about why Kit had threatened to kill him. It was a damn annoying reaction. His mouth tightened. "Yes," he said coldly.

Kit shook his head. "No, it wasn't that one either."

"Okay. How about the Day of Accord and Reconciliation in Russia? The Day of the Nationalization of the Oil Industry in Ecuador? National Salvation Revolution Day in Antigua? Tomb Sweeping Day in Korea?"

"People like celebrating revolutions," noted Kit. He added, sadly, "You've found the website."

"Google is our friend." John nodded. "You were pretty casual about which ones you chose, weren't you? Did we celebrate any of them on the right date?"

Kit shrugged. "I just liked the names. Didn't matter about the dates."

"Ah. Makes sense in Kit-land, I guess. So which one were you going for this time?"

"Svetitskhovloba in Georgia."

"Sevetits-what?"

"Svetitskhovloba. In Georgia. Not our Georgia, mind. The one over beside Russia somewhere."

"Svetitskhovloba." John shook his head. Trust Kit to choose the exotic-sounding one.

"You've got it."

"In Georgia."

"I swear I'll kill you," said Kit, glowering. "They will never find the body. And if they did, no one would blame me. I'd get off."

"What the hell does it mean?"

"I dunno. I just thought it made a brilliant excuse to have sex with you."

John grinned at him. "Kit, why in hell do you need an excuse?"

Kit looked suddenly very shy. "I know. But I never want it to be just ordinary for you, John. I know we've been together... huh, fifteen years. Can you believe that? Longer than any straight couples we know have been married. Since we were in college."

"Fifteen years," John said and smiled. Almost of its own volition, his hand lifted to play with Kit's thick brown hair. He loved Kit's hair.

"Fifteen great years." Kit nodded. "I just want it always to be fun and exciting and wonderful for you. Not just the same old, same old. Not just boring and everyday."

"Oh, it is, Kit. It is. It always is." John smiled and leaned forward to kiss Kit. When he pulled back, Kit no longer looked shy but disgustingly complacent. John didn't care. "It's all the boring, everyday things that make it real. It's always fun and exciting and wonderful. You're always wonderful for me."

Kit pretended to blush. "Aw shucks." He grinned. "Don't say the L word. I'll just get all mushy."

"Mushy won't do. I need you hard-edged. We have a lot to celebrate. Fifteen years and a lot of revolutions. You on for a little—what was it? Svetits-something-or-other? Peace and Accord? National Revolution Day?"

"You bet!" said Kit with unfeigned enthusiasm. "All of them." He gestured to his groin. "I tell you, Johnny, I've got quite the revolutionary upswing going on here!"

John grinned. He'd take any sucker's money on that. What's more, he knew just the man to take care of the upswing.

And he did.

ANNA BUTLER learned early that life is wonderful if you live it always drunk on words. As a child she preferred books to toys, disdaining dolls for Enid Blyton and the Famous Five. She started scribbling stories almost as soon as she first learned to write; first to amuse her little sister, later to savor the richness and flavor of the words for herself. After years of working as a communications specialist for the UK civil service, she's now living with her husband and Molly the cockerpoo in London's East End, writing full time and combining her love of m/m romance with her love of science fiction.

Anna's website is http://annabutlerfiction.com. You can also find her on Facebook at http://www.facebook.com/anna.butler.9822. E-mail her at annabutlerfiction@gmail.com.

The Responsible One

Eva Clancy

Tom

"Why don't you go without me?" Tom said. "Or you could call Andy and see if he wants to go?" He kept his tone light and his attention fixed on the coffee machine, but he could sense the waves of resentment coming off Owen as he ate his frosted cereal at the kitchen table. Frosted cereal. Ugh. Just thinking about that much sugar made Tom's teeth ache.

There was a brief silence. Then, "I wanted to go with you," Owen said. His voice was tense with anger. "You promised last weekend we'd spend some time together."

"I know, babe, and I'm sorry. If I could avoid going to work today—"

Owen clattered his spoon down on the table. "Please don't pretend there's nothing you can do. We both know that nobody else goes into your office at the weekends—you spend long enough moaning about it."

Tom sighed. Okay, maybe he had an overly developed sense of responsibility, but he couldn't let everything slide just because that was what everyone else was doing.

"I spent ages planning a route and getting the bikes ready," Owen continued. "You watched me do it, Tom! You knew this was important to me, but you still let me down at the last minute. Again."

"I'm sorry," Tom said again, but this time he didn't try to suppress the resentment in his tone. Was it really too much to expect Owen to be in his corner over this? He wearily ran a hand over the back of his neck, wincing at the tension he carried there.

"You're always sorry," Owen muttered.

They lapsed into a strained silence, broken only by the *drip, drip, drip* of the coffee machine. It was an ancient thing, and it produced a lethal caffeine-heavy brew that Tom loved and Owen couldn't stomach.

When the machine eventually stopped, Tom reached for a mug, pausing when he caught sight of the time. Shit, was it almost ten already? This morning's argument had set him back more than hour. He'd hoped to be at the office by now.

Well, he could always have breakfast at his desk. It was probably better than being glared at by Owen across the kitchen table, wasn't it?

Decision made, he began raking through the kitchen cupboards for something to put his coffee in, finally unearthing a big vacuum mug Owen had bought him a couple of Christmases ago. The reindeer on the front was a bit unseasonal for April, but it would keep the coffee hot, and it held almost a pint, which should help him stay awake after his crappy night's sleep. He gave the mug a quick rinse under the tap, then filled it almost to the top with coffee, adding a cursory dash of milk before screwing the lid on. Another rake around in the larder scored him a couple of cereal bars.

"You're not even having breakfast before you go?" Owen's voice, tinged with disbelief, caused a stab of guilt.

Tom glanced at his lover, taking in the rigidity of his shoulders and the tight line of his mouth. Owen looked as though he was trying to suppress his anger, as though he was only just keeping it in check, and Tom's resentment flared again.

"I thought I might as well have breakfast in the office," he said. "It's not as if we'd be eating together—you've already had yours. Such as it is."

"Oh, sorry, should I have offered to cook you some bacon and eggs before you head off to work again?" This in a sarcastic voice.

Clearly, Owen was spoiling for a fight, but he wasn't going to get one. Even if Tom hadn't had far too many other things to do, he didn't have the energy for another argument. "I need to get going," he said instead. He paused before adding more gently, "I really do wish you'd go cycling without me."

"Well, like I said, the purpose of going was to spend some time with you, so I don't really see the point. Besides, someone needs to clean this place up, and it might as well be me—it usually is."

"Please don't do cleaning. We can do that tomorrow. Together."

Owen gave a bark of disbelieving laughter. "Oh right, so the one day a week we have together we're going to spend *cleaning*? No thanks, I'll do it today, and maybe we can salvage something out of this weekend tomorrow. Assuming you don't have to work again." He turned on his heel and stalked out of the kitchen, throwing over his shoulder, "You have a great Saturday at work. I'll be sure to have your dinner on the table when you get back like a good little wife."

Tom sighed, grabbed his reindeer mug, and made for the door.

Owen

IT WASN'T the Saturday Owen had been hoping for. He'd been so looking forward to taking the bikes out again—it'd been months since they'd been cycling.

Now that Tom was gone, Owen felt like shit. He was still pissed off, still furiously angry. He knew Tom wasn't having an easy time at work, but this seemed to be turning into the new normal for them—and it felt like Tom didn't even get why Owen was so angry about being let down again.

Tom acted like Owen was being a brat over not getting his own way, but the truth was Owen just fucking *missed* Tom. And frankly it didn't feel like the sentiment was returned. Right now it felt like he was a duty to Tom, an afterthought. Another job on Tom's long list of jobs to be done: *spend time with Owen.*

The stress Tom was under wasn't just preventing them spending time together. Owen only had to look at the state of the house to see that. It really was a horrible mess. The laundry basket was overflowing—no clean socks for either of them—and the kitchen was a pigsty. The bathroom needed a good scrub too. Without a doubt, it would take most of the day to sort out.

Ah well, he might as well get to it.

Donning a pair of sweat pants and a ratty T-shirt, Owen got busy, going at the place like Snow White on steroids.

By midafternoon, the house was transformed. The bathroom and kitchen shone, the carpets were vacuumed, and the laundry was well on its way to being up to date. He'd even finished his most hated job of the day: ironing. He normally didn't bother ironing his stuff, and Tom tended to do his own, but in a fit of generosity—or maybe, more honestly, martyrdom—Owen had decided to tackle Tom's work shirts. Now, as he added the last shirt to the neatly folded pile and unplugged the iron, a sense of satisfaction washed over him. Once he'd put this stuff away, he was done. A cold beer while he watched this afternoon's England game on TV would be ample reward for his efforts.

The cleaning spree didn't exactly match a twenty-five-mile bike ride in the activity stakes, but it seemed to have helped to work off some of his temper. For the first time, the thought of his argument with Tom that morning didn't make him want to grab something and throw it at the wall.

Instead, he felt the familiar pall of worry settling on him. Tom was working far too hard. Coming to bed late every night and getting up early every morning too. The occasional attacks of insomnia he suffered when he was stressed were becoming noticeably more frequent. It wasn't healthy, and they both knew it, but so far neither of them had mentioned that fact. Not explicitly. Maybe it was because they'd both thought it was just a temporary blip to start with. Till the days had turned into weeks, then the weeks into months.

They were going to have to have a proper talk about it, Owen decided. Things had to change, and not so they could go on bike rides together. Bitching wasn't the way to go about it, though.

Tonight he'd show Tom how much he appreciated him with a good meal, and when they were nice and relaxed, Owen would explain that the reason for his bad temper this morning was that he was worried about Tom. That he missed him.

He'd make steak and peppercorn sauce—Tom's favorite—and pop to the independent wine shop down the road to get a nice bottle of red. And after they'd had their chat—and maybe some sex—they could watch a flick. They'd agreed at New Year that Owen would watch Tom's top ten film noir flicks in exchange for Tom watching Owen's top ten horrors. Tom had dutifully sat through most of Owen's list already, but Owen had only watched one of Tom's.

Owen frowned at that thought. They'd laughed about it just the other night when Tom had suggested putting on *The Big Sleep*. Owen had whinged, the way he always did when he didn't get his way, and Tom had laughed and given way. When Owen thought about it, Tom always gave in over stuff like that.

Well, not tonight. Tonight, they'd watch Tom's choices. All nine of them back to back, if Tom wanted.

With that decided, Owen lifted the pile of ironing and headed for the bedroom. Tom's shirts, still warm, gave off the satisfying fragrance of clean laundry as he climbed the stairs. He inhaled the scent, smiling, a smile that widened when he saw how good the bedroom looked. For the first time in ages, the floor was clear of Tom's discarded socks and boxers, and the ancient carpet was as spruce as it could be after a good vacuuming. The bedding was clean, the windows shone, and the furniture was dust free. It was a very different room from the one he'd woken up in this morning.

Owen laid the ironing on the bed and opened up the doors of the big double wardrobe. He put his own stuff away first—there wasn't much. As an IT guy in a big company with no customer-facing responsibilities, he could pretty much dress as he liked for work. Jeans and T-shirts were his uniform, so his side of the wardrobe was pretty low on dress shirts. His one and only suit, purchased for his sister's wedding last year, sat neglected at the back of the rail, going swiftly out of date.

Tom's side, by contrast, was bursting with suits. As a criminal lawyer, he lived in them. Owen frowned as he considered just how full the space was. The newly ironed shirts were going to get crushed all over again if he tried to shove them into the tightly packed space.

Hadn't Tom been talking about having a clear-out just the other day? There were clothes in there he hadn't worn for years, he'd said. Well, maybe Owen could help out. Even if he just made a pile of possible things to chuck out that Tom could look at when he got home, it'd be a start.

Owen began to shuffle through the hangers, quickly identifying a dozen garments Tom hadn't worn in ages and tossing them onto the bed. He'd fill a charity bag in no time at this rate.

The last third of the rail was taken up with suit bags. For all his untidiness, Tom generally did take care of his suits. There was probably at least one among all these Tom would never wear again. Owen thought of a suit with wide pinstripes he'd always hated. Now would be a good time to persuade Tom it had to go.

Owen lifted out the suit bags and laid them on the bed. Methodically, he began unzipping them, peering inside to ascertain the contents of each one.

The first four were fine. No sign of the offensive pinstripe yet. Maybe Tom had already ditched it? The fifth suit bag, though, felt oddly heavy when Owen moved it. He frowned, wondering at the unexpectedness of the weight.

He unzipped the bag and peeled the sides open. The first thing he noticed was a lump inside the jacket. He frowned, wondering what it could be, and unbuttoned the jacket to investigate further.

Hidden inside was a dark-blue plastic bag, the handles hooked over the top of the hanger.

Owen gently unhooked the bag. His stomach clenched as he shook the contents out onto the bed, wondering what was inside. When he saw what tumbled out, he let out a choked laugh. Strange that was his first instinct. His second was to feel weirdly empty.

He organized the items—the three magazines and two DVDs—in a tidy line. A bit tired and dated, they nevertheless declared the same interest. Dominance. Submission.

Slowly, Owen picked up the first magazine. The cover bore the date October 1999, and the pages were well thumbed and crumpled. It had been bought years and years before Owen had even met Tom. If Tom had bought this in 1999, he'd have been twenty at the time.

Owen had been ten.

He flicked through the magazine, glancing at the pictures: a man suspended in bondage, impaled by a dildo, clamps on his fleshy nipples; a leather daddy with his boy over his lap, the man's arse reddened from being spanked; a slender submissive sucking his tattooed master's cock, the master's hand fisted in his hair.

One or two of the pictures were unexpectedly tame. Owen couldn't look away from one picture Tom seemed to have marked with a turned-down corner. A stocky blond submissive sat, leashed and naked, at his dark-haired master's feet. He leaned his fair head against his master's leather-clad leg as his master stroked his fingers through the sub's hair. The sub looked blissed out, the master lazily satisfied.

The sub looked quite a bit like Owen.

He flicked through the other magazines and looked at the DVDs. They were all from around the same time and all D/s in nature. The pictures didn't disgust him—far from it, his cock was rock hard from looking at them. And there was nothing particularly violent or worrying in the material. So far as kinky stuff went, it struck Owen as fairly mild.

So why were they hidden away like this, in a suit bag in the wardrobe? Why had Tom never mentioned he was interested in this kind of thing? It wasn't as though Owen was the repressed type. They'd watched plenty of porn together. Had Tom thought he'd be disgusted by this?

Or perhaps Tom had just forgotten about them? Owen glanced in the suit bag again. He recognized the navy suit inside—it was one of Tom's favorites. He'd worn it just the other day.

So that was one theory shot, then—Tom had to know this stuff was in there.

Owen grabbed one of the DVDs, leaving the other things lying on the bed with the garments he'd pulled out of the wardrobe and the pile of freshly ironed shirts. He went downstairs to the living room and stuck the DVD in the machine, his heart thudding as he waited for the movie to load.

The weirdest sense of disbelief suffused him. If there was something he'd never worried about, it was his and Tom's sex life. They both liked sex, and they had it all kinds of ways. When they did anal, they switched up who topped and who bottomed. They both liked fucking, and they both liked being fucked—and sucked and rimmed and wanked. Everything was good between them, open and easy. He'd always felt lucky, having a boyfriend like Tom, who didn't seem to have hang-ups or limits. Even now, when Tom was as busy as he was, they always found time for sex. Owen had thought it was a measure of how strong their relationship was. If everything was okay in the bedroom, everything else would be okay.

Wouldn't it?

Owen made himself comfy on the couch, skipping past the trailers to the main event. His cock quickly grew hard as he watched the opening scene. It was pretty standard stuff. An American flick set on a college campus. Geeky college student meets dominant professor. The actors were buff and toned and actually pretty unconvincing as a geek and an academic respectively, but Owen's cock didn't give a shit about plausibility. He was hard within a minute, leaking precum within two.

The professor spanked the student for handing in his assignment late. Then he forced him to his knees and stuffed his cock in the lad's mouth, fucking it for a long time before coming on his face. He tied the guy up, spanked him again, harder. Rimmed him. Fucked him. Brought in another guy and double-teamed him.

Owen's cock was as hard as a stone as he watched, but for all the wrong reasons. He didn't see himself as the student. Or the blond sub in the picture in the magazine, leaning against his master's leg. He tried to imagine Tom bending him over like the dom professor did to the student. Tom spanking and fucking him. Telling him what to do.

It didn't... work for him.

Thinking of fucking Tom worked, though. Thinking of Tom choking on his dick, like the student was doing right now, worked.

He liked that so much that it only took a few more strokes of his hand and he was coming, all over his belly.

Regret followed closely on the heels of his orgasm.

He sat through the rest of the film with a limp dick, thinking *That's what Tom wants*, and as the credits rolled up the screen, he realized something: Tom wasn't like him. He wasn't satisfied with their relationship.

If he was, he wouldn't have this stuff hidden away, would he?

Tom

TOM threw an armful of files onto the passenger seat and wrenched his seat belt on. Jesus. Six o'clock. He'd worked the whole day, a full extra day, and he was still behind.

It wouldn't be so bad if anyone else had come in, but, as usual, he was the only one who'd turned up, and now he felt as pissed off as it was possible to be. He'd hoped to get away with working three or four hours max, but it hadn't happened. Too much to do. He turned his head and stared at the buff-colored files. Was he seriously going to look at those tonight? Tomorrow?

Ever since Kate had gone off sick, it had been like this. Latimer & Brown was a small practice, and the four partners had agreed to absorb Kate's work among them. Except it seemed Tom was the only one actually honoring that agreement.

Simon, the senior partner, was perennially lazy and had been since Tom joined the firm. He viewed himself as semiretired and rarely put in a full week. While Tom found Simon's idleness irritating, he'd long ago realized Simon would never have offered him a partnership if he hadn't needed a young deputy to pick up his slack. Tom had known Simon's work pattern wouldn't change just because Kate was off, no matter what platitudes he mouthed in partners' meetings.

Rosie and Paul, though—they had been the big disappointment. The three of them had always got on, all having joined the firm around ten years ago, and all being made up to partner around the same time following a rash of partner retirements. They regularly met for drinks—usually to let off steam about Simon—and had dinner at each other's houses. But when things had blown up with Kate, neither Paul nor Rosie had done more than the bare minimum to keep things ticking along. Whenever something big needed to be done, it was always Tom stepping in.

When Tom had finally brought up the problem with them a couple of weeks ago, Paul had gone into a long explanation about how he and Rosie both had families, which—Paul said—made weekends and evenings so much more difficult to manage for them than Tom.

Rosie hadn't said anything, just sat next to Paul, silently backing him up, and somehow Tom knew they'd talked about this. Agreed how to approach it. Discussed—and agreed—that Tom's personal life wasn't as important as theirs.

Somehow that had stung more than if they'd just been completely thoughtless, like Simon.

He hadn't told them that, though. He'd calmly pointed out they weren't being fair and that they had to do more. And they'd agreed—a little resentfully, but he could live with that. Until, that was, he realized they were just like Simon—their promises were empty. When the shit hit the fan, they all disappeared, leaving Tom to deal with the crisis.

Well, he was fucked if he was going to do it any longer.

Tom sat in the front seat of his car, leaning his arms on the steering wheel and staring out the windscreen. Suddenly it all seemed very simple. Come Monday morning, he was going to call a partners' meeting and give them one last chance—they'd agreed at the outset that they couldn't afford any temporary help, but they could afford it if they all agreed to reduce their monthly salaries. And if the rest of them weren't up for that, he'd pick up the phone to Jo Kennedy and arrange to meet her for that coffee both of them knew would have a business proposition at the end of it.

For a few minutes Tom sat there, contemplating the hugeness of that decision, taking stock of how it made him feel. Weirdly, as scary as it was, he felt as though a weight had been lifted off his shoulders. In fact, he felt better than he had in ages. Better, but angry. Angry at his partners for their behavior and even angrier at himself for putting up with it.

He'd let down Owen again today, after promising all week to go cycling with him. He'd watched Owen plan the route on Thursday night, watched him get the bikes in from the garage and check them over, even watched him mend a puncture on Tom's. Tom had been too busy working to do much more than grunt his agreement to Owen's happy chatter at the time. He'd worked till after midnight that night, determined to get ahead so he could leave at a decent time on Friday and guarantee Saturday free, but on Friday morning, one of Kate's cases had gone tits up, and it had put him behind again.

But then, one of Kate's cases always went tits up. Why should Owen's plans be upset every time it happened? Why couldn't Paul or Rosie deal with it? Or even one of the others? Why was it always Tom?

It had to stop.

And he had to show Owen he was sorry for taking him for granted so much over the last few months.

When Tom got home, he'd make a start with an amazing blowjob. Just lead Owen straight into the bedroom and go down on him for ages. Tom shifted in his seat, his cock growing hard at the thought. Five years together, and just the thought of blowing Owen still made him hard. Just the memory of the other man's taste in his mouth, musky and sweet.

At first he'd thought it couldn't possibly work between them. The age difference had bothered him a lot. Owen had been nineteen when they'd met, Tom a decade older. Both sets of parents had freaked out, particularly Owen's dad. Tom had understood. Owen had only come out six months before and was still a teenager when he'd brought home his bearded twenty-nine-year-old boyfriend.

Tom still winced when he remembered that first meeting. He'd lost the beard the next day. He'd started wearing too-young clothes and listening to new music too. He'd even bought a fucking skateboard in his quest to bridge the chasm of that decade. And why? 'Cause the alternative—giving up on each other—wasn't an option.

Tom loved Owen way too much for that.

It had been one of those clichéd love-at-first-sight things. He'd seen Owen across a crowded bar—a beautiful young guy, just a little shorter and a bit broader than Tom with that dark-blond hair—and his heart had cranked to a standstill. Of course, it wouldn't have been love at first sight if Owen had turned out to have a crappy personality, but he hadn't. Owen had been clever and funny and self-deprecating too. Just as Tom had known he would be from that first glance across an empty bar. He'd looked at Owen and felt like he knew him, inside and out.

Five years on and look at them: Owen had spent today cleaning the house. It wasn't what most twenty-four-year-old guys would be doing. Christ, when Tom had been twenty-four, he'd been doing, well, everyone. He'd had a lot of lovers. Owen had only really ever had Tom. Other than some het sex with his one and only girlfriend and a couple of exploratory blowjobs with a guy at uni, he'd done nothing before they got together.

Tom had been his teacher.

Quite a responsibility, that. Especially when he found himself in love for the first time, so that everything they did together felt new to Tom too. New and beautiful. Innocent. He'd wanted to protect Owen's innocence. Had felt entrusted with it, especially when he'd looked into the worried eyes of Ken, Owen's dad, at that first meeting.

It's okay, he'd wanted to say. *I'm a good guy. I'm not going to hurt him.*

He smiled to himself, remembering that. Owen certainly wasn't innocent now. The only worry Tom ever entertained these days was whether he was preventing Owen from trying out new things he wanted to experience. Like last week when Owen had brought a ménage flick home. Did that mean he wanted to bring another guy into their bed? Tom didn't think he could handle that. And yet he'd had quite a few threesomes himself before he met Owen. Was it hypocritical to want Owen to forgo trying that out?

Owen was enough for Tom, but Tom had gotten all that experimentation stuff out of his system long before they'd met. What if Owen decided one day that he wanted other lovers, new experiences Tom couldn't give him?

And then there was the age difference.

When Owen was his age now, Tom would be forty-four.

Forty-four. Christ, nearly fifty.

Hell, right now, he might as well be ninety for all the fun he was giving Owen.

Well, that was something Tom *could* change, and he'd take the first step toward sorting it out on Monday morning. He was going to start putting Owen first for once.

Suddenly he couldn't wait to tell Owen what he'd decided.

He turned the car onto Cedar Drive, excited to be nearly home. He was on autopilot now, slowing down on cue for the speed bumps, turning right, then left, before cruising down that one last stretch of road and swinging into the drive in front of the house.

The lights were on, the blinds down. The place looked warm and inviting, and Tom smiled as he locked the car up and walked to the front door.

He toed off his shoes in the porch and hung up his jacket, calling out, "Babe, I'm home."

No answer.

"Owen?"

He pushed open the door to the living room and came to an abrupt halt at the sight that greeted him. Owen. Naked. Kneeling. Eyes downcast. And on the coffee table beside him, some very familiar magazines and DVDs.

"Owen—oh Jesus, you found—" Tom broke off, face flaming, voice dying in his throat.

Owen didn't even look up. He just knelt there, in a classic submissive pose, hands at the small of his back.

"Owen," Tom pleaded. "Please look at me!"

At last Owen raised his head. "Why didn't you tell me?" he said softly. "Did you think I'd be disgusted or something?"

"No, I—" Again Tom broke off, distracted by Owen's nakedness and submissive pose. "Could you get up? I can't think with you sitting like that."

Owen didn't move an inch. "You should have told me, Tom. I don't want you to hide stuff like that from me. If you want this, I'm cool with it. You know I trust you."

"Yes, I know," Tom replied, and he did. "I just—look, seriously Owen, get up. I just can't—I can't stand it! Please!"

Owen started at that, a hurt expression growing in his silvery eyes, but somehow Tom couldn't find the words to apologize for his sharp words. He rubbed the back of his neck, watching as Owen slowly got to his feet, his gut clenching and unclenching.

"Sorry," Owen muttered. "I just thought it might be a nice surprise for you, coming in and finding me waiting for you, like one of the boys in your magazines. After you've been working so hard, and I was such a brat this morning and—"

"Owen—"

"And then I find out you've got this secret kink I didn't even know about—"

"Owen—"

"And I just thought if I could show you that I'm okay with trying—"

"Owen, I'm not a dom!" The words burst out of Tom's mouth before he could think through the wisdom of saying them. He just had to stop Owen talking. Had to stop him standing there, expecting Tom to start ordering him around or something.

Owen immediately fell silent.

"I'm not a dom, okay?" Tom repeated more quietly. "So, thanks for"—he gestured at Owen and the stuff on the coffee table—"all this. But it's not me."

Owen just stared at him. Christ, what must he think? Tom couldn't bear to look into those watchful gray eyes a moment longer. He turned on his heel and headed for the door. "I'm going to take a shower."

"Tom, wait! Does that mean—?" Owen stopped midsentence, as though he couldn't think what to say next.

Tom stopped walking, but he couldn't bear to turn round, to look at Owen's disappointed face. "It means that when I was into that stuff—a long time ago—I preferred to be the guy on his knees." The silence that greeted that assertion was towering. After a moment Tom huffed out a sigh. "And it's all ancient history, so please don't make this into a big deal, Owen. I got over that little obsession a very long time ago."

And with that, he left the room, taking the stairs to the bathroom two at a time in his hurry to get away.

Owen

OWEN watched Tom leave the room, torn between humiliation at Tom's rejection and stunned disbelief at what he'd revealed. He realized, intellectually, that Tom wasn't rejecting *him*, just what he was offering. But not once had it occurred to him that Tom might see himself in the sub role.

How could Owen have been so blinkered? Because Tom was older and more experienced? Because he'd taught Owen everything he knew about sex? Because he was fucking *taller*?

Even more stupidly, why had Owen assumed Tom would want him to take the submissive role?

And why hadn't it occurred to him to tell Tom what *he* wanted? When he'd watched that DVD this afternoon, it had been the professor he'd identified with, not the student. It was the thought of control, not abandon, that had moved him.

God, had he really thought he could make everything all right with Tom with a gesture like this? Taking his clothes off and dutifully offering himself up for a spanking he didn't even want? It wasn't as though he'd want that from Tom. Damn. He should have *thought* about what those magazines and DVDs meant, what Tom wanted.

It was just that Tom was always in control. Always. Tom did everything. He sorted all the bills and paid the lion's share of them too, and when Owen protested, he'd gently point out that Owen's salary was much lower than his, promising they'd change the contributions in future, when Owen's salary went up.

Tom had guaranteed the loan Owen took out for his car too, and actually, come to think of it, he'd renewed the tax and insurance for it as well. He was the one who remembered everyone's birthdays—even Owen's parents—and made sure the cards and presents were sent on time.

Had they fallen into bad habits? Tom always taking responsibility and Owen always letting him? If so, it had been easily done. Tom seemed to naturally assume control. And, in fairness, maybe Owen naturally relinquished it. After all, he'd only lived away from home for two years before he'd moved in with Tom, and even then it had been in a flat-share that was one step up from a pigsty. Moving into Tom's well-appointed suburban home had felt like moving back home again, with lots of hot sex thrown in for good measure.

God, Tom. How must he be feeling right now? Without bothering to don his clothes again, Owen followed Tom upstairs.

The shower was already running, and when he pushed the bathroom door open, a fog of steam enveloped him. Tom stood in the shower cubicle, his dark head bent under the driving water and his back to Owen, the stiffening of his shoulders the only sign he'd heard him enter the room.

Owen paused for a moment, absorbing the beauty of Tom's lean frame under the water; then he eased the shower doors open and stepped inside, slid his arms round Tom's waist, and brushed his lips against the back of Tom's neck.

"I'm sorry," he whispered against Tom's golden skin. "I'm an idiot. I should have thought before I jumped to conclusions."

Tom's shoulders were rigid. "You don't need to apologize," he muttered. "I'm the one who hid stuff from you." He turned then, and his expression was unhappy. "I'm so sorry."

Sometimes Owen went weeks just living life, and then he'd have a moment like this one when he'd see Tom—really *see* him—and he'd realize how much he loved him. It got him all over—in his heart and his gut and his cock all at once. He wished he could explain the feeling to Tom, wished he could put into words how full his heart was.

"Come to bed," he said instead. "Let's make love."

Tom's eyes glittered; he looked half surprised, half turned on. He let Owen turn off the water and tug him out of the shower, let Owen scrub a towel over his naked body and lead him, unresisting, into their bedroom, guiding him to the bed.

"Lie down," Owen said.

Tom settled himself down on his back, and for a moment, Owen let himself just look. Tom was perfect, so perfect. Long and lean, his chest furred with dark hair, his abdominal muscles evident but not overdeveloped, a faint olive tone to his skin. Matched with the dark eyes and hair that he'd got courtesy of his Italian mother, that perfect olive skin gave Tom a Mediterranean look Owen loved. Tom always looked amazing when they went on holiday, his skin toasting deliciously in the sun. Not like Owen, with his blond hair and fair skin that freckled and burned scarlet at the drop of a hat.

He straddled Tom's hips and leaned down, beginning his journey at Tom's throat. Tom loved being kissed there, loved being bitten too, farther down, at the tender spot where his shoulder and neck met. Owen licked him, gathering up droplets from the shower on his tongue, loving the rasp of stubble against his face and the fresh, just-showered scent of Tom's skin. Loving too the moan from Tom's throat.

Their cocks brushed, greeting each other, and Owen shivered. He moved lower, cataloging all the joys of Tom's body. Hello, small, light-brown nipples. Hello, golden, muscled flesh. Hello, dark treasure trail. He licked and kissed his way over Tom's body, the journey brisk, a sprint rather than a stroll. When he reached Tom's cock, he drove his mouth over it, relishing the rude arrival of the bulbous head at the back of his throat.

"Oh *fuck*, that's good." Tom groaned above him, his fingers twining into Owen's hair, and Owen moaned his own pleasure around the dick in his mouth, slurping inelegantly, though effectively if Tom's moans were anything to go by.

After another minute of sucking dick, Owen pulled off and moved down to explore Tom's balls, licking his sac with the broad flat of his tongue, teasing the bollocks inside before pulling them gently into his mouth and mouthing them. Christ, he could never get enough of Tom's body.

He kneeled up and took hold of Tom's lower legs, pushing them up to his chest.

"Hold them up," he ordered roughly. "I want to rim you. Then I'm going to fuck you."

Tom moaned his agreement, dark eyes gleaming with something beyond the obvious pleasure of the moment. Something Owen hadn't noticed before. Or rather, something he'd noticed but hadn't put a name to before.

And right then, he paused.

Something clicked into place.

He realized his words just now were more to Tom than a mere statement of intent. They were a command. And that Tom moaned not only from the anticipated pleasure of being rimmed and fucked, but from hearing—and obeying—Owen's orders.

Owen watched as Tom lifted his legs, gripping the backs of his thighs and tipping his hips up to expose his hole to Owen's gaze.

Owen didn't move straightaway. Until just now, he'd been racing toward the finish line, desperate to get his cock inside Tom, but now he paused, his heart beating fast as he considered the potential of this. Of Tom's suddenly obvious desire to submit and his own desire to control.

He let his gaze move over Tom, traveling from his exposed arse, up the backs of those muscled thighs, and all the way up to Tom's flushed face.

"More," he said softly. "Come on. Pull those legs back and show me that hole."

Tom whimpered. He shifted, gripping his legs even tighter and lifting his arse a tiny bit higher. And God, what a filthy, sexy picture he presented, lying there, as exposed as a man could be.

"More," Owen said again. "Show me how much you want it."

Tom's dark eyes were glassy with his lust, his breath coming in short, shallow gasps as he struggled to obey. He probably couldn't get his arse much higher but he did his best, and Owen loved watching his earnest struggle to please. He laughed softly, and that seemed to prompt another moan from Tom.

"Good boy," Owen praised at last. "Now, don't move a muscle. I want you to keep your arse just like that for me while I get you nice and wet." Tom moaned again, closing his eyes, a flush of red over his high, sharp cheekbones.

Owen got himself comfortable. He rubbed his hands over Tom's arse, then dipped his head and teased at his pink hole with his lips and tongue. Working up some spit, he gradually softened his tongue till he was lapping at Tom's hole in broad swipes, Tom moaning his pleasure. He'd always loved rimming Tom, loved the way Tom lost control. Now, as he feasted on Tom's body, licking and probing him in the most intimate way possible, he began to acknowledge to himself why he loved it so much. He was controlling Tom, mastering him, owning him.

"Please, Owen—" Tom whimpered.

Owen lifted his head. "Please what?"

"Please—please fuck me."

"Open your eyes and ask me again."

Tom obeyed him. His eyes, those beautiful, liquid eyes, were soft with surrender. "Please fuck me, Owen."

Owen could hardly suppress a groan of his own at that. "I'm gonna fuck you so hard, Tom. And I want to hear you while I'm doing it. I want to hear how much you love my cock in your arse."

"Yes, yes," Tom agreed frantically.

Grabbing the lube, Owen coated his dick in the stuff, leaving Tom's hole alone. Tom liked a bit of burn, and he was more than ready to be fucked, loose and open from the rimming.

"You keep that arse nice and high for me, you understand?"

"Yes—" A gasp of agreement.

Owen slid his hands up the backs of Tom's legs and pressed forward, pushing past the ring of Tom's muscle and letting the head of his cock settle for a moment. Tom's muscles gripped him almost painfully tight before he thrust all the way home. The meaty arrow of his dick plunged into the hot grip of Tom's body, his balls meeting Tom's in a prickly kiss. They both grunted with pleasure.

"Jesus, Owen, fuck me hard. I'm gonna come in about ten seconds."

Owen took him at his word. He fucked Tom brutally, letting go of a part of himself he wasn't sure he'd ever let entirely go before. He thought, *This body belongs to me*, and he stamped his ownership on it, on Tom, without holding back anything.

And Jesus Christ, but Tom loved his roughness. He howled as he came, squirming on Owen's dick and shooting spunk all over his belly. His arse quivered and pulsed on Owen's dick, drawing an orgasm from Owen that was longer and more intense than any Owen remembered. Better even than that magical first time with Tom.

He slumped on top of Tom as Tom's legs dropped to the mattress, and for a minute they simply lay there, panting. Then Owen said, mumbling the words into Tom's ear, "I love you, Tom. And I promise, things are going to change. I'm going to be the boyfriend you deserve from now on."

Tom

TOM shifted, pushing at Owen's shoulder till he lifted his head.

"What are you talking about? I don't want you to change, Owen. I love you just as you are."

Owen flopped over onto his back. "I know you do." He sighed. "But you know what? You shouldn't. You deserve better than you've been getting from me."

What?

Tom sat up and looked down at his lover. Owen's expression was troubled, and Tom realized he was serious. A sickening suspicion bloomed inside him. Why the hell would Owen feel *guilty*? His heart clutched, and a lump rose in his throat as he contemplated what might be coming.

"What have you done?" he whispered, even as his mind raced forward. Owen had said he'd be a better boyfriend, so he wasn't planning on going anywhere, right? But what if his regret was over something Tom would find difficult to forgive?

Owen's blue eyes widened in astonishment at Tom's expression, and he sat bolt upright. It might have looked kind of funny if Tom hadn't felt like he'd just been stabbed.

"Hey, I've not done anything!" Owen exclaimed. "What, you think I'm trying to confess something here?" He scowled then, looking offended. "Why would you even think that?"

If the fear had felt like a heart seizure, the relief felt like jumping off a bungee platform. Tom blew a blast of air out of his lungs that turned into laughter. "God, you scared me then!"

But Owen was still scowling. "I mean it. Why would you think that?"

Tom stared at him, bewildered by his irritation. "Um—because of what you *said*?" he offered in a tone of voice that suggested Owen was asking him to confirm the bleeding obvious. Which he was, in Tom's opinion.

Owen didn't smile. "I didn't say anything to suggest I'd done something bad. Just that I was going to be a better boyfriend. Why would you immediately assume I'm talking about, what, *cheating* or something?"

It was a fair question. The answer was easy too, though not to admit to.

"I suppose," Tom said slowly, "because it's my biggest fear."

Owen looked shocked at that. "What? Why? What reason have I ever given you to worry about that?"

Tom sighed. He flopped back down on the mattress and covered his eyes with his arm. He couldn't look Owen in the eye as he admitted the truth in flat voice. "You're twenty-four. When I was your age, I was fucking everything that moved."

"Oh right, so obviously that's what I want be to be doing?"

Tom laughed without humor. "I don't know, but I wouldn't blame you if you did. You were just a kid when we got together—"

"Yeah, and that's how you've always seen me, isn't it, Tom? It's still how you see me! Christ, you act like you're my father sometimes."

Tom moved his arm away from his eyes. Not that Owen noticed. He was too busy contemplating the duvet, apparently fascinated by the swirling pattern.

"That is *not* how I see our relationship, Owen."

"Oh really?" Owen sounded unconvinced; then he looked up and met Tom's gaze, his own unhappy. "You know what I realized today, Tom? Much as I love you, the fact is, we don't have an equal partnership."

"Of course we have an equal partnership!" Tom protested. "Didn't I transfer half the house to you?"

"Yes, you did," Owen agreed. "Even though I pay way less than you toward the mortgage. You've always been incredibly generous, Tom. That's not what I'm talking about."

"Then what are you talking about?"

"You take care of everything. You indulge all my whims."

"I like taking care of you—"

"Whenever we go out, you drive. You arrange all our holidays because I'm too lazy to search for flights on the Internet. Last week you spent two hours finding the best car insurance deal for me because I was busy playing FIFA 13."

"I don't mind."

"You should mind. You sent my mum flowers for Mother's Day and let me take the credit when she phoned up to thank me. You always pay when we go out."

Tom laughed. "This is silly."

Owen turned a serious look on him. "You don't admit to me that you're stressed at work. You always tell me you've got everything under control, as though I can't handle the truth. As though I haven't noticed you're not sleeping properly."

"Owen. I—" He broke off, seeing for the first time that this wasn't just about who paid the bills.

"And," Owen continued, lying down to settle his head beside Tom's on the pillow, "you never told me that you like to submit."

Tom closed his eyes.

All true.

"I'm sorry," he whispered.

"We've been together for five years, Tom. You couldn't tell me in all that time?"

Tom shook his head, eyes still clamped shut. "You were so young when we got together," he whispered. "How could I corrupt you with all that? It was bad enough I was ten years older. I just wanted us to have a normal, healthy relationship. God, Owen, your dad was already looking at me like I was some kind of pervert!"

Owen gave a bark of laughter. "What are you talking about, you idiot? My dad loves you!"

Tom opened his eyes. Owen's blue eyes were dancing with amusement.

"He didn't love me then," Tom said. "Believe me. We had a couple of very uncomfortable conversations at the start."

"Christ, Tom, he *is* my dad! It wasn't easy for him. He didn't see the gay thing coming at all. I play rugby, for God's sake!"

Tom laughed weakly at that.

"But he does love you. He was just saying to me at Christmas how glad he was I met you so early on. Probably thinks meeting you stopped me going out and fucking half the gay men in the free world."

"Lesser of two evils?"

Owen chuckled. "Probably, yeah. Well, what parent wants to think about their child having sex with anyone?"

"Or vice versa," Tom agreed, shuddering.

"The thing is, though," Owen said, gently moving them back to the subject, "for whatever reason, you still treat me like some immature kid who can't take care of himself. Who you can't corrupt by asking for sex the way you really want it."

"No!" Tom interrupted. "Don't you dare start thinking that I've been secretly longing to be spanked all this time! It's not like I was in the lifestyle and gave it up to be with you."

"Well, what was it like?"

"It was nothing! I found it sexy, so I bought some mags and DVDs to wank to. Oh, and once, I went to a club, though I only watched."

"Did you do anything with any doms?"

"Nope. I let one boyfriend spank me a couple of times, but it wasn't anything much. He wasn't a dom."

"You never wanted to try it out properly? Be honest, please, Tom. You went to a club, so that tells me you wanted to do more than just wank about it."

Tom felt himself flush but forced himself to be honest. "I suppose I was interested in exploring it at some point—with the right partner."

"And that's not me?"

Tom thought of the way Owen had just fucked him. The effortless way he'd taken control, reducing Tom to a heap of quivering need. His cock hardened again, just at the thought.

"If you wanted it, you'd be my perfect partner," Tom admitted, flushing even hotter. "But I would never ask you to do anything you don't want to, and I don't need it anywhere as much as I need you."

Owen paused. "And if I want it too?"

Tom returned Owen's searching look, his heart suddenly beating way too fast. "Do you?"

Owen gave a soft laugh. "Oh yeah. I watched one of your DVDs this afternoon, the college student one. And God, did I want to be that professor!"

"So why did you present yourself like a sub when I got home tonight?"

Now it was Owen's turn to look discomfited.

After a brief silence, he said, "It didn't occur to me that you would see yourself in the sub role."

"Why?"

"For the reasons we've just been talking about. You've spent the last five years taking care of me. The idea that you might ever want to give up control just didn't occur to me."

"So it was nothing to do with you wanting to be the sub?"

If Tom had entertained any doubts, they were dispelled by Owen's reaction.

"God, no! Wasn't that obvious from the way I just fucked you?"

Tom smiled, embarrassed and pleased at once. "That was hot."

"Fucking hot. I want to do it again. I want to do everything to you, Tom."

"What do you mean 'everything'?"

Owen gave a grin, inching closer and palming Tom's arse firmly. "I want to spank this. Hard. I want to hear you beg for my cock in your mouth and your arse. I want to tie you up and torture you with pleasure and refuse to let you come. How's that for starters?"

Tom moaned.

"But that's not all I want," Owen continued, more seriously. "I want us to be equal partners the rest of the time. Which means no more indulging me like a kid. And no more hiding your problems from me. You have to *talk* to me, Tom."

Tom's heart swelled in gratitude. Owen wasn't going anywhere. He was in this for the long haul, just like Tom. "You're right. And I want that too. I'm so sorry I treated you like a kid, Owen."

"Yeah, well, I'm sorry for behaving like one."

"But can I still indulge you sometimes? I like organizing our holidays, and you know you hate trawling the Internet for deals."

Owen laughed. "So long as you let me indulge you back. And tell me what's going on in here." He kissed Tom's forehead.

"Yeah, well about that. I've decided to meet up with Jo Kennedy. Speak to her about making a move."

"Really?"

"Yeah. I was going to call a meeting of the partners first, but you know what? I already know how it'll turn out. So I'll text Jo tomorrow and set up a coffee for Monday."

"Wow. Look at you being all decisive!"

"You know me. It might take me a while to make a decision, but once I do, I commit."

"Yes," Owen agreed, smiling. "You do."

They lay there for a while, entangled in each other's arms, sharing occasional kisses and love murmurs.

"Fancy watching a flick?" Owen said at last. "I could bring up a DVD and some beers and snacks."

Tom smiled. "What were you thinking of? We've still not watched *Final Destination 4*, have we?"

Owen got out of bed and grabbed his robe. "I was thinking of *Double Indemnity*, actually," he said casually. "That's your favorite, isn't it?"

Tom grinned. "Ah, yes. Barbara Stanwyck and Fred MacMurray. It's a great movie. Not quite my favorite, though."

Owen's face fell. "Really?"

"Yeah," Tom said casually. "It's not a patch on *Swedish Sub Slut 3: The Whole Smorgasbord.*"

Owen burst out laughing. That fabulous big, generous laugh of his. He dived back onto the bed, landing on Tom and knocking all the air out of him. "I fucking love you, you nutter," he said happily.

"Yeah, well, I fucking love you too," Tom replied. "So kiss me again before you go and get that porn."

"Ya know," Owen mused out of the side of his mouth, Bogey-style, "this could be the beginning of a beautiful friendship."

"*Casablanca* isn't film noir. Though some of the shots—"

He never reached the end of that sentence. Owen's lips pressed to his, and their tongues tangled.

It was just him and Tom.

The rest of the world would just have to wait.

EVA CLANCY is a long-standing lover of all forms of romance but most particularly M/M. She traces her love of the genre back to reading *Maurice* by E.M. Forster in her last year of school in 1990. Although it was not a set text for her sixth-year English exam, she wrote about it anyway and likes to think that was why she got an A!

In between working her day job, looking after her two children, and arranging the occasional date with her husband, Eva writes sexy, romantic fiction featuring both contemporary and historical heroes. Eva lives in the UK with her family.

Visit Eva on her web site: http://evaclancy.blogspot.com

Twitter: @Eva_Clancy

E-mail: authorevaclancy@gmail.com

Home on the Range

Anna Martin

GRAY filled his paintbrush and carefully loaded the paper in front of him with color. Rich and bright, the paint filled his ink drawing and completed a section of the detailed diagram of an esophagus he'd been working on for several hours.

Although the heat outside was oppressive, here in his studio the air conditioning was cranked up as high as it could go, as Gray liked it. He allowed himself a moment to stretch his neck from side to side and scratch at his beard before continuing with the illustration.

Gray didn't look like an artist; he knew that. He didn't look much like a rancher either, although he seemed to be roughening into one of those with time and age. Lean muscles graced his tall frame, toned from physical labor and living with a man who made his life on cattle and horses. Gray could handle a horse just fine—the cows he avoided, where possible.

Outside his window the ranch spread away into the distance, the heat shimmering on the horizon. If Gray were to look up, it would be laid out for him, the endless miles of dirt and sky, but even though he'd set up his drawing board so it faced toward the wide windows, he was rarely distracted by the scenery. Not when he had a job to do.

Technically the ranch didn't belong to him. It was owned by his husband of seven years, the same husband who had been away for nearly four months now. The economy had gone to shit, and in an attempt to save his business, Colt had been forced out of the county to do research, network, and hopefully find an investor or two.

Gray missed him something crazy.

But he didn't think about that either.

Kings of Leon blasted through the stereo—Gray found their mix of rock and country blended into the background while he worked, just as he liked it. He had a playlist on his iPod and played it on shuffle. The band's back catalog was large enough to allow him several hours before he heard a repeat. Mostly he ignored the ranch hands who teased him about his choice in music—he was only just forty. Not too old to enjoy the modern stuff.

Tuned in to his work as he was, Gray didn't notice when the sleek black truck came down the long drive and pulled to a haphazard stop in front of the house. What he did notice was the blaring of a horn, cutting through "Day Old Blues." When a familiar face popped up through the sunroof, he dropped his paintbrush with a start, laughed in delight, and ran barefoot through the house, down the stairs, and out onto the deck.

"Colton Maverick, you ugly motherfucker," he drawled, slowing to a halt and leaning his hip against one of the posts that surrounded the veranda, his arms crossed over his chest.

Colt jumped down from the cab of the pickup he affectionately called Betsy and lifted his wide hat from his head. His sandy-brown hair had been cut, cropped short to his head, and he'd trimmed his beard back short too. Gray decided he liked it.

"Alastair Graystone," he responded, using the full name he knew Gray hated.

"Come here," Gray demanded.

Within moments Colt was in his arms, hot lips on his, wide hands cradling his waist.

"I missed you," Colt whispered into Gray's neck as they clung to each other.

"I missed you too."

It was all they needed to say.

"How's work?" Colt asked as they settled down into the porch swing with a couple of bottles of beer, both sore from the quick but incredible fuck they'd both needed before anything else. The need to reconnect always seemed to override everything else—food, water… a shower.

"Good," Gray said absently. "Busy."

When he'd graduated with a doctorate in medicine (a discipline his parents had blackmailed him into), there was an expectation that he'd follow the family business and open a local practice as his father and grandfather had done before him. Then he'd come out as gay, and it didn't matter what Gray did anymore. His family wouldn't notice or care.

The one thing he'd excelled at through his training was a keen eye for detail and an ability to turn the three-dimensional and grotesque into bold, often beautiful diagrams. Although he'd been approached while studying to provide illustrations, there had never been time—he was too busy.

Then when there was no medical practice to open, he found the time to take on a few jobs. Gray got an agent, took a booking, and from there a career sprang up around him. He provided drawings for medical journals and children's books and a range of different publications in between. He liked high school textbooks the best—he could be accurate but simple, a delicate balancing act.

"I wasn't expecting you home quite yet," Gray said. They'd last spoke on the phone a few days ago, Colt mentioning that things were still rough and he'd be back as soon as he could.

"There was a turn of events," Colt said. "I've picked up an investor."

"Really? What did they take?"

"Five percent of the business over the next five years, and two acres to build a house on. In return for a seventy-thousand investment over the same time."

"Where did you give them?"

"Not decided yet. He's going to come out to finalize the deal, but he wants this area specifically, and I was the only one willing to sell."

It would stick, and stick hard, Gray knew, for Colt to have to give up some of his precious land. But times were tough. They'd take what they could get.

When Gray noticed Jared's red truck coming down the drive, he groaned internally. This was not the right time. Colt stayed silent as a fair head leaned out the window. The engine shut off.

"Hey," Jared called as he slammed the door of his truck closed.

Colt stood, frowning at the newcomer.

"Howdy," he called back.

"I didn't recognize the new truck," Jared said, ambling toward the house. "Thought I'd just come down and check everything's okay."

"Everything's fine," Colt said, his voice cool now. "I'm Colt Maverick. This is my place."

"Oh!" Jared said. "Gray said you wouldn't be back for a while yet."

"Yeah," Colt said, eyeing Gray suspiciously. "Surprise visit. Look, sorry, man, but who the hell are you?"

Gray jumped to his feet before Jared could answer, sensing it was too late. Colt was already on edge. That didn't mean he couldn't try.

"Listen, Colt," he said, "I know what you said, but it's been crazy out here. I have no talent with the horses at all, and I have my own career too, you know? I couldn't run the ranch and do my own work as well. I tried, and I was working fourteen hours a day."

"I'm the ranch manager," Jared supplied.

Colt raised his eyebrows. "No, you're fucking not."

"Colt...."

"I trusted you," Colt said, rounding on him, furious now in sharp contrast to the peace they'd shared only a few minutes before. "You said you could take care of it."

"And I tried. But it's too much for one person to do on their own. Even Jared said so."

"Don't tell me there are more," he said slowly, dangerously.

"No," Gray assured him. "Just Jared and your workers. No more."

"Clearly we need to talk about this," Colt said, turning back to Jared. "There seems to have been some confusion. But you can go back to wherever it is that you're staying and pack your fucking bags, because no one works my horses except me."

He stormed back into the house and slammed the door behind him—a very final full stop.

"We'll talk tomorrow," Gray said, turning to Jared with the apology ready. But Jared shook it off.

"It's no problem," he said. "I understand."

Gray nodded and turned back toward the house, hoping to go some of the way toward placating his husband.

THE bedroom door was closed and locked from the inside. Gray considered for a moment banging on it, breaking it down. He'd done that before. Colt had done the same thing too. More than one new set of hinges had been installed on that doorframe over the course of their marriage. More like five or six sets of hinges. It was a good way of marking the time passing.

A good boot to the handle would generally cause the lock to give, but Gray decided to try the old-fashioned way first and knocked sharply three times.

"What?" Colt demanded.

"You wanna go for a ride?"

It was a strange thing to ask. Gray wasn't quite sure where it came from, but it was enough to make Colt open the door and give him a wary look.

"Yeah," Colt said, nothing more. "Let me get my hat."

When Colt was home, riding the fences was a job they did together of an evening a few times a week, allowing the ranch hands to skip off early. Once two horses were saddled up, they took off over the ranch so Colt could cast his eye over his property before his employees turned up the next morning.

Technically, Thunder was another one of the ranch horses, but Gray had taken a shine to her early on, and she had quickly become his horse of preference when he went out riding. Over the past few months, he hadn't been out quite so often; he loved riding, but Colt had been the one to teach him how. He'd never been on a horse before moving to the ranch. It meant riding without Colt by his side felt awkward, uncomfortable, just all wrong.

Colt wasn't fussy about which of his horses he took out. Generally there were two or three he rode on a day-to-day basis, rotating so they weren't worked too hard. He picked Mirabelle, a chestnut Arabian who was one of the older horses still working the ranch, and Gray guessed the choice was only because her stall was next to Thunder's.

The prickly heat was still bearing down as they rode out over the ranch. While Colt took them on a circuitous route around the land and through the grazing area, Gray felt the sweat start to trickle down his back. So *this* was why he never came out during the day—he'd almost forgotten.

"Did we lose any cows while I was gone?"

"Nope," Gray said. "They're all fine."

"Good. Good."

Gray tugged on Thunder's reins and sidled up next to where Colt was peering out across the plains.

"Whose great idea was it to go riding a couple of hours after I'd been fucked senseless for the first time in months?" he asked, wanting a reaction.

Colt's head whipped around, and he smirked. "Not mine," he said.

Colt fell silent as the sun started to finally dip beyond the horizon, setting most of what he owned alight in red and gold. They used to do this all the time just after they'd got married, sit out here on horseback, or kick back with a few beers and watch the sun set.

There was no one around for miles. Gray leaned in for a kiss, pleased when Colt's hand wrapped around the back of his neck and their tongues slid together. Even if there were people around, Colt rarely cared. He would kiss his husband wherever and whenever he chose to.

"Did you fuck the kid?" Colt asked in a low voice, his hand still on Gray's neck.

"What?"

"The kid. Jared. Did you fuck him?"

"Jesus. No!" Gray exclaimed, pulling away from the touch.

"Did he fuck you?"

"What? No, Colt. He didn't fuck me. The only man who's fucked me in the past nine years is you. And you know it, you bastard."

He pulled on the reins and set Thunder at a steady gallop back toward the stables. Colt was calling at him to wait, but he didn't feel like complying, kicking at the horse's rump to urge her on. He had forgotten Colt had the advantage both as a superior rider and because he had a faster horse, and the two men drew in to the homestead around the same time.

"Gray," Colt called out again. "I'm sorry."

Shaking his head, Gray dismounted and led Thunder out to a paddock where the other horses had been set to graze. He'd leave Colt to deal with the tack, knowing there was no way Colt would just abandon two horses that were fully saddled up when it was still hot outside. It meant he could storm back into the house, tossing his shirt on a sofa as he passed on the way to his studio.

"I'm sorry," Colt said, grabbing on to Gray's arm and stopping him as his foot landed on the first stair. So Colt *had* just left the horses. He wasn't sure how to interpret that. "It's just…. I'm just…."

"Jealous? Callous? Unpredictable?"

"Yes," Colt said. "Worried? You can add that to your list too. I spent months missing you and come back to find out you've replaced me with another man. What am I supposed to think?"

"You're supposed to trust me!" Gray yelled. "You're supposed to know that I'm your husband, for fuck's sake. I promised you forever, Colt. I'm not about to throw that away."

Colt nodded. "Okay. But you fucked up too, Gray. This place—it's all I have. It's my life. And I trusted that to you."

"If I'd called you and told you what I needed to do, you would have said no. Or you would have come home and not found an investor, and we would be totally in the shit. I did the only thing I could, given the circumstances."

"That doesn't give you the right to make it without my input!"

Gray walked away a few paces, lifting his hat and running his hands over his head in frustration. Then he replaced his hat and walked back.

"I'm sorry for not calling you," he said. "I thought it was the right decision at the time."

"I didn't really think you fucked him," Colt said in a small voice.

"That's not an apology."

Colt looked at him evenly with his big, expressive brown eyes. "No," he said. "I need to go and check some things out. Find out what's happening around here."

"Fine. I have work to do."

The cool interior of the house only reminded Gray how hot and sweaty the ride had made him. He headed to the bedroom first to put on a clean shirt before carrying on up to the attic studio, realizing he'd left paint on his brushes and probably wrecked at least one of them.

It was getting darker now, and he flicked a light on to move around the room, setting his brushes in a pot of paint thinner in the hope of saving them and neatly filing all his paints in the drawer where they belonged. He'd made the cabinet himself one winter when they'd been snowed in; each compartment was carefully labeled with the color that lived inside, the drawers split up with dividers that sectioned off oils and acrylics and watercolors. His brushes were stored similarly in the upright part of the cabinet, each held in place with a tiny clip.

If he was a bit obsessive over his tools, then so what? Gray spent most of his working life in this room; he wanted it how it made sense to him.

There was a computer desk set up in the corner where he could do research, if he needed to, and most of the correspondence with his agent came via e-mail, so this was where he picked up jobs. Next to the computer desk was his little library. Some of the books were ones he'd illustrated himself; others were there for reference. It was a good setup, as far as he was concerned.

After checking his e-mails, he returned to the painting he'd been working on when Colt had interrupted with his arrival home. The piece was nearly finished. It only needed a few more hours' work before it would be ready to scan into the computer, ready to be sent off to his agent. There were a few other commissions he needed to get going, though, and he sat down at his desk to start the initial sketches.

This work was calming in its familiarity, allowing Gray to think as his pen flew over the paper. The instruction to create a diagram of a human heart, suitable for studying by third graders, was easy. He didn't even need to think about it anymore. The illustrations seemed to flow out of his hand without any particular guidance from his head.

In all the months he'd been waiting for Colt to finally come home, this was not how he imagined their reunion. The brief moments of calm were overshadowed by the decisions they had both made while away, things that were in the past with no way of being changed.

Then again, the whole situation, from the moment Colt had told him he had to leave, had been fucked up. They'd fought then too. Gray had been adamant that he couldn't cope running the ranch on his own, and he'd been right, of course.

He pushed the sketch aside and put his head down on the cool surface of his desk, desperate for a glass of the iced tea he'd made and set to cool in the fridge, but too stubborn to risk running into Colt downstairs.

Instead he stood and walked over to the huge window, looking down on the paddock where the horses were now being brought into the stables by Colt's workers. Thunder and Mirabelle were already gone, and Gray guessed they had been the first ones to go in. Either that, or Colt had gone back and done it himself. Colt's truck was still parked where he'd left it earlier.

The overhead light flicked off, then on, then off again. Gray's eyes snapped to the doorway; when the light came back on, Colt was framed in the light, his hat abandoned—he was wearing a sheepish expression now instead.

"Hey," Gray said.

Colt opened his arms. Gray took a step forward, then another, realizing it was his turn to fall into his partner's reassuring embrace.

"I'm sorry," Colt whispered, his fingers brushing back and forth at Gray's nape, teasing the straggly hairs there. "I didn't mean to yell."

"That's okay."

And it was.

Colt had a short temper. Gray had known this from when they'd first met ten years before. After his family had all but disowned him for coming out as gay, Gray had wandered from Chicago to Texas, up to DC, then over to Nevada, crisscrossing the country trying to find somewhere to settle. Home, it turned out, was a big bear of a man in a bar somewhere south and west of Illinois.

After watching the man for most of the night from the opposite side of the bar, drinking beer and eating peanuts and waiting for his chance, he learned that sometimes opportunity ambled up, tipped its hat, and offered a fuck in the back of a pickup.

That one fuck led to another, then another, and then, without meaning to, Gray fell in love. It wasn't just a fluttering of love either. It was full-blown, heart aching, sweaty palms, head over heels in love. And because of the way Colt kept all his emotions so well concealed, Gray was convinced the other man didn't feel the same way.

It took time for their relationship to settle around them, each piece slipping into place over a number of years. They had married during a vacation to Canada, took the term "husbands" back home when many around them refused to accept that two men could be in a legal, loving relationship.

They looked like a good couple—people had said so. Gray wasn't a small man, although he didn't have anything on Colt's bulk. In fact, when they'd got the tape measure out, Colt was only a half inch taller, but probably twenty pounds heavier. A lifetime of academics had molded Gray into a quiet, reflective man who could iron his own shirts and always combed his hair and knew how to treat a lady right.

"I'm sorry about the ranch," Gray said, wanting to make it clear that he never meant any harm.

"No need to apologize," Colt said roughly as his arms tightened around Gray's body. "I should be the one 'pologizing, for yellin' at you like that."

Gray was smiling as he straightened up, pulling his hands out of the embrace so he could play with the unruly hair that fell over Colt's forehead.

"You wanna go to bed?" he asked.

"I'm sure tired. Someone wore me out."

"Come on, then," Gray said with a laugh.

Their bedroom was a sanctuary. No one ever came up here except the two of them; it was a space where they were happy to be just who they were, and fuck anyone who didn't like it. Gray had painted the walls a soft, dusky blue, tossed rugs on the floor, and had made the lamps that sat on the nightstands himself. It was designed to be a peaceful place for two very tense men.

Gray started to unbutton his shirt, until Colt batted his hand away and took over the task of the undressing. His lips roamed over each exposed inch of Gray's skin, taking the time to appreciate the toned, tight body. After all these years, Colt still felt the same. Solid. Safe. *Home.*

Colt's hands spread out over Gray's ribs as he leaned in for another kiss, his lips slowly teasing until Gray's parted and allowed his tongue to steal inside. Laughing into the kiss, Gray tugged at the hem of Colt's shirt until it was tugged up and over his head, tossed in a corner somewhere, and forgotten about. He'd always loved Colt's chest—strong and broad and covered in that light dusting of hair.

When Colt's hands wandered farther, down to Gray's jean-covered ass, and squeezed, Gray leaned away and raised his eyebrows.

"Don't you think once in an afternoon is enough?" he asked.

"Nope."

"Well, my poor, sore ass certainly does."

Colt chuckled, his eyes crinkling at the corners. It was amazing, Gray thought, that after all this time, a simple smile from his husband could make him feel like a teenage girl in love. Aware he was smiling back, probably looking like an idiot, Gray reached up and cupped Colt's cheek and drew him into another slow kiss.

While Colt steadied his waist, Gray shucked off his jeans and underwear, enjoying standing naked in his lover's arms while Colt still wore his own beat-up jeans. Completely against the odds, Gray felt his cock start to stir again. He decided he was younger than advertised and definitely still virile. Maybe having Colt home would reenergize their sex life.

It had simply been too long since they last had any decent time alone like this. Colt kissed down his chest, slowly sinking to his knees and nuzzling his face into the crease between his stomach and thigh. Gray threaded his fingers through Colt's thick, softly curling hair and dropped his head back when Colt licked a wet stripe from the root to the tip of his cock.

He gasped, then groaned when Colt swallowed him down, licking and sucking while fingers teased the still-sore rim of his ass. It was a sweet pain, though, and Colt never pushed inside, just stroked in time with the rhythm of his mouth.

Gray forced his eyes open and looked down at his husband, on his knees, looking back up with big brown eyes filled with lust and love and sex and desire. All the things that made them perfect for each other.

Colt had his own cock out too—Gray wasn't sure when that had happened—but he didn't seem to be paying much attention to it. That was Colt all over, though. He got off on giving. And he was just so fucking good at it.

When Colt's mouth picked up a more enthusiastic rhythm, Gray started to pinch at his own nipples, knowing that would tip him over the edge.

"Colt," Gray said, a harsh whisper, a warning. Colt nodded, almost imperceptibly, but enough for Gray to know it was okay. He started to thrust, short, intense pulses over the smooth flat of Colt's tongue, and cried out as his orgasm spilled over Colt's lips.

"Holy shit."

"Mmm." Colt hummed low in his throat and allowed Gray to tug him to his feet.

"Want me to return the favor?" Gray mumbled against Colt's lips, tasting himself.

Colt shook his head and kicked off his jeans. "No. I need a shower, though...."

There was a clear offer there, and Gray followed him through to their adjoining bathroom to get wet and slippery. Colt loaded up his toothbrush to take into the shower, a strange habit Gray had almost forgotten about.

Clean, but tired, they emerged some time later and slipped on pajama bottoms. Colt set the AC to run through the night, then fell into bed. It had been too long since they had been able to do this, and Gray relished the feel of his partner's arms around his waist, the calm, solid reassurance.

With the moon shining cool light into the room, they slept.

THE next morning dawned brighter. Even though Gray slept in, he still got up before Colt. The dark shadows under Colt's eyes told Gray he'd been working hard while away and was probably stressed as hell about the business. It wasn't just a business, after all; they lived here, worked the land, worked some of the horses, and sold the rest on. Even though there was no mortgage on the house—Colt had inherited it from an uncle who had never married—there was no way they could ever leave. There was no situation that would make them want to.

It was a beauty of a house. Colt's uncle had built it himself with his father, and it sprawled low to the ground, open plan. From the top of the stairs, you could see down into the living area with its huge brick chimney stack, leather couches, and deep fur rug. Floors, doors, and the magnificent staircase had been made by the Mavericks by hand with the wood from their own land. The kitchen ran the length of the back of the house; family legend had it that even though Uncle Riff never took a wife, there were plenty of women who had come through over the years.

Gray fixed a breakfast of coffee, pancakes, and fruit—strawberries and oranges, since that was all he had in the house. He toasted near on half a loaf of bread and carried the whole lot back up to the bedroom, where Colt was beginning to stir.

"That coffee?" he grunted.

"Yes, sir. Come get it yourself, you lazy ass."

Colt heaved himself up in bed, scratched his belly, and emptied nearly half a mug of black coffee in one swallow.

"Damn, that's good. You cooked for me, baby?"

"Yeah, but don't get used to it. I've got better things to do with my days than wait on you hand and foot."

The sniping was in good humor; this was how they communicated. The easy teasing back and forth contained an abundance of affection, something that was reinforced by the slow kiss they shared as Gray settled back into their bed.

They picked at the food, eating the hot stuff first while rubbing their bare legs together under the sheets. The conversation about Jared hung over them, though, spoiling the easy morning quiet.

"He's a good kid," Gray said eventually, cradling his mug to his bare chest. "He works hard and knows his way around. I was going nearly crazy before I hired him to take over."

"I asked for too much of you."

"That's for damn sure." But he gave Colt a small smile.

"What are you paying him?"

Gray named a figure.

"Shit."

"You mad?"

"Not really. Not anymore."

"If you want to fire him, at least let me give him a few weeks' notice and good reference so he can move on to somewhere else."

"Well," Colt said, heaving himself up out of bed. "S'pose I better talk to the kid before I make any decisions."

After turning his face away so Colt couldn't see, Gray smiled.

GRAY returned to his kitchen while Colt went out to meet Jared to discuss horses and cattle and all the things that bored Gray to death. When he was working to a tight deadline, little things like housework would be cast aside in favor of finishing a commission. Colt had offered, again and again, to get someone in to do the cooking and cleaning for them—a housekeeper, he called it.

Although it was eternally tempting, Gray said no, every time. His family didn't know much about what he did and where he lived now, but his youngest sister did come to visit a few times a year. Out of three siblings, she was the only one. He didn't want her turning up and thinking he couldn't handle one house on his own, or worse, that his parents were right and he did need a woman in his life.

They mostly split the chores between them; Colt liked to cook, when he wasn't out late in the evenings, and didn't mind running the vacuum cleaner around on a weekend. Gray ended up cleaning the kitchen most of the time, and the bathroom too, and since Colt's attempts at washing clothes usually resulted in something being shrunk or shredded, Gray did that as well.

Their daily routine was pretty well worn, but since Colt was out negotiating with Jared, Gray wasn't sure what to do. He wanted to be around in case Colt came back in another foul mood and he needed to defuse it.

From his previous experience with Jared, Gray thought the ranch manager was calm and levelheaded, which was one of the main reasons why he had hired him in the first place. He was hoping the two of them would be able to sit down and work things out between them, Colt's hot temper cooled by Jared's practicality and common sense. That wasn't to say that Colt didn't have common sense; it was just... well hidden, sometimes.

Jared knew his job was likely only temporary until Colt came back, so he wouldn't be too shocked if he did get asked to leave. In some ways Gray wanted Colt to ask the younger man to stay; the extra help would be good for Colt. God knew he wouldn't be able to keep doing it forever. He was only seven years older than Gray, but years of physical labor had been hard on his back, and he'd already had one operation to treat a torn muscle.

Gray had fixed sandwiches and a big salad for lunch and set it all in the fridge, then indulged himself with a cop drama on the TV until Colt rolled back in.

"Hungry?" Gray asked, poking his head up over the back of the sofa.

Colt smiled and leaned down to brush a soft kiss over Gray's lips. "Sure. I'll go fix something."

"I already did it."

"I knew I kept you around for a reason."

Gray laughed and went to swipe at Colt's shoulder, but Colt was faster and jogged away to the kitchen, where he started making a new jug of Gray's favorite peach tea. Gray set the plates of food on the breakfast bar, where they could look out over their wide backyard while they ate.

After pouring two glasses of the tea, Colt sat down, hooked his ankle around Gray's, and took a big bite of his sandwich.

"So, did you talk to Jared?" Gray asked.

"He's gonna stay," Colt mumbled around a mouthful of food.

"Yeah?"

"Mhmm. Gonna work the cows while I take the horses."

"That sounds like a good plan. Are you happy?"

Colt grunted.

"Okay," Gray said with a short laugh. "Happy was the wrong word."

"I am happy," Colt insisted. "It's just… been a long time since I was here. It feels like a lot has changed."

"I haven't changed."

"No," Colt said with a fond smile. He reached over and brushed a few stray hairs away from Gray's face. "You never do."

ANNA MARTIN is from a picturesque seaside village in the southwest of England and now lives in the slightly arty, slightly quirky city of Bristol. After spending most of her childhood making up stories, she studied English Literature at university before attempting to turn her hand as a professional writer.

Apart from being physically dependent on her laptop, Anna is enthusiastic about writing and producing local grassroots theatre (especially at the Edinburgh Fringe Festival, where she can be found every summer), going to visit friends in other countries, baking weird and wonderful sweets, learning to play the ukulele, and Ben & Jerry's New York Super Fudge Chunk.

Anna claims her entire career is due to the love, support, pre-reading, and creative ass kicking provided by her best friend Jennifer. Jennifer refuses to accept responsibility for anything Anna has written.

2nd place winner of the 2012 Goodreads M/M Romance Member's Choice Award "Best Musician / Rockstars" for *Tattoos & Teacups*.

Website: http://annamartin-fiction.com
Twitter: https://twitter.com/missannamartin
Tumblr: http://annamartinwrites.tumblr.com
Facebook: https://www.facebook.com/annamartinfiction
Goodreads: http://www.goodreads.com/author/show/5251288.Anna_Martin

The Cat's Out of the Bag

Rowan McAllister

I.

THE scene was set. The lights were out, leaving only the faint orange glow from the streetlamp outside. I was perched just so in our mustard-yellow, overstuffed, midcentury-modern vinyl swivel chair, affecting an air of indifference I most certainly wasn't feeling. I had a glass of shiraz next to me on the little antique table we'd bought on our first trip to New York together. And I was dressed to kill in my white linen slacks, kelly-green sweater, and matching plaid button-up: the outfit Joel and I had picked out for me before our last cruise to the Bahamas because he said the green matched my eyes.

Now, if you're picturing some lean, sexy model wearing a famous designer's spring collection in a magazine spread for Rolex or something, I'd love to say you were right on the money. But unfortunately that isn't the case. And that fact is kind of important to our story, so, alas, I cannot allow that little fantasy to go on—much as I would like to.

It pains me to admit it, but I'm not really all that much to look at. I'm average in almost every way: cock, looks, height… pretty much everything. I've even gained a few extra pounds around the middle over the last few years that I've been trying desperately not to think about. I'd have to say my eyes are about all I have going for me—deep green and very expressive, or at least that's what I've been told. Hence why I took the extra hour to find that green sweater and went so far as to apply just a teeny bit of eyeliner in preparation for the role I'd be playing. I did decide against mascara, though, because I knew I'd be crying at some point, and I was *not* going to make my grand exit with raccoon eyes. I wanted Joel—my soon-to-be *ex*-boyfriend of six years—to remember me looking my best as he watched me walk out the door.

All this setup and preparation for my breakup might sound a bit theatrical, but I didn't spend most of my free time volunteering at the community playhouse because I liked the coffee. The theater was in my blood. And besides, I deserved a little drama after what had to have been the worst weekend of my life.

I'm sure *some* people might say I should count myself lucky that the worst weekend of my life only involved a false-alarm heart attack for my dad and learning that my boyfriend was cheating on me. But I'm sorry, at that particular moment that kind of wisdom and perspective was simply beyond me. I'd just spent the previous night in a hospital, holding my mom's hand in a waiting room, terrified for my dad and unable to get hold of the one other person in my life who meant the world to me... *after* finding out he'd lied to me about his work trip and was off who knew where, doing who knew what, with who knew who. And believe me, while I sat in that awful, cold, sterile room comforting my mom and trying not think of my dad barely clinging to life, I had plenty of time to picture the whos, the wheres, and the whats, and it wasn't pretty. Let me tell you.

So there I was, waiting in our living room in the dark, all dolled up and ready for my scene—and it was *going* to be a scene, because *dammit*, I was shattered. Joel had broken my heart, and I was going to make one hell of an exit... one he wouldn't forget anytime soon.

I know what you're thinking.

If I was so shattered, how could I coldly plan out my own breakup like I was directing a play?

The answer is simple. I *needed* to plan it out, because it was the only way I could stay in control, to not crumble into a million little pieces, beg him to forget whomever he'd been sleeping with and come back to me. If I didn't have my little drama planned out, I wouldn't have been able to make it through the night with any self-respect or pride left. And at that point, self-respect was all I had, fragile, pathetic little thing that it was.

The sound of keys in the lock made my heart jump in my chest. I could almost hear a director whisper "Action" as I watched Joel shoulder his way through the door, his pale gold hair highlighted by the overhead light from the hall outside our condo.

Our condo. My lips trembled, and I stifled a sniffle.

Don't be fooled into thinking I was too embarrassed to cry. I would definitely be turning on the waterworks. I'm not one of those stoic guys who keeps everything bottled up. When I'm upset, *everybody* knows it. I just didn't want to spoil the effect of the scene I'd set before it was time, that's all.

Joel switched on the light in the entryway after setting down his suitcase, laptop bag, and a large, almost cube-shaped box, draping his coat over the box as if to hide it. He stretched his arms above his head and groaned a little, forcing me to stifle a groan of my own. Even after six years together, the sight of that man still got to me: six foot three inches of solid muscle and masculine beauty. He could have been a pro football player with those massive shoulders and rippling abs. He was smart, successful, charming, and gorgeous, so far out of my league that a little part of me had always believed it couldn't work between us, at least not forever, anyway. The fact that it had lasted this long had always been a bit of a surprise to me… and therein lay most of our problems.

But I'll get to that later. Just then, I was geared up for a confrontation about *his* unworthiness, because that was what I needed to focus on so I could stay angry and not break down into a weeping, wailing mess.

Joel didn't see me waiting for him, so after he stretched, he threw his keys on the hall table, kicked off his shoes, and wandered into the kitchen. A moment later, I saw the refrigerator light come on and heard the clink of a bottle as he pulled out a beer. He twisted the cap off as he wandered into the living room. In the dim light from the entryway, I saw him bend to turn on the small lamp by the couch, and I took one last deep breath. Picking up my wineglass, I let it dangle nonchalantly from my right hand and waited for him to finally see me.

Joel sprayed his mouthful of beer all over the couch and the rug as he sputtered and coughed. "Holy shit, Michael! Why didn't you say something to let me know you were there? You about gave me a heart attack!"

I watched in haughty silence as he wiped his face on the back of his hand and stared at me with those heart-wrenchingly beautiful soft brown puppy-dog eyes. His thick blond hair was a rumpled mess, smooshed a little on one side and sticking up in those adorable spikes on the other. The spikes I'd always loved to play with first thing in the morning. He'd obviously slept on the plane, probably because he hadn't gotten much sleep over the weekend, the bastard.

I stifled another whimper and stiffened my spine. I wasn't going to crumble. I was mad, and justifiably so.

"Baby? Aren't you going to say hello?" His voice was all deep and sultry, and I had to clench my hand around my glass to keep from reacting to it.

"Where were you?" I asked quietly, not moving from my pose in the chair, raising my eyebrows just slightly, as if the answer didn't mean the world to me.

Joel's eyebrows came together in a frown. It was really unfair that the man could still look gorgeous even when confused.

"Where. Were. You?" I repeated with a little more bite.

I wanted to give him a chance to come clean before I dropped my bombshell. Part of me still hoped he'd tell me the truth and it would be something silly. He'd drop to his knees in front of me, and I'd forgive him for what he'd put me through, and the nightmare would be over.

But he didn't.

"Honey, you know I was in Atlanta for work. I got off the plane and came straight home, just like I said I would. Right on time. I texted you when I landed," he said as he walked closer and leaned in to kiss me hello.

I dodged the kiss, stood up, and stepped behind the chair, putting some space between us.

Joel frowned. "Baby, what's wrong? I'm sorry I missed your call yesterday. I knew you were supposed to be at the playhouse last night, so I waited and called this morning, as soon as I got moving, but you didn't pick up."

There it was, my cue. It was time for my big line.

I set my drink down and tilted my chin up so I could look him in the eye. "Don't you 'baby' me! I want to know where you were, and don't lie this time. Because I *know* you weren't at work. They told me when I called."

"What?"

Now he looked worried. And was that guilt? Good. He *should* feel guilty for what he did.

"I called your office, Joel. Dad was on the way to the hospital. We thought he was having a heart attack, and I needed you! Your cell was off, so I called your office, and they told me you were on *vacation*. You were off somewhere without me, and I had to find out from a stranger while my dad was possibly dying in an ambulance. You lied to me, and you weren't there when I needed you the most!"

"Oh my God, Michael! I'm so sorry, baby. Is your dad going to be okay?"

He took a step toward me, but I put my hand out like I was one of the Supremes. "He's going to be fine. It was a false alarm. But that's not the point. The point is that you lied to me. Who was it, Joel? Who were you with? Do you even know his name? Please don't tell me it was one of our friends."

He blew out a breath, set his beer down on our coffee table, and put his hands up, waving them and shaking his head. "It's not like that, baby. Please."

Now he looked nervous as well as guilty. Also good. He was playing his role as I'd expected, and that would help me continue to play mine.

"What's it like, then? You tell me, Joel, and no bullshit this time. Where were you?"

His gaze dropped to the floor, and he chewed on his lip for a moment, obviously trying to come up with some sort of story to get his ass out of trouble. Unfortunately, what he came up with wasn't nearly good enough for that.

"I wasn't with anyone like that, baby. I didn't cheat on you. I'd *never* cheat on you. I just needed a little time away. That's all."

Even if I had believed him about the not cheating part, I was so wrapped up in my scorned lover role that talking things out like a grown-up was pretty much beyond me.

"Away from *me*?" I screeched. I could feel the tears coming, but I didn't want to break down yet. I wasn't ready to make my exit, and I was supposed to be angry, not hurt, dammit. "Is living with me so bad? Am I that much of a monster that you felt you had to lie to me in order to get away from me for a few days?"

Okay, so my voice broke a little on that last part. Sue me.

Joel shook his head emphatically. "Baby, no! I *love* you. Things have just been really stressful at work lately, and you've been doing all those long hours at the office and then at the playhouse. I didn't want to bother you with it. That's all."

I hated to admit it, but he had a point. Neither one of us had made much of an effort to spend time together recently. We'd slept in the same bed at night, but that was about it. Lately, it seemed like we were both too tired for anything else. It was one of the reasons I'd assumed he was cheating, because we hadn't had sex in months.

I started to melt. My righteous indignation was fading under his pleading voice, puppy-dog eyes, and my own insecurities. I began to revert back to thinking everything was my fault and I was just being a big ol' drama queen, making something out of nothing. I even started moving toward the wall to flip the light switch and get rid of the whole "dramatically shadowed room" thing I had going on so we could sit down together like adults and discuss things rationally. But as I moved toward the front hall, Joel made a weird noise, and his gaze shifted to the box on the floor by his suitcase, and my scorned diva came rushing back again with a vengeance.

The box. That stupid fucking box that had traveled with us through the first two crappy apartments we'd shared and then on to the condo we had now. The box that was always locked and that Joel would never give me a straight answer about when I asked.

For six years I'd let him have his privacy. I hadn't pushed about it, because I loved him, and I didn't want to rock the boat. And honestly, the box had stayed in the storage units at all of our places, so I actually forgot about it most of the time.

But now there it was, in my face, another lie, another secret he wouldn't share with me. I was in enough of a snit that I didn't give a shit about his privacy anymore. He'd taken *that box* on his getaway weekend, not me. And this time, I wasn't going to let it go without finding out what was inside. *I* was the injured party here, and *I* deserved some fucking answers.

Did I mention I was a little dramatic?

I stormed over, all pinched lips, narrowed eyes, and righteous fury. I snatched Joel's coat off the box and threw it in his face as he came after me. The box wasn't locked. For once, TSA security measures actually worked in my favor. I crouched down and flipped the latches on the case, all the while glaring at Joel, daring him to stop me, as I threw open the lid with the flair of a Las Vegas magician.

Joel stopped dead in his tracks and made a little noise of protest. His face even paled a little. The look and that sound were so odd coming from him. He was my rock—solid, confident Joel—and seeing him like that almost made me reconsider my actions, but it was too late to go back at that point.

I'm not sure what exactly I was expecting to find inside, but I have to tell you, the sight that met my eyes was so beyond anything I had imagined that it took me a solid minute of looking at it for me to comprehend what I was seeing.

Giant green slitted eyes glowed up at me from beneath a set of tufted pointy ears. Whiskers poked out in every direction around a heart-shaped hot-pink nose. And a huge mouth, full of blunt white teeth, grinned at me, mocking me with its lolling pink tongue.

It was a head… a head in a box.

A cat's head, to be exact—a giant purple-and-blue-striped fuzzy monstrosity of foam, plastic, and fake fur.

"What the fuck is that?"

I looked back and forth between the head and Joel, and when I lifted it out of the box to get a better look, Joel flushed and looked away. Beneath the head was what looked like a bodysuit in the same electric-blue-and-purple shaggy fur, with a curled fuzzy purple tail, a pair of fluffy clawed gloves, and matching booties. This time, I was the one left with my mouth hanging open. I was so confused and surprised I even forgot to be angry for a while.

"I can explain." Joel's shaky voice broke me out of my stupor, and I looked at him with my eyebrows raised.

When he didn't say anything else, I wafted a hand in his direction, gesturing with all the regality of the queen herself for him to please continue.

He cleared his throat and licked his lips. Normally the sight of his pink tongue wetting his nearly perfect lips would've distracted me, but the last thing I wanted to think about was sex at that moment. Not with a giant purple-and-blue cat head in my hands.

After a few moments' hesitation, Joel blew out a breath and let his massive shoulders slump. "There *was* actually a work conference in Atlanta. But... but it got canceled. Things have been so crazy around here, and I already had the ticket, so I just decided to go anyway."

"And this?" I asked, shaking the head at him.

He grimaced and blushed. "There's this, uh, con in Atlanta... at the same time as my meeting was supposed to be, and I decided to go."

I put the head back in the box and stood up with my hands on my hips. "What kind of con?"

I knew already, but I wasn't going to let him off that easy.

Well, scratch that, I didn't *know* exactly, but I was sure it was some kind of kink convention by the way he was acting.

"Furries," he whispered.

One word, no embellishments or explanations, but it certainly called to mind all kinds of images, from the comical to the utterly disturbing, and I had to take a second to rub my eyes to make them go away.

"Baby, please look at me," Joel pleaded. "I'm sorry I lied. I made a mistake. Can we talk about this? I love you."

My lips started trembling. "Not enough to tell me the truth," I whispered. Then I looked up at him and searched his face. "You do this? You get dressed up in this, and what? Fuck other guys in costumes while your partners stay home, clueless? How many, Joel? How many times have you done this and I was too stupid to realize?"

The waterworks started then. Was that on cue? I don't think I even cared anymore. My scene was supposed to end with him admitting he'd fucked up with some nameless trick in a Holiday Inn somewhere and begging me to come back while I grabbed my bag and stormed out. Now, not only was my relationship fucked up, but my dramatic exit was too. I was at a loss, and I hated it.

"Baby, you have to believe me. I didn't fuck anybody. The conventions aren't like that, not unless you go looking for it. It's just a chance to let myself go, to be somebody else for a while. That's it."

"I *have* to believe you? When you already admitted to lying to me for weeks, even years, about this? You tell me how I'm supposed to do that, Joel!" I yelled through my tears.

He shook his head and threw his arms out. "Dammit, Michael! I knew you wouldn't understand. I just knew you'd go all *diva* and make it all about you somehow! I just knew it!"

Okay, now, it's one thing for me to call myself a diva. It's completely another for Joel to call me one in the middle of an argument, as an *insult*. After six years together, he certainly knew how to hit my buttons.

"Diva? You did *not* just go there! And for your information, of course I made it about me! Because *I'm* the one who was lied to, in case you forgot that part!" I stormed past him, picked up the suitcase I'd packed that morning, and headed toward the door. "You want to see diva? Well, here you go! I hope you and your little furry friend have a blast together, because obviously I'm too much drama for you!"

And that was my grand exit. It wasn't as satisfying as I'd made it out to be in my head. Slamming the door behind me felt kind of good, but the long slow elevator ride to the garage and the quiet walk to my car were a bit of a letdown.

II.

ONCE I closed the car door and started the engine, the tears began to fall in earnest as reality set in. The scene was over, but the rest of my life wasn't. I didn't even make it a block away before I pulled my phone out and hit number two on speed dial.

"Hello, dear."

"Mom? Can I come see you?" *Sniffle*.

"Sure, honey. What's the matter?"

Sniffle. "I'll tell you when I get there." *Hiccup*. "I just wanted to check before I came, in case you were too tired or busy taking care of Dad."

"Your dad's asleep, sweetie. The trip to the hospital and the new blood pressure meds he's on wiped him out. I fell asleep as soon as we got home this morning, and I slept most of the day, so I'm wide-awake now. Besides, you know I'll always have time for you, honey. Come over and tell me what's wrong."

Sniffle. "Okay. I'll be there soon."

I turned off my phone and drove the rest of the way on autopilot with tears blurring my vision. Luckily, I didn't run anybody over on my way there.

Mom was waiting for me in the kitchen with a cup of tea and a hug when I arrived. I squeezed her tight for a long time while I cried. She was shorter than I remembered her being the last time I did something like this. Joel had been the one to hold me when I cried for the last six years. But she still smelled like home, and her soft gray-brown hair still felt warm and comforting against my cheek.

When I'd cried myself out, she handed me my cup of tea, and we sat at the little island in her kitchen. She didn't push for details, knowing I wouldn't hold back once I got control. She just sipped her tea and waited quietly until I could bring myself to start.

As I spilled the events of the last twenty-four hours, beyond what she already knew, there were a couple of times when it looked like she wanted to say something, but she knew I needed to get everything out before I'd be able to listen to what she had to say. We worked well together like that. It was comforting, and I found myself relaxing and even feeling a bit silly rehashing some of what I'd said and done. I didn't tell her about the whole "furry" thing. We shared a lot, but if my boyfriend was into kinky faux-animal sex, I didn't think my mom needed to know that. I just told her he'd gone to some kind of secret convention that I didn't really understand and that I wasn't sure I could believe him when he said he hadn't cheated on me.

When I was finished, she put her hand over mine and looked into my eyes. "Honey, I can't tell you whether you should believe him or not. All I can tell you is that I know he loves you. If there's something he hasn't shared with you, it might be because he's too ashamed or embarrassed by it, and he's afraid of what you might think of him. We all have things we'd rather our partners didn't know."

I couldn't help but snort in disbelief. "Mom, we're talking about Joel here. Prom king, voted most likely to succeed, youngest VP in his office, so gorgeous he has guys practically falling all over themselves for him. Even if he is into something a little weird, I can't picture him ever being too embarrassed to talk to me about it. I mean, look at me. I can't exactly cast stones here."

Her lips twisted in annoyance. "That's just it, honey. You're a wonderful, beautiful person, and you don't seem to have any idea of how lucky Joel is to have you."

I rolled my eyes. "You have to say that. You're my mom."

"I'm serious, Michael. You spend so much time thinking he's too good for you that maybe you miss the fact that he's human too. Sometimes it hurts me to think I did something or didn't do something, when you were growing up, that made you believe you weren't good enough. If I did, I want you to know that I'm sorry."

Well, shit, there went the waterworks again.

"Mom, you didn't do anything wrong. I'm just being realistic. I have eyes. I know what he could have if he wanted to."

"Realistic for who, honey?" She set her teacup down and grabbed both my hands. "You are an incredible person, my darling. Joel knows it, even if you don't. You might think he's perfect, but that's only because you love him so much. He's got his flaws too. Everybody does."

I gave her a skeptical look, and she laughed. "You remember that first time we were all supposed to go to dinner together, and you got stuck in traffic, and Joel had to meet us without you? I have to tell you, I thought he was a good-enough-looking guy, but kind of stiff and dull. I was afraid things were doomed between you two, because you were just too vibrant a soul to be chained down to someone like that for very long. But then you showed up, and he lit up from within. It was like a switch had been thrown, and he got more animated and open and *funny*. I wouldn't have recognized him as the same person if I hadn't seen the transformation myself. All I'm saying is, don't sell yourself short. You aren't doing either of you any favors when you do that."

I bit my lip and nodded. She might just possibly have a point. Maybe I was so busy being down on myself that I'd missed the part where Joel actually needed me as much as I needed him. Maybe I'd put him on so high a pedestal that he was afraid to fall off it by telling me the truth.

"What should I do?"

"Talk to him."

"I don't know if I can ever trust him again," I wailed in true Michael fashion.

Mom humored me by pouring me some more tea, handing me a tissue, and patting my cheek. "Honey, you won't know unless you talk to him. All I can say is, when your father was in that hospital yesterday and I was terrified that I'd lose him, I wasn't thinking about any of the times he might've failed me or any of the bad times we'd had over the years. I was thinking about the good times and how much I loved him. I was thinking that the only regrets I had were the times I'd missed out on telling him how much he meant to me or that I might never get a chance to make any more of those good memories with him."

I couldn't let that speech go without a hug. I might be a bit selfish and self-centered at times, but I knew my mom had been through the wringer the day before, just like me. She needed a little love and understanding too. We held each other for a long time, and we cried a little more. My mom started that round, and I couldn't let her cry alone, now, could I?

After the weeping, we both started laughing for no reason, and she gently pushed me away. "Look at us. We're a mess," she said, wiping tears from her cheeks as I did the same with mine.

She'd left me with a lot to think about, so I was actually pretty quiet while I finished my tea.

I know, right? Who'd have thunk it?

Anyway, Mom sent me off to bed with one more little tidbit of advice.

"You have to decide what's more important to you—staying mad and making Joel pay for hurting you, or the fact that you love him and he loves you."

"If I choose the second, can I still make him pay just a little?"

She swung a hand at my arm, and I grinned as I danced out of range.

"You can, but I don't suggest you let it drag on too long, or you might regret it," she said as she wagged a finger at me.

I leaned in and gave her a peck on the cheek. "Thanks, Mom. I owe you."

She smiled. "I'll add it to your tab. Now, go on. Go to bed and sleep on it. I'm sure things will look better in the morning."

She was right. They did.

Despite how worked up I was, the stress of the last two days caught up with me pretty quick, and I slept hard. I don't even remember dreaming. The next morning I was thinking a little more clearly, and I regretted storming out on Joel. All I could see was his puppy-dog eyes pleading with me to understand.

Okay, maybe some big green cat's eyes found their way in there a couple of times, but I did my best to shove those back into the box. I wasn't quite ready to deal with the whole furry thing. I didn't understand it. It wasn't a kink I had ever even considered, and I wasn't sure Joel and I could meet in the middle on that particular subject. But my mom was right. I loved him. The furry thing was only a small part of him, and while it still hurt that he felt he had to hide it from me, I could understand why he'd done it. No one, and I mean *no one*, would ever picture big, buff, toppy Joel in a purple-and-blue fluffy kitty costume, least of all me. It changed things. I just wasn't sure how at the moment. But I didn't really have to figure that out just then. The only thing I needed to decide was whether or not I loved him enough to put in the work to get past this rough patch.

My mom was right about that too. Go figure.

So, I want you all to be proud of me. I didn't go rushing back to finish having it out with Joel. I didn't even torture Joel by making him wait all day before I returned his numerous messages on my phone. I was actually a grown-up, at least for a few hours, and I called him and told him I wanted to get together at our place for dinner after work. Then I took a mental health day off from my own office job and spent the rest of the day in quiet contemplation about everything I had said and everything that had been said to me.

Of course, I had to put on my best pair of yoga pants, take two classes at the studio, and spend a couple of hours in the Zen rock gardens with my favorite soy latte to get in the right mindset. But I got there, *eventually*, and the new and improved Michael was ready to set another scene for Joel by five o'clock that night… after some extensive last-minute shopping for props.

III.

THERE I was again, sitting in the dark, waiting for Joel… at least until I lit the tapers on our dining room table and a few more candles scattered about the living room and bedroom. Everything was set for the evening I had planned. The tablecloth was pressed, the wine was on ice, and the casserole was in the oven. There were a few other surprises in store for Joel as well, but we'll get to those in a little bit.

My heart leaped in my chest once again when I heard Joel's key in the lock, but it was a good feeling that time. Our night was going to be great. I'd made sure of it.

Joel's eyes sought me out the second he walked in the door. When he spotted the candles and me standing next to the romantically set table, he smiled, and some of the creases marring his forehead eased. He dropped his briefcase and tossed his keys toward the table as he rushed across the room and wrapped me up in a bear hug.

"Baby, I'm so sorry," he whispered into my ear before he kissed it and buried his face in my hair.

I started to get a little choked up, and that simply would not do. I pushed at his shoulders until he eased up a little and said, "No more of that tonight. If you really want to show me you're sorry, you'll stay quiet and enjoy the evening I have planned for you. We can talk about all the rest of it tomorrow, okay?"

Joel looked puzzled, but he nodded. "Okay, baby. Anything you want."

I grinned and arched a brow. "Anything?"

To my relief and joy, Joel's shoulders visibly relaxed, and he grinned right back at me. "Yeah. Anything."

"Good. Then you'll sit right down here and eat a little something for me." I pulled out the chair in front of me and waved Joel into it before going to get my casserole out of the oven. When I got back to the table, I figured Joel must have noticed there was only one place setting, because he looked confused again. I just smiled and put a large serving of the casserole on the plate. After clicking the remote to turn on the stereo, I removed my navy-blue "Actors speak louder than words" apron and sat down at the end of the table, facing him.

"Open wide," I said, loading up a fork and offering it to him as Andrew Lloyd Webber's "Memory" wafted from the speakers.

He lifted an eyebrow at me but did as he was told, chewing and swallowing the bite I gave him while I fed myself.

"Tuna?" he asked.

I smiled. "Mmhmm. Do you like it?"

"It's great, baby. I just don't think you've ever made a tuna casserole for me before."

I smirked. "I know. I have all kinds of surprises waiting for you, so shut up and eat."

He laughed and accepted the next bite I offered him. Every time he tried to speak, I shoved food in his mouth until he got the hint that I really didn't want to talk, and we finished the plate and a glass of wine each in silence.

When the plate was empty, Joel lifted his eyebrows and waited like a good boy to see what was next. I knew he'd play along. And he knew if he put himself in my hands and went along with whatever crazy scheme I'd come up with this time, he'd be rewarded in the end. It had always been that way for us, but I hadn't spent anywhere near enough of my energy on my man lately. I'd finally realized that, and I was going to do my best to change it, starting that night.

I stood up and reached out a hand to him. His eyes were a bit damp when he wrapped his big hand around mine and rose to his feet, but I blamed it on the candlelight. Otherwise, I would have started crying, and that would have just been silly.

"I want you to take the dishes and the food into the kitchen. And when you're done, I want you to get undressed and meet me in the bathroom, okay?"

Joel nodded and pulled me to him for a quick kiss before letting me go and gathering the plate and glasses. I didn't stay to watch. I had things to do.

By the time Joel joined me in the bathroom, the tub was nearing half-full and the air was fragrant with scented oil and candles. He walked in, not in the least self-conscious about the fact that he was completely and gloriously nude. Of course, with a body like his, what did he have to be self-conscious about? I could spend days just looking at him naked.

"Babe, why do we have a tiger-fur bedspread?" Joel asked as he crossed the floor and stood next to the tub.

"Don't you worry about that. Just shut up and climb in the tub."

He smiled indulgently at me and rolled his eyes as he stepped over the edge, easing himself into the warm water with a sigh.

"Now close your eyes and just relax and enjoy," I said as I shut off the water and puttered around picking up the things I was going to need.

I put a towel on the floor and knelt down on it as I filled a cup with bathwater and poured it over Joel's head. When his hair was good and wet, I massaged shampoo into it, luxuriating in the feel of it and the sound of his voice as he groaned in pleasure. When I was done rinsing it clean and conditioning it, I set to work with a washcloth and scented soap, caressing every inch of his body until Joel's always impressive erection arched up to meet his belly button. He reached for me then, but I dodged away and searched for the little vial of oil I'd used to scent the water, adding a little more to the bath to chase the scent of the soap away.

Joel sniffed. "What is that?"

"Lemongrass. I wanted to buy the catnip essential oil, but the sales guy said the lemongrass would be a better idea."

"Catnip? Baby, what…?"

I put a finger to his lips and gave him a quick kiss before getting up and grabbing a towel. "Nope. No talking, remember? Now dry off and meet me in the bedroom."

Joel gave me a bemused smile and shook his head before taking the towel and climbing out of the tub. When he met me in the bedroom, I told him to lay his hot body down on the bed, facedown. He tried to reach for me again, but I swatted his hands away and scrambled backward until my back hit the dresser. When he kept coming at me, I finally had to resort to threatening him with the purple fluffy feather-tipped whip I was saving for later in the evening. He backed down then and flopped onto the bed. But I think it was my pout over my surprise being spoiled more than the threat of the whip that did it.

I started to undress then, but Joel was watching me from his spot on the bed, his head pillowed on his arms, and I got a little self-conscious. There was no hope for it, though. Once again, I'd set the scene, so I had to keep going, kicking off my shoes and socks, pulling off my polo, and dropping my trousers to the floor. I did blow out a couple of the candles I had lit, but apparently Joel could still see just fine, because his eyes widened when my new fancy undies were revealed.

To his credit, he didn't laugh as I walked to the bed in my leopard-print boxer briefs. In fact, he looked almost as turned on as he was amused. There'd been a leopard-print thong at the shop too, but I wasn't going to go there, not even for Joel. I would have had to blow out *all* the candles to walk across the room in that thing, and then I wouldn't have been able to see Joel in all his glory waiting for me.

I reached under the bed for my last surprise before I climbed onto the mattress and straddled his hips. He wiggled his ass a bit under me, rubbing my cock across his exceptionally firm glutes until I had to give them a firm swat to get him to stop. He peered cheekily over his shoulder at me, completely unrepentant.

"Close your eyes and put your head down," I ordered sternly, "or you don't get the last surprise."

He chuckled. "Okay, okay."

When I was sure his eyes were closed, I opened the box, pulled on the fuzzy mittens I'd bought, and started smoothing my hands over his broad back as Tom Jones's husky baritone belted out "What's New Pussycat" from the living room.

Joel let out a noise that seemed to be caught between a laugh and a moan, but eventually the moan won. "Oh my God, Michael. What are those things?"

I grinned. "Mink massage mittens. You like?"

"I'd start purring if I didn't think it would ruin the mood."

I kept running my hands over him in sensual circles. "But that's the point, my love. I want you to purr if that's what you want to do. I'm trying to meet you halfway."

Joel sighed and rolled over, grabbing my wrists and holding my mittened hands to his chest. "I know what you're trying to do, babe, and I love you so much for it. I can't even tell you what I'm feeling right now. The catnip, the music, dinner, and the fur blanket… not to mention those sexy undies of yours, which are just… *damn*." He shook his head and reached for me, pulled me all the way down onto his chest, and wrapped me tight in his arms. "I love you, Michael. I should have told you about the furry thing a long time ago. But, after I met you, things were so great that I didn't mind walking away from all that for a while. It was just recently that everything got really stressful. And when I saw an opportunity to let loose, I took it." He cupped my chin and lifted my face until he could look in my eyes, and the warmth and love I saw there made me want to cry. "I appreciate what you've done here, but being a furry isn't really about sex for me. It's more about living in the moment and pretending to be someone completely carefree and simple for a while, if that makes any sense. When I think about sex, it's you and only you, babe. I promise."

I kissed him then because I didn't have any words, and Joel didn't waste any time ridding me of my mittens and my fancy new leopard undies.

Naked and so hot for each other I'm surprised the bed didn't catch fire, we made love like animals for the rest of the night. When Joel pressed inside me that first time, we were both on our knees, my back to his chest. Joel's arms were wrapped so tightly around me, I felt completely surrounded and filled by him until I couldn't tell where I ended and he began.

Angels wept.

The new tiger-fur bedspread needed to go to the cleaners after our little lovemaking marathon, but I didn't mind. We'd only be breaking it out on special occasions anyway, since it clashed horribly with the rest of our décor. But I have to admit, rolling around on all that fuzzy softness was kind of luxuriant and sexy. It almost made me want to try fucking Joel in his costume... *almost*. I still couldn't quite get over the giant grinning foam head.

For now, though, I decided to just let him go to his cons every now and again to scratch that, uh, furry itch—as long as he promised to keep it zipped up in his fuzzy bodysuit, that is.

And I definitely had a "no strays" policy for the condo.

ROWAN MCALLISTER quit her day job in 2007 and moved to her dream home in the woods of Virginia to follow her muses and explore her creative side full time. She's a firm believer in practical romanticism, requires a strong cup of coffee every morning to be even remotely human, and has a healthy obsession with romance and fantasy fiction, small (and not so small) furry creatures, and anything to do with working with her hands. She can be found most days either hunched over her sewing machine or hunched over her laptop. Though she has spent a lifetime making up stories in her head when whatever task she was occupied with failed to keep her full attention, she only recently discovered the challenge and reward to be found in committing those stories to paper. Now that she has, there's no going back.

Contact Rowan at rowanmcallister10@gmail.com.

Like an Old Sweater

Elizabella Gold

I.

"Keys, keys, keys. I put them here somewhere...."

"Did you check your pocket, Ethan?" Jeff called. He tilted his chin up and checked in the mirror to be sure he'd gotten rid of the stubble. He glanced into the hallway and smirked as he watched his boyfriend bumble around.

"Oh." Ethan dug into his jacket pocket and produced the jangling ring of keys. "Thanks, babe."

"No problem." Jeff hurried over to Ethan and kissed him on the cheek. "When will you be back?"

"Well." Ethan frowned. "I'm hoping to get home around six. *But it's possible I'll be later than that.*"

"Uh-huh. Should I just assume you will be? Later, that is."

Ethan tapped his chin and jiggled his keys. "Yeah, probably. Sorry. I'll definitely try to make it home for a late dinner, though."

Jeff's lips tightened; then he smiled. "That's okay. You've got to do what you've got to do."

"Hey, you know I'd rather spend time at home with you," Ethan said, wrapping his arms around Jeff's waist and nuzzling his neck. "But I've got to go to that conference, and then do the book signing, and—"

"I know. It's okay. I'll see you later." Jeff kissed him quickly on the mouth.

"Hmm. You need to brush your teeth."

"Yeah, thanks." Jeff rolled his eyes.

"You should do that before shaving. I always tell you that. The toothpaste might sting any little cuts you have if you get some on your face." Ethan shook his head.

Jeff put his hand to his heart. "I'm touched by your concern, my love. It will serve me well for the rest of my days."

"As will your gratitude for me and my wisdom, darling. Okay, I'm going. See ya!" Ethan grazed Jeff's head with a kiss and darted down the hall and out the front door.

Jeff smiled to himself, then began brushing his teeth. When a little bit of the toothpaste got onto his skin, it did sting a little. He shook his head. *Next time, learn from the master, Jeff.*

"Hey, uh, has this liberry got that, uh, movie about... uh, there was some kind of monster in it." The man frowned, then belched. "A vampire, maybe? Or a werewolf. That's all I remember."

Jeff winced but forced out a smile. "I'm afraid if you can't give me more details about it, then I'm not sure which one you mean. There are a lot of movies with vampires and werewolves. We have a horror movie section right over there if you want to check it out. Maybe you can find what you're looking for there. Or something else you might like to see." He pointed to the shelf several feet away.

"Huh. Some help you are," the guy mumbled and waddled over to the horror movie section.

Jeff leaned against the counter and sighed. *If the guy said squid movies or piranha movies, I'd be in a much better spot to help him.*

He heard the front doors open, and when he glanced to see who had come in the library, his breath froze in his throat.

It was him again. The man who somehow made Jeff's stomach flutter even though he looked nothing like Jeff's dream guy—who was supposed to be Ethan. He had short, spiky blond hair, light-blue eyes, and a seemingly permanent tan. Jeff never tanned. Ethan didn't either.

"Hi." The guy smiled at Jeff, walked up to the desk, and leaned against the counter. "You're always working. Don't you ever get any time off?"

Jeff tried not to grin like a goofball. He shrugged. "Eh, it's not so bad. I work full-time. Nothing more, nothing less. Well. Generally."

"Mm." The guy drummed his fingertips on the countertop. "Still, it must be hard, dealing with people who just want to take advantage of all the free stuff you guys have here. I've seen some of the people giving you a hard time. It sucks, man."

Jeff nodded, but his mind went back to Ethan. Ethan had sympathized with his complaining about unruly or demanding patrons, but would sometimes argue that he had it worse, because his readers had paid money—most of the time—to read his books, except for his blog, of course, which was free, and thus they expected more from him.

He cleared his throat. "So, ah, can I help you with anything?"

The guy's brow furrowed for a second. Then he opened his backpack and got out a couple of books. He set them on the counter. "I just wanted to return these. I think they're a little late."

"Oh, okay, no problem." Jeff scanned the books and set them on the return shelf. He headed back to the computer and peered at the screen. Hmm. So the guy's name was Timothy Wallace. Probably went by Tim. That suited him. "It's fifty cents."

"Darn. Well, library fines are the cheapest things I've come across lately, so I guess I'll pay it." Timothy grinned and handed Jeff a couple of quarters. Their hands touched briefly, and Jeff tried to hold back the shiver of warmth that sparked inside him.

Get a hold of yourself. He's a patron, he's probably just being friendly, and hey, buddy, you've been in a relationship for seven years. Remember your boyfriend?

Jeff hoped someone would come up and distract him from the spiky-haired grinning guy, but the flow of patrons seemed to be slow for a change. The vampire/werewolf man was still perusing the movies, and there was a small group of kids singing a song with the children's librarian in the back of the library. But otherwise things were quiet. Too quiet.

"Okay, your fine is all taken care of," he said, putting the change in the cash drawer. "Your record's clear. Would you like a receipt?"

"No, that's okay. I trust you. I just hope you can trust me not to be late with your library books again." Tim's smile deepened. "So hey, I'm Tim. Well, you probably already figured that out when you scanned my card."

"Ha-ha, yeah." Jeff felt his ears turning red. *Get a grip! Even if there were no other impediments, he's probably too young for you. I bet he's still in college.*

He tried to discreetly look at the computer screen and saw the guy's age: twenty-four. Right. Only five years younger than him. Not that it mattered, of course.

"Um, what's your name?" Tim had lost the grin and was rubbing the back of his neck and biting his lip.

Oh! He was supposed to answer him. Right. Of course. Duh. "Heh. Sorry. I spaced out for a second. Not a good thing to do at work," Jeff joked lamely. "My name is Jeff." *Please don't ask for a last name. Not yet, anyway.*

"Jeff. I like that name. Do you go to college?" Tim leaned against the counter again, closer this time. There were only a few inches between them now.

"I, uh, no. I graduated"—Jeff winced—"some time ago. I just work here now."

"Oh wow." Tim's eyebrows raised. "I thought you were my age. You look really young." He laughed. "I mean that as a compliment. How old are you?"

"Twenty-nine." And turning thirty in less than a week. Barf.

"I bet you still get carded all the time. You look great for your age."

"Thank you." Jeff could feel his insides melting. He had to stop this fast. "My boyfriend says I look great too." *There, that wasn't totally and completely obvious or anything.* And actually Ethan had never commented on it one way or another. But this guy didn't need to know that.

"Ah." Tim leaned back a little and moved his elbow off the counter. "Well, he's right."

Silence abounded, and Jeff was almost happy to have vampire/werewolf man come up to the counter and set down some

DVDs. Tim hesitated for a moment, then gave him a quick waggle of fingers and headed off toward the row of study rooms.

Jeff felt a wave of disappointment wash over him. But what right did he have to be upset that a guy had quit flirting with him as soon as he'd shot him down, especially considering he had a boyfriend?

"I found my movie, no thanks to you," the vampire/werewolf man informed Jeff.

"Oh, that's good," Jeff said, biting his tongue as he scanned the DVDs. "What movie was it?"

"*Swamp Thing.*"

Jeff desperately wished he could headdesk himself.

"YOU look frazzled, Jeff," Kristy said, clamping her hand on his shoulder and giving him a firm squeeze. "You're never going to make it to being library director like me if you're ready to collapse when it's only just going on five o'clock."

"Well, I'd hate to take your job away from you, Kristy," Jeff said, straightening his posture and giving her a wide grin. "I'm just a simple day worker. Didn't even go to liberry school like you."

"There's still time for you to get your master's degree, bud." Kristy nodded, sage-like. "You're still young enough to get the attention of all those cute college boys who come in here. Like that spiky-haired one."

Jeff flushed a little. So she'd seen that. "Oh, I think he was just hoping I'd take his library fines off for him."

"Or his pants," Kristy deadpanned.

Jeff blushed harder and shook his head. "Are you sure you wouldn't have been better off as a sailor with that mouth, Kris?"

"Nah. Somehow I think most of those men wouldn't have been interested in my mouth. Or any other part of my body."

"Oh! Come on now. Don't stereotype."

"Yeah, you're right." Kristy slapped herself lightly on the cheek. "That was lame and no doubt inaccurate. So, off home to your star writer husband, then?"

Jeff winced. "Not right away," he said. Psht. As if he needed to prove himself to his boss in some way. "Might pick up a sandwich or something on my way home."

"That's good, that's good. Don't let that man tell you what to do just because he's a big shot and you're stuck working for me. You get that sandwich. Get five of 'em!"

Jeff swatted at her hair. "You're really obnoxious sometimes, you know that?"

She chuckled. "You come for the money, but you stay for my awful jokes."

"Well, not today I don't. My time here is up. See ya tomorrow." Jeff waved and headed toward the employees' coatroom.

When he got to the parking lot, he saw Tim sauntering toward a beat-up gray junk bucket.

"So his car isn't as hot as he is," Jeff murmured.

As if he'd heard him, Tim turned around. He spotted Jeff and smiled and waved.

Eep. Jeff gave a quick wave and darted toward his car.

"Great, now he knows which one is mine," he muttered as he started the engine.

But he wasn't really worried about Tim stalking him. Really, he kind of hoped he'd show up at the library again. Just because it was so boring there, of course. Yup.

JEFF sighed as he pulled into the driveway. Ethan's car wasn't there. But he hadn't really expected it to be.

"He won't be able to snag any of my roast beef sub, then," he said aloud and turned off the engine. After he'd gone inside, gone to the bathroom, and changed into more comfortable clothes—he always thought of Mister Rogers when he put on a cardigan and took off his shoes—he settled down with his e-reader and his roast beef sub.

But he couldn't concentrate on the book, and he'd only eaten about half of his sandwich in the past few minutes. Ethan liked to tease him that he could eat ten footlongs in as many minutes, and Jeff couldn't disagree with him. Jeff found himself wondering if Tim liked to eat a lot.

He was pretty thin. Didn't look like he was a gym buff. But maybe he had great metabolism.

Jeff's phone buzzed, and he picked it up.

Sorry babe, but the line here is really long, and the bookstore owner said I could stay an extra hour to make sure everyone gets an autograph. Will call you when I'm done. Love you!

"Fine," Jeff said aloud. "That just means I can watch my zombies in peace. No screeching housewives tonight. Your loss, buddy."

But as the hours scraped by and Jeff busied himself with television, reading, and even—shudder—doing the dishes, he kept glancing at the clock more and more. He texted Ethan: *You're going to have to bring a pair of pajamas with you next time you go to one of these things, so you're ready for bed when you finally get home.*

An hour later he got a reply: *Haha. You know I sleep nude. A few people here have actually asked me what I wear to bed. Anyway I'll be home soon, J-J. Hold your horses.*

So Ethan knew he was impatient. Well, he hadn't exactly tried to hide it, had he? He should probably cool it. He wouldn't want Ethan sending him angry texts while he was working at the library.

No problem, babe. See you soon xxx.

Jeff lay back on the couch and thought of some of the fun times he'd had with Ethan. He could remember very clearly, though it'd been seven years earlier, when he'd spotted Ethan at the university café, looking absurdly good with that luscious chocolate-brown hair, and later, when he'd gotten closer, those beautiful honey-brown eyes. His stomach rumbled as he thought of the many, many jaunts they'd made to Spoony's ice-cream place, often followed by some glow bowling, then a few slices from Mick's Pizza since they'd had such a workout. And he remembered the time they'd first had sex—made love, really. How long they'd waited before finally giving it a go.

He thought of how Ethan had kissed him for the first time, had cupped his face so gently, like he couldn't believe he'd been gifted with such a man as Jeff. And Jeff had trembled, feeling as if he'd never loved anyone the way he loved Ethan. Anything before had been puppy love. He'd been out since he was sixteen and had had a few boyfriends, but how they had flown from his mind when he first laid eyes on Ethan. All he could think was *Why didn't we meet sooner?* And he was thankful he hadn't graduated yet.

He heard a car pull in the driveway and nearly jumped in excitement. He went to the window in the front hall and almost cheered. His boyfriend was home. Yes! Suddenly he wished he had prepared an awesome three-course meal, because for sure Ethan would be starving after all that signing and smiling.

When Ethan entered the front hall, Jeff flung his arms around his neck and hugged him tight.

"Well! Someone sure missed his baby while he was away," Ethan said, giving Jeff a firm but brief squeeze in return. "Good to see you too. Hey, listen, I've got to take a shower. I wouldn't have thought sitting and smiling with gritted teeth for five hours would make me so smelly, and yet it has. I guess I was nervous."

"You don't smell so bad," Jeff said, but he stepped a bit farther away from him.

"Mm-hmm. Your actions speak louder than your words," Ethan teased.

"Hey, I could join you in the shower," Jeff said. "I could use one myself."

"Hmm. That sounds nice, but I am seriously stank. I don't know how long I'm going to be in there."

Jeff stared at Ethan in surprise. "You're refusing a shower with me?"

Ethan stared back. "What? No, I'm not refusing. You can join me if you want. I just thought you might appreciate me at my best, rather than my stinkiest."

"We've been together for seven years, Eth. I accepted you at your best and your worst a long time ago." Jeff shook his head.

"Well, I feel the same about you, babe," Ethan said, his voice low and smooth. "I mean, hey, try not to take what I said the wrong way. I've just had a *really* long, tiring day and wanted some time to myself. You know. Just to unwind in my little 'man cave'. You like that too, don't you?"

"I guess so," Jeff muttered.

"Hey, look." Ethan put his hands on his hips. "I had people telling me they wanted to marry me. People begging me to have kids with them.

Even a few straight women thinking they were hot enough to 'change me'. It's been annoying, okay, and I don't need any grief from my boyfriend as well."

"Did you accept any of their propositions?"

Ethan closed his eyes and took a deep breath, then let it out slowly. "I'm going to take a shower. Hopefully you'll be in a better mood before we go to bed. See you later." He turned around and headed toward the bathroom. He shut the door with a firm click.

Jeff sighed and went back to the couch. He flipped through the TV channels and even tried to watch a few videos on his phone, but nothing appealed to him. He looked at the bathroom door. It was still closed.

He trudged up to bed. If Ethan didn't want to sleep next to him, he'd just have to go onto the couch himself.

II.

ETHAN yawned and rolled over onto his right side. He smiled as he saw Jeff asleep on his back, whistling softly through his nose. He reached out and brushed Jeff's sparse copper chest hair with his fingertips.

Jeff stirred in his sleep; then his fingers closed over Ethan's. Ethan smiled, and with his other hand he brushed a strand of that sweet curly red hair away from Jeff's face.

"Mmm. Morning," Jeff mumbled.

"Good morning, my love," Ethan cooed, continuing to stroke Jeff's chest and stomach.

"What time is it?" Jeff moved onto his side and smiled sleepily at Ethan. "I'm glad you're not mad at me anymore."

A lump formed in Ethan's stomach. *He had to bring that up?* But he smiled. "Oh, how could I possibly stay mad at you? You're too freaking adorable." He pinched Jeff's cheek, which caused Jeff to swat at him, and they rolled around on the bed, occasionally hitting each other with pillows.

Ethan's alarm sounded, and he groaned. *Just five more minutes, please.*

"Time to get up already, Superstar?" Jeff said.

"It is for you too, Jeff," Ethan pointed out. *And don't call me Superstar.*

He sighed. "I know. It's just I was enjoying myself." He snuggled close to Ethan. "Let's call in sick today."

"Aw. I wish I could, babe." Ethan ruffled his hair. "But duty calls. I've got a live chat on my publisher's site in an hour, I've got to update my blog, I have to talk to some bookstores about stocking my books...."

"Point taken. Maybe I'll see you at dinner. Or breakfast. Tomorrow." Jeff got up from the bed, stretched, and rubbed his eyes. "I've got to check the adult fiction stock today anyway."

"Too bad my stuff is too adult for you guys." Ethan grinned and winked.

Jeff rolled his eyes. "Yeah, they just can't handle your brand of truth."

Ethan blanked on a comeback. But then he lit up. "Hey, why don't we take a shower together now. I'm game if you are."

Jeff smiled but then said, "Actually, I'd better make it a quick one. I just remembered I told Kristy I'd try to be in a little early today to help her with the interloan book delivery. I don't really have to, but we've been short of workers lately." He shook his head. "We can't let people work as much as they want to because of budget cuts. I'm one of the lucky ones." He paused. "I guess."

Ethan felt a thud of disappointment hit his stomach. *Wish I'd let him get in with me last night.* "Oh well. We'll do it later. I mean hey, it's the weekend tomorrow. We have two and a half days of fun."

"Until you get called away by the computer."

Ethan felt annoyance prick his insides. "I'm going to make some coffee," he muttered and headed to the kitchen.

Half an hour later, they'd barely said more than a few words to each other as they got ready for their respective days. Before Jeff headed off to the library, he graced Ethan with a grazing kiss to the cheek. "See you later."

"Bye. Hey, I love you." Ethan gently slapped him on the bottom as Jeff headed past him.

Jeff turned to him and smiled. "Love you too." Then he was out the door.

Warmth kindled in Ethan's stomach as he headed toward the living room, where he'd left his laptop. He put on his favorite music—eighties pop—and tried, as he did every day, to get into the mindset of an enthusiastic, no worries, saucy and sassy blogger and author extraordinaire. Even when he just wanted to say *Screw it, I'm going back to bed*, hiding meant fewer sales. One needed to establish a rapport with one's readers. One couldn't hide out for weeks at a time and expect them to stick around.

The chat with fans and fellow authors breezed by, and Ethan had several people begging him to publish again soon, which warmed his heart more than chicken soup or his favorite beer.

He updated his blog, promising his next entry would be hilarious and amazing. Then he remembered he hadn't had much of a breakfast, just half a protein bar and a gulped-down cup of black coffee. And he'd done pretty well so far for the morning. He deserved a break, for sure.

Ethan headed to the kitchen, and it occurred to him it was almost lunchtime. Jeff would be on a more fixed schedule than him. He hadn't noticed whether Jeff had packed a lunch for himself or not; maybe he'd go out for his break instead. But he could surprise Jeff with a nice homemade lunch. Good, tasty stuff he hadn't had in a while.

Ethan tapped his chin. "Let's see, when did he last have a quinoa and asparagus salad? With some olives thrown in there.... Yeah, that sounds good. I should make one for myself too. And a toasted baguette with garlic butter.... Oh man, I'm drooling now. And a caramel latte to drink. Damn! I need to treat myself like this sometime."

Humming to himself, Ethan set to work making his boyfriend's fabulous lunch. When he'd finished, he looked at the clock.

"Almost noon. Perfect. Too bad Jeff only gets half an hour for a break. I wonder if he'd be receptive to doing it in my car? Nah, probably not. Wouldn't want to get his clothes wrinkled. Or his birthday suit. Ha! Burn! Oh, he'd hate me if he heard that one."

As bad as he knew the time and place was for such things, Ethan couldn't help but feel a little amorous as he drove to the library. He'd just have to make sure to get all his work done by the time Jeff got home, and then he'd lead him to the bedroom with candles and smooth jazz playing softly. He'd forgo the Adam Ant and Culture Club, just for Jeff.

Ethan whistled as he jogged up the stairs to the library entrance, though he knew he'd have to cut it out in a few seconds. Kristy looked built for noise, but she wouldn't tolerate it in her library home.

Ethan pushed open the front door and smiled when he saw Jeff at the circulation desk. His smile faded when he saw the spiky-haired blond man leaning against the counter, practically oozing all over his—damn it, *his*—boyfriend. Smiling and laughing like a buffoon. Where was Kristy to stop this disgusting nonsense? And how long had this guy spent in the tanning booth?

When the orange jerk caressed Jeff's arm, Ethan sucked in his breath with a fury. "Hi, Jeff," he boomed as he walked up to the two.

To his simultaneous satisfaction and dismay, Jeff jumped away from Orange Jerk and gawped at Ethan. Orange Jerk smirked and stared at him. "H-hi," Jeff stuttered. "It's—it's good to see you."

Ethan nodded slowly. "Thought I'd bring you lunch. I made it for you." He held up the tote bag, into which he'd carefully packed those lovingly made items in plastic boxes decorated with Jeff's favorite superheroes, and the thermos. He wanted to pour the coffee—which couldn't be too hot anymore, anyway—onto Orange Jerk's head. "Seeing as I'm your boyfriend and all," he added.

Jeff's face softened. "That was really sweet of you, Eth. I'm on break in five minutes. Will you wait for me?"

"You sure you don't already have other plans?" Ethan arched a brow and side-eyed Jeff's companion.

Orange Jerk shook his head, then turned to Jeff. "I've got to go study. See you later, Jeff."

To Ethan's grim approval, Jeff ignored him. Orange Jerk walked off.

Jeff tightened his lips and glowered at Ethan. "Wait here, please. I'll be right back." He disappeared into the staff room. Ethan could see him talking to Kristy. She laughed and nodded, and Jeff came out, glaring at Ethan. He leaned in close and continued to stare as if he could eviscerate him with his face. He took hold of Ethan's arm. Ethan went with him outside, and they got into Ethan's car. Once safely inside, Jeff gave him a little shove.

"What's your problem, you asshole? Are you trying to get me in trouble? Do you think I wanted all the patrons to know I was gay?"

"Oh?" Ethan arched a brow. "Are you ashamed? Like no one's ever seen us together before? I think they can figure it out. And anyway, I think you already blew your cover with Mister Frosty Spikes."

Jeff rolled his eyes. "Tim is just—" He stopped.

Ethan gave a mock gasp. "You're on a first-name basis. That's good."

"Oh, come on, Ethan. I check out books to him. I can't help but notice his name."

Ethan wanted to make a joke about checking out other things about him but held his tongue. He leaned back in the seat, stared out the windshield, and sighed. This was silly. Wasn't it? He'd been with Jeff for seven years. They'd graduated from college together, purchased a house together, and informally but solemnly pledged their love to each other in front of family and friends. If he didn't trust him now, could he ever?

He held up his hands. "Okay. Okay. My reaction may have been a little… whatever."

"Obnoxious? Premature? Absurd? You're the author. Stuck for words?"

Ethan grinned sheepishly at his boyfriend. "Yeah. It was all those things. But." He bit his lip. "Do you think he's cute?"

Jeff stared at him stone-faced. Finally he said, "I don't ask you about all the guys you meet at your signings and whether or not you like them, do I? Even though they apparently propose to you and want to suck your dick."

Ethan blushed. "Well, it's not like you've never asked me about…. I mean, last night you…. Okay, fine." He held up the tote bag. "Look, I really want you to eat this lunch I made for you. It's quinoa and asparagus, with a nice hunk of baguette. And a latte."

Jeff's eyes lit up. "Nice. Thank you." He took the bag from Ethan and peered inside. He opened the plastic containers and tore into his meal, then drank his latte down.

Ethan chuckled. "It's glorious to see you transform from a prim and proper librarian to a ravenous beast at the sight of some noms."

When Jeff had finished wiping his mouth, he gazed up at Ethan. "That was some truly excellent grub, man. You should make me turn into a ravenous beast more often."

"Hmm. I like the sound of that. How many hours till you get off work?" Ethan ran his finger up and down Jeff's sleeve.

"I get off at five." Jeff's breathing had gotten a little labored. His gaze bored into Ethan's.

Ethan tingled. "Well, I just have a few more things to do today, and you know how fast I work when I'm motivated… and how slow I can work when I'm stimulated."

Jeff smiled. "I'm tempted to tell Kristy that I want the rest of the day off. But it's just me and her working today. Well, and the janitor. But I don't think we can get him to work the circ desk."

"Damn. I guess that means I'll just have to occupy myself for the rest of the day."

"Are you going to cook me something else?" Jeff asked, making puppy eyes at him.

Ethan chuckled. "Maybe. But I was thinking more along the lines of…. Well, you'll just have to wait and see."

"Aw." Jeff pouted.

"Hey now. No pouting. It'll be worth it. I promise."

"I trust you." They stared at each other, and Ethan knew they both recognized the importance of those words. "I'd better get back to work." Jeff leaned over and kissed Ethan gently on the mouth. "And I just want to tell you, you don't have to worry about Tim. He's cute, and his attention to me is flattering, but he's not you. And you're the one I want."

"Gosh, excuse me while I melt all over the place here." Ethan kissed him again, letting his lips linger on Jeff's. "I'll see you soon. Can't be soon enough."

"We'll make it special," Jeff promised. He got out of the car, waggled his fingers at Ethan, and headed back to the library. Ethan watched as Jeff's jeans hugged his ass. He gently rubbed his burgeoning boner.

"Patience, my love. We'll be rewarded soon."

III.

"I'M GLAD you and Lover Boy got to make up," Kristy said to Jeff, nudging his arm.

And how whipped am I that the first thought "Lover Boy" brings to mind is my boyfriend's love of cheesy eighties music? "Yeah. We always do."

"Well, I think that's really good." Kristy sounded serious for a change. "And don't worry. If you get any more trouble from Frosty Flakes"—Jeff guessed she meant Tim—"you just let me know, and I'll deal with him."

Jeff smiled. "Thanks, Kris. Your Mama Bear attitude helps during crises like these."

"I hope you feel you can come to me when something's not awesome. And hey, I know what it's like to be stalked by a patron," she said with a shrug. "Did I ever tell you about my psycho fan?"

"Yeah, you did. About fifty times. Per week. Ever since I started working here four years ago."

"Yes, I'll never be able to forget that," Kristy continued, as if Jeff hadn't said anything. "He was just a few inches above five feet tall, and he always smelled like a mixture between pot and puke. Like he'd just come from a big outdoor music festival. Once a week he brought me an orange flower. I told him I hated orange, and he told me I would learn to love it, just like I'd learn to love him."

"Kristy, it's five o'clock now. I'd better get—"

"And then, after months of that crap, one day he came in and told me, rather haughtily I might add, that he no longer loved me and had taken up with a woman who worked at a ringtoss booth at that carnival they have out in Woodville. You know it?"

"Yes, but Kristy—"

"I told him I was happy for him, and he looked at me sternly and said I would never see him again, and I would cry for what I had so foolishly let go. And I never did see him again, and the last time I cried, it was because they stopped making those cheese and jalapeno chips I like."

Jeff put his hand gently on her elbow. "That's awesome, Kristy, but my time is up, and I need to get home because my boyfriend is going to rock my socks off. And maybe make me another nice meal."

"Oh, he'll make a meal out of you, all right. Have fun, tiger." Kristy slapped him on the back. "Don't do anything I wouldn't—oh wait, actually you're probably doing a fair few things I wouldn't do. Well, off you go then."

Jeff grinned. "Thanks. See ya."

JEFF opened the front door to his house and sighed in happiness as the smell of garlic wafted toward his nose. "Mmm. Nice."

"That you, babe?" he heard Ethan call.

"Yep," he called back. He peered around the front hallway and the living room. Everything looked the same. But then, what had he been expecting? For a circus to be taking place? A bunch of balloons and streamers everywhere?

Ethan entered the hall and lit up when he saw Jeff. "Hey, honey." He came over to him and wrapped his arms around Jeff's waist. He gently pushed their noses together. "It is so good to see you. I hope you're hungry."

"I certainly am." Jeff nuzzled Ethan's neck, moving back his luscious brown hair to do so, and twining the strands through his fingers. "What did you make?"

Ethan leaned into his touch and nibbled his ear. "Garlic chicken with scalloped potatoes. Oh, and some more nice buttery baguette hunks."

"Yum. You're a star."

"You're the star, my contrarian librarian." Ethan kissed him, and for a moment they forgot the food as they wrapped their arms and tongues around each other. Their breathing became more harsh, more urgent.

Before they could get too lost in each other, Jeff's stomach rumbled. They both laughed.

"Better soothe the savage beast first. Well, the one that wants food, anyway." Ethan rubbed Jeff's tummy, then took his hand, clasping it gently. "Come on."

Jeff let himself be led by his love to the kitchen. He sucked in a breath when he saw what Ethan had done to it.

It was nothing absurd, nothing ostentatious. Ethan had gone for subtlety: two long white candles lit and placed in Jeff's favorite rose-shaped candleholders, and his iPod was playing some Miles Davis on low. The food laid out on the table made Jeff's stomach rumble again.

"Aww." Jeff hugged Ethan and kissed his cheek. "You're so sweet, Eth. You've relinquished A Flock of Seagulls and canned spaghetti tonight just for me." He kissed him again. "But seriously, this is great. You're the best."

Ethan leaned into him, then pulled back and gazed into Jeff's eyes. "It was my pleasure. You know, I am so lucky to have you in my life. And as my partner. Not everyone is fortunate enough to find the love of his life at such a young age as we were." He chuckled. "I was so afraid you weren't gay. And when I found out you were, I was afraid you'd think I was totally lame."

"Who says I don't think that?" Jeff nudged him.

"Hey. I made lunch and dinner for you. Watch it, buddy." Ethan nudged him back. "Anyway, sit down and enjoy it before it gets cold."

"You don't have to tell me twice. I'm starving. Kristy didn't want me to leave," Jeff said as he sat down and unfolded his napkin. He took a sip of water and marveled at Ethan's preparation. He'd thought of everything he'd wanted. Not that Ethan had never made him dinner before; he had, plenty of times. But it was usually something like slapdash pasta or frozen food.

Ethan pointed to the glass of merlot he'd provided. "Drink up. You're going to need to be nice and drunk for the things I have planned for later."

"Pssht. Somehow I don't think my vanilla baby has anything too sinister in store for me."

Ethan grinned and shrugged. "Wait and see."

Jeff felt a shiver go down his spine.

They ate and drank mostly in silence. Jeff would take a sip of his wine and feel Ethan's gaze on him. During those times, they'd lock eyes, smile at each other, and Ethan would continue to stare at Jeff as if he were with the most amazing man on earth. Well, maybe he was. And Ethan was amazing too.

When they'd finished eating, Jeff set down his napkin. "So, what's for dessert?"

"Ah. Dessert. That's in the bedroom." Ethan winked at him as he stood. He gathered up the dishes to put them in the sink and refused to let Jeff help, saying he wanted to take care of him. When they'd both washed their hands, Ethan laced his fingers through Jeff's and led him toward their room. Jeff's heart began to pound with excitement and anticipation.

Ethan pushed open the door, and Jeff grinned.

His boyfriend had decked out the place in candles of red and purple, Jeff's favorite colors, and had spritzed the air with sandalwood, one of Jeff's favorite scents.

"Okay. You've seen it. I'm done seducing you," Ethan said, and pushed Jeff onto the bed.

He fell with an *oomph* onto the black down comforter. Ethan straddled him and raised his eyebrows. "Uh-oh. I've got you now."

"You won't for long," Jeff declared and began tickling Ethan's ribs.

Ethan yelped and jerked out of Jeff's grasp. But Jeff persisted, and soon the two were engaged in an all-out tickle war. They gave up and lay back on the bed, panting.

"Well," Jeff said after he'd caught his breath. "You are a master of seduction, my dear man. You've utterly and completely conquered me."

"Hey, there's no reason why we can't still be fun and young at heart, even if we are nearly old thirtysomethings." Ethan ran his fingers over Jeff's chest.

"You've still got five months left of your twenties," Jeff grumbled.

"Doesn't matter to me, babe. We can pretend our ages are reversed, if you want, and I'll be the older one."

Jeff nodded. "Sounds good to me."

"And this sounds good to me." Ethan wrapped his arm around Jeff's waist and loomed over him, then kissed his throat.

"Mmm." Jeff tilted his head back to give Ethan better access to his neck. He sighed in happiness as Ethan licked and sucked at the hollow in his throat. *So good.*

"Hey," he managed to say, though he was beginning to find it hard to breathe, "so is this the dessert you promised me?" *Washing the sheets will be so worth it if he's brought ice cream and chocolate too.*

"It's not all of it. I promise there's more." Ethan took off his shirt, then coaxed Jeff's shirt off. He ran his fingers over Jeff's chest hair. "So masculine. So hot."

"So are you."

"I was talking about me." Ethan pulled a serious face.

"Oh, ha-ha. No more talking unless it's along the lines of 'oh yes' or 'fuck me harder'," Jeff ordered.

"You're the boss." But the sparkle in Ethan's eyes told Jeff they'd both be taking charge throughout the night. He knew very well from past experience that Ethan was great at holding out on the good stuff, sucking Jeff some, but not enough, making Jeff beg for more. And Jeff was an expert in causing Ethan to make more noise than one of his beloved synthesizer bands cranked to eleven.

They kissed, slow and sweet at first, then deep and hot, moaning and sighing as they ran their hands over each other's bodies. Jeff grasped Ethan's ass and squeezed gently, then harder. Ethan pushed into Jeff's touch and made a murmuring sound.

Ethan lifted off of him and began to undo Jeff's belt buckle. Jeff helped him and then let Ethan unzip his jeans. He arched off the bed and let his boyfriend do away with his clothes until he was naked. Ethan, meanwhile, still wore his jeans and....

Jeff smiled as he pulled back his love's waistband. "No underwear. Yet still you have on socks? Weird."

"I won't in a second," Ethan said and tore off his socks and tossed them in the clothes hamper. "You want to do the honors, babe?"

"Absolutely." Jeff guided Ethan to his feet and ran his hands up and down Ethan's abs. "Mm. Nice."

"It's all for you, honey."

Once they were both naked—that meant no socks either—Ethan held up his hand. "I think now's the time for the dessert."

"Excellent."

Ethan gave Jeff's back a loving caress, then headed over to the closet. He pulled out jars of chocolate sauce and marshmallow fluff.

"Are we making s'mores?" Jeff joked.

Ethan smirked. "We can be the graham crackers. I'll put the filling on us." He opened the jar of chocolate sauce, dipped his finger in, and wiped some on Jeff's stomach.

"You're too slow," Jeff said and dipped his hand in the chocolate, then smeared it all over Ethan's chest. He followed with the marshmallow fluff. He bent his head down and began to lick the mixture of sugary coatings off, making little noises of contentment as he did so.

Ethan sighed. "That feels nice."

When Jeff had finished his impromptu dessert, Ethan suddenly growled and pushed Jeff back onto the bed. He rubbed his pelvis against Jeff's. Both went from simply aroused to hard as stone in seconds.

"I'm so glad we don't have to use condoms anymore since we're monogamous," Ethan whispered in Jeff's ear. "I love to feel you against me and inside my body." He stroked Jeff's hair. "I'm so happy with you, Jeff. I couldn't ask for a better partner or a better man."

Jeff's heart melted faster than the sauce had. "I'm happy with you too," he said, surprised at how choked his voice sounded. "You make me feel so great. So important, even when I mess up. I love you."

Ethan smiled. "I love you too." He kissed him. The kiss was deep, wet and hot. Jeff wrapped his arms around Ethan's back and stroked his lean muscles, moving down to cup his ass. Ethan arched into his touch.

Jeff sighed in happiness as Ethan sucked and kissed and nibbled his neck. He rubbed his hard cock against Ethan's pelvis and grinned as Ethan responded in kind.

"I want you," Jeff whispered.

"I want you too. Always." Ethan ran his hands up and down Jeff's sides and squeezed the side of his ass. "Are you ready?"

"Never readier," Jeff said.

"Excellent." Ethan lubed him up, whispering how much he wanted him and how hot he was, and when Jeff was relaxed enough for him—which never took much time or effort, given how long they'd been together—Ethan entered him. Jeff groaned and moaned as Ethan moved in and out of him. After many minutes of thrusting and caressing and kissing and grasping and pleading, Jeff orgasmed first, followed soon by Ethan. They collapsed on each other in a sticky, sweaty mess.

THEY cuddled underneath the comforter, arms and legs wrapped around each other.

"Thank you for this. For everything," Jeff said, gazing into Ethan's honeyed eyes. "You've really made tonight special for me."

Ethan's eyes crinkled. "Well, I'm glad I succeeded. Because you are special, Jeffy."

Jeff's eyes prickled. "Did you bring onions in here too?" he joked.

Ethan laughed and kissed him. "Yeah. Damn onions, they get in everywhere."

They lay there together in silence, basking in the warmth and touch of each other.

"Are you still upset about turning thirty?" Ethan asked, tracing Jeff's arm with his fingertip.

Jeff considered it for a moment, then shook his head. "Well. I mean, maybe a little." He laced his fingers through Ethan's. "But I think if I've got you with me, I can deal with it." He kissed Ethan's nose, then his chin, then his lips.

"Well, if you can deal with having me, then you've got me," Ethan promised.

Jeff snuggled closer to him. "I think I can." He rubbed his leg against Ethan's. "We fit each other really well."

ELIZABELLA GOLD has enjoyed reading and writing since she was young. She is passionate about literature, history (with a particular affection for the medieval and Victorian eras), and exploring the many ways human beings communicate. She loves learning new things and finds excuses to do research whenever she can.

Elizabella Gold can be found at:

Twitter: @ElizabellaGold

Livejournal: http://elizabellagold.livejournal.com/profile

Blog: http://elizabellagold.blogspot.com

Facebook: https://www.facebook.com/elizabella.gold

Change of Heart

Rhidian Brenig Jones

"HE'S been flirting with him all night, the slimy little prick."

Charlie Langridge felt around in his pocket for a tissue. Someone had poured cement into his skull, and his lungs were on fire. He leaned back against the seat, wondering why he'd agreed to go out, longing to be home, wishing to Christ she'd shut the fuck up. His eyes began to water again. "I don't think so," he croaked, mopping.

"Think what you like. I'm telling you, he's all over him like a rash. If he didn't have that stupid ponytail, he'd be twirling a finger through his hair. And Finn isn't exactly beating him off with a stick, either."

"Keep your voice down, for God's sake. They're just friendly, Steph. What d'you expect? Finn's his mentor; they're bound to be close—"

"Close? They're bloody close now. Just look at them."

Stephanie was a good friend, but Charlie felt a sudden wave of dislike for her. With the greatest reluctance, he swiveled around in his seat. Finn and Alex were leaning on the bar, elbow to elbow, waiting to be served. "What? What am I supposed to be seeing?"

"Are you serious? Just look at them, you idiot. You wait," she said, eyes cold above her glass. "I bet you he'll touch him. Any second now, he'll touch him."

As he stared, it struck him how similar the two were—both dark-haired, slender, taller than average. Finn couldn't claim classic good looks, but the edgy, fine-boned angularity of his face had its own low-key attractiveness. Alex was simply and straightforwardly breathtaking.

He said something that made Finn incline his head to listen for a moment, then slowly straighten, seemingly pleased. He was still smiling when Alex held his wrist to glance at his watch.

"Told you," Stephanie said with sour satisfaction.

"Leave it now," Charlie muttered anxiously. "They're coming back."

She smiled brightly at the approaching beers. "Oh, Charlie," she said through her teeth.

"SURE you've got everything you need? You warm enough?"

"Yeah, think so."

"Right, then." Finn took a last glance around the bedroom, rubbing his hand over his chest. "Call me if you need anything—you know, oxygen tent, iron lung." He blew Charlie a kiss as he reached for the light switch. "All you're getting, Typhoid Mary. Night."

Quite right, Charlie told himself stoutly, *only sensible*. But he couldn't quite dismiss the thought that at one time Finn wouldn't have left him. Flattening Charlie's protests, he'd have climbed into bed, worried and fussing, no matter what shitty virus had laid him low; he'd have stayed if Charlie had had Ebola. But that was then. Five years; things changed. By its very nature, the euphoria of new love was transitory, a blaze of glory subsiding to a warm and comfortable glow. Love faded into the background, its presence taken for granted. It just... was. And yet an odd sense of having been abandoned persisted. Charlie pushed his pillow onto the floor and dragged one of Finn's across. Too high, too firm, but blessedly cool under his boiling cheek. Little ticks and creaks as the old house settled itself for the night. No other sounds from the room next door. Charlie lay in his clammy sheets and wondered what Finn was doing, alone and unobserved on the other side of the wall. What was filling his mind, there in the dark? Whom did he see as he reached down under the covers? A slim young man, the rack of his ribs visible under smooth muscle. Long hair, loosed from its ponytail, slipping forward, concealing. At Finn's hoarse command, the quick tuck behind an ear. The dark head rising and falling, rising and falling. The glossy wing of hair, dislodged again, caught in Finn's fist, held tightly at

Alex's nape. The first gasping moan, then another and another and another.

Charlie turned the pillow over and closed his eyes against the night.

"OFF your feed? Not like you, Charlie. Cassoulet not up to scratch?"

"It's fine. Just don't seem to have much of an appetite today."

Martin Goddard patted his mouth with his napkin. "A state of being with which I am happily unfamiliar." He tilted his head appraisingly. "You've lost weight. Not on a diet, are you, dear? God forbid."

"No, I'm just not hungry." He speared a bean but then thought better of it and laid his fork down.

"Hmm. Old joie de vivre's conspicuous by its absence. Out with it. What's up?"

Not for the first time, Charlie thought how unnerving it must be for some hapless defendant to face Martin across a courtroom floor. The cultivated drawl, the jolly fat man persona thrown off, and the predator revealed in that pale, forensic stare. "I, uh… I'm not sure anything's up. That's the point, I suppose. I feel a bit stupid even saying it."

"I don't make my money from intelligent clients, dear."

"Is that what I am? A client?"

"For now."

"Just between us, then."

Martin waved a dismissive hand.

Still Charlie hesitated. Once said, it could never be unsaid. Once said, it would become real. And if it was real, he would have to do something about it. But do something about *what*? A suspicion? A feeling? When all was said and done, it wasn't as if he'd walked in and found them with their cocks out. In all probability he was doing Finn an injustice. And yet, and yet… Stephanie had seen something too. He dotted a fingertip over the tablecloth, sticking breadcrumbs. Martin watched him, content to let the silence stretch to shrieking point if necessary; they always cracked in the end.

Charlie raised his head and looked miserably at his friend. "I think Finn's fallen for a guy he works with."

Folding his hands on his gargantuan belly, Martin asked, "And what makes you think this?"

"Something Stephanie said."

Martin considered this, keeping his eyes on Charlie as he turned the matter over in his mind. *Ah, Stephanie. One wonders about women like Stephanie. Do they hope to turn us, to get us to appreciate the exotic pleasures of the vagina? Hardly; it's our being homosexual that excites them, poor things. And of course, the thrill of fancying themselves in love. How blind you can be, Charlie.* "I should take what Stephanie says with a pinch of salt. She might well exaggerate what she would perceive as a threat."

"A threat?"

"Undoubtedly. To her relationship with you two. If there's any possibility of a third pillow, Stephanie would want it for herself."

Charlie's lip curled in distaste. He shook his head. "It wasn't just Steph. I saw it too. The way they were flirting."

"Flirting? One frequently flirts. Hardly a hanging offense."

"It's not only that. It's the way he's been lately, with me. Kind of… off."

"Off?"

"I'm not explaining this very well."

"Make an effort."

"He's distant, as if his mind's on other things. Well, not so much distant, although he *is* distant. It's more that he's preoccupied, as if he has some massive secret that he's hugging to himself."

"And you think it's to do with this…?"

He forced the name out. "Alex. He's a new graduate trainee at Finn's firm. Finn's a grad mentor, and this year he's got him and another kid, Keir or Kyle or something, can't remember. Doesn't matter. He's from Leicester, Alex is—doesn't know anyone in this part of the country. Finn's been looking after him. Or so he says."

"Tell me about him."

"He's young, twenty-one, twenty-two. Superbright, got a starred First from Oxford, by all accounts. Good-looking. He's cool, full of himself, totally up his own arse. He'll be there Saturday—you can see for yourself." Charlie moved his wineglass back and forth, tracing invisible tracks on the cloth as he struggled to find words to convey his meaning. "It's the way they are when they're together. You know when two people are.... You can tell. It's the way they stand, the way they look at each other. Or don't look at each other. There's this.... It's like a magnetic field. It's hard to describe, but you can't mistake it when you see it."

Perhaps you're not as blind as I thought. "Quite so. Very well, let's assume for the sake of argument that the threat is real. What do you intend to do about it?"

"That's the point. What can I do? If he wants out of our relationship, he wants out. Nothing I *can* do about it. "

You could try growing a pair, for a start. Picking his words with care, Martin asked, "Apart from this recent... wobble, how have things been between you?"

"Fine. Ordinary."

"Ordinary?"

"Ordinary."

"What does that mean?"

Charlie frowned. "You know what ordinary means, Mart. Normal life. We go to work. We go to the pub. We do stuff. Just... get on with things."

Martin pursed his lips. "And sexually?"

Giving the lie to his reply, Charlie's eyes flickered momentarily. "Fine. No problems there."

"I see. When did you fuck him last?"

"Christ." A stain of color crept from his shirt collar, which Martin ignored; he'd asked worse questions in his time. "We, uh, don't.... We've never been into doing that."

"Let's try another tack. When did you last buy him flowers?"

For the first time in the conversation, Charlie grinned, imagining the look on Finn's face if he walked in with a dozen red roses. "Give me a break—hang on, are you serious?"

"Perfectly serious."

"What, you buy Luke flowers?"

"I do, yes."

Their glasses were empty. Martin poured more wine and set the bottle down. Evenly, he said, "Let's see if I can summarize the situation accurately. A relatively long-standing relationship. If not connubial bliss, then quiet contentment. Happy enough, thank you very much. *Ordinary.* Small surprise gestures of affection no longer feature, but then again, why should they at this mature stage in the relationship? Sex occurs, probably less frequently than hitherto, stuck at the adolescent stage, but pleasant nonetheless. On the whole, life is nicely arranged. Such a relief after the hurly-burly of the chase to have caught one's man, to be able to settle back, put one's feet up, loosen one's corsets, and have a damn good scratch." He took a sip of wine. "Into this exemplar of domestic harmony strolls a young man. Good-looking, clever, ambitious. Probably sexually voracious, as these young things so often are. Certainly with an eye on the main chance."

"What are you suggesting? It's all my fault because I've stopped trying?"

Ten thick fingers spread themselves carefully on the tablecloth. "One surmises, dear; one merely surmises."

Charlie stared into his wineglass. *Okay, yes, maybe I've taken him for granted. But isn't that what being in a relationship means? Being able to take it for granted?* Beneath his indigo cotton Boden sweater, fear crawled up Charlie's spine, cold and ripplingly unpleasant. *Finn's bored. He's bored with us. He's bored with me.* A picture flashed into his mind: two dark-haired men, fiercely erect, sinewy arms around each other, rooted, motionless except for their mouths, their sliding, fluid tongues. "Oh God," he whispered.

WHISTLING tunelessly, Finn stood at the mirror raking his fingers through his hair. He turned his head this way and that, checking it. The towel around his waist slipped, and he rewrapped it, pulling it tightly. *Don't. Let it fall.* With a sinking sense of unhappiness, Charlie realized that not so very long ago, Finn would have walked from the bathroom naked, his pale skin damp and rosily flushed from the heat of the shower. He would have sauntered across to the bed and waited, hands on slim hips, smiling down at the sudden ferocious hunger in Charlie's eyes. And because he adored the sensation of Finn stiffening in his mouth, Charlie would have taken his cock quickly, before it was fully hard. Finn would have leaned back a little so he could see the thrusting length of it and watch his lover's, reared rigid in response.

"Does this shirt need ironing?" he asked, holding up a hanger.

"No point. Linen, it'll crease to buggery in two minutes."

"You bought shares in poly-cotton or something?"

Charlie got off the bed. "I'm going down. Don't be long—they'll be here any minute."

As would *he*. Charlie ran a cloth over the kitchen counters and tried to quell the queasy churning in the pit of his stomach. Cool as fuck, a smirk on his face, looking around with interest at Finn's home, *their* home, the arrogant piece of shit. Later, when all eyes were turned, brushing his fingers against the back of Finn's hand, his arse. Waiting, maneuvering. Seizing any opportunity to be alone with him. Cupping Finn's balls. A swift check over the shoulder. A squeeze, a gleeful grin, and a final hasty kiss before reluctantly rejoining the party.

With a perfunctory rap on the door, Louisa and Simon came into the kitchen.

"Hello, darling. God, what a wonderful smell. What is it?"

"Garlic and rosemary. I'm doing crushed potatoes," he said, pecking her cheek.

"Oh yum, I'm starving. Anyone else here? Are we the first?"

"Someone has to be."

"I'd have paid good money to get here after breakfast." Simon handed Charlie a bottle of Australian Shiraz. "Some lesbian ever asks you to donate sperm, remember my words: kids are hell."

Louisa slapped his arm. "Isabella's teething, poor thing. So where's the birthday boy?"

"Just getting dressed. He'll be down in a sec."

"Here he is!" Circling her hips in a salacious bump and grind, she gave a throaty little purr. "Happy birthday, sexy! Give me a big sloppy kiss, with tongue."

Finn strode forward and hoisted her a foot into the air, growling and nuzzling into her cleavage as she squealed.

Lanky and fair, her husband peered at them like an inquisitive heron. "Don't start something someone else'll have to finish. I've got a bad back, remember."

Finn swung her around in a circle. "Look and learn, boy, look and learn."

Visions of loveliness in eyeliner and Shalimar, Ned and Jake sashayed through the door. "A barbecue *and* an orgy? Divine!"

Charlie looked around for the corkscrew. If the Dolly Sisters had arrived, the party was underway.

NEAR midnight, and Finn was Baker's Man for the latest round of Pat-a-Cake. The Dollies, consistent losers in any game that required a degree of bodily coordination, flopped and giggled, neither quite able to work out who belonged to which arm, let alone which was right and which left. Catching sight of Charlie, Finn waggled an empty Finlandia bottle in the air. Stonily sober, Charlie walked back into the kitchen and took another from the freezer.

"Don't drop it," he told Stephanie, handing it to her. "Mart, maybe you should take it."

"Give it here. I'm not that drunk. You coming? We're going to play Knees." They watched her veer across the lawn until she arrived at the patio to table thumping and cheers.

Martin asked, "Shall we?"

"I just need to finish this." A ziggurat of walnut brownies stood on the table, awaiting its candles. Charlie shook them out of the box and began to fix them in place, counting.

"Different," Martin remarked, eyeing it doubtfully.

"A lot of people don't like birthday cake." He took a cigarette lighter from a drawer and flicked it once, twice, studying the flame. "What's he doing now?"

"Alex? Talking to Luke."

Charlie took off his glasses and polished them on the hem of his shirt. When he replaced them, his hands were shaking slightly but his jaw was set. "I'm going to have it out with Finn tonight."

Martin's face creased with concern. "Is that wise? On his birthday? And he's had a lot to drink."

"*In vino veritas*, isn't that what they say?" He leaned heavily on the table. "I was talking to him earlier. Alex. Thought I'd better make an effort. I mentioned we're going to London next month, just a few days, nothing spectacular. There's a Manet exhibition on at the Royal Academy that Finn wants to see. The look on his face, like I'd said I'd arranged a tour of a fucking tractor factory. He gave this kind of superior smile and said he knew—Finn had already told him. I wanted to punch his lights out. I can't go on like this, Mart. Okay, okay, maybe not tonight. Definitely tomorrow." He picked up the lighter and the plate of brownies. Grimly, he muttered, "Happy birthday, Finn."

TOUSLED and bleary-eyed, Finn padded into the kitchen, barefoot in a pair of faded orange board shorts. He took a bottle of water from the fridge and swigged thirstily, squinting into the reflecting glass of a cupboard. "Christ, talk about piss holes in the snow."

Charlie asked, "Feeling rough?"

He ran his tongue over his teeth. "Nah, I'm all right. Why are you up so early?"

"It's gone eleven."

It seemed to dawn on Finn that the room had been restored to its usual pristine neatness, the only traces of the previous night a few brownies wrapped in cling film and a bulging plastic sack of bottles. "I'd have given you a hand," he said.

"Sit down a minute, will you?"

"Ah, don't give me a hard time, babe. My head's splitting. I didn't know you were up."

Charlie felt an odd sense of disassociation, of unreality, as if he were an actor in a badly directed play. He looked at Finn slumped at the opposite side of the table, long legs sprawled. Pale, unshowered, his hair spiking wildly in all directions, he appeared to Charlie peculiarly beautiful then, so desirable. His heart began to thud at the thought that he might be about to bring the temple crashing down on their heads. Better, perhaps, to leave it, to wait and hope that the scenery would eventually change? Better to settle for part of this lovely man, to share him for a while, rather than risk losing him entirely? Better to retreat into the background like patience on a fucking monument, smiling at grief?

"What?" Finn asked, smothering a yawn.

"Are you planning on leaving me?"

"What?"

"Are you planning on leaving me?"

Pushing himself slowly upright, Finn said, "What the hell are you talking about?"

"Straight enough question."

"Why the fuck would I be planning on leaving you?"

"Alex."

"Alex? What about Alex?"

"That's what I'd like to know."

"What, you think there's something going on between him and me?"

"Isn't there?"

"No! Christ, Charlie!"

There was an unmistakable ring of truth to it, but it wasn't the whole truth. "But you'd like there to be. Wouldn't you?"

Finn Lydiard was an imperfect creature. Fabulously untidy, he had a tendency to snappishness, to sulk when thwarted. Some miswired neural connection made him laugh when he received a shock or unwelcome news: he'd laughed when he heard his father had been admitted to a coronary care unit. He laughed then, right in Charlie's face, a short, nervous bark. But set in the balance, outweighing his flaws, was his essential honesty: at heart he was a truthful man, and he had never lied to Charlie. And so, for one fatal second, he hesitated.

Charlie got to his feet. His legs were shaking as he walked past Finn and headed for the stairs.

"Charlie!"

If he had been a character in a play, he would have dragged a suitcase from the top of the wardrobe and flung a random selection of clothes into it. Tearful but dignified, he would have swept past his lover, pausing only to spit out one last killer remark. But Charlie simply sat on the bed and stared at the floor, so dumbfounded by pain he was unaware Finn had come into the room.

"Charlie, can I explain?" Bone-white, only two hectic spots of color high on his cheekbones, Charlie's face remained utterly impassive. "Please."

Even to himself, his voice sounded like an old, old man's. "What's to explain? You want him, have him."

"I don't, that's the point. I don't want him."

Charlie lay back on the bed and closed his eyes. "Just fuck off."

"No."

The poisoned silence held, baleful, pregnant with impending disaster. Tentatively, Finn put his hand on Charlie's ankle, jerking it away as he kicked out.

His voice clotted with tears, Charlie said, "Will you just leave me alone?"

"Oh God, don't cry." He reached out to the bedside table and yanked a sheaf of tissues from the box. "Don't cry, Charlie, please. Here."

Charlie ignored him. He took off his glasses and swept the heels of his hands under his eyes, then stared through Finn as if he didn't exist.

"Okay. I've fucked up big-time, I realize that, but you're going to listen. Will you listen? You owe me that, at least."

"I don't owe you anything."

Finn took a degree of comfort from the fact that Charlie had stayed on the bed. "I don't want Alex. He's nothing to me. I've never laid a finger on him. I've never done anything with him. Yes, yes, I admit for a time I was tempted—*Jesus, will you stop fucking crying and listen to me!*" After a moment, he started again, keeping his eyes on Charlie, ready to pounce if he moved. "A couple of weeks after he joined the firm it, was obvious he was... well, he was interested. And I was flattered. I admit it, I was bloody flattered, a guy like Alex interested in me. I enjoyed the banter, just messing around, having a bit of fun. It was a game, nothing serious, like you and the guy with the eyes in the deli. And anyway, I reckon what really turned him on was the thought that he might be hooking the CIO. Career-enhancing move. Whatever. But... well, after a while I began to think, *why not?* You'd never have known. It was exciting; the thought of it excited me. I'm sorry, Charlie, but I'm trying to be truthful here. I thought, one time, just once, before he moves on. He'll be off to Dresden in a couple of weeks, working with Helen. He'll be gone by the time we get back from London."

Charlie focused bloodshot eyes on Finn. "Once? What d'you mean, once? Once what? Take him to dinner once, fuck him once, what?"

"I don't know. *I don't know.* I just thought… something… different, something new. A change."

"A change from me."

"A change from being… settled."

"A change from me. Dull, steady, boring Charlie, tying you into our dull, steady, boring relationship. Our *unexciting* relationship." He sat up and patted the quilt for his glasses. "Finn, if that's what you want, that's what you want."

Finn took hold of Charlie's wrist and hung on, gripping hard enough to bruise. "But it's not what I want. That's what I'm trying to tell you. Yes, it would have been a… a kind of thrill, to be with someone different. These last few weeks, I've been pulling away from you. I've been trying to think it through. Would it be worth it? Really? To risk wrecking what we have, everything we've built together, for a cheap screw? Come home to you knowing what I'd done? I could have, but I didn't. *I didn't*, Charlie. I didn't want to, not when push came to shove." He smiled faintly. "As it were."

But he *did, didn't he? He'd have had it up your arse any day of the week. And you'd have loved it, wouldn't you? Getting fucked?* Charlie felt a visceral clench of loathing for Alex so intense he thought he might throw up. "So this is why you've been so off with me. I see it now."

Finn uncurled his body from the bed and walked to the window. He stood, arms raised, spanning the glass, looking down into the garden. "It's more than that. I've never really thought about us, you know, *really* thought. It was like, I'm coming up to thirty-four, forty just around the corner, then fifty, sixty. The thing with Alex was a kind of wake-up call. Did I intend to spend the rest of my life with you, because if I did, it would only be you. One man, for always. Decision time." He turned and leaned a shoulder against the wall. He smiled, a shy, almost humble smile that poured a little balm on Charlie's sore and battered heart. "Not a tough decision. It's you I want. It's you I've always wanted. I'm sorry. I've been a total twat."

Charlie swung his legs over the edge of the bed. He stared at the floorboards. "It's not all down to you. If you've been looking around, that's got to be something to do with us, with me. I know what I am. I'm just an ordinary bloke. Thing is, I don't know what to *do* to be exciting, to be the kind of bloke you're looking for."

"I'm not looking for any kind of bloke. I've already got him. Okay, maybe you're not going to set the world on fire, but who wants to burn to death? You're kind and warm and loving and... gentle and... steadfast. That's what I'll want when I'm sixty. It's what I want now. I love you, Charlie Langridge, always have, always will." Catching Charlie's quick flush, Finn pressed home his advantage. "Forgive me?"

Charlie sighed. "Go make me some breakfast. Then we'll talk."

THE concourse at Paddington station was its usual frantic whirl of activity: business types sweeping by, frowning into phones; bemused tourists studying the departure boards; a gaggle of Chinese teenagers, all multicolored hair and attitude, craning their necks to take in Brunel's airy spans of iron and glass. The only thing missing was a nun with a guitar.

Finn shifted his bag to his other hand, waiting for Charlie, who had been held up at the barrier behind a stout, striking woman in a Nigerian *gele* who'd mislaid her ticket. "Bakerloo line," he said. He set off toward the entrance to the Underground until Charlie tugged his sleeve.

"No, we'll get a taxi. Come on."

"It's only a few stops on the Tube."

"Finn. Am I organizing this or what? It's your birthday present. We're getting a taxi."

He shook his head in mild exasperation, but it wasn't worth arguing, spoiling Charlie's treat. He seemed so happy, almost fizzing with excitement. It couldn't be the mere fact of their being in London; they'd visited the capital dozens of times, for business and pleasure. More likely it was relief, a joyous rebound from the worry and strain of the past weeks. Remembering Charlie's grace, his generosity of spirit in forgiving his... lapse, Finn felt an almost overwhelming urge to take him in his arms and kiss him. *Sweet, sweet guy.* Instead he blew softly on the back of Charlie's neck as they waited, shuffling forward in the queue until the taxi marshal beckoned.

"You get in," Charlie said and gave brief directions to the driver.

After a minute or so of crawling through the traffic, Finn hunched forward and looked out through the window. "Hang on. Isn't this Marylebone Road? This isn't the way to Piccadilly."

"No, it's the way to St. Pancras."

"St. Pancras? Why are we going to St. Pancras?"

"It's where the Eurostar leaves from."

Charlie grinned at the blank expression on Finn's face. Timing it just right, he added, "I always thought it was weird. You've been all over the world, but you've never been to Paris. How can you never have been to Paris, for Christ's sake? Everyone's been to Paris."

"I was meant to go once when I was a kid, but I broke my leg. Charlie?"

"That famous Manet? The one of the naked woman on the grass? It didn't come over for the exhibition. It's still in the Musée d'Orsay."

"*Le déjeuner sur l'herbe*, yes...."

"I thought you're bound to want to see it."

"Oh, you—" Heedless of the driver's fascinated glances in the mirror, Finn kissed his lover, a soft kiss, prolonged and lingering, until suddenly he broke away with a jerk. "My passport."

"In my case." Charlie threaded his fingers through Finn's and pulled his hand down to the seat. "Relax, everything's taken care of. All you have to do is enjoy the trip."

"MESSIEURS." With a sweeping gesture of his hand, the urbane gray-haired *patron* indicated that they should precede him into the suite. For sure, an unusual set of requirements for this agreeable young couple but nothing that had really tested his ability. He glanced briefly around, checking that all was in order. "*Est-ce que tout vous convient?*"

Charlie smiled, his eyes on Finn. "*Un rêve devenu réalité, m'sieur.*"

"*Je vous en prie. Ce sera tout?*"

"*Oui. Merci.*"

The door closed with a soft click. Charlie came up behind Finn and slipped his arms around his waist, resting his chin on his shoulder. Ahead of them, between tall, elaborately dressed windows, a magnificent pier mirror caught and reflected all the exuberance of a Belle Époque sitting room, gorgeous in cobalt and jade, aquamarine and milky eau de nil. Twin cameo settees, upholstered in moiré silk, one either side of a low console table, formed the focal point of the room. To the left was an imposing Empire sideboard and opposite, two low armchairs, their glossy hide a rich peacock blue. Dotted here and there, small tables in the Louis XVI style held a variety of objets d'art, bronze figurines and little boxes inlaid with ivory and mother of pearl. The crystal drops of a deep bowl chandelier trembled from an ormolu rim, old diamonds flashing, and in every corner of the room porcelain pots held lush sprays of maidenhair fern.

Charlie pressed his lips to Finn's throat. "What d'you think?"

"A bit understated, maybe." He gasped and jerked, laughing as Charlie dug him sharply in the ribs. "Okay, okay!" Turning so that he faced him, Finn gently stroked his cheek. "It's amazing, beautiful. What made you think of it? How did you find it?"

"Oh, you know, just...." He caught Finn's hand. "Come on, let's see the rest."

The twining wisteria pattern of the wallpaper carried through to the bedroom. They stared at the bed, its carved walnut headboard cradling a blowsy extravaganza of pillows. A teal silk coverlet fell in folds to the floor. Finn gave a low whistle, but Charlie's gaze focused on the small spray of white flowers, modest and unassuming, almost lost in the splendor of satin and brocade.

"Jesus. And what's that lovely smell?"

Charlie pointed. "There, look, between those pillows."

Finn picked up the little nosegay and twirled it under his nose. "I wonder what it is."

"I think it's called Cherry Pie."

"Is it? How do you know that?"

"You know me, a mine of useless information."

"Come here, mine."

It was crucial that everything continued according to plan, so when their embrace threatened to develop into something neither of them would want to stop, Charlie eased away and planted a kiss on the tip of Finn's nose. "Steady on, handsome. I've ordered room service for half past nine. Just time to shower and unpack. You go first."

"I've got a feeling," Finn said, rubbing his palm on Charlie's zip, "that there's going to be an old-fashioned bath in there, very big, very deep, and there'll be oils and lotions and... unguents."

"*Unguents?*"

"Sure. Bound to be."

Charlie gave him a slap on the arse. "Don't take too long."

WRAPPED in bathrobes, they sat in a loveseat at the larger of the two windows, Charlie's legs on Finn's lap. Charlie said, "If we go to the museum tomorrow morning, we can get a boat on the Canal St-Martin in the afternoon. They go from there. They're nicer than the bateaux mouches—not so touristy."

"I want to be touristy. I want to see it all. I want to go up the Eiffel Tower and buy one of those snow globe things you shake. God, this is fabulous champagne."

"Belle Époque. Name seemed to fit, somehow. We'll see everything you want. We'll get a tour bus, hop on, hop off. Fancy going to Père-Lachaise, visit Oscar's grave?"

"Yeah, I do."

The knock at the door was so soft they nearly missed it.

"Dinner." *God, please, God, let them have got it right.*

"SO WHAT do we have?" Finn looked at the domed covers on the sideboard with a grin of anticipation. "Something fabulous, bound to be. Can I look?"

"Go ahead."

As he lifted away each cover and set it aside, his hand slowed, and his expression changed. Solemnly he considered the food, touching a fingertip to each silver platter. "Those little flowers. What did you say they were called?"

"Cherry Pie." He gave it a few beats. "Heliotrope."

"White heliotrope."

"Yes."

"Oysters. Foie gras. And that'll be partridge, I think. Oranges, pineapple, bananas."

"Yes."

His voice shaking, full of wonder, he said, "It's *Teleny*. You've made *Teleny* for me."

Charlie smiled.

When Finn returned his smile his eyes were glimmering with tears. The classic piece of Victorian erotica had long been a favorite. "Oh, Charlie."

"It's not all down to me. There's this Web site. You tell them what you want, and they fix it all for you, well, as best they can. I know the room should be red, and we skipped the bearskin, but it's as near as, damn it."

"It's.... It must have cost—"

"Ssh, don't." Gently Charlie kissed Finn's forehead. "Cheap at twice the price just to see your face. You do like it, don't you?"

"I bloody love it, but what gave you the idea?"

"I was cleaning the bedroom, and it was in your pile of books. I looked at the cover, that fabulous arse, and it just... came into my head: *Teleny*, Paris, Manet."

Taking hold of Charlie's hand, playing with his fingers, Finn said, "This is the best present I've ever had, but I don't want you to think you have to do stuff like this. You don't have to prove anything to me."

"Once in a while won't hurt. Anyhow, this is for me as well."

Finn thought, *For you? But who are you, Charlie? I don't know you, not you as you are now. I thought I did, but I don't. All this time. I thought I knew everything there was to know about you, but what I see now is a stranger, a lovely, entrancing stranger. And, oh God, I want you.*

"Hungry?" Charlie murmured. He picked up an oyster shell and lifted it to Finn's mouth, a sharp thrill knifing as he watched him swallow. "Good?"

"Mmm."

Down, down between Finn's pecs, Charlie drew the shell, grazing to the base of his cock. Up again, zigzagging his belly in a delicious scrape against the grain of hair, from one nipple to the other. "You remember what happens in the story? After they've eaten?"

As Finn finally grasped the entirety of what Charlie intended, his heart began to thud wildly in his chest. "Yeah."

"Remember what Teleny does to Des Grieux? Turns you on, doesn't it, reading about it? So fucking sexy. Beyond erotic." Charlie's gaze bore into him, only a halo of gray visible around the fathomless pupils.

Finn's cock lost its heavy curve, rapidly straightening, lengthening. "You've never.... I didn't think you wanted to."

"I didn't think I did, but things change. People change."

"So we'll... like in the book?"

"Yeah, just like in the book. But I won't make you bleed."

Finn slid his palms along Charlie's collarbones and pushed the robe off his shoulders. He shrugged out of his own and rested his hands on Charlie's waist. Naked and beautiful, they stood, brow to brow, each breathing the other's breath. Softly Finn murmured, "I'd like it if you did."

Neither man told the other that he loved him; during the past weeks, all that needed to be said had been said. Time now to show their love in the age-old joining, male uniting with male in power and passion and pain. The first fluttering touch of tongues became a crushing of mouths, kisses as only two men can kiss. Arms gripping, strong as steel hawsers, slamming chest to chest, thigh to thigh. The desperate press of cocks, shifting, rolling, hot, and engorged.

"Where? The bedroom?"

"No. Here."

Hoarsely, Charlie said, "Sit on that chair."

At first touch chilly, the leather seat grew warm from Finn's body. He looked around him: Wilde's exquisite imagining made real—if it had been Wilde; it had never been proved that he had written the book. *Did it excite you, baby?* He smiled at the thought—Charlie irritably straightening the stack on the bedside table. Picking one out and riffling through the pages. Pausing, sitting on the bed, elbows on knees, becoming engrossed in the story. The scene in the carriage. In Teleny's red room. Briancourt's party and its unspeakable ending.

"Don't stop." Charlie had been watching him. He came out of the bathroom and walked across to the chair, dropping his glasses on the arm of a settee. Without taking his eyes off him, he knelt between Finn's legs, his hands on his thighs. "Don't come."

Little slicking sounds as Finn's hand slowed, the swollen head of his cock revealed, concealed by his gripping fist. He held the skin squeezed tightly down at the root of his cock, and the head bulged, the delicate V of its tie pulled taut. Consciously he relaxed the muscles of his belly and back, shutting his eyes as the first glimmers of orgasm receded.

"Slide forward." As Finn worked his hips over the leather to the edge of the chair, Charlie pushed his palms under his buttocks. "Bring your legs up."

He smelled so fucking good. No matter how thoroughly a man soaped himself, his body scent lingered. Faint, faint, but intoxicating, as much a part of him, as essential to his sexuality as his balls. Blindfolded, Charlie could have picked Finn out of a hundred men merely by his scent. He pressed his palm hard against the underside of his shaft, the tremendous vein, and licked the sac, working his tongue, sucking first one, then both balls into his mouth. Beautiful balls, tight, swollen with semen—

"Fuck me, Charlie."

And just there, pink and perfect.... Charlie sat back on his heels. Not yet. He stroked a finger along the firm ridge of Finn's perineum and touched it to the little rippled slot, his own cock cramping as Finn gave a low moan of pleasure. So soft, damp velvet like the gills of a mushroom. Tiny.

"Please."

"What, baby?"

"Kiss it."

He'd recoiled from this for so long. Why had he? It was clean and lovely and tasted faintly of salt from the soap. He circled his tongue, and then, parting the cheeks, he began to suck, rhythmically drawing the flesh into his mouth as he did with Finn's nipples. It was nothing, then, to take the further step. As he pressed the tip of his tongue inward, the thought came with a force that ratcheted his arousal to delirium. *I'm inside him, I'm licking inside his arse, I'm—*

"Change places." Finn stood, straddling Charlie's thighs, and watched him squeeze a thick coil of lube onto his fingers. Slippery cool as Charlie prepared him, fingers brushing around, around and pressing in. "Let me," he said, taking the tube and stroking a glistening veil of gel over Charlie's shaft, stark and upright in his lap.

"Tell me if I hurt you. We can stop."

"It's part of it." His thighs wide, Finn shuffled forward and lowered his hips, pausing to let Charlie center his cock, the blunt head seeking entry. A twinge of warning when he pressed down.

"Open for me, Finn. Push."

"Ah, fuck, ah fuck—"

"Push me out."

"Oh God—"

A brief moment of splintering pain and a slithering glide.

Finn's throat arched as he took Charlie high into his body. Sweat broke out on his back, sticky under Charlie's stroking palms, but when he opened his eyes to his lover's gaze, he already knew the truth of it. This was what he had yearned for, all unknowing. To be mastered. To be penetrated. To have the void in him *filled*. Shock had softened him, but when Charlie clutched his arse, easing him forward, hot blood returned in a rushing flood. Rocking, gently rocking, Finn felt the stiff shaft slide, friction igniting nerves, flashing spangles of pleasure through his gut, his cock. He raised up, thigh muscles quivering, and sank down again, his body moving in the age-old rhythm for which it had been made. "I want to feel it. Feel you come in me."

Charlie groaned, already teetering on the edge. "Not yet. You first."

"Do it." Finn wrapped Charlie's hand around his cock, as rigid now as the shaft impaling him. "Get me there."

Hard, fast, Charlie stroked his lover. He watched the muscles of Finn's belly ripple and clench and heard the cry he always gave moments before he came. All control lost, he thrust violently again and again into Finn's arse and then stilled, so racked by the ecstasy of his orgasm that he hardly felt the spurts of Finn's semen raining on his face; it wasn't until he opened his eyes and smiled that he licked them from his lips.

"Hurting?" Charlie ran his foot up and down Finn's shin.

"A bit." He lifted his hips to straighten the towel under him. "Don't know if I'll be able to walk tomorrow, big boy."

"Have to. Busy day." Strong and steady, Charlie felt Finn's heartbeat under his palm. He rubbed his face into the dense mat of hair, finding the nipple and giving it a teasing bite. "Have to get used to it."

"You reckon?"

"No doubt about it."

Charlie shut his eyes and pulled the coverlet over their shoulders. He was drifting pleasantly into sleep when Finn's wakeful fidgeting roused him. "It *is* hurting you, isn't it?"

"No. It feels… odd, but it feels good. I like it. I can feel your sperm, kind of seeping out." After a few moments he went on. "It wasn't only Teleny fucked Des Grieux, you know."

Charlie's eyes snapped open.

Finn raised himself on one elbow and hovered over him, a handsome shadow in the dark. "Des Grieux fucked Teleny too. A lot."

"Yes." Charlie turned onto his back and opened his arms. "He did, didn't he?"

RHIDIAN BRENIG JONES is a Welshman who has herded sheep in New Zealand, taught English in Poland, and run a bar on the Costa del Sol. Now settled back home in Wales, he leads an adult literacy program and writes whenever he can snatch a spare hour or two. Rhidian lives with his partner, Michael, and their two arthritic old Labradors. He is still trying and failing to master the acoustic guitar.

The Thing I Love Best About Mitch

Dawn Douglas

"Dammit, Tyler."

The words were delivered in Mitchell's best intimidating growl—usually reserved for undergraduates who thought three science credits, less than minimum wages, and free room and board as volunteers at one of Mitch's environmentally at-risk sites meant they were going to have a summer of ease playing grabass and running around on the beach picking up pieces of trash every now and then. Too bad for him, I was immune to the tone.

"Honey, I'm home," I replied, voice deadpan, and shrugged my backpack off one shoulder, depositing it on the chair by the door beside my shoes.

My lover shot me a dirty look, shoved one hand through his hair, and paced a back-and-forth circuit of our entryway. Watching him, I was pretty sure he hadn't just started the pacing thing. I was also pretty sure he didn't really appreciate my humor either.

"Have you been doing that since I left?" I asked, careful to keep my tone light. I didn't expect an answer, but experience has taught me that the best way to deal with Mitch when he's in a mood is not to let myself get drawn into it.

Ignoring the question—big surprise—Mitchell shifted his attention away from my face. He turned his glare on the backpack. "You need a briefcase," he announced. "You shouldn't be carrying that ratty thing. I could get you a briefcase. I'll buy you a damn—what's the brand that Pete in marketing totes around? Larry Wilson? Lucas Winston?"

"Louis Vuitton?"

He waved a dismissive hand. "Yes, that. I'll buy you one of those briefcases."

I couldn't stop the scoff that rose in my throat. "Mitchell, if you buy me a $3,000 briefcase, I'll kill you. Besides, I don't *want* a briefcase. My backpack works fine. It's got sentimental value."

He knew I was talking about the fact that he'd gotten me the pack eight years ago, when I'd been one of the annoying undergrads spending his summer interning for credits and slave wages at the Biofield Watch Project. Although in my defense, I hadn't been expecting to play grabass when I joined the project. I'd actually been excited about the job.

At twenty-eight years old, Mitchell Masters had designed and built the most innovative oil spill cleanup technology on the market today, and the fact that it had turned into a resounding commercial success and made him a very rich man when he sold it just meant he had more time to spend out in the field, working on-site to manage cleanup efforts at actual spill sites.

That first summer for me was his third moonlighting as a wealthy philanthropist in environmentalists' clothing, and I'd barely been a blip on the guy's radar. He'd thrown a worn North Face backpack at my head one afternoon when the strap on my cheap pack broke, and I had to scramble not to drop the three gallon jugs of drinking water it had been holding into the swamp our team was trudging through at the time. That night, fooling around with my roommate in the crappy furnished studio apartment Biofield Watch used to house their interns, I'd had to bite my lip not to say Mitch's name when I came. Because giving me a backpack had definitely been inadvertent fuel for my crush. Probably my roommate, Robert, wouldn't have cared too much, but still—it seemed a little rude.

Mitchell took me a little more seriously my second summer. Apparently, not many volunteers came back for more after they realized just how hot, miserable, and exhausting the work was. But I was heading into grad school at Duke's Wetland Center the next fall. Biofield Watch, and therefore Mr. Masters, were loosely affiliated with the center. That, plus my small crush and vague sense of hero worship, meant that unlike the other undergrads, Mitch would have had to beat me off with a stick to keep me from coming back to the project. He and I had even had a few offhand talks about my future career goals during set up week, nothing overly serious, but considering I hung on pretty much his every word, they'd felt significant to me. We were sloughing around, planting soil probes, when we had our first actual deep conversation.

"Hey, kid, is that my backpack?"

At twenty-three I was less than ten years younger than Mitch and didn't exactly consider myself a kid, but since we were the only two people in shouting distance, and since it was, in fact, his backpack, I figured he was talking to me. "Yeah—actually. You gave it to me last year. Did you, um, want it back?"

He'd given me a look like he was actually seeing me for the first time, his gaze running up and down my body from head to toe in a way that made me feel decidedly tingly. Then he said no and went back to work.

At this point in our lives together, I can admit that "deep conversation" might be a bit of a stretch, but hey, it was a turning point. Kind of. It actually took me two more summers, a master's in chemistry with a thesis on soil science, and said backpack full of smuggled bottles of tequila and beer at a spill site off the coast of Florida to convince Mitch to fuck me. But he had, and we'd been together through my entire PhD. As it always did, reference to the pack prompted in him a dual reaction—irritation because it reminded him that he'd been an ass when I met him, and fondness because I'd been too tenacious to give up like a sane person would have. It takes a special man to smile and frown at the same time, but Mitchell could do it.

It was one of the things I loved best about him.

"Fine, then." He crossed his arms over his chest, still not happy, but with a slightly mellower growl. "How about a nice watch?"

"Mitch."

"A Montblanc pen?"

"*Mitchell.*"

"A motorcycle?"

"Damn it, Masters!"

There was a heartbeat of silence, and then we were both laughing. Mitchell's chuckles were deep and quiet, and they sent a shiver of awareness through my stomach. I loved to hear Mitch laugh. He didn't do it often enough, and when he did, he almost seemed surprised to find out he remembered how.

The laughter didn't last long, but it was enough to lighten the mood. Before Mitchell's half smile could melt away, I reached up and grabbed his wrist and pulled him down onto the sofa with me when I flopped onto my spot on the couch. I landed with a grunt and sank into the cushions. It wasn't much to look at, but the old plaid couch in the center of our family room was damn comfortable. It's funny. I knew academically that Mitch had something like as much money as God, but you sure as shit couldn't tell it from looking at his furniture. Or his clothes. Or his car. That was another one of the things I loved best about him.

Mitchell opened his mouth to say something, but I held up a hand before he could. "I love that you want to get me something, Mitch, but it isn't necessary."

"I think that's up to me, isn't it? It's not every day you're awarded your doctorate, Mr. Freeman."

I raised an eyebrow. "Mr. Freeman?"

"You haven't walked the stage yet, Doc," Mitchell countered.

"Semantics." I reached out and threaded my fingers through his, then raised his hand to my lips and kissed the back of it. "But you can call me Mr. Freeman as long as you want. I like it. Usually means I'm going to get lucky," I finished with a grin.

Mitchell's eyes darkened from aqua to turquoise, and I took that as my cue. Lifting up, I put one knee on either side of his hips and straddled his lap, resting my weight on his thighs.

"Tyler—" Desire warred with frustration in his voice.

"Mitchell—" I replied, teasing, and brought my face close to his neck. I intended to lick his pulse point—he loved that—but I paused for a second and breathed deeply. As it always did, the familiar smell of him touched something deep inside me.

"We have to talk about this."

"We already did," I said into his collar. "I told you what I wanted."

Then I was kissing him, my lips blazing a trail down the side of his throat. Maybe it was unfair, but I didn't care. I wanted to distract him, and in the two years we'd been living together, I'd learned exactly how to do it.

"It's not a good idea, Tyler." But he ended on a moan, and I felt a flash of triumph when his hands drifted down my body to grasp my hips. He pulled me toward him, grinding the panel of my fly into the erection clearly outlined beneath his jeans.

"This feels like a very, very good idea," I countered, then pushed his head to the side so I could nip at the cord on the side of his very sexy neck.

"You know what I mean."

I ignored the words and moved in to bite his earlobe as I started unbuttoning his shirt. Mitch had an amazing body. Tanned and muscled from almost constant work outdoors, his chest was a thing of beauty. He let me push the shirt off of his shoulders and sucked in a breath when I leaned down to lick and then pull at his nipples.

"Christ," he hissed, but let me play for a few minutes before his hands moved up, fingers delving into my hair. I felt a thrill of excitement when he tugged me away and pushed me down to the floor between his spread knees.

"What do you want?" Mitch demanded, voice rough. My cock strained against the front of my pants in response, and I leaned forward, trying to press my face into the apex of his thighs, but he wouldn't let me.

I struggled against his hold, letting myself fall easily into the game, and answered, panting. "I want you. I always want you."

A smile played at the corner of his mouth, and he pushed me gently away. "Hm. You want me? Stand up, then. Let's see what I'm getting. *If* I decide to let you have me."

I rolled eagerly back on my heels and stood. Mitch's playful-with-a-side-of-domineering mood was absolutely one the things I loved best about him. I waited impatiently to see what he was going to do next. He didn't make me wait long. His voice, we he spoke, was deliciously bored.

"Well, I can't tell anything with you dressed like that. Take off your shirt."

I grinned and rushed to pull my T-shirt over my head. "Is that better?"

"A bit," he replied dismissively. "But I think I need to see more before I decide. Pants, please."

My fingers fumbled a bit with the button, and I started to pull my jeans down.

"Wait." Mitch said sharply.

I froze.

"Turn around, and do it slowly."

My heart sped in my chest as I *slowly* did as I was told. Swiveling to face away from him, I could see myself reflected in the dark television screen over the fireplace. No one but Mitch had ever made me look that way—fucked out and blown away before he even really touched me. The fact that he could get that kind of reaction from me was without a doubt one of the things I loved best about him.

"Now, push them down." His voice was a soft growl, velvety and firm.

I slowly pushed my pants down my legs and stepped carefully out of them, barely breathing as I waited to see what my lover would do next. I jumped a little when I felt his rough palms reach up to cradle my hips, pulling me backward. His breath was hot against my ass through the fabric of my briefs.

"Oh, that is lovely." He squeezed my cheeks, kneading them, letting his fingertips slip beneath the cloth. He was clearly having trouble holding on to the bored role-play, and with his hands on me, I was fine with dropping the game and getting down to business.

"Mitch," I moaned, reflexively pushing back into his palms to encourage him to move faster. "Please."

"Hush," he ordered, voice gentle. "I'm still deciding." His hands pushed farther into my underwear, fingertips meeting in my cleft and dragging down, brushing roughly across my hole until they bumped into my balls from behind. Using his thumbs, he hooked the waistband of my briefs and pulled them down. They caught on the head of my leaking dick, but Mitch didn't let that stop him. He forced them off and down my thighs, sending my cock snapping up against my stomach before he let them drop to my ankles.

"Spread your legs for me."

I whimpered. And I obeyed.

One of Mitch's hands slipped between my legs. He fondled my balls, tested their weight in his hand, and then squeezed lightly. "These are very, very full."

"I haven't—it's been—days," I panted. And it had. Between putting the finishing touches on the paper, presenting, and defending my dissertation, I'd fallen into bed exhausted only to drag myself back to the lab after a few hours of sleep for almost the past two weeks. I'd dimly registered Mitch holding me in the night, wrapping his big body around mine, and he'd been there every morning with coffee and something for me to eat as I rushed out the door. It was a different kind of intimacy, one I'd never really experienced before. Mitch and I were past the stage where we couldn't keep our hands off of each other for more than ten minutes at a time, but two weeks was a very long time for us to go without making love, and I hadn't even considered jerking off alone. I'd definitely missed the sex, though, and I was ready to make up for lost time.

He squeezed again, harder this time. "Well, we'll have to do something about that, won't we?"

His hand moved away, and for a second my heart stopped. Then I heard the slide of a drawer and the snick of a cap opening. "Bend forward for me, Tyler."

I was halfway to hyperventilating, but I did as I was told, bending slightly at the waist. My obedience was rewarded when I felt slick, cool fingers brush against my opening. Mitch pushed inside me carefully, cognizant of the fact that it had been a couple of weeks since I'd been penetrated. Dimly, I realized I was babbling as he slowly stretched me, working first one and then a second finger into my body, widening me.

"Yes. Yes. God, yes. I've needed this. Needed you. Please, Mitch, more. I want more. I'm ready now."

"Patience, love. I don't want to hurt you."

"You won't, I swear. Oh God, more." He slipped a third finger in, and I started rocking back and forth on the balls of my feet, fucking myself on the hand half-buried in my ass. My cock was leaking a steady stream of precum, and I could feel my balls swinging between my spread legs as I moved.

Behind me, I heard Mitch fumble to unzip his pants one-handed and the rustle of cloth as he lifted up and pushed them down. The fact that he was coordinated enough to strip himself while he finger-fucked me into oblivion was bar none one of the things I loved best about him. Never losing the rhythm that was slowly driving me out of my mind, he pushed in farther, his thumb going between my legs, across my perineum, to push into the back of my balls. I keened, moving faster on his fingers.

"Deeper. Deeper, Mitch, please." I was begging, but I didn't care. I trusted this man to give me what I needed. And he didn't disappoint me.

"All right, baby." His free hand was at my hip again, and he was guiding me backward. "Come back to me. I've got you."

I let him move me, let him lead me. His fingers slipped from my body just in time to line his throbbing erection up with my hole. The head breached my opening, and then his slick hand was in front of me, wrapping around my cock before pushing me down in one solid, firm slide, until I was impaled on his cock, my back flush against his muscular chest, head lolling on his shoulder.

"Mitch! God, Mitch!" I screamed. I couldn't help it.

It felt like a bar of warm, solid steel was driving into me, deeper than I'd ever been taken. I writhed, legs splayed on top of Mitchell's while one of his hands worked my cock and the other one my balls.

"That's it. Take what you need, baby. I've got you."

Mitch's pelvis was moving slightly in short, rocking thrusts that kept him pressed into my prostate, forcing a stream of liquid from the head of my penis that he used as lubricant. I couldn't even begin to form words, pleasure and trust that he would take care of me melding and letting me give him everything as I went wild in his lap.

"Squeeze for me, inside. There you go, rock with me. Your ass is so tight, baby. So hot. I've watched you these last weeks, missed you so much."

"I'm sorry. Sorrysorrysorry. I missed you too. Needed you. God. Please."

"It's okay. Nothing to be sorry about. I'm proud of you. So damn proud of you. Always. Always."

His hand was moving faster now, and I could feel both of our ball sacs drawing closer to our bodies.

"Going to cum in you. So deep you'll be able to feel it in your stomach."

"Want that, Mitch. Want to keep you in me all the time. Want you. Want everything with you." I was gasping now, close, so close, and then he gave one last hard tug on my balls, at the same time the head of his cock pressed into my prostate, and I was coming, shooting jets of semen into the air that landed all over my chest and stomach. As my body rippled around his, I felt and heard Mitch roar beneath me, then latch his mouth onto the side of my neck and suck fiercely to muffle his shouts. I threw my head sideways to give him better access, encouraging him to mark me. Then he was slamming up and grinding my hips down as his cock exploded inside my stretched ass.

And God, the way he clutched me and whispered how much he loved me as the aftershocks rippled through both of us was so much one of the things I loved best about him.

Afterward we lay on the couch, quiet for a while, just enjoying the feeling of each other's skin. We'd cleaned up with the baby wipes kept carefully positioned beside the lube in the coffee table drawer. I was on top of Mitchell, my head on his chest, and he was rubbing my back as I drowsed. Mitchell moving inside me was maybe the most amazing feeling in the world, but the cherishing afterward stuff was a close second.

Every now and then the pads of his fingers traced a scar that curved down one of my shoulder blades, the result of an injury I'd gotten my fourth summer working with Biofield. Whenever they did, I felt him lean up to press spontaneous kisses into my hair.

That particular scar was special to me, an integral part of my history with Mitchell. I'd woken up in a hospital bed after I'd gotten it, Mitch sitting beside me, holding my hand. His eyes were bloodshot. There were bags under them big enough to double as checked luggage, and his face was lined and covered with ragged stubble. His voice, the first time he told me he loved me, was rough with tears and exhaustion, but even fuzzy from the painkillers, I'd never forgotten the way he pressed the back of my hand to his lips whispered over and over, "God, I love you. I almost lost you. I can't lose you. Jesus, I love you."

And anytime he was nervous about something to do with our relationship, he gravitated to the scar. I don't know if he realized I recognized the action as a tell, but it was. It was why it didn't surprise me when the silence didn't last. I'd known it wouldn't the second he started tracing my scar.

"Tyler, you know I'd do anything for you, don't you?"

I sighed and sat up. "But?"

If I'd been born without ears, I would have heard the "but" at the end of that statement.

Mitchell followed my lead and pulled himself up beside me with a roll of his neck. "*But*, I don't think you've thought this through. Besides, I've already met your parents."

I shot him a look, trying to keep frustration at bay. "Mitchell, twenty minutes in a hospital waiting room after a scaffold fell and nearly decapitated me *does not* count as 'meeting' my parents."

"Twenty-five minutes," Mitchell replied, not meeting my eyes. "And that didn't go particularly well."

This time I couldn't quite keep my tone modulated. "Give me a break."

He blew out a sigh. "Fine. I'll admit the circumstances weren't ideal. But this is a happy occasion. They're coming all the way here to see you walk the stage to get your doctorate. Do you really want to spring the fact that you're in a homosexual relationship with a man they tried to sue for negligence when you nearly *died* on your family at a time like this?"

I stood up, acutely aware of the fact that I was naked, but not willing to do anything about it. "One, you and I and even my parents know that was a freak accident no one could have predicted. They reacted badly at the time. It wasn't Biofield's fault, and it certainly wasn't your fault. In fact, if you hadn't been there, I probably *would* have died—"

"Tyler." He cut me off, paling under his tan, and I felt a flash of guilt. I knew how much he hated talking about the accident. Unable to stop myself, I leaned forward and brushed a soft kiss across his lips.

"You're right. Ancient history." I soothed for a second, then firmed my voice again. "Anyway, I would have told them about us sooner if I could have. We agreed to wait until I finished my doctorate. I understand why that was important to you, so I didn't have a problem with it. But that reason is going away in two days."

"I realize—"

I held up a hand. "No. Listen to me. It's just—I'm tired of hiding. It's not that I have to run screaming down the street and shout it to the world, but I want the people I love to know how happy I am. Is that so much to ask?"

Mitch rubbed a tired hand across his forehead but didn't answer. I was tempted to apologize, to tell him I didn't mean it, but I couldn't. Because I did mean it. I did want it. Badly. I understood that this was scary for him. The people who mattered in our daily lives just sort of knew. There hadn't been any major coming-out scenes. There hadn't been any conflict. Mitch's parents were both gone, and he had no significant family who would have cared either way if he was gay, straight, or bi. But asking him to publicly acknowledge our relationship to my parents, who weren't necessarily going to be thrilled about it, but who I loved anyway, was a whole different ball game.

We both knew I'd wait if I had to, though. Because more than anything else in the world, I loved Mitch. And I wasn't going to let my family come between us even if it took him another two years to be ready for that. Even if it took him another ten.

I took a step toward the sofa and rested a hand briefly on his shoulder, squeezing. He leaned silently into the touch, clearly torn and drawing comfort from the contact. "Whatever you decide," I said, voice soft, "I'll live with it. But if you want to get me something I really, really want, then let my parents come to the house before the ceremony. I want them to meet the man I love."

Silence stretched, and finally I realized he wasn't going to answer. I was disappointed but not surprised. I started to move away, thinking a shower sounded really good, but Mitchell's hand stopped me.

"Next time you get a PhD, I'm not going to ask what you want for graduation. I'm just going to buy you a damn Harvey Weinstein."

My head whipped toward Mitch so fast, I think I gave myself whiplash.

He'd said yes. That was absolutely Mitchell for "yes," but I had to make sure.

"You mean—"

"We'll have to have Helen come in and clean tomorrow instead of Thursday, and—"

Whatever else Mitch might have said was lost against my lips.

He didn't seem to mind being interrupted.

When we finally pulled apart to breathe, Mitch was smiling down at me. I reached up and cupped his cheeks. "Thank you so much," I whispered.

Gently, Mitch brought his forehead to mine and spoke against my lips. "I meant what I said. There's *nothing* I wouldn't do to make you happy, Tyler. Nothing."

And I kissed him again. Because I knew that. Because the thing I really loved best about Mitchell was the way he loved me just as much as I loved him.

DAWN DOUGLAS moved to suburban San Antonio, Texas, from Illinois in 2004. She realized she wasn't in Kansas anymore when she went to a meeting of her local Democratic party and she and the organizer were the only ones there! Dawn was a reporter for several years but now works in marketing. Next to spending time with her husband and daughter, writing anything from freelance news features to fiction is her favorite thing to do. In 2010, Dawn placed third in a national humor writing competition sponsored by News Portal Corporation.

You can write to Dawn at dawndouglas1981@gmail.com or follow her blog at http://dawndouglas.blogspot.com.

Looking Back

Rob Rosen

TEN years, ten thousand dollars. It was a grand for each year, though this past year had been anything but, well, *grand*, hence the rather expensive anniversary present. In other words, money well spent—fingers crossed.

"I don't understand," my husband, Mack, said as he read the gift certificate. "Memory Merge? What memories are we going to be merging, Glenn?" He managed a crooked smile, but his eyes went all squinty on me just the same. "Merged bank accounts not enough for you? The shared mortgage? Christmas with not one but *two* sets of crazy families?"

I sighed, knowing passive-aggressive when I heard it. Though with Mack it was always light on the former and sledgehammer heavy on the latter. "Do you ever wonder why we got married, Mack?"

His sigh echoed mine. "Really, Glenn? It's not obvious by now?"

I patted his shoulder. "Humor me, please."

"Because I loved you." The sigh repeated, a distinct groan edging its way in.

My chest tightened at hearing him say it. "Past tense or present?"

"You asked me a past-tense question; I gave you a past-tense answer." He took my hand from his shoulder and held it in his. "Loved, love, will *always* love, hon." He paused. "Is the feeling not mutual? Does one of our His & His towels need to be incinerated? Timeshare sold?"

My hand hung loosely and unconvincingly in his as I stared into his eyes. There was a time, I remember, when doing so would send butterflies swarming inside my belly. Now said belly merely gurgled for lunch. "It just seems like we've become, well, *complacent*, is all. Love, but maybe not so much *in* love. His & His towels are safe, but I want to make sure they stay in the same bathroom."

Thankfully, he at least had a concerned look on his face, as if what I was saying was suddenly hitting home. "And this Memory Merge will keep them draping happily side by side?"

I nodded, then shrugged, then glumly shook my head. "Not a clue." And then I forced a smile. "But it's worth a shot. I mean, timeshares have absolutely *no* resale value."

He chuckled and leaned in for a peck on my lips. "Then thank you for the anniversary present; I look forward to merging memories with you." The grin faltered. "You didn't spend too much on it, though, did you?"

A cough worked its way up from my suddenly Saharan-dry throat. "You're well worth it, Mack. That is to say, *we* are."

Again, fingers crossed I was right about that—and some toes to boot.

WE ARRIVED at Memory Merge a week later, both of us nervous if not excited. I mean, it was certainly more fun to visit your past than, say, take a glimpse of an uncertain future. Besides, I already knew how the past turned out, and it wasn't all that bad. Not all sunshine and lollipops, no, but that mortgage he mentioned was for a split-level in a nice neighborhood, and that timeshare was in Maui, and though Christmas with the families was, um, *severe*, at least we loved said families—for a few days a year, at any rate.

In any case, we had little time to worry, seeing as they took us to our reserved room almost immediately. Mack was seated in a dentist-like chair, and I was facing him in an identical one. The tech strapped us in, placed a rather fetching helmet on each of our heads, and explained what would happen next.

"Welcome to Memory Merge," Chloe, the tech, began, all smiles, fake as rhinestones. "We're here to help couples reconnect, for loved ones to see what they might have forgotten, to glimpse happier times in the hope that the future might become brighter." She grinned and chuckled, the laughter so canned that I looked to see if it was coming out of some sort of body speaker. "And, if nothing else, to show you why you should never have bought those clothes buried in the back of your closet." She flicked on some switches and continued with her pat speech. "Now then, you will only be seeing shared memories. The computer will take both sets and combine them as one, filling in the gaps as best it can, so that, instead of looking at the scenes through your own eyes, you'll be seeing everything as if a spectator, like watching TV, uncensored."

I gulped. "Um, only we can see these scenes, correct?"

Again she laughed, clearly accustomed to those sorts of questions. "Only the two of you and the computer." She paused for effect. "And he's not telling anyone." Suffice it to say, she didn't get the desired effect she was hoping for, though I wasn't so sure my groan was all that stifled. "So sit back, relax, and enjoy. You have one hour. Scenes will unfold at whatever pace you desire, right on up to this very moment."

And then she was gone.

I paused as I got comfortable in my seat. "Ready?" I then asked, the whirr of the machines filling the room, the helmet suddenly warm atop my head, a light pulsing from deep within my subconscious, spreading like wildfire.

"Not really," Mack replied, a nervous edge to his voice. "But here goes nothing."

Well, here goes ten grand and our combined futures, I thought, but who was I to mince words?

In any case, all at once my head filled with a sole vivid image. We were at a mall. It was our first shared experience together, I quickly realized. He was sitting across the food court eating from Panda Express, while I was devouring a low-fat, lactose-free, sugar-free—and, suffice it to say, flavorless—gelato. Despite the unenjoyable snack, I was smiling, both then and now.

Look how young we look, I thought. *No gray in our hair, no extra layers of bulk, and why did I ever get rid of that goatee?*

"What's with the facial hair?" Mack asked with a chuckle. "You look like an ax murderer." He backtracked, if only by a smidge. "Um, a sexy ax murderer, I mean." Which explains why I got rid of said goatee.

And then the me from yesteryear noticed the him of yesteryear, and I could actually see the twinkle in my eyes, my heart suddenly racing as I sat in the memory chair. God, he was stunning. Oddly, he still is. Older now, true, but no less handsome. "Did you notice me staring?" I asked him.

"Nope, not yet," he replied. "Jump ahead twenty minutes."

Why then? What happens in twenty minutes? Odd that I haven't a clue. In any case, I jumped, or at least my mind did. We were now in The Gap. Or, that is to say, he was in The Gap, and I was standing outside looking in, obviously searching for him. The old me smiled, anxiously, nervously, as the old him shopped. "That's not where we met, though," I said. "Did you see me standing out there?"

He laughed. "Hard to miss an ax murderer cruising you, hon." I grimaced. I clearly wasn't his type. *Why didn't I realize that?* "Jump ahead thirty more minutes. That should just about do it."

Again my mind raced, the vision going blurry, fading to white and then color again. I was now sitting on a bench just outside the mall, looking none too happy. Mack came out, shopping bags in hand, and walked past me while I stared on, sure I'd missed my last opportunity. He tripped, landing on his palms, bags flying out in front of him. This part I remembered. This was when we met. This was when my hand touched his, as I ran to help him up, as flesh met glorious flesh.

"Wait," I said, noticing now what I'd missed back then. "Did you trip on purpose?"

Again he laughed. "You followed me to three different stores, Mack."

"Why didn't you ever tell me?"

"I didn't want to embarrass you," he replied. "Then time passed, and it never seemed that important to bring up. I mean, we were together by then, right?"

But I'd always thought our meeting was by chance, by fate: he tripped, and I came to his rescue. Then again, he'd tripped on purpose to meet me, so I let it go. Besides, I saw the way he looked at me when I helped him up, saw the way I looked at him. It was like, from this vantage point, I could see the spark. Like witnessing the Big Bang.

"And my goatee?"

He sighed. "Your eyes canceled it out. So much blue, I thought. Like looking into the sky." He paused, watching the scene unfold. "Notice how I'm not blinking."

"Funny," I said. "At the time, I thought you were just mortified that you fell like that. I wish you'd said something."

"Like what? Like 'How does anyone have eyes like that?' Like 'I fell on purpose because you'd obviously been following me for close to an hour'? Like 'I was impressed by your stick-to-itiveness, curious as to why'?"

Weird how I could watch all this now and still misinterpret what he was thinking, feeling. Even then, I thought he was a bit distant. That I remember. And it explains why I didn't let go of his arm at the time, why I walked him to his car, why I handed him my business card, clearly afraid to let him slip through my fingers.

"I wanted to kiss you, right there in the parking lot," I managed.

"I know." I watched as he pulled away, remembering how my heart was racing, wondering if he'd ever call. "And I would've let you too." Again he chuckled. "I held on to your card all the way home. It smelled like your cologne."

"I don't wear cologne."

"Just like you don't have a goatee anymore."

Ah. "Where to next?"

He paused as the helmet went white again. "Next day, lunchtime."

And then I paused, trying to remember why he chose that specific day and time. It didn't make sense. "Our first date was three days later."

"Just jump to tomorrow before noon."

I nodded, my mind rushing ahead, the vision inside the helmet a blur before the image took on form and shape and color. I was at my old job, heading outside the building on my way to pick up lunch. "How can I be seeing this?" I asked. "It's not a collective memory."

"Really?" he asked. "Look across the street."

I spotted him in the corner of my vision, the old me oblivious. "Why? You didn't work anywhere near me at the time."

"I didn't even remember this until a minute ago," he replied. "I had a lunch meeting downtown that day. It was near your office. I didn't think I'd see you, but then there you were. See, I'm still holding your business card in my left hand."

My heart raced again, that old familiar gurgling in my belly returning. "Why… why didn't you say hello?"

"I didn't want you to think I was stalking you," he told me. "Besides, we'd already made a date for a couple of days later." I stared at the old him now as he was staring at me then. He was smiling, so bright as to make the sun jealous. "I should've said hello."

Yes, he should've. Then again, those three days apart only made me want him more, so maybe not. Who knows? Maybe if he had, we wouldn't still be together today. Weird how a split second of difference can change everything. Weirder still how watching him stand there like that made me miss him, even though, in reality, he was sitting across from me at that very moment.

Again my belly gurgled, heart racing through a furlong, knowing what the next scene would be.

"I miss that restaurant," I told him, watching us as we sat down to dinner a couple of nights later.

"Are you forgetting what happened next?"

My mind raced ahead of the video. I laughed as I did indeed remember, as the scene blurred and unfolded a few hours later, with us back at his apartment, so much of our now joined furniture mixed with the stuff we'd discarded over the years. I half grinned, half groaned as I recalled the fights that ensued with each table and chair that went out with the garbage.

I laughed again as I watched him patting my back, my head in the toilet, body retching. "Oh, I guess I don't miss that restaurant all that much."

"See."

I nodded, amazed at the look of concern on his face, at the tenderness he showed me: a virtual stranger and potential ax murderer. The computer had to have been filling that in based on what I was feeling and hearing, but it seemed so real, was, I knew, real. That was Mack, the man I'd fallen in love with.

And then I remembered what was to come next, or, that is, *who*, and I shifted in my seat, crotch suddenly throbbing. "Are we really going to watch this part?" I asked, a trickle of sweat working its way past the metal helmet.

"Not curious?" he replied, voice thick as molasses.

I nodded. I was, as he said, curious. Was what was about to happen as beautiful as I remembered it? And what if it wasn't? What if it was just awkward and my memory would forever be shifted? In any case, I let the scene play out, cock now ramrod stiff inside my jeans—both now and then, if memory served correct.

When I'd finished emptying my dinner into the toilet, Mack had given me a new toothbrush and some mouthwash and tenderly wiped the sweat and muck off my face with a damp towel.

"You okay?" he'd asked.

The old me looked down at my rumpled clothes, my hands clammy, a chill running through me. I suddenly remembered all that clear as day. "Okay," I'd replied. "Though as first dates go, I think we might be leaning toward the worst one on record."

At the time, he chuckled and continued patting my back. "Well then, things can only get better." Then he'd noticed I was shivering. "You, um, cold? Need to warm up a bit?"

A grin worked its way up my sweat-soaked face. "Post-barf chills. I'm sure it'll go away." Though I distinctly recall I wasn't so sure. Dinner, after all, had really done a number on me.

"Maybe a hot shower will help," he'd suggested. "Lucky for us, I have one right here."

"Us?" I'd managed. Though *us* is exactly what I was thinking as well, as he stood there, hand on my back, face next to mine, the bathroom barely large enough for the two of us. He nodded, sheepishly, *hotly*. "Let me just, um, brush my teeth and gargle a bit."

The current me watched as the past me gargled and brushed, noticing that Mack never took his eyes off of me, that my hand was shaking as I brushed my teeth, that I stared at him through the mirror as he turned on the shower. Both old and new me watched intently as he shucked off his shoes and began to undress, a new land opening up before me, so much promise in each inch of newly exposed skin, of swatches of hair previously unseen, at the crooked grin and the blush of red working its way up his neck.

Then he was in his white cotton briefs, the tenting obvious, a flash of curly bush poking out from above the band, stomach and chest etched in dense muscle, all covered in soft down. It was a body I now barely recognized, so much younger and leaner, like what I'd find if I peeled away the layers of age and time.

"Look at me," Mack said from across the room. "Was I really ever that thin?"

I nodded. "Apparently." And then the old me was undressing, bashfully, shyly, haltingly, until I too was in my tenting briefs. "Guess we both were. Maybe it's time for a diet and a new gym membership, huh?"

He chuckled. "I like the men we are now, Glenn. Those, after all, are barely boys back there." The chuckle grew. "*Horny boys*, by the look of things, but still."

Which didn't even begin to cover it, as I recalled. Judging by how I was looking at him, almost salivating, *horny* was about as gross an understatement as ever there was. In fact, I jumped him about two seconds later, my mouth devouring his, our bodies and boners pressed up so tight together that it was impossible to tell where he ended and I began.

"Shower time?" he eventually asked, my chill almost all gone by then, replaced by an intense inner heat.

I'd nodded my hearty yes as the briefs got shimmied out of, both of us standing there with raging hard-ons, eyes glued to the prizes, both of us grinning again, thrilled to at last be naked together. That feeling would last years into our relationship. Now seeing him naked barely got a sideways glance, despite his still being so damned handsome.

He coughed from across the room, his helmet lifted up so he could stare my way. "I… I still feel that way for you, you know."

I lifted my own helmet. "No, I didn't know."

He nodded. "It's just grown into something else. A natural progression. Comfort and ease replacing… well, *that*, back there." He pointed to his helmet. "One isn't necessarily better than the other."

I slipped my helmet back down and watched in rapt wonder as I watched myself on my knees, his steely prick buried deep inside my throat, my hand working my cock like a well-tuned machine. "No?" I asked. "What we have now is better than *that*?"

He also slipped his helmet back down, a groan ricocheting around the room. "Fine, so 'better' might not be the word for it. Still, it was hot because we both found what we were looking for. Now that we have it…." He trailed off.

"What?" I asked, still watching as he face-fucked me, his head tilted back against the tiled wall, mouth in a pant. "Now that we have it, there's no need for *hot*?"

He cleared his throat. "You're oversimplifying, Glenn. Life is not that black and white, and hot naturally grows to warm."

I frowned. "Unless you stoke the fire from time to time."

His sigh now filled the room. "Jump to our wedding, Glenn."

"Before you come?" I replied, barely in a hoarse whisper.

"I came. It was wonderful. Just jump, please."

I nodded and did as he asked. We were married five years later in a field in the countryside, both families there, about fifty friends happily watching on. There wasn't a dry eye to be found, the two of us included. What I saw standing there was a man deeply in love, two men deeply in love, both professing just that.

"I will love you for all time, Glenn," he'd said, after we exchanged vows and slipped the rings on. I remembered the butterflies in my stomach, the salty tears dripping into my mouth. "I will love you for all time, Mack," I'd replied, his hands in mine, our faces mere inches apart.

Again I slipped the helmet off. "Did you mean that?"

He slipped his helmet off too. "I did. I meant it then and I mean it now." He stared across the room at me. "I'm just sorry if you don't believe it like you did in that shower, in that field, like you did the countless times in between."

Those same butterflies of mine at last returned, swarming as they flitted about. "It's not that I didn't believe it, Mack; it's just been so long since I've heard you say it that I wasn't so sure *you* still believed it."

His frown turned to a grin. "I believe it, Glenn. Guess it just took a little looking back to be able to look ahead, is all." His smile grew and grew. "Maybe we should come here every year on our anniversary, though, as a booster shot."

I coughed, loudly. "Um, I have all I need right here." I pointed to my head and then my heart.

He did the same, grabbing his tenting crotch for good measure. Then he hopped off the chair and closed the gap between us, his lips on mine in a heartbeat, the familiar warm glow burning its way through me. "Still…."

"Still?" I replied, gazing up at him.

"Still, might be nice if you grew that goatee back," he told me with a horny-boy smirk. "For old time's sake."

I chuckled. "You have a thing for ax murderers all of a sudden?"

"No, hon," he replied, the kiss repeated again and again. "I have a thing for you."

ROB ROSEN is a novelist, short story writer, anthologist, and editor. He began writing fifteen years ago the very second he got his first personal home computer, a very clunky and heavy HP, and hasn't stopped writing since. To Rob, writing is like breathing: it's something he must do and he does it with ease, with just the occasional hiccup, groan, or sharp exhale. He's twice been nominated for a Lambda Literary Award and was the winner of the 2010 TLA Gaybie for Best Gay Fiction, the winner of the 2012 BEARy Award, and The Romance Studio's 2012 CAPA Award finalist.

Rob Rosen can be visited at http://www.therobrosen.com.

Quarter Moon Over a Ten-Cent Town

Stephen Osborne

EVERY town has at least one Gossip (capitalized, as it is an honored profession), and Flemyng, Illinois, (population 1100) had Mrs. Eleanor Gardner. Mrs. Gardner's age had been a matter of much discussion among the citizens of Flemyng. The women who worked at the Flemyng Bank on the corner of Main and 3rd insisted she was at least seventy, as she'd been a customer at the bank longer than most of them had been alive. The staff of the Coffee Hut maintained she had to be somewhat less than that, reasoning she was still somewhat spry and wielded a mean pair of scissors—Mrs. Gardner was the owner of Clippers, the hairdressing salon next to the bank—and had yet to gouge someone's ear and draw blood. One of the librarians in town stated with confidence that Eleanor Gardner was a mere fifty-six and just looked old. Tommy Watkins, the young lad who worked part-time at the gas station after school, was of the opinion that she was hundreds of years old and that a voodoo doll Mrs. Gardner kept in her dresser drawer aged instead of her, but he was alone in this contention.

Whatever her age, Mrs. Gardner was ideally suited in her role as town Gossip. With her salon right on Main Street between the bank and the veterinary clinic, Mrs. Gardner watched the people who passed her storefront with interest. And those who came in found themselves not only getting their hair done, but pumped for information about nearly every denizen of Flemyng. These intelligence reports were then broadcast to anyone Mrs. Gardner could corner for five minutes.

And if Mrs. Gardner couldn't dig up gossip on someone, she would conjecture. And these conjectures would then be spread about as if they were gospel.

One beautiful spring morning, Mrs. Gardner, finding herself without a customer, sat in a chair placed so she had a clear view of anyone strolling down Main. Her eyebrows rose when she spotted young Dylan Reed out walking a somewhat tubby basset hound. "What's this?" she said aloud, as was her custom. If there was no one around to hear her ruminations, she entertained herself with them. "The fags have got themselves a dog?"

It must be pointed out that Eleanor Gardner used the word "fags" with no animosity or ill will—or at least, not much. It was, for her, a term of endearment. After all, how could she not like Dylan and his boyfriend, John Mackelby? They provided her with so many stories that she had quite a soft spot in her heart for them. It was hard not to like Dylan. He was a slight, not very tall man of thirty-two and was the head librarian. His lover, John, was even shorter of stature but had a thick chest and impressive biceps, a legacy from his stint in the Marines. John had been a leatherneck back even before Don't Ask, Don't Tell, his own policy at the time being It's None of Their Business. After leaving the Marines, he opened up an auto repair shop with a little monetary help from his parents. Part of the basement of Dylan and John's modest house was devoted to John's home gym, which he used daily. He'd also participated in a few MMA fights, much to the surprise of many of the townsfolk, who were shocked that not only would a homo enjoy fighting but be fairly proficient at it.

Their surprise at learning that John Mackelby enjoyed putting on board shorts and beating the crap out of his opponents was nothing compared to their amazement when John and Dylan bought a little cottage together just south of Main Street on Walnut Avenue. As Mrs. Gardner had said at the time, while she had been teasing Mary Lightner's hair until it screamed, "I always knew it, mind you. I mean, it's no surprise to find out that Dylan is One Of Those," she said, punching up the phrase for emphasis as she nearly ripped out a tuft of Mary's locks. "He always was a little light in the loafers, as my old dad used to say." Here Mary Lightner frowned, trying to imagine the ancient Mrs. Gardner having a parent who had been around by the time of the invention of loafers. "And I always knew about John. No one ever believed me, but I always saw how he watched the boys as they walked down the street. Especially Dylan Reed. He had a thing for Dylan even in high school, but he was too afraid of what people would say to do anything about it. Like we would! We're enlightened around here, even if we are a backwater town. What do we care what two little queer boys want to do behind closed doors?"

Mrs. Lightner would have replied, but a sudden tug at her coiffure brought tears to her eyes, and whatever she would have said about Dylan and John will never be known.

And in the years that passed, Dylan and John had become Mrs. Gardner's favorite subject. Oh, there were other "queers" in town—Mr. Parsloe, the druggist, sprang to mind—but none of them were as high profile as John and Dylan. They had a joint bank account! They bought a house! When at parties, they introduced each other as "my boyfriend" or "my better half"!

"It's almost like they're regular people," Mrs. Gardner said one day as she squirted perm solution over Penny Carter's scalp.

"They *are* regular people," Penny protested. She'd been a classmate of both John and Dylan and had always felt a little protective of them.

"I suppose they are," Mrs. Gardner admitted. "In their way."

After that day, Penny Carter always drove to nearby Dixon to get her hair done.

As Mrs. Gardner watched one of her favorite subjects coming down leading a dog on a leash, she smiled to herself. Things were obviously not happy in Gay Paradise, if Dylan Reed's expression was anything to go by. God had given basset hounds a mournful, naturally sad expression, but the dog at the end of the lead was being outdone in the woeful department by the man next to him.

Indeed, Dylan's outlook was gloomy. The May sun was beaming down, doing its best, but even the lamp of the heavens was finding bringing a little cheer to Dylan a daunting task. Birds chirped merrily in the trees behind the drugstore, but their song fell on deaf ears. Mrs. Lightner passed Dylan on her way to the bank, and her cheery hello received only a grunt in return. When Dylan and Spider—for that was the hound's unlikely name—got to the corner and waited for the crossing light to change, the dog looked up at his master as if to say, "Dude, you're bringing me down!"

The light changed, and Dylan and Spider moved on, eventually going out of sight of Mrs. Gardner, who wondered what was behind the young man's furrowed brow. "Trouble in the bedroom," Mrs. G said aloud. "Mark my words. He and John have stopped having sex. I've seen that look before."

Incredibly, for once Mrs. Gardner's conjecture had hit the nail on the head.

DYLAN walked on, deep in thought. He was vaguely aware of life going on around him, but the comings and goings of the folk of Flemyng held no fascination for him. His mind was occupied on The Problem, specifically why John had recently been giving him the cold shoulder. They hadn't fought. In truth, they'd hardly spoken since the end of April. John was spending more and more time at work, often coming home after Dylan had already given up and gone to bed. It seemed, at least to Dylan, that John was scheduling appointments, workouts, and meetings at times when he knew Dylan would be free in an attempt to keep away. And on the few occasions when John crept into bed while Dylan was still awake and Dylan tried to instigate some action, John had just muttered, "Not tonight. Okay, babe? I'm just not feeling up to it." And that had been that.

Dylan had tried everything. He'd made a special dinner for John on Saturday night, cooking like a madman all day while John had been at work. By the time John had come home, his coveralls stained with grease, oil, and other mechanical mishaps, Dylan had set the table with candles and had Emmylou Harris—a favorite of both of theirs—playing on the stereo and was pouring the wine.

"Go hop in the shower," Dylan had said. "Only don't take too long. I don't want the casserole to cook much longer. I put it in a little too early, I guess, thinking you'd be home before now."

John gave Dylan the briefest of pecks on the cheek. "I'm sorry, babe. I got tied up at work. Everything looks wonderful." He started to peel off his clothes as he headed down the hall to the bathroom. "But I'll have to eat quick and run. Town board meeting tonight."

Which put to a halt any hopes Dylan had that the evening would end up with a sexual wrestling match in the bedroom.

Even the addition of Spider to their household had done little to ease the situation. Dylan had thought Spider would rekindle their romance as the two of them fawned over the animal, but John had done little fawning. And Spider's habit of sleeping between the two men in bed hadn't helped the coital situation. "Not," John would mutter if Dylan's hands began to stray, "in front of the dog."

Dylan suggested a trip to Hawaii. "Too much work right now, babe," John had replied.

Dylan thought throwing a party might lighten the mood of the household. "Who would we invite?" John had grumbled. "Penny? Eric? Those two are steps away from a divorce, from what I've heard. No thanks on the party idea, Dylan. I don't need the drama right now."

Dylan ran out of ideas and decided his only option was to brood. And he brooded well. He and Spider traipsed across the street and wandered over to Tinker Park. There Dylan sat on a bench thinking black thoughts while Spider watched squirrels and wondered if it was worth stirring his admittedly large ass to give chase to them. He decided against it.

So immersed in thought was Dylan that he didn't even notice Cody Brewer's presence until the young man had sat down next to Dylan on the bench. Cody had apparently just been out for a run. His tank top was soaked, and as he crossed his long legs, he wiped a hand through his hair, nearly showering Dylan with a spray of perspiration from the motion.

"Hey, buddy, how's it going?" Cody's voice was a little hoarse from his recent exertions, making his normally gravelly voice even more so.

"You talking to me," Dylan asked glumly, "or the dog?"

"The dog. You sound like a whole lot of no fun right now."

"I'm not."

"Still trouble at home?" Cody asked, his eyebrows raised.

Dylan nodded.

Cody put a damp, sweaty arm around Dylan's shoulder and pulled him closer. Dylan thought it sweet that Cody was comfortable enough, as a straight man, to engage in such a public display of affection in a town that boasted the likes of Mrs. Gardner. "Cheer up, buddy," Cody said. "Things could be worse."

A sour look to his face, Dylan merely grunted in reply. In truth, though, he felt comfort in Cody's friendship, although he could do without the wet arm draped about him and the musky smell coming from Cody's armpit. Cody, technically, was more John's friend than Dylan's. Cody and John had been Marines together, worked out together, and practiced their martial arts together. Up until recently, Dylan had felt there was little in common between him and the athletic—and presumably straight—Cody. However, at a party several weeks ago, Cody and Dylan, spurred on by the crowd and aided by a few too many beers, had kissed. It had been a mere lip-lock with no tongue, but everyone had a good laugh over it. Cody had joked, "You're a pretty good kisser for a dude," and Dylan found himself liking the guy.

Strangely, it had been to Cody that Dylan had told his troubles in the following weeks. Cody's had been a welcome shoulder on which to figuratively cry.

"Has he said anything to you?" Dylan asked hopefully.

Cody shook his head with a sigh. "Afraid not. I've not really seen much of him these last few weeks. He hasn't been to the gym much."

"No, he's been using the equipment in the basement a lot. He locks himself down there and turns up the stereo. All I hear is the clank of his weights and Steve Earle blasting out of the speakers."

"I don't know what's wrong with the guy."

"I do," Dylan said sadly. "He's gone off me. I'm no longer what he wants."

Cody scoffed. "Dude, he thinks the world of you. Always has. This is just a phase he's going through."

"I don't think so. I think he's realized that what he really wants is someone like you. Someone athletic. Someone he can hit the gym with. Someone who likes those MMA fights you guys do instead of someone who would rather see *Wicked*."

"Well, then he's crazy," Cody replied with feeling. "You're the best thing that's ever happened to him. Back when we were in the Corps—"

Dylan winced. He hoped this wasn't going to be a long harangue about the good old Marine Corps days.

"You were all he thought about. Of course, I'm the only one he talked to about you. Back then, he kept his gay side firmly under wraps."

Something clicked in Dylan's brain. All John's closest friends were either ex-Marines or guys who worked out a lot or were into martial arts. And then there was small, thin, weedy Dylan. Dylan sat up so suddenly he startled Spider, who had been sitting quietly on the grass throughout the proceeding dialogue, contemplating an anthill. "Can you," Dylan asked Cody, "teach me how to box?"

"Say what?"

Dylan repeated his words slowly.

Cody shook his head, as if trying to dislodge a reservoir of water that had decided to camp out there since his morning shower. "It sounded as if you said you wanted me to teach you how to box."

"I'm glad that's what it sounded like, because that's what I said."

"You're crazy!" After seeing Dylan's hurt look, Cody quickly added, "I mean, I think you're jumping the gun here. John doesn't want some macho idiot for a boyfriend. He wants you."

"The last few weeks would seem to point in another direction," Dylan grumbled. "So you're telling me you can't do it?"

Cody removed his arm from around Dylan's shoulders, leaving behind faint patches of wet on Dylan's shirt. He sat forward, contemplating. "I could teach Richard Simmons to be butch," the ex-Marine boasted. "I just don't see that—"

"Then it's settled." Dylan was adamant. "When do you want to start?"

Cody sighed. Gays, he was quickly learning, were every bit as weird as heterosexuals when it came to their relationships.

HISTORY has had some great brooders. Lincoln was, from all reports, a pretty melancholy guy. Napoleon went about with a scowl so often most of his army thought his face was frozen that way. In literature we have Hamlet, with his "to be or not to be" stuff—really, make up your mind!—and nearly every character John Steinbeck created. None of these, however, could hold a candle to John Mackelby when he really had a brood going. Lincoln, upon seeing John sitting at his desk in his cluttered office at the repair shop, would have spotted the lined forehead and the clenched jaw and muttered, "And I thought I had problems." Hamlet would have gasped and said, "Dude, lighten up!" Napoleon would have attacked some poor army somewhere in an attempt to forget the sight entirely.

John was good at brooding, and he had a lot to ruminate over. He was in turn angry, crushed, puzzled, and perturbed. And to make matters worse, he knew he had to talk the situation over with Dylan. He was just afraid to do so.

Because once he voiced his concerns, they would be out there. They would take on a life of their own. They would be real.

And John wasn't ready to face that.

On the other hand, he knew he couldn't keep dodging the issue. He had to know, one way or another. Even if it meant he and Dylan were over.

No! That, he told himself, *won't happen.*

He remembered when he and Dylan had first started dating, once he'd finally gotten enough nerve to actually ask Dylan out. John would have done anything for the guy. He'd once told Dylan, on a night when they'd been walking in the park at twilight, that he'd buy him anything, even the moon. Not that he'd had the money for much of anything in those days, let alone Earth's satellite. Dylan had laughed, thinking John was misquoting Jimmy Stewart in *It's a Wonderful Life.*

John knew that, by avoiding talking with Dylan, he was exacerbating the problem, driving a further wedge between them. He had to act.

John looked up from the invoices that were scattered across his desk, through the window of his office into the garage itself. Three cars were there, still awaiting repairs. And he had a brake job, a tune-up, and an alternator to deal with the next morning. For over a week now, he had been *overbooking* the garage, agreeing to do more repairs than he and his two assistants really had time to do. But John wanted to get some extra money so he could buy Dylan season tickets to the Broadway in Chicago series. That meant working late. Every night.

And it wouldn't be enough.

He had to do something more. He was losing Dylan. He felt that in his bones. John just had no clue as to how he should proceed. So he brooded.

Will Helton, the youngest of his workers, opened the office door and popped his head inside with the manner of one who is prepared to duck immediately if John decided to throw a projectile his way. "Um... boss?"

"Yeah?" John knew he was speaking through clenched teeth, but he couldn't help it.

"You want us to stay on and help out with those last jobs?"

John shook his head. "No, that's all right. You guys can go."

"We can stay. We don't mind. You don't have to pay us overtime or nothing. I don't got nothing going on tonight."

John's first instinct was to curtly correct Will's grammar. He stopped himself in time. *Good God,* he thought. *If I'm scaring my workers this badly, so much so that they're volunteering to work for free, what effect must I be having on Dylan?*

John knew he had to talk to his lover. But even thinking about doing it sent shivers into his very soul. *This is silly,* he told himself. *I was a Marine. I've had six mixed martial arts fights and won five of them by KO! Why am I so afraid of dealing with Dylan? Sweet little Dylan, who doesn't weigh 140 pounds soaking wet?*

Because, John told himself, *you love him. And you're afraid you're losing him.*

A WEEK later found Dylan at the gym, dressed in baggy sweats and attempting to keep a speed bag going. The first hit he found, no trouble. His fist hit the little bag, and it thumped back and forth, but when he went to punch it again, the bag didn't seem to be where his fist went.

"You've gotta keep your eyes on the bag," Cody told him. He was dressed in shorts and a sleeveless T-shirt. "And don't try to go so fast at first. You'll pick up speed once you get used to it."

Dylan frowned. So far on their trips to Rockford to use the boxing gym—there was no such establishment in Flemyng—Dylan had shadowboxed, hit the heavy bag, and done more rope skipping than a bevy of ten-year-old girls would do in a lifetime. After four boxing lessons from Cody, Dylan was disappointed he hadn't actually *boxed.* He had hit no one, and no one had tried to hit him back. "When am I going to get into the ring?"

In about a decade or two, if I have anything to say about it, Cody thought. He liked Dylan. For that matter, he liked John, even if he was acting like a butt. Cody felt protective of the small, thin librarian, and the thought of someone punching him, even with gloves on, did not sit well with the ex-Marine. "Soon, soon," he said just to placate Dylan. "Let's get you over to the heavy bag for a while. We'll come back to the speed bag. I want you to work on that right hook of yours."

Dylan sighed but moved over to one of the heavy bags hanging from a chain. Cody held it in place, hardly necessary, as Dylan's hardest punches barely moved the bag, and shouted out encouragement, and Dylan slammed his fists into the thing.

Dylan's arms soon felt like rubber. His back hurt. His legs ached. And he was sweating. Sweating! Then he thought of John and ramped up his adrenaline, punching the bag with everything he had.

Do it for John, he told himself. He thought of better times, when he and John would snuggle on the couch and watch movies on TV. Their usual position on the couch would have Dylan leaning against John, with John's arms wrapped tightly around him. Every now and then, when the movie hit a lull, John would kiss Dylan's neck. If the movie turned out to be a snorer, the necking would escalate until they were kissing passionately. Soon all thoughts of the movie would vanish, and the two would be peeling off items of clothing in between kisses. Dylan recalled one time when they'd abandoned a particularly unfunny Will Ferrell movie and things started to get hot and heavy. "Let's go to the bedroom," John had whispered. But Dylan had smiled mischievously and hadn't budged. Instead he started to give a nearly naked John head. John had sighed contentedly and said, "Or here on the couch is good."

Dylan had to get those days back.

"Are you with me here, Dylan?" Cody's voice broke in on his reverie.

Dylan nodded and began beating the hell out of the heavy bag.

THAT night, Dylan finished up work at the library as quickly as possible and was home by nine thirty. It was supposed to be John's day off from the garage, but he'd said he had to go in for a few hours "to get some stuff done." Surely, though, he'd be back by now.

Dylan entered their little house with anticipation. It had only been a week since he'd started training with Cody, but he was already feeling a change. His arms ached so much that at times they twitched spasmodically, but, in his mind at least, he was becoming buff and macho. Just the kind of guy to make John stand up and take notice. In more ways than one.

As soon as he stepped into the house, though, he knew John wasn't there. Spider, not being the most demonstrative of dogs, didn't run to the door, barking his greeting, but he did lift his head from his spot on the couch and wag his tail. This seemed to exhaust the basset, who then put his head back down with a sigh.

Dylan walked down the short hall to the bathroom, peeling off his shirt as he went. He dropped the garment into the hamper and then stood bare-chested before the mirror. He first checked his phone so see if John had texted him. Nothing. He placed the phone on the toilet tank and returned to the mirror. He ran a finger along his right bicep. Feeling a little foolish, he looked behind him to make sure no one could see him, even though he knew he was alone in the house. He then turned back to the mirror and flexed. *Still too skinny,* he mused, *but getting there. I'm getting... muscular. Not bodybuilder muscular, but toned muscular. It's starting to show.*

He was so engrossed in taking stock of his body that he didn't even hear John come in. When John's slumped body came to the bathroom doorway and Dylan saw his reflection, he nearly jumped out of his skin. "You startled me," he said breathlessly.

"Sorry," John said softly. "I didn't mean to." He attempted a smile, but he was out of practice, and it was a feeble effort. "Were you flexing?"

"No!" Dylan knew his cheeks were flushed a deep crimson.

"That's what it looked like."

"Well, it wasn't."

John tried the smile again, with better results. He came up behind Dylan, wanting to wrap his arms around his lover. Doubt kept him from doing so. What if Dylan shrugged him off? Instead he felt his lover's thin upper arm. "You're getting a little bicep there. You been using my weights?"

A little bicep? Dylan wanted to scream. *It's a monster bicep!*

At least they were talking, although the small room was charged with indecision and words unsaid. Dylan opened his mouth to speak, but John beat him to it.

"We need to talk."

"Yeah," Dylan said. He felt shaky and a little ill. "We should."

"I just want to say—"

At that moment Dylan's phone rang. John, being closer to the toilet, picked it up. He handed the phone to Dylan after checking the caller ID. He knew he shouldn't have looked, but he couldn't help himself. "It's Cody," he said tonelessly.

"Oh. It's okay. I'll talk to him later."

John's whole manner changed. He'd been on the verge of spilling his guts, but now the gloom had returned, and he slunk out of the bathroom. "No, go ahead and talk to him. I need to go take a walk anyway."

Dylan tried to stop him, tried to speak, but he hesitated. By the time he said, "John, wait a minute!" his boyfriend was already out the front door.

THE following day Dylan went to Rockford with Cody and was hitting the heavy bag with a defeatist attitude. Cody barked encouragement, but his words fell on deaf ears. After ten minutes of Dylan smacking the punching bag as if he was afraid he'd hurt it, Cody finally could take no more. "What's the matter with you today?"

Dylan lowered his hands. His head followed. "This isn't working for me."

Inwardly, Cody breathed a sigh of relief. While he enjoyed spending time with Dylan, he couldn't help but think the librarian was woefully out of place in a boxing gym. "Well," he said, "since you've got the whole evening free, we can take in a movie, or—"

"No, I mean hitting some stupid bag isn't working for me. I want to box!" Dylan looked around the gym at the other occupants, most of whom were skipping rope, hitting bags of various sizes, or shadowboxing. "I want to hit someone! What about that guy over there? He's about my size!"

Cody's eyes widened. "Him? You've got to be kidding!"

"He's smaller than I am!"

Cody knew the young man in question, at least enough to say hi to. "That's Pedro Machias. He's pretty good, Dylan."

"He looks like a kid."

"That's the trouble. He's seventeen. He's got boundless energy. You're over thirty."

"And?"

Cody sighed. "And you put books on a shelf really, really well."

Dylan was adamant. After the blowup with John the night before, he was full of pent-up frustration and anger and wanted—at least he was pretty sure he wanted—to fight. To actually use his fists and hit someone. And if he got hit in return, he was fine with that. He was pretty sure of it.

Before his reason kicked in and he changed his mind, Dylan strode over to Pedro, who was skipping rope with an easy grace. "Excuse me."

Pedro, who had just started and hadn't even broken a sweat, ceased the rope skipping. "Yes?"

"This is going to sound insane," Dylan said. And, now that he was actually standing next to the young man, the words really did sound like those of a lunatic. "But I've never actually boxed anyone. And I want to. Have an actual boxing match. And I was wondering…." Dylan trailed off. How did you ask someone if they'd put on gloves and hit you and possibly be hit in return?

"You want to box me?" the kid said.

Cody came up behind Dylan and took him by the shoulders, pulling him back a pace. "No, he doesn't," he told Pedro.

"Yes, I do," Dylan insisted.

Pedro shrugged. "Sure."

Cody's grip on Dylan tightened. "You just can't decide you want to box someone. It's not that easy. There's a lot of preparation that has to be done, and—"

Dylan had spotted the club's owner, Bob Underwood, nearby, talking with another gym member. Bob, or so the rumor had it, had once been a boxer himself. If so, it was entirely possible he'd taken a few too many punches to the noggin, as his thought processes were slow. When you asked Bob a question, he first looked at you blankly, as if it took a moment to register that someone was speaking. Then you could see understanding dawning in his eyes, and finally the words would sink in, and he could formulate a reply.

"Bob, can we use the ring for a boxing match?" Dylan asked.

Bob stared at Dylan blankly. A muscle twitched in his cheek. This was a hard one. Finally the words sank in. "If anyone gets hurt, I'm not responsible."

"You got it."

Cody sighed. "This," he muttered under his breath, "is going to be bad. Really, really bad."

JOHN, meanwhile, had been busy. He'd called into the shop and told Will he wouldn't be in and was taking a day off. "But I need a favor," he had added.

Will, pleased that the boss was actually going to relax for a change, eagerly said he'd do anything John wanted.

"I want to borrow your car for the day. I'll leave you mine."

Will was perplexed but agreed. Shortly after the call, John showed up, and they exchanged keys. John then drove away in Will's beat-up Chevy Nova like a man on a mission. Which, it must be admitted, he was. His mission was to follow the love of his life, Dylan, and find out, once and for all, just what was going on. No more guessing. No more listening to rumors. John was going to learn the truth, even if it broke his heart.

If someone had asked John "How do you feel, spying on Dylan?" he would have been surprised by the question. It wasn't spying. Spying was devious and secretive. This was just a mission to gain intel. True, he was doing so in a car that wouldn't be recognized, and he was keeping back so Dylan wouldn't see him, but that wasn't *spying*.

And when he saw Dylan pull up in front of Cody's apartment building and go inside, John's worst fears were, he thought, realized. But then he frowned as, minutes later, Cody and Dylan emerged and got into Dylan's car, carrying gym bags. John then followed them as they headed north and eventually drove to a boxing gym in Rockford. As they got out of the car and went inside, John, who had pulled up a little too close to the entrance, had to slink down into his seat to avoid being seen. Not that he was spying, of course. He just had to know.

And he'd been *so* sure he'd known what Dylan had been up to. Now, as he watched Dylan and Cody going into a gym, he wasn't so sure. Cody, yes, but *Dylan*? In a boxing gym?

John had to know. He got out of the car and followed the two inside.

Although he hadn't been to Underwood's Boxing Gym for weeks—in fact, not since The Party, when Dylan had kissed Cody—John was well-known there. He hoped no one would spot him and shout out his name, as that would alert Dylan to his presence. As best he could, he slunk in, at first hiding behind a potted palm and then moving to a secluded spot behind one of the heavy bags. A young black man, working on a nearby bag, raised an eyebrow at the guy standing plastered to the wall wearing street clothes, but he didn't give the game away.

John peered around the bag. What was going on? He watched as Dylan and Cody disappeared into the locker room. His mind was whirling. Could he have been wrong all this time? No, he had walked into the room at The Party and caught Cody kissing Dylan. Dylan had tried to laugh it off as a sort of truth or dare game, but John knew better. More than that, he knew Cody. Nice guy. Good friend. But he'd fuck anything with a pulse.

And after that, Cody and Dylan had begun hanging out *all* the time. True, John had been working a *lot* at the time and hadn't had time for Dylan, and, if he was honest with himself, John had been stewing over The Kiss and hadn't wanted to talk to Dylan, but… still. And then it all went downhill. Did he have himself to blame? Had he pushed Dylan away, into the waiting arms of Cody?

John perked up as Dylan and Cody emerged from the locker room, now dressed in sweats. His eyes widened when Cody led Dylan over to a vacant heavy bag and Dylan—*Dylan!*—started punching away.

Dylan? Dylan couldn't even stomp on a spider. He liberated them, placing them outdoors when he found one in the house. Dylan didn't hit things. Dylan was sweet, kind, and mild. No, this was Cody's doing. Cody was trying to beef Dylan up, for....

Well, John couldn't think of a reason, but obviously Cody had some Machiavellian plot going.

And what was going on now? They were moving over to the ring. Cody was putting boxing gloves onto Dylan's wrapped hands. And Pedro Machias, whom John had seen in the ring before, seemed to be gloving up as well. Surely....

Was Dylan climbing into the ring? John nearly rubbed his eyes in disbelief. *This has got to be a dream,* he told himself. *No, a nightmare.*

John listened carefully. He could just make out Cody asking Dylan to put on some headgear. Dylan's reply was easy to hear.

"No, thanks."

John moved away from the wall, no longer caring if anyone saw him. His mouth gaped open as Cody helped put a mouthpiece past Dylan's lips. "Sorry," Cody said. "It's mine, but there's no way I'm letting you get your teeth bashed in. Literally."

"No problem," Dylan replied. Actually, with the hunk of plastic in his mouth, it came out as "Nuh arblem," but John got the idea.

Most of the guys working out in the gym, only about seven or eight guys, saw some action was about to take place and stopped what they were doing and gathered at ringside. Bob Underwood, standing near the bell, looked up, first at Dylan and then at Pedro. "You guys sure about this?"

Pedro shrugged. "Sure. Why not?"

Dylan, who looked more than a little shaky, said, "Uh-huh."

And then Bob rang the bell.

John, aghast, rushed forward. Although his feet were moving quickly, it seemed to John that things were going in slow motion. He'd never reach the ring in time. Even his shout of "What the fucking hell do you think you're doing?" sounded like it was distorted, as if spoken underwater. John couldn't feel his feet slapping against the floor. He realized someone had grabbed him by the arm, and he vaguely knew that person was Cody and that Cody was saying something to him, but John couldn't be bothered by anything but stopping Dylan from getting the stuffing beat out of him.

"He's doing this for you, you imbecile." Cody's voice finally penetrated John's skull.

John brushed off Cody's restraining arm. "What are you talking about?"

"You've been ignoring him. He has this stupid idea that he's got to be He-Man for you. So he wants to box someone. I've been giving him lessons for the past few weeks."

He felt weak in the knees, but John still managed to glare at Cody. "And what else have you been doing to him?"

"What?" It took Cody a moment to figure out John's implied message. "You think that Dylan and I—"

He would have gone on, but at that moment things exploded in the ring.

IT WAS at least mercifully brief. Dylan, his heart pounding so much it seemed to echo against the walls, stepped to the center of the ring and touched gloves with Pedro. Pedro gave him a brief smile and then shot out a quick jab that connected with Dylan's nose.

Hey, Dylan thought. *That hurt. A lot.*

And so did Pedro's left to the side, which was followed by a right to Dylan's jaw. Dylan stumbled backward, but Pedro pressed forward, hitting Dylan with a right-left combination to the stomach. The pain from those shots had barely registered in Dylan's mind before he got clobbered by Pedro's right hook, which felt like it had ripped Dylan's chin right off his face. Dylan was only barely aware of his knees giving way and falling to the canvas.

"CAREFUL!"

John smiled and said, "Sorry."

He'd been trying to shower Dylan with kisses, which was hard when the whole lower half of Dylan's face was a mass of pain.

They were sitting in the front of John's car, parked on Main Street just across from Mrs. Gardner's salon. On their way back into town, John had coordinated the transfer of vehicles with Will, and they had agreed to meet just outside of The Tobacco Shop. Dylan's car was still at Cody's, but they could deal with that later. The sun had gone down, and, as was typical of a small town like Flemyng, with the disappearance of day, the streets were all but deserted. Ordinarily John wasn't the type to kiss in public view, but as there was no public to view, being outside in a car didn't really count.

John leaned in again to attempt to kiss Dylan, gently, but was stopped when Dylan put a restraining finger to his chin. "You thought," Dylan asked, with more than a touch of amazement, "that I was having an affair with Cody?"

"Well, yeah." John felt his cheeks flush. It wasn't easy to admit he'd been wrong. So very, very wrong. "I mean, you guys kissed. I walked into the room, and there you were, lip-locked with my buddy!"

"It was more a dare than anything else! I told you that!" Dylan rolled his eyes heavenward. "And besides, Cody is straight."

"He isn't!"

"He has a girlfriend!"

John snorted. "That wouldn't stop Cody. Cody will screw anything with a pulse."

"Well, he didn't screw me. He never even made a move." That puzzled Dylan. "I wonder why?"

"And then you were spending all that time with him."

"Because you were ignoring me!"

"Well... I was mad," John said. "And then I kept getting madder the more you were with him."

"You were working all the time, and when you weren't, you never talked!"

"Okay, I was wrong! I admit it!" John took Dylan's hands in his and gave them a loving squeeze. "But what the hell were you thinking, getting into the ring with Pedro? He could have killed you!"

"You're always with Cody and your old Marine buddies and guys who are into fighting and stuff. I figured that's why you were… well, growing tired of me."

"So you thought you'd get the crap beat out of you to prove to me how tough you were. Makes perfect sense." John's sarcasm was gentle but pointed.

"Hey! He was a little guy. I figured I had a chance."

"Good thing he took it easy on you."

"*That* was taking it easy?"

John nodded. Smiling, he released Dylan's hands and put his own around Dylan's neck. He pulled Dylan's face to his, and they kissed. "Did that hurt?" John asked when they eventually broke off the kiss. Dylan's lips *were* fairly swollen, and there was a dark bruise on his chin.

"Terribly," Dylan said. "Do it again."

John did. "Promise me you won't do anything that stupid again."

"It wasn't that stupid."

"It was," John assured him.

"Well, you were stupid for thinking I was sleeping with Cody."

"Okay, we both were stupid."

Another kiss followed, this one lasting what seemed an eternity and yet was over much too soon.

"Let's get home," John said. "We'll get your car tomorrow. We've got makeup sex to engage in. God, how long has it been since we—"

He would have gone on, but Dylan's lips were on his, making it hard to talk plainly. "Let's just do it here," Dylan said with a mischievous grin.

John started to chuckle but then realized Dylan was serious. "Here? On Main Street?"

"It's dark. No one's around. And I always keep lube and emergency condoms in my gym bag." When John's face began to darken, Dylan playfully punched him on the shoulder. "Not for *that,* you idiot! For us. Let's face it, before I asked Cody to train me to box— something I'm thinking he didn't do all that well at—the only time I used my gym bag was when you and I would go camping."

John looked around outside the car. True, there was no one around, but… making out right there just felt wrong. Strangely titillating, but wrong. "I don't know. The hair salon is right across the street, and you know what a gossip Mrs. Gardner is."

"The shop is dark and closed, scaredy-cat." Dylan shifted around, laughing lightly, pressing John back until Dylan was almost lying on top of him. "Come on, chicken. You won't believe how horny I am."

"Oh," John muttered, wrapping his arms around Dylan, "I think I can imagine."

Dylan began to pull off John's T-shirt, but the steering wheel and their relative positions made this a herculean task. Laughing, Dylan suggested they retire to the backseat. "More room," he said.

They scrambled into the back, John taking one last look outside to make sure no one could see them. There was no one, just the moon and stars shining in the sky.

"Remember when we first started dating," John said as they got comfortable and both their hands began roaming, "and I told you I'd do anything for you, even buy you the moon?"

Dylan's eyes twinkled. He looked out the rear window. "It's just a quarter moon tonight. You're getting off cheap."

MRS. GARDNER had been working on the books in the back room, but it was late and she wanted to go home. She shuffled through the dark shop, heading for the front door. She was fishing in her pockets for the keys when she paused. Something caught her eye. She looked out the window. What was going on? That was John Mackelby's car parked across the street, and there seemed to be movement within. She crept up to the window and peered out.

There was something white bobbing up and down in the backseat. Mrs. Gardner pressed her face to the window, cupping her hands around her eyes to get a better view. That was John's—no, Dylan's bare butt, going rapidly up and down. In sight and then out of sight. And those must be John's legs sticking up. Eleanor Gardner's mouth fell open. Right there, on Main Street! In front of her shop! For shame! *Mind you,* she thought, *gay boys don't have the same sense of decorum as regular folks.* But still! How shocking! Disgusting!

As quick as her old legs would take her, Mrs. Gardner went over to the reception desk. The bottom drawer had her personal belongings, and she rustled around until she found the item she was looking for. She returned to the window, binoculars in hand. Her hands trembled as she got them up to her eyes and adjusted them.

Disgusting! Shocking!

Oh, don't stop yet!

STEPHEN OSBORNE has been an improvisational comedian, a pizza restaurant manager, and a bookseller. Other than writing, his addictions include British television shows, reading mysteries, and (a recent addition) Broadway musicals. He lives in rural Illinois with Jadzia the One-Eyed Wonder Dog.

Visit him at Facebook: http://facebook.com/stephen.osborne2 and Twitter: http://twitter.com/southbendghosts. You can contact him at leftyIN@yahoo.com.

Reboot

S. H. Allan

JOSH FLOHR was sitting in his living room hunched over his laptop. He was deeply focused on programming a new algorithm to streamline data processing in his company's SQL databases. He chewed his lip as he went through the debugging log, frustrated that the script wasn't working correctly. He barely noticed when his boyfriend, Flynn, came into the room, a big smile on his face.

"Hey, Josh? Candice and Mike want to meet up in about half an hour at the Mug Shot to inhale some caffeine before they go to the opera."

Josh looked up and blinked.

"I know, right? Who thought Mike would be cultured enough to go to the opera? He's probably the one who needs the coffee. Anyway, I was thinking we could meet up and then maybe catch dinner and a flick after, just you and me." Flynn looked hopeful.

Josh glanced at his program. "I don't know…. I really should get this done by Monday, or I'll be even more bogged down than usual." He turned to meet Flynn's eyes. "Maybe just dinner?"

Flynn looked disappointed. "C'mon, Josh, it's Saturday. Do you really have to work? I can make it worth your while; we could come back here after for a special dessert featuring chocolate, caramel, and a whole lot of licking. Please?" He batted his eyelashes.

Josh laughed. "Oh God, stop that thing you're doing with your eyes. I'll go if you knock that off. It's so disturbing, I may lose my appetite for dessert sauces."

The other man grinned, and Josh's heart skipped. Feeling all squiggly inside, Josh smiled at his boyfriend's words and took a moment to linger. Even out of his rocker duds, dark-haired, dark-eyed, gorgeous Flynn looked rebellious and a little dangerous. Neither matched the sensitive and sweet person who lay inside. The public was used to tight black clothing; leather, chains, and studded things; guyliner, black lipstick, and nail polish; and brightly streaked hair. Wearing an old, loose pair of blue jeans and a faded T-shirt, sans makeup and accessories, Flynn was in camouflage and at his sexiest.

Josh stood and put his arms around his boyfriend. "You know, Mike is always at least half an hour late to everything. We could do a lot in an extra half an hour." He raised his eyebrows suggestively.

Flynn chuckled. "Yeah, okay. I can think of a few things." Josh's lover grabbed his hand and pulled him toward the bedroom. Josh stopped them long enough to hand Micro a chew toy and order her to stay; then his lover dragged him down the hall, both of them shedding clothes along the way.

"I'M JUST saying that it's easier than being, say, a doctor or something." Mike's nasally voice was even more annoying when he was trying to assert opinion as fact.

"That's like saying it's easier being a brain surgeon than the president. 'Course there are jobs that are more difficult than others. That's not the point. We're talking about how hard a guy works, and being a musician is hard work." Flynn's voice was never annoying, but it was increasing in decibels.

Josh wanted to tune both of them out by chatting with Candice, but she was too busy listening to them. She had a big grin and wide eyes as she watched and kept score on a napkin. Seeing someone best her husband in an argument gave her some kind of vicarious, inexplicable thrill.

Josh took a sip of his Caffé Medici and watched the customers line up at the counter. Unlike coffee shops that catered to business people or students, Mug Shot's clientele were eclectic. The shop was all the better for it, and he enjoyed people-watching there. He surveyed the line until his phone alerted him to a text message from his coworker Ian, a new systems operator who covered the weekend shift.

"*yo dud. server crash. wont start right*"

Josh opened his phone and texted, "*Be more specific.*"

"*reboot but database no go*"

He texted back, "*You rebooted the physical server and now you can't start up the SQL server?*"

"*thats what I sed*"

Josh closed his eyes and took a moment to ground himself. That wasn't at all what Ian had said. There were also a number of steps to get the main server up and running before starting SQL. "*Did you rerun all the shell scripts after you rebooted?*" Nearby, he could hear Flynn breathing faster. Josh glanced over and saw his partner dragging the handle of his teaspoon along a groove carved into the wooden tabletop. He appeared to be making the gouge larger.

Ian texted back, "*u think im stupid?*"

Well..., Josh thought, then checked himself. Ian was fairly new at being a systems operator.

He caught snatches of the conversation between the others. "You really think being a rock star is hard." Mike managed to sound both condescending and sarcastic.

"You really think being an accountant is hard?" Flynn shot back.

Josh figured his boyfriend could defend himself and focused on how to help the rookie sysop. "*Which script did you run last?*" He didn't use shortened speech when he texted. It was important to always be clear, especially with Ian.

"*datarun.bat*"

"*Did you wait ten minutes after you ran the shell script to restart the SDI batch processes first?*"

A long pause followed before Ian replied. "*10 min?*"

Josh sighed. The shop was warm and smelled of rich coffee and the cedar of the walls. The atmosphere was homey, the friendly people treating Flynn like everyone else, not a famous rock musician. Josh loved the place and wanted to enjoy it, not spend his time dealing with someone not really qualified for his job.

Mike was chuckling. "How hard can it be? You get to travel, you hang around in luxury hotel suites all day drinking champagne and eating caviar, play a couple of hours in front of people who adore you—you don't even have to sound good—and then party all night long with gorgeous women—sorry, men—hanging all over you. When you get back, you can sleep all day if you want to."

"What the fuck are you talking about? Man, you're so fucking clueless. Yeah, all a big party. We don't rehearse or write songs; there're no long days or spending fucking hours on a bus with a bunch of sweaty assholes. Yeah, it's fucking fabulous to be gone from home, my family, my friends, my *dog*; being away from my boyfriend all the time, no sex for weeks or sometimes months." Flynn's voice was growing louder. "I bet you and Candice would be all over that."

"That's different."

"Why?" Flynn growled.

"Because we're married."

Josh heard that. *Uh-oh.*

On the other side of him, Candice snickered and stage whispered, "Ooo, come on, Flynn, step it up a notch! Put him in his place."

Josh moved his coffee cup away from Flynn in case his boyfriend felt like throwing something. He also pushed Flynn's tea out of the way for good measure.

Flynn's voice was suddenly low and slow. "You fucking prick." He breathed in deeply and calmed visibly. "I'm gay. Unless I switch teams—ugh." He shuddered melodramatically. "I can't get married. Doesn't mean I don't love Josh as much as you love Candice."

"Sure it would be hard to be away from her," Mike conceded, "but if I made that kind of money, she wouldn't have to work, and I would just bring her with me."

That, at last, invested Candice emotionally. She flushed and opened her mouth to respond, but Flynn spoke first. "You think Candice would put up with that? Really?" he snarled. "Josh isn't my houseboy, he's my partner. He's got his own shit, like an awesome job he loves and kicks ass at, his own buds he hangs with. He'd hate being on the road all the time. And I wouldn't want him to, 'cause he'd be miserable. Me and Mr. Happy hate being away from him, but Josh needs to have a life too. I can't take that away from him. I won't."

Candice was bobbing her head with a scornful smirk on her face as Flynn talked. "Mmm-hmm. Tell it to the man," she urged. Then she leaned over to Josh and whispered, "Is Mr. Happy his—?"

Josh's phone beeped, saving him from replying.

"reran sh script. Still cant access db"

"Are you reading the reboot procedure list?" Josh asked Ian.

Another long pause followed. *"what list"*

Josh took a deep breath and exhaled slowly. *"Start over."* The list hung right next to the server in question, a laminated card on a chain. *"Go step by step through the list. Confirm that you do every item by checking it off with the attached grease pen. Make sure you wait for each process to complete before going on to the next step. Text me when you're done."* He had to split that text into two, it was so long.

"All right, so you miss your boy toy." Josh heard Mike's words and cringed. Candice giggled. "You probably miss having your nerdy lover hanging off your arm in front of the press too." The dig was directed at Flynn's decision to make his homosexuality very public. He would never be closeted and felt that as a semicelebrity, it was his job to be a role model. Mike thought it was all a publicity stunt, which was asinine. But that was a different argument.

"I'm gonna ignore that 'cause you're an idiot and an ass. And for the record, Josh is the hottest guy, nerd or not, who's ever used a computer." Josh couldn't help smiling. He knew he wouldn't win any beauty contests; even when wearing his boyfriend's trendy clothes, he was ordinary-looking. But all that mattered was that Flynn, one of alternative rock's hottest lead singers, thought Josh was sexy.

"Mike…," Candice interjected, knowing enough was enough. Josh was pretty sure Mike was trying to get a rise out of Flynn, which really wasn't too hard by that point. Mike couldn't even claim his obnoxious behavior was due to being drunk. They were in a coffee shop drinking overpriced caffeinated beverages with pretentious names. Maybe he'd brought his own flask.

"Never mind. I gotta take a leak." Flynn got up and stormed to the back of the shop.

Mike laughed victoriously, which irritated Josh, so he put the phone aside for a moment. "Mike, Flynn works very hard. Going out on tour is difficult for any musician, but these folks are not big rock stars.

Bugs Are Nervous is a good alternative band with a large following, not the Hollywood crowd. They can't afford to stay in really nice hotels and eat gourmet food."

"You guys have plenty of money. I know Flynn makes a lot."

"Mike!" Candice admonished.

Josh continued. "We aren't hurting, because we both make good money; we're well off but not rich—and Flynn earns every dime he makes."

Mike was shaking his head.

"Mike, I've been on tour with him, and it's grueling. They're on the road all the time, sometimes having to sleep as they travel instead of staying in a hotel. Then they work eighteen-to-twenty-hour days, so they're always exhausted."

"What do they do with all that time?" Candice sounded genuinely curious.

"Well, when they first arrive at a concert location, they have to go over the concert hall/arena/whatever. The band meets with their manager, tours the venue, and discusses the set list. They meet with the opening band and figure out how to arrange two sets of equipment onstage to minimize how much has to be moved between sets. Each venue is different, so they have to do this every time. They then help set up the equipment, test, and adjust it. They practice a bit to get a feel for the acoustics. All of that takes hours and hours."

Mike grimaced. "Sounds boring."

"They're too busy to be bored. Sometimes they have to leave to do a quick interview or even an unplugged gig at a local radio station after setting up and before the show."

"Yeah, but that's it, right? Then they go rock out?" Mike was still trying to win the argument without Flynn present.

"No. They do their own hair and makeup. Flynn meditates to get himself ready. He also listens to the first act to get a feel for the audience. Then they do their set, which is exhausting. You try singing and playing a heavy guitar while running around and dancing onstage. He's really good at it and engages the audience to put on a good show. That takes a lot of work and skill."

Mike rolled his eyes, and Candice punched him. "Go on, Josh."

"After the show, they head backstage and go over the performance while it's fresh. Often they have to entertain a local who won a radio contest. They help pack away the gear because they don't really trust anyone else to keep their instruments safe. When possible, the band goes to a hotel and gets a few hours of sleep before hopping back on the bus at the crack of dawn."

Mike had the decency to look uncomfortable, at least. Candice looked embarrassed. "I never really thought about all that."

Josh nodded. "I didn't really get how hard it was until I took some time off work to go travel with them for a couple of weeks. It's really exhausting; I couldn't do it. I think I lost twenty pounds just watching them work. I no longer complain about his hours, especially since he always finds time to call me before bed."

Mike made a noncommittal sound just as Flynn rejoined them, his head cocked as though he had remembered something. "Mike, what did you mean by 'You don't even have to sound good'?"

Josh's phone signaled another text, distracting him.

"*dunno if scrip ran, froze*" It hadn't been more than ten minutes. How had Ian messed up already? He'd thought the procedure was idiot proof. Apparently not.

Josh sighed. "*Which script are you on?*"

"C'mon, Flynn. A rock st—a 'rock musician'"—Mike's words dripped with sarcasm—"doesn't have to be able to sing—"

Helping Ian, Josh tuned out the conversation, only catching snippets.

"The bass and drums mostly drown out—" Mike stated.

"Are you serious?" Flynn's voice was loud, catching Josh's attention.

He heard Candice say something and, figuring she could handle it, texted Ian back. "*How much time has it been since you started it?*" Damn, was he going to have to go to work just to reboot a server hardly anyone used? He really didn't want to go in today.

"*dunno,*" Ian replied.

"*Well, you may need to run the shells scripts again.*"

"I'm not saying that rock stars are bad singers, just that they don't have to be good. In a studio, the—what are they called, sound engineers?—can play with the voice, make it on-key, make it sound good. Out at a show, they can't do that, so they amp up the instruments so it's mostly noise—" Mike's voice was rising too. Candice's was the only calm one in the storm.

"*tryed that, dint work,*" Ian texted.

"Are you fucking kidding me? You saying I can't sing?" Flynn yelled.

Josh didn't register Flynn's anger, nor did he clue in as to why people were starting to stare. Ian was an idiot—that's why the man had to work weekends. If Rosita had been at the office instead of Ian, Josh might have been able to enjoy a day off, maybe even turn off his phone.

"'Course not, just that there's a reason you're part of a band and Amy Winehouse is a solo artist—"

"*going 2 reboot again*" How many times had Ian done that now? Josh had lost count.

"Are you hearing this? Josh? Can you fucking believe what this asshole just said?"

Josh looked up. "What?" Flynn and Mike were both looking at him, Flynn red-faced and furious, Mike smugly annoyed. Even Candice was chewing on her bottom lip. Damn. What were they arguing about now? "Uh, Mike, Flynn works very hard. He gives his best."

All of them looked surprised. Mike started to nod and Flynn exploded. "What the fuck, Josh? I *give my best*? I fucking *work hard*?" He jumped up, his chair falling backward on the floor. More heads turned.

Josh gaped at him, realizing he had said precisely the wrong thing. "Flynn—"

"Fuck you, Josh. Fuck you, Mike. Fuck you both. Not you, Candice, I don't swing that way." Flynn flew out the door, making the normally sweet bell clang atonally.

"Flynn! *Flynn!*" Josh jumped up, but his chair was wedged in by the wall, and by the time he got outside, Flynn was long gone. Crap. Josh turned and saw an anti-marriage-equality poster glaring at him from a nearby telephone pole. He felt like throwing something at it. Instead, he went back inside. His phone buzzed, but he ignored it and sat down again.

"What were you guys arguing about?" He had to know how badly he'd hurt Flynn.

Mike shrugged. Candice answered Josh but didn't take her eyes off her husband. "Just whether rock musicians can really sing, and thereby Mike implied Flynn can't." She was fuming, and Mike was trying to avoid her glare.

Shit. Josh closed his eyes and leaned back for a moment. Why hadn't he just admitted he hadn't been paying attention? He had screwed up big-time. He was going to need an even bigger bouquet of condom roses this time around.

IT WAS well after closing time at the bars when Flynn got home that night, reeking of alcohol and cigarettes. Josh was sitting on the couch waiting for him. He was working on his laptop, writing a new batch script to simplify that particular server's reboot even further, a solution hopefully even Ian could handle.

"Flynn, I—"

His lover walked right past Josh without acknowledging his existence.

"Am so sorry." Flynn was already out of sight, so Josh followed. He found his lover lying on the bed fully clothed, only his leather jacket discarded on the floor. "Flynn, honey—"

"Shhhh. Tryin' ta sleep."

Josh moved to the bed and pulled off Flynn's boots. When he moved up to unfasten Flynn's belt, though, his boyfriend rolled away from him.

"Leave m' 'lone." Flynn buried his face in the pillow.

"Honey—"

"Don' touch me!"

Josh's chest tightened.

Flynn turned toward Josh long enough to say, "Jus'... 'm tired."

"Okay, Flynn... okay." Josh stripped off his clothes slowly, opting to leave on his T-shirt and the briefs with the smiley face on each ass cheek. He climbed in bed as Flynn moved back over to his own side. Josh ached to hold him. Instead, he hugged himself and curled into a ball facing the back of the man he loved, careful not to touch him. It was a long time before he fell asleep.

JOSH was eating lunch and sharing half of it with Micro when Flynn finally dragged himself into the kitchen. "The coffee is a couple of hours old. I can make you a new pot."

"I got it."

"Want me to make you something to eat?" Josh tried to sound as ingratiating as possible.

"Not hungry."

They both remained silent as Flynn made fresh coffee. Josh waited, barely moving except to pet Micro, anxious to see what his lover would do when he was done. He tried not to sigh in relief when Flynn came over and sat at the kitchen table with him.

"Flynn, I—"

"'S okay," his boyfriend mumbled into his coffee.

The chest tightness came back. "No, it's not, Flynn. I'm so sorry; I wasn't paying attention." He reached out and touched the other man's hand, but Flynn only pulled it away.

"I can sing, Josh."

This time a needle of pain stabbed through his heart. "Of course you can, Flynn. I would never say otherwise." He was no longer hungry and gave the rest of his sandwich to the dog.

Flynn finally looked at him. "No, you wouldn't, would you? But you believe it."

The look on his boyfriend's face would have had Josh on his knees if he had been standing. "No! No, I don't! I know you can sing. You sing to me all the time."

"Yeah, but not like Amy Winehouse."

"Plenty of people who are great vocalists can't sing like Amy Winehouse. Your voice is—"

Flynn slammed his palm on the table. Micro slunk underneath Josh's chair and licked his hand. "Fuck, man! I didn't say I can't sing like her. I said I don't sing like that to you. You never want me to sing that shit." His face was tight with anger.

Josh wasn't sure what would be best to say, so he didn't say anything. Micro nudged at his hand, and he clutched her scruff.

Flynn deflated. "I know you weren't even listening to Mike and me. You were too busy working."

"Yeah. I'm a jerk. I'm sorry." Josh didn't try to make any excuses.

"You're always on that phone, or on your laptop, or at work. It's like you don't have time for me anymore, like your job is more important than me." Flynn looked so sad. Josh wanted to take him in his arms and just hold him, but he knew that wouldn't help.

"Honey, nothing is more important than you are. I just… get wrapped up in my work. The servers are running and being accessed 24/7." Micro abandoned him and moved to bat at Flynn's hand with her muzzle.

"Can't someone else deal with it?"

Josh shook his head. "That's the problem. We've got… less than competent people working nights and weekends, and when something goes wrong, they call me."

"Yeah, but can't they call someone else? Can't Rosita help? You said she's real good." Flynn was almost pleading.

"Uh… yes. Yes, I can work on that. We used to have a schedule, but no one followed it. Everyone just calls me. I can try to get people to go back to it."

Flynn just looked at him.

"I mean, I'll make it work so I'm not on call all the time."

"Baby, I love you, but you're a workaholic. That's not going to change."

Josh cringed. "Yes, it will. I mean, I'll just be a workaholic when I'm not with you." He had a hard time believing it himself.

Flynn stared at him with sadness. "What's happening to us?"

A sucker punch wouldn't have hurt as badly as that sentence. "What do you mean?" Micro sensed something was wrong and whined.

"You're working all the time; I'm on the road. You don't care about what I do. I try to care about yours, but I don't get it. I feel like an idiot around you."

Josh rubbed his chest to ease the discomfort. "You're far from an idiot, Flynn. You're brilliant, just in different areas. My work is just specialized. And I do care, very much. Ask people at work—they're sick of your music because I play it all the time. I brag about you and your latest awards and special gigs. When you appeared on the Colbert Report last spring to sing your song about marriage equality, my team had an actual intervention to get me to shut up because it was all I talked about."

"Really?"

"Scout's honor."

"You were kicked out of the Boy Scouts for being queer."

"No, I was kicked out because I went to the awards ceremony wearing a dress to protest their position on gay rights."

Flynn snorted. "Same diff."

"Yeah, well, I still swear it: Your work is very important to me. Your music matters. You write and sing about real issues and real people. I am so proud of you. I'm sorry I don't always show it."

Flynn looked at Josh for a moment, then said to himself, "I gotta fix this." He stood up. "I'm gonna get dressed." When he reached the doorway, he turned just a little. "I can sing, Josh. There's lots of stuff I can't do, but I can sing."

Before Josh could reply, Flynn was gone. And if Micro then had to lick unexplained water off Josh's cheeks, it was no one's business but his own.

OVER the next few weeks, Josh made an effort to change. He made up a backup support schedule at work and got the team to agree to follow it. At first, people called him anyway, but he would ignore the phone and text back the name and number of the person who was on call that night. By the beginning of the second week, Ian et al., stopped phoning and texting him when it wasn't his turn.

He tried not to work at home, but sometimes it couldn't be helped. On those nights, he apologized profusely, and Flynn said he understood. Josh tried to make it up to him by doing something special the next night. A couple of times, he surprised his boyfriend with a gift or a fancy dinner or tickets to a show. By the middle of the first week, Flynn was letting Josh touch him again, and by the weekend, they were back to having sex, thank the universe. When Flynn asked Josh if he would help him work on the marriage equality campaign, Josh readily agreed; it was something they could do together that was important to both of them.

But Flynn still seemed distracted and bothered by something. Josh knew his boyfriend, and something was off-key. He caught Flynn mumbling to himself saying things like "I've gotta fix this" and "I'm gonna do something about us." His boyfriend claimed everything was fine, yet he wouldn't sing to Josh anymore, no matter how much he begged and cajoled. Flynn always had a reason: his throat hurt, he'd just had ice cream or milk, his ears were clogged, he was too tired. Finally, Josh stopped asking. He was at a loss. He loved Flynn, and it hurt to see his partner unhappy. Somehow, he was the one who had to fix it, but he had no idea how. His old standby, a box of penis-shaped chocolates, just wouldn't cut it this time.

"I LOVE you."

Flynn smiled. "I love you too."

"I mean, I really and truly love you." Josh held his boyfriend tightly, feeling his lean muscles through his thin T-shirt.

"Baby, I know. I gotta go. Band's waiting." Flynn tried to push Josh away. It took three tries before Josh finally let go and stood back. His boyfriend climbed the steps into the smelly bus looking at him like he was being weird, which he probably was.

"You're an amazing singer, and your fans all know it."

At that, Flynn's smile faded a little.

Damn. "And you know I'm your biggest fan. I mean it; you're wonderful."

"You too. I've got a plan."

Anxiety pounded in Josh's chest. "What do you mean?"

"Nothing. Never mind. Love you."

Flynn was still acting funny, and it scared Josh. "Please come back."

Bemused, Flynn replied, "Of course."

"Promise?"

Flynn cocked his head and narrowed his eyes. Then he nodded. "Promise."

For some reason, Josh only felt worse. He didn't have any tissues. Where was Micro when he needed her?

RING. Ring. "You missed me. I'm partying like a rock star. Leave a message." *Beep.*

"Hi. I'm just wondering if you're okay. I haven't heard from you in a couple of days, and I—" He what? If Josh said he was concerned, would that come across as too clingy? "I'm just checking in. Call me." Crap. That sounded demanding. "I mean, if you want to." He hung up the phone.

Josh was worried. It had been over a month since the tour started, and he'd only spoken with his boyfriend a few times. When Bugs Are Nervous was on tour, Flynn usually called him every single night. They'd talk for a while and then often had phone sex. Even when Flynn was really tired, they'd talk for a little bit. The few times they'd spoken on this tour, Flynn sounded harried and exhausted, begging off after only a minute or two, saying he was dealing with something. They'd only had phone sex once, and Flynn had fallen asleep midway through.

Was he having an affair? Josh felt a stab of pain, and suddenly he couldn't breathe. Hadn't Mike mentioned something about beautiful guys "hanging all over" rock musicians? Flynn hadn't argued with that. Oh God... what if he was leaving? Five years was a long time, especially for gay men with the societal pressures they faced. It was forever in the entertainment business. Long-distance relationships were hard, and when Flynn was home... well, Josh was hard to live with, no denying it.

No, he wouldn't think about that, because if it was true, if his boyfriend was leaving him, his world would fall apart. As Flynn had said, Josh had a job he loved, friends, a home, but without Flynn, it was all pointless. Flynn was his everything. If Josh lost him.... He couldn't go there; he just couldn't. He sat down and stared at the phone, trying to breathe. *Flynn, I love you. Please call me so I can remind you.* The phone didn't ring.

ANOTHER two days passed before Flynn called. "Sorry, babe, we're in the middle of nowhere. No reception."

Josh struggled to get his breathing under control. "You couldn't have used a landline?"

"I didn't have time during the day, and I swear, no phones in the rooms. We're in this lodge thing, real rustic. Like, quilts on the beds and no TV either, not like I have time to watch it. It's been like this all week. Gary got us booked in all these hotels in like Siberia, so we don't get bugged by fans, and none of them have reception. We waste hours just driving back and forth to the venues. I'm so exhausted I can't think straight." He snorted. "I mean, I can't think gay… and that's really bad." He laughed, sounding weary, but Josh was filled with doubt.

Was Flynn telling the truth? "Aren't there any phones in the lobby? And none of the places you've stayed had phones in the rooms?" Josh knew he was nagging, but he couldn't help it.

"Baby, why the third degree? Yeah, some places have phones, but by the time I get back to my room, I'm too tired to even get undressed, and I forget to call you. As for calling from the lobby, I don't want to talk to you with other people around. It's not the same like when it's just us."

He forgot to call? "You could have at least phoned to let me know you were okay."

"Josh, don't be like that. Your last message said to call 'if I wanted to', and you never called back. I mean, I just got your messages, and I called because I did want to, but still. It's not like you've been calling off the hook. You could have called Gary if you were really worried."

Like Josh would call the band's manager to check up on his boyfriend. But it was time to back off. "I know. I'm sorry. I just miss you so much. I love you."

"I miss you too, baby, and I love you too." Flynn chuckled sleepily. "What are you wearing?"

ON THE day the marriage equality bill passed, Flynn's phone rang and rang. Josh tried three times that night, and his boyfriend never once answered. Although Josh joined the rest of the volunteers in a big victory bash, his mood was subdued. He kept thinking about Flynn and what he was doing, who he was with, who he was doing….

"Stop. Just stop," he said aloud. He knew Flynn and knew he was loyal; he wouldn't cheat. Josh was sure of it. Really, he was. Really.

IT WAS another three weeks before Bugs Are Nervous returned to finish their tour at a local arena. Josh was waiting when Flynn stepped off the bus. He wanted to fly into his lover's arms, but he wasn't sure how he would be received. Flynn looked exhausted and disheveled, but he smiled, put his arms around Josh, and kissed him.

"I'm so glad I'm home. I've missed that hot ass." Flynn punctuated his point by squeezing the cheeks in question.

Josh felt a lot better and grinned. "It's missed you too. Let's go home, and I'll show you how much."

Flynn drew back. "I'm so tired, babe; I'm going to have to take a rain check. All I want is a shower and a nap, not necessarily in that order. Shit, the others even want to get another rehearsal in tonight. We've got some new material we're trying out at the show tomorrow."

Josh tried to keep the disappointment off his face. "Sounds good. Let's get you home."

"Sorry, we're staying in a hotel tonight. The house is too far away. The commute would take too long. I'm so sick of traveling."

Josh couldn't help the ache that centered in his stomach. "Am I going to see you before the show?"

"Yeah, yeah, of course." At the words, Josh felt reassured. "You can stay at the hotel with me. We'll be up late, though, which is why I need a nap. You might not get a lot of sleep. I'm not sure you want to come."

And like that, Josh's relief was gone. "No, I better get home. I have to take care of Micro."

"Micro…. Fuck, I've missed her. Okay, but I want you to come see me before the show, okay? I really need to see you before I go onstage. You're my good luck charm."

It wasn't enough. Josh couldn't keep the sadness out of his voice. "Okay."

"Josh, please. It's real important to me that you be there."

"I said okay; I'll be there." He tried to sound more upbeat.

In a weird reverse echo of the last time they saw each other, Flynn asked, "Promise?"

Josh never broke a promise, ever, and Flynn knew that. "I promise."

THE arena was fairly large. As a homegrown band, Bugs Are Nervous drew a big crowd. Mainstream stations played their music here, not just those featuring alternative rock. It was very affirming for the band, and they always ended their tours with a concert in town.

Josh took a taxi, and even though the opening band, Vegetarian Meat, was already starting, the streets were packed. By the time he made it backstage, that set was half-done. When Josh entered the dressing room, Flynn's expression was a mask of stress, his body tight with tension, until he looked over and saw Josh. Then his face lit up as he strode over with a big grin. "You came!" He sounded like a little boy who had just been told Santa was coming this year after all.

"I—" Josh's phone rang.

Flynn froze, his expression flat. The ringtone told Josh it was someone from work, probably Ian. He didn't care. He pulled the phone out of his pocket, held it up between them, and ceremoniously turned it off. He stuck the phone back in his pocket.

"As I was saying—"

Flynn grabbed him in a bear hug. He kissed Josh on the neck and then whispered in his ear, "Thank you."

Josh squeezed back. He hoped he had proven his point; Flynn came first, his work a distant third, after Micro, of course. He used to be sure he rated higher on his lover's list, back before his boyfriend thought Josh's priorities were messed up, but now he was unsure of how Flynn felt. He just hoped he hadn't blown it and was still actually on his lover's list at all.

OUT in public in his hometown, Flynn could be a normal person, but after an incident backstage with an obsessive fan many years ago, he got a bodyguard. He used her when away from home, at any public event, and at all his shows, even those close to home. Many times over the years, Missy had proven worth her paycheck. The name couldn't be less apt. She was very tall, very wide, and all muscle. She couldn't have been less prissy. In a matter of seconds, she could flatten both Flynn and Josh at the same time. She was the best bodyguard Flynn had ever had, and he had run through quite a few that first year.

However, by all accounts she hated Josh. She had never said as much, but her cold reserve, her inability to talk to him, and the glares and snarls pretty much nailed it. He tried to convince himself it was just jealousy—she had been there first, and who wouldn't be attracted to Flynn? The man was a dark-haired Adonis. But by now, Missy should have come to terms with the fact that the rocker was gay and would never be anything else. Josh had always thought she should accept that he was there to stay too, but now he wasn't so sure himself, and it terrified him. He was absolutely positive the woman would blame him for any breakup, and in turn, break up his face—although, if he messed up and lost Flynn, Josh would let her.

At the break between acts, Missy escorted Josh to his assigned seat in the audience. The bands had a section roped off for their guests, and apparently she thought he was too dumb to find it himself. He was too scared of her to do anything but follow. He was surprised when she sat down beside him. He looked at her face, but she was staring straight ahead, expression unreadable. Damn. Flynn didn't trust him not to work while at the concert. Or maybe he thought Josh would take off. He sighed and settled into the less- than-comfortable seat.

Soon, the set started, Flynn jumping around the stage like he was on a pogo stick. The band started with one of their biggest hits, "Melting Through a Memory," a song about PTSD. Then Flynn took a moment to greet the audience and thank them for being there. Bugs Are Nervous began playing more hits, a Linkin Park cover, and a couple of lesser-known tunes. Flynn took time between songs to play to the audience. The fans ate it up. There was a lot of audience participation, and Flynn got cheers when he praised them and the state for voting for and passing the marriage equality law. The singer knew how to work a crowd, and people were screaming along to the music.

Flynn was moving nonstop and singing hard, belting out the songs with the band playing loud behind him. He was sweaty and probably exhausted, but it never showed. Josh thought his boyfriend had never looked sexier, and he sat entranced. When Flynn threw his hands over his head to urge the audience to sing along, his shirt rose above his low-slung leather pants, revealing an expanse of skin, a bit lower than normally shown in public. The smooth white was a contrast to the black clothing. Josh gasped and had to put his jacket in his lap. He was in love with the man inside, but he was also in love with the body.

Throughout it all, Missy remained indifferent, sitting stiffly upright in her chair. Josh asked himself again why the woman was there, as she didn't appear to be enjoying herself. He idly wondered if she ever watched the shows. Maybe she was used to watching from backstage and didn't appreciate having to sit with the commoners. He tried to ignore her and pay attention to his lover.

Near the end of the show, something unexpected happened. The guitar and bass players put down their instruments, grabbed stools, and picked up acoustic-electric guitars. The drummer sat back and crossed her arms. Flynn headed to the microphone stand.

"Thank you for being the best fans ever. It's always so good coming home!" The crowd roared. Flynn waited for the noise to die down before continuing. "We're going to try something quite different now, and we hope you'll like it." There were a few whoops and cheers, but the audience waited quietly for what would come next.

Josh was confused. When Flynn mentioned trying out new material, Josh just thought the band had a new song or two. He didn't expect anything out of the ordinary. He looked at Missy, who was smirking. A momentary flash of jealous pain washed through him; the bodyguard knew what was going on, and Josh didn't. He pushed it down when a second thought occurred to him. What if this was how Flynn was going to announce he had a new lover and was leaving Josh? It would be just like him to do something dramatic and public, like invite the new guy onstage and introduce the interloper as his new lover. Josh pushed the thought down. Flynn wouldn't do something that cruel. He wouldn't. This time he really was sure.

Josh shook his head and focused on his boyfriend. The band members were picking out a light melody, quiet, more like background music than anything. Flynn was nodding along to the tune a bit, like he was gearing up for something. He looked decidedly nervous. Flynn anxious? During a show? That was weird—really weird.

Finally, Flynn turned to the audience. "As you folks know, I'm gay and out and proud." Lots of cheering and catcalls followed. "I've hit the jackpot and have a wonderful, amazing man in my life." Josh tried to swallow the lump that suddenly grew in his throat. "When I'm on the road, I miss him so much it hurts." The fans were absolutely silent.

Finally, Flynn moved his gaze to look at Josh. With all the spotlights on him, it was unlikely the singer could even make out where Josh was in the crowd, let alone meet his eyes. Yet somehow, Flynn was staring right at him.

"While on this tour, I wrote a song to let him know what he means to me and how hard it is being away from him all the time. I hope you like it."

There were a few claps and more whistling, but mostly people remained silent. Flynn put the microphone back on its stand, adjusting it a little. He took a deep breath, opened his mouth, and let forth the most beautiful voice Josh had ever heard. It wasn't the half scream or growl or shout the audience was used to. It wasn't the soft croon he heard at night when he was sung to sleep. It was the voice of an angel.

Josh was frozen, transfixed, as Flynn began his song a cappella. After the first chorus, the guitarists began to play again, but the instruments were soft and distant, providing only background to Flynn's singing.

The lyrics were beautiful, talking about his undying love, the loneliness he felt while on the road, how he ached for his lover's touch, and the joy he felt when he heard Josh's voice. Flynn sang about how frustrating the long hours were. He loved his fans and didn't begrudge the need for hard work. It was just that he was often so exhausted when he finally got to the hotel, he only had a few minutes to talk to his boyfriend he adored. Sometimes this reality was too much to bear, and he wrote his feelings down in a song instead of calling and having to hang up so soon. At those times, he would lower his head, ashamed for being a coward.

Genuine pain ripped through Josh as he realized what Flynn was saying. This tour had been particularly hard and time-consuming, and rather than having an affair, Flynn was just too distraught to talk. He was spending his time writing this song instead. Josh felt like the worst kind of heel for doubting this man who loved him so much. The feeling with which he sang the song left no doubt.

But it was the beauty of Flynn's voice, the range he had, and his ability to sustain long, high notes that was the most amazing part of the song. During the dark parts, the melody sank deep in his register. When the words turned to great passion, Flynn's voice rose higher and higher until his voice hit notes at the very top of the possible male register, and

Josh had to remember to breathe. Flynn's range was extraordinary, and the power of his singing mesmerized the crowd. In Josh's opinion, Flynn was better than any Amy Winehouse.

Little could be heard from the stage other than Flynn singing, and not a sound came from below. The piece ended on a very high note, which his boyfriend sustained longer than Josh thought possible, and when he finished, there was dead silence until the audience erupted. Anyone who had been sitting was now on his or her feet, and the applause and yelling were deafening.

Josh stood but swayed, dizzy with emotion and shock. Flynn could really sing. Josh had never doubted it, not really, but still, he hadn't been prepared for that incredible ability. He'd make sure Flynn stopped hiding his talent; Josh would make his boyfriend sing to him every night. That was if Josh didn't have a stroke from the excitement and collapse and die first.

A strong hand grabbed his elbow to steady him, and he glanced at Missy. The expression on her face was unfamiliar, but he thought she might have smiled for a moment. Then she helped him sit, as his legs were too weak to keep him upright. Once seated, he quickly turned back to the stage, where Flynn was looking almost bashful as he waited for the noise to die down again.

"Thank you, thank you. You are all incredible, and we appreciate your support. A lot of people are unable to be out and proud, or they suffer alone without anyone standing by them when they face the cruelty of the ignorant." Flynn could be eloquent when he wanted. "I am profoundly grateful for my bandmates"—he gestured to the rest of Bugs Are Nervous—"and to you, our fans. You have embraced who I am." There were more cheers and shouting. "I have just one more thing I need to do. Would you all like to meet the man who inspired that song?" Again, the audience screamed and stomped their feet. "All right, people, I give you Josh Flohr!"

Josh stopped breathing for real this time. He couldn't move. He hated crowds; he hated being the center of attention. He really hated being the center of attention in front of a crowd. What was Flynn doing?

The crowd began pounding their feet and clapping their hands in rhythm. "Josh! Josh! Josh! Josh!"

He felt like he was going to faint. Missy clutched his arm and pulled him to his feet. The sudden action got his lungs somewhat working again, and he struggled to keep breathing as the bodyguard led him to the aisle. He followed along only because he would fall if he didn't; his legs were still noodly. When he got to the steps leading to the stage, he could see Flynn, halfway down, grinning at him. Josh tensed his jaw. No one was getting any tonight. His boyfriend would pay for this, angelic singing or not.

Halfway up the stairs, Missy had to put an arm around his waist to steady him as he grew more and more terrified. Josh focused on Flynn's face and concentrated on taking one step at a time. The singer's expression was completely supportive. Josh could imagine Flynn was saying internally, "You can do it, you can do it." *Fuck you, Flynn.* But his eyes were also full of love, and Josh glommed on to that as he stumbled across the stage.

When he reached his lover, he grabbed for the outstretched hand as though he would die if he didn't. Flynn whispered, "Look at me—don't look at anything else. It's just you and me, baby." Josh tried; he really did. He was still terrified, but he held his boyfriend's gaze and tried to calm himself. Somewhere along the way, Missy had disappeared, and Josh gripped Flynn's hand like a lifeline, taking strength from his boyfriend in order to remain upright.

Flynn adjusted the microphone, and the crowd quieted. "Josh, the first time I saw you, you took my breath away. I knew I had to get to know you, so I did everything I could to make that happen. We became friends. Within a very short time, I knew you were the one, no doubt in my mind." There wasn't any sound, so the audience must have been hanging on every word. Josh tried not to think about them and focused instead on what Flynn was saying, which was making his cheeks flame.

"You are the smartest man I've ever known. No one can make me laugh like you do. Your kindness and generosity blow me away. Sometimes I get jealous because you do so much for everyone, but I always know it's who you are, and you could no more turn away a person in need than you could stop breathing." Josh wasn't sure about that. He was having a hard time breathing right now.

"You've been there for me through everything: celebrating with me during the good times and being my rock through the bad. When I'm in your arms, I feel safe and loved. Every day I wonder how I got so lucky that the man of my dreams loves me back." What? Didn't Flynn know that Josh was the lucky one?

Suddenly, Flynn sank to one knee, and all thoughts left Josh's head. "I want to spend my life with you. I want to be there for you as you've been there for me. I want to be yours and you to be mine forever." There was something in Flynn's hand, which he was holding out. "Joshua Doren Flohr, will you make me the happiest man on the planet and marry me?"

Josh's legs gave out, and he fell to his knees too. He didn't even have to think about his answer. "Yes! Oh God, yes, yes, yes," he whispered. But his words were amplified by the microphone, which apparently worked just fine picking up sound down there. As his boyfriend—*no, fiancé*—slipped the ring on his finger, his ears filled with the sounds of the fans showing their support with great gusto at great decibels.

Flynn's smile took over his whole face, and Josh was shocked to see tears in his lover's eyes. Flynn gently placed his hands beneath Josh's jaw, leaned down, and kissed him, slow and deep. If the crowd had been loud before, the sound was positively ear-splitting now. Josh barely heard them. He pulled Flynn into his arms and lost himself in the embrace. He needed Micro's cleanup service again.

Eventually, Flynn pulled them to their feet. He kissed Josh's hand and whispered, "Love you, baby, so goddamn much." The fans were too loud to hear that, so it was just for Josh. He couldn't speak over the lump in his throat, instead trying to convey his love with his eyes. Then Missy was there leading him offstage. He held Flynn's gaze until he stumbled, and then let the bodyguard herd him out of sight. He tripped on a cord and she had to catch him. He looked up to thank her and saw her hiding a grin. She could grin? His thoughts left that wonder as she hoisted him up and carried him back to the dressing room. He was too overwhelmed to be embarrassed. Mostly. Behind him, the crowd was back to normal loudness again as Bugs are Nervous began playing another hit, "Digging Her Grave," about a Tulalip tribeswoman coping with life on the reservation.

Missy put him down. "Congratulations. You've made Flynn very happy and that makes me happy." Josh blinked. Was he in an alternate universe? No, this was too fabulous. He must be dreaming all of this. Still smiling, she said, "If you break his heart, I will break every bone in your body." She didn't look like she was joking, and he was relieved when she left.

Marriage. It was now legal in this state. He was marrying Flynn. He was marrying Flynn! His heart soared. He had never been happier.

"I NOW pronounce you husband and husband. It's time for you to kiss." The Unitarian minister smiled as Flynn grabbed Josh and pulled him into a tight embrace, proceeding to try to suck his throat out through his mouth. Around them, family and friends applauded and whistled. When they separated, Josh knew he was grinning like a lovesick puppy. His husband was the most beautiful man he had ever seen, the most amazing person he'd ever known. He reveled in his good fortune.

Josh took Flynn's arm and turned down the aisle. Everyone was standing and smiling. Even his usually stoic father joined in and tossed rose petals over their heads as they walked. Flynn was clutching him back, finally stopping midway along to pull Josh in for another kiss.

Out in the foyer of the little chapel, they kissed once more; then Josh dragged his husband into the room they had gotten dressed in. Micro, their Best Dog and ring bearer, followed, slipping in just before Josh closed and locked the door. Flynn narrowed his eyes, and Josh gave him a sly smile.

"We're alone." Josh smirked. Flynn nodded slowly. "We need to take our clothes off to change into our other outfits for the reception."

"We're guys, Josh. We only have one outfit." His husband's clothing was custom-made and looked more like something Sid Vicious would have worn than the more traditional tuxedo Josh was wearing. Just looking at Flynn in the outfit made Josh's heart beat faster.

"Hmm. Well, we shouldn't be the first ones to the reception. That just isn't done." Micro barked in agreement.

Flynn narrowed his eyes. "Okaayyy...."

Josh reached for the fastener on his husband's pants. "I think it's time we consummated our marriage."

"So soon?"

"Sweetheart, as soon as I saw you in those clothes, all I could think about was taking them off you." He demonstrated his feelings by untucking the shirt and tugging at the pant zipper. Micro sighed and hopped up on a chair for a quick snooze. She was familiar with this routine.

"Well, I can't deny you anything." Flynn laughed into Josh's mouth and pulled him closer.

When they came up for air, Josh stopped his husband's roving hands for a moment. "Flynn, this is the happiest day of my life. I don't even want the party. I just want to take you and Micro home and start our lives as husbands."

Flynn laughed again. "Baby, don't worry. We have forever. You're never getting rid of me."

"No kidding. Missy said she'd kill me if I even tried to leave you. She's one scary woman." Then Josh grew more serious. He pulled his husband closer and buried his head in his true love's neck. He whispered, "I'm never letting you go. You're all I've ever wanted." He breathed in Flynn's scent; it smelled like home. "You're my one and only. Now make love to me." And so his husband did.

S. H. ALLAN has been a therapeutic foster parent for almost fourteen years, focusing on teenagers—which is a lot like herding cats, but a lot more rewarding. Dogs make her happy, and the senior dogs for which she provides hospice have to tolerate a giddy younger pup or three. Whenever possible, she ignores them all in favor of reading smutty gay love stories. S. H. knew writing was her destiny when her classic, *Mr. Cuke and Mrs. Tomato*, was put in the school library in third grade (coincidentally, along with the stories written by all her classmates). Politically active and socially conscious, with a useless M.A. and over twenty-five years working in high tech, S. H. fits in well in her beloved Pacific Northwest, except for that health conscious stuff. Tofurkey is one thing, but she says, "Seriously, no donuts?"

S. H. loves to hear from readers. She can be reached at shallanmm@yahoo.com or https://www.facebook.com/shallanmm.

The Making of a Family

Caitlin Ricci

TIRED, hungry, and sore from the long plane ride, Arden barely made it up to the front step of his town house without stumbling on the way up. The only thing that kept him going was knowing that his boyfriend, Serio, was waiting for him. He'd have dinner ready, and they could spend the evening on the couch watching old movies like they always did when he came home from a business trip.

He put his key in the lock, but before he could turn it, the front door opened wide, and Serio stood before him.

"Hey," Arden greeted him, smiling as he dropped his suitcase on the front porch and reached for the tall Latin man. But his smile quickly died on his lips as Serio stepped away from him.

"Arden... I...."

His gaze dropped to the duffel bag at Serio's feet. "What were you—"

"You weren't supposed to be home yet." Serio shifted away and stuffed his hands into the pockets of his jeans as Arden continued to stare at him.

"I took an earlier flight to get home sooner," he explained. "Were you...." He swallowed thickly, his throat refusing to make the sounds. "Were you leaving?" The thought of the thing he'd said was nearly impossible to bear. If Serio had any family, he'd have thought he was going to visit them. Maybe someone was sick. But that wasn't the case.

Serio refused to look at him. "I left you a note."

"*Mi cara...*," Arden whispered, the endearment easily leaving his chapped lips. "Don't go. Please. We'll talk. Work this out. Don't leave me."

Serio's face pinched as he shook his head. "It's too late."

Arden didn't believe that for a moment. "Never. I'm here now. Let me know what I did wrong. I'll fix it. Right now. Whatever it is."

"There's no fixing it. Not this time." His mouth set into a firm line, Serio bent down to pick up his duffel bag, but Arden's hand on his arm stopped him.

"There's always time," he quietly insisted. His lover had tears in his eyes, making the warm chocolate-brown of his irises look like they were about to run. "Oh, *mi bella,* don't cry. We'll get this sorted." He stepped forward, taking Serio's face in his hands and laying a gentle kiss on his cheek. "Talk to me. Give me a chance to make it right."

Shaking his head, Serio backed away. Arden followed him, though, staying close to his partner of the past five years. Anything was fixable; they'd promised each other that. No matter what, they could fix this. They had to. He closed the front door behind him. "Serio? Tell me what's going on," Arden softly demanded, putting his hands on Serio's muscular upper arms.

"You weren't supposed to be home yet," Serio whispered, his voice breaking through his tears. "This was supposed to be easy."

Arden shook his head. "What? Leaving me?" When Serio didn't correct him, Arden's mouth fell open. "With only a note to explain everything?"

Flushing, Serio turned away from him. "It was a good note."

"It was still a fucking note!" Arden loudly snapped at him. Serio flinched, and Arden sighed. "All right. I'm sorry. Look, I'm tired. I've been traveling most of the day. Let's talk about this. "

"But see, that's the problem," Serio said, stepping around him. Though he was damn tired, Arden moved to quickly block his path. "Move out of the way. Please."

Arden shook his head. "No." He tried to wrap his arms around Serio's stomach, but his lover stepped out of his way. "What's the problem?"

Serio pursed his lips. "You can't keep me here. I want to leave. Get out of the way, Arden."

He tried to catch him again, and thankfully this time Serio didn't get away. Though he didn't let go of the duffel bag in his hands, he let Arden hug him. "Talk to me," he pleaded, his face pressed against the hard planes of Serio's broad chest. He breathed deeply, letting his lover's familiar scent fill his nose, and smiled. "You used the new soap I got you before I left. The goat's milk stuff."

The duffel bag fell to the floor, and Serio's arms came around him. "I did. And I liked it a lot. It made my skin really soft."

Arden nodded, glad he'd been able to get him something that helped his perpetual dry skin. "If you drank more water...," he lightly teased him.

Serio snorted and kissed the top of Arden's much shorter head. "You still have to let me go, babe." He tried getting out of Arden's hold, but Arden refused to let him.

"No," Arden stubbornly refused.

"The taxi is probably already waiting out there. I can't just leave him there," Serio argued.

Arden shook his head. "Yes, you can. Let him go. Talk to me. No notes, no trying to leave right now. Just talk to me." He took a breath. "Please. I love you."

Serio sighed deeply against his cheek. "I love you too. But it's not enough anymore. We can talk, though. So many years...." He stepped back, and this time Arden let him. Serio shook his head. "A note doesn't seem adequate anymore. Not now that you're home."

"Damn straight," Arden agreed. He took Serio's hand and let him lead him to the living room. He took the other end of their big cream sofa as Serio sat down. "This is all coming out of nowhere. I had no idea that you were thinking about going," he softly said, reaching for Serio's hand.

Serio took his fingers in a loose grip between them. "No. Maybe not. But we've been having trouble for months."

Arden nodded. "Ever since I took this job. But we've talked about the time away, the long business trips. I thought we were okay. Not great. But okay. So what changed about today?" With a sigh, Serio pulled his hand back even as Arden tried to cling to it. "No, please don't pull away. We're talking now. I can make this up to you. I'll be better. Do more. Whatever you need. Just stay here with me. Right here in this moment." Arden knew he was pleading, practically begging, and also knew he'd do a whole lot more than this to keep Serio in his life. They weren't perfect. Not by a long shot. But no couple was, and they'd been through a lot together in the past few years. Moves, losing friends, family rejection—everything had taken its toll. But they'd gotten through it. "We can get through this too," Arden said, giving voice to his desperate thoughts.

Serio roughly wiped at his tanned cheeks. His eyes were already puffy, as if this hadn't been his first time crying tonight. Arden moved closer, hating to see his lover upset by anything, but especially because he'd somehow caused the hurt he could see glistening back at him through Serio's brown eyes.

"You don't even know what's wrong," he whispered.

Arden shook his head. "No, I don't. But I would if you told me."

"I shouldn't have to tell you, though," Serio grumbled.

"Now, that's not fair," Arden said, sighing. Sure, it would be great if he could figure out what had made Serio upset enough to leave a note and want to walk out on their life together. It would make things easier at the very least. But nothing was coming to mind. Of course, maybe if he'd actually had a good night's sleep in the past few months, his brain would work better. As it was, he was barely able to concentrate on their conversation.

Serio got up, but he didn't go far. Instead he went to their dark oak mantel and stared down at the pictures there. They were sort of photo junkies, taking pictures of everything and keeping it all right there on display. Arden didn't know what frame Serio was holding, but by the way he smiled, he was sure it was a good memory. They all were.

"Tell me. Please," Arden begged. "I'm not perfect—"

"No one asked you to be." Serio put the picture back.

"But I'm trying," Arden continued. "For you."

Serio joined him on the couch again, though this time he sat much closer, and Arden wrapped his arm around Serio's shoulders as he turned to rest his head against Arden's chest. His arm came around Arden's stomach, and he pulled Serio close. He kissed Serio's forehead and laid his cheek against his lover's spiky black hair.

"I didn't forget our anniversary or your birthday," Arden said aloud. But there wasn't too much else that would have upset Serio so much.

Serio shook his head and sniffled. Arden squeezed him tighter, hating to see his partner so upset. "She'd have been two today."

And there it was, the reason Serio was so upset. Arden felt like an ass for forgetting their would-be daughter's birthday. "I'm sorry. I hadn't thought about it."

"You don't think about her?" Serio sounded surprised.

Arden shook his head and frowned, feeling not only like an idiot for not remembering, but also like an ass for not thinking about the little girl who was almost theirs. "No. You do?"

Serio nodded. "All the time." His shoulders shook, and Arden held him tighter. "Think she's okay?"

"Of course she is." Arden was adamant about that. Just as he'd always been so. "If there's a heaven, she's there."

"Thank you," Serio whispered. "Why don't you still think about her?"

Shrugging, Arden looked out the large bay window to his left. It was fully dark now, and the old iron streetlights were coming on. "She's gone. Has been for years. Thinking about her won't bring her back."

"But it doesn't erase what she was," Serio replied, his voice muffled by his tears and Arden's jacket.

"No, it doesn't," Arden agreed. "And I'm so sorry I forgot. We can go to her grave tonight if you want. Or tomorrow morning. There's the little flower shop on the way. We could pick up some white roses. Or yellow ones." He took a breath. "And I'm so sorry for not calling you.

For not remembering her birthday. It's not because I don't remember her. Or what she meant to us."

Serio wiped his eyes on Arden's shirt and slowly sat up, though he didn't move away any more than that, for which Arden was grateful. He'd really screwed up this time and needed the reassurance that Serio was going to stay nearby. Even if it was just while they talked.

"She was so small," Serio whispered. He spread his hands apart a few inches. Then, after appearing to reconsider his measurements, he opened his hands a bit wider.

Arden nodded. "Yeah, she was." He went quiet, remembered pain drawing him back to the memories he so rarely visited. The smell of the hospital room came back to him first, a young woman's hand in his, her shaky words as she apologized for something none of them could have prevented. A simple car accident, a driver skidding on ice and running into her as she waited to cross the street, had taken away their dreams of being a complete family.

He reached for Serio's hand and gave his fingers a light squeeze. "Do you want to call Jenny? I'm sure she's probably hurting too."

Serio's fingers went still in his. "Damn," he whispered. "I didn't even think to call her. Last year she called us; we had lunch and cried. Today all I could think was how you weren't here when I needed you."

"That's going to change. Starting today," Arden promised him.

Serio's brown gaze lifted to his own. "How?" he asked, sounding cautiously hopeful.

The answer was simple, though it would probably involve a lot more than he was considering with his sleep-addled brain. "I'll quit."

"You can't," Serio protested, his mouth falling open.

Arden frowned at him as his partner pulled away. "Why not? Won't that fix everything?"

He shook his head. "You love your job. You're good at it. You've even won awards. People like what you write."

Snorting, Arden shook his head. "It's a travel magazine, not some groundbreaking news. They won't miss me. Besides, we'd talked about me quitting or working from home writing articles back when Jenny got pregnant. It's not an impossible goal to have us both here."

Serio slowly nodded. "Yeah, we did. But that was when we were planning on having a baby. Now…."

Arden leaned forward and quieted his concerns with a gentle kiss. "You were going to leave me tonight, and I didn't remember something pretty damn important to us both. If that's not a wake-up call to bring me back to the reality of what's actually important in my life, then I'm not really sure what is."

Still, Serio looked uncertain. "I don't want you to quit just for me. That's not fair to you."

"It's not just for you, darling. I'm going to quit for both of us. Because you're right. I've been away a lot since I started this job, and it's not fair to you or us. I'll call my boss in the morning, and I think we should call Jenny tonight. Just to check up on her. I'm sure she's probably pretty lonely right now." Arden's decision was made, and with it he felt stronger, like he'd taken the first giant step to putting their relationship first again. Right where it belonged. They'd had some rough times since the accident, and though he'd always believed they'd get through it in the end, that their relationship was strong enough to fight through anything, tonight had been the reality check he'd needed.

He silently rose from the couch and held his hand out for Serio to take. "Let's go to upstairs." It was Serio's choice whether or not to join him, to want to be with him again so soon after packing up his things and wanting to leave, though Arden seriously hoped they could put that behind him tonight.

Serio took his hand, and Arden helped him to his feet. He wrapped his arms around Serio's narrow waist and caressed his slim hips. "You had every right to want to leave," Arden whispered, kissing along his lover's stubble-covered jaw.

"No, it was rash," Serio softly said, lowering his chin just enough for Arden to lick it.

Secretly, Arden agreed with him. But he also knew Serio had his reasons, and Arden promised himself he'd do everything possible to make these past few months up to Serio. Quitting his job so he was around full-time might have seemed like a big thing, and to others it probably was, but for Arden it was a small price to pay in order to make their relationship work.

His long fingers went to the buttons of Serio's shirt as he opened his mouth for a kiss. Serio's arms settled around his shoulders, and his hands went to the back of Arden's hair, pulling him closer and deepening their kiss. Arden's fingertips slipped over Serio's chest, seeking the smooth planes of his muscles and the soft nubs of his nipples. He found them and scraped his short nails over their points, getting a hiss from Serio in return.

"Let's stay down here," Serio whispered, helping Arden unbutton his shirt the rest of the way until he was able to strip it off. It fell to the sofa beside them, and Arden brought his mouth to Serio's neck before trailing soft kisses down his collarbone. He rested his cheek against Serio's heart, listening to the erratic beat with a soft smile.

"I don't ever want to lose you," Arden said, turning his head and kissing Serio's chest right above his heart.

Serio shook his head. "I don't want to lose you either. Thanks for coming home early."

Chuckling, Arden went to his knees to continue kissing down Serio's stomach. "Thanks for listening instead of simply walking out."

Flushed, Serio shook his head and trailed his fingers through Arden's hair. "I'd have come back. I thought leaving would help me think, figure out why it was that I was so fixated on her birthday and why it was so important that you didn't remember it too."

"Because it's the day she died," Arden softly answered him. "She lived all of three hours outside Jenny's body. We each got to hold her once the doctors realized there was nothing that could be done for her, and that's a memory I'll cherish for the rest of my life. But her birthday is still the day she died. I prefer to think about the day Jenny called us a few months before that, so happy that her voice was high-pitched and hard to understand as she tried to explain to us that the fertilization took. That she was pregnant with our child. We went out to dinner and a movie, held her hands, rubbed her belly even if there was no visible sign that she was pregnant yet. Do you remember?"

Serio nodded and wiped his cheeks. Arden was surprised to realize he'd started crying as well. "We all got manicures the next day and pedicures the day after. We made up reasons to spend time with her, the mother of our future child. I don't think I'd ever spent that much time with a woman before that. Back then she was bubbly and bright, quick with a smile and a laugh."

"She was happy," Arden confirmed for him. "Not only because she was having a baby, but because she was having our baby. She always said that. Remember? That it wasn't just that she was pregnant, but that, in her eyes, we were the perfect dads."

Serio gave his hair a playful tug. "We would have been great dads. Our daughter would have been loved, cared for. Cherished."

Arden licked his lips and tilted his head back so he could better see Serio's face. "We could still be," he whispered.

"Yeah. We should get a puppy or something," Serio said, nodding.

Arden shook his head and took hold of Serio's hands. He was serious about this and needed his partner to listen. "No. I mean it, darling. We could be great parents. We would have been. We could still be that for some lucky little kid out there."

Serio's breath sucked in on a loud hiss, and he fell to his knees in front of Arden. His brown eyes were wide and wet as he stared into Arden's. "What are you saying?"

Arden pulled Serio's hands into his lap. "Exactly what you think I am." He smiled softly, his heart beating wildly as he considered it all. Two years ago they'd had everything planned out. Could they get there again? Was it the right time, the right place? Were they the same as they had been? He didn't have all the answers, but he knew talking about the idea was the right thing at that moment.

"It wouldn't replace her," Serio quickly said, his voice taking on a stern edge.

"No, of course not," Arden replied. "What happened with her was tragic, and nothing will ever replace her for us. But maybe it's time to consider being a family again."

Serio appeared to consider his words. He pulled his lower lip between his teeth and looked to the mantel. This time Arden looked along with him and his gaze landed on a simple framed black-and-white photograph. He rose, his unsteady steps taking him over there even when he hadn't really thought of picking up the old image. By the time he thought better of putting his hands on the photo he rarely looked at because the memories were too painful, he was already holding it and belatedly wondering why his hands were shaking.

"She was so tiny," he whispered, echoing Serio's earlier words as he stared down at the grainy ultrasound. His thumb brushed against the curve of her skull. There was a time when he'd been able to see her in various stages of growing up all over their home. She'd be coloring at the table, trying on dresses in the bright-yellow bedroom they'd decorated for her, eating popcorn with her friends and watching a scary movie in the living room, or being tucked into bed. His gaze went to Serio, still kneeling on the carpet and smiling across the room at him.

"I used to picture her," he said, admitting something he'd never told him. "Before the accident, I saw her everywhere. And you with her."

"Was I good to her?" Serio asked.

Smiling, Arden wiped at his tears. "You were great." He put the ultrasound back and returned to him, sinking down on his butt next to him. "Really gentle. She giggled at just the sight of you."

Serio nodded and curled his fingers into Arden's. "I bet you were good too."

Arden shrugged. "I was okay. As much as I want to be there for the baby parts, and I plan to be, the toddler times are when I think she and I would have had a lot of fun. Coloring, painting, dressing up, doing our hair...." He shook his head and pressed his lips together as his shoulders shook. "We would have been great dads."

"Yeah, we would have. I think we could be again, though," Serio said, his voice sounding lighter and more hopeful than Arden had heard it in a long time.

Arden nodded. "I think so too. I'll call Jenny tomorrow. I haven't spoken to her in over a month. It'll be good to hear her voice."

Serio smiled. "It really will. And then we can ask her again. No pressure; she doesn't have to go through it again. Losing the baby was rough on us, but Jenny damn near broke."

"Things will be different this time, though," Arden promised him, giving his hand a squeeze. "We'll be parents. Someday, somehow, we'll get there. I love you, and we will make this work."

Serio leaned against him and gave his shoulder a light bump. "You know, I think you might just be right. And I love you too, Arden."

Smiling, Arden leaned his head back against the sofa and looked forward to the future for the first time in years.

CAITLIN RICCI was fortunate growing up to be surrounded by family and teachers who encouraged her love of reading. She has always been a voracious reader and that love of the written word easily morphed into a passion for writing. If she isn't writing, she can usually be found studying as she works toward her counseling degree. She comes from a military family and the men and women of the armed forces are close to her heart. She also enjoys gardening and horseback riding in the Colorado Rockies, which she calls home with her wonderful fiancé, their dog, and their blue-tongue skink. Her belief that there is no one true path to happily ever after runs deeply through all her stories.

Remember When

River Clair

"So. We didn't do anything on New Year's Eve because you were in the middle of a project for your internship."

"Mmhmm."

"And we missed Valentine's Day because you had a paper due."

"Mmmm."

"And of course the last two hundred and seventy-six or so weekends were spent on various other projects and papers and whatever else since you started on your scholarly path to enlightenment, or 'master's in social work', as you like to call it."

Ben waited for another distracted hum from his boyfriend, but Aaron had apparently found something extremely interesting in the ridiculously thick textbook he was reading while also balancing his laptop on his long legs and scribbling in a notepad by his side. Ben sighed and slid his bare feet across the sofa and under Aaron's thigh. If his man was going to ignore him, at least he could help him stay warm. And why was it so damn cold anyway? This was supposed to be California, not some godforsaken cold-ass place with snow and other unmentionable horrors. Ben gave an irritated glance out the window at steady gray rain and shoved his cold toes farther under Aaron's leg before continuing.

"So anyway, my *point*, since you insist on dragging it out of me, is that a certain date is coming up, and we're going to celebrate even if I have to hire three bears and a drag queen dressed as Goldilocks to kidnap your skinny ass for a day away."

Ben paused again, but there was still no response from the other end of the sofa as Aaron chewed on the cap of his pen and frowned at whatever he was reading. As irritating as it was to be ignored, Ben couldn't help admiring the view of Aaron's profile—high brow and long slim nose, soft thick honey-colored curls an unruly mess that Ben wanted to mess up even more. But he forced himself back to the topic at hand, determined to get Aaron's attention.

"Also, those three bears I mentioned?" Ben continued. "They're coming along with us, because I'm pretty sure the five-year gift is supposed to be a big furry orgy, or at least that's what my Gramma's etiquette handbook said."

This last statement seemed to have the desired effect, because Aaron finally stopped writing and looked over at Ben with a confused expression.

"What about your grandmother? Did you say she's going on a date?"

Ben couldn't help laughing. It really wasn't fair of him to try to get Aaron to participate in a conversation while he was studying. On the other hand, Aaron was pretty much always studying, so whatever. Ben was going to keep teasing him, but something about Aaron's sincerely bewildered expression and the tired shadows under his beautiful brown eyes stopped him, and instead he scooted forward and pressed a kiss against Aaron's unresisting mouth.

"No, my precious nerd, my Gramma is very still very happily married to my grandfather, and the date I'm talking about is one for you and me. A date to celebrate a certain date of our own. Ringing any bells?"

Aaron stared at Ben with the same intensity he had when faced with a particularly challenging test question, and Ben was just wondering how many more hints he'd have to drop when his boyfriend's eyes widened with sudden recognition.

"Our anniversary!" Aaron exclaimed and grinned as Ben rolled his eyes and nodded. "Oh my God, I'm so sorry. I swear I would have remembered, baby."

"Of course you would've," Ben said. "Just as soon as that Google alert popped up in your e-mail." He winked and waved away Aaron's attempt at a protest. "But never mind that, because I want to tell you what I've got in mind for us to celebrate. Well, not exactly *tell* you, because most of it is a secret. In fact"—Ben thought for a moment—"in fact, I really can't tell you anything, other than I'll be picking you up after your Saturday morning class next week for a little whirlwind getaway."

Ben sat back to let Aaron absorb this news, but when he saw Aaron's eyes dart to the open textbook, he clapped a hand quickly to Aaron's mouth and spoke before Aaron could start with the excuses.

"I know what you're thinking, and I happen to know that you have a quiz on Tuesday and a paper due Thursday, but then you've got a week before anything major. And I also happen to know that you deserve a break, and *we* deserve to celebrate five fucking years together, and all work and no play makes Aaron a dull boy, and a stitch in time saves nine and et cetera. *And* I know that I won't take any excuses this time, so don't even. Do *not* even."

Ben eyed Aaron warily until he felt a smile twitching under his fingers, and he drew his hand away, only to have Aaron grab it and kiss his palm.

"No excuses, I promise. And thank you. You're kind of awesome, you know that?"

"Well, duh!" Ben said. "Of course I'm awesome. My boyfriend has excellent taste in men."

Aaron laughed, and Ben took advantage, quickly moving textbook, notepad, and laptop onto the coffee table before maneuvering himself into Aaron's lap and silencing any potential protests with another kiss, this one with more intent behind it. There was more than one way to get warm on a cold gloomy day, and over the past few years Ben had learned how to make his boyfriend forget his studies for a while and focus on something less cerebral. He might be a lot smaller than Aaron, but it wasn't brute strength that helped Ben get his way in these matters; it was finesse. Or at least really skillful kissing.

Leaning back after a few moments to gauge the effect, Ben was gratified to see the heat in Aaron's eyes and to feel Aaron's fingers tighten on Ben's hips, drawing him closer. He ran his fingers through Aaron's loose ringlets—*cupid hair,* Ben always called it, which made Aaron roll his eyes and counter that it was *stupid* hair. Ben had realized long ago that his boyfriend might be smart in many ways but he was also amazingly dumb in others, such as recognizing how hot he was. Which is where Ben came in. And soon enough the rain and the cold were swept away by the heat building between them, and textbooks were forgotten as they studied each other's bodies with hands that were knowledgeable but still always finding new things to learn.

TEN days later, Ben watched Aaron walk out of the campus library chatting animatedly with a group of students, and he leaned on the horn to get his boyfriend's attention. Aaron's face lit up when he spotted the car, and he waved quickly to his classmates and left them behind as he broke into a trot. The autumn sun turned his hair gold, and he was wearing the soft red sweater Ben had gifted him that morning, which looked fabulous on him, if Ben did say so himself.

"Hey." Aaron grinned as he got into the car, wrestling off his bulging backpack. Ben reached over to help him, hefted it into the backseat, and leaned over the console to greet him with a hearty kiss.

"Hey to you. Have I told you how smoking you look in red?" Ben waved away the self-deprecating answer Aaron was ready to give. "Whatever, whatever, just accept it."

"Well, I got a ton of compliments on the sweater, so thank you," Aaron said. "And you're looking quite delicious yourself, my love," Aaron swept Ben with an appreciative glance that warmed Ben's heart. "I love that blue shirt on you. Matches your eyes."

"So you've said. But are we going to sit here and pay each other compliments or get this show on the road?" Ben teased. "Okay, listen— here's the rules for today: no studying, no thinking about school, no worrying about tests. This day is about you and me. Deal?"

"Deal," Aaron agreed readily, and Ben, satisfied, patted his head and kissed him again. He glanced into the rearview mirror and ran a quick hand through his own dark hair, checking to see if all the effort he'd put into crafting soft spikes hadn't been wasted; then he checked to make sure Aaron was wearing his seat belt and pulled away from the curb.

"So where are we going?" Aaron asked.

But Ben refused to tell him, so Aaron had to be content with waiting until they got to their first destination. About twenty minutes later, they reached the outskirts of the city, and Ben pulled into a small parking lot. Aaron raised his eyebrows.

"The antiques store where I used to work?"

Ben grinned at him. "Okay, so here's the big reveal: the theme of the day is 'a walk down memory lane', and we're going to revisit some of the places where we had relationship milestones."

"Milestones?"

"Yeah, like significant moments. The memories that really stand out, you know?"

"Okay." Aaron nodded. "That sounds fantastic. I hope you remember that I have a really shitty memory, though."

Ben laughed. "Don't I know it. But I promise, these are the real highlights. Unforgettable. And this little antiques store is the site of memory number one. What happened here?"

"Well, I worked here for a couple of years," Aaron said.

"And?" Ben prompted.

"Um, and then I got a better job with potential for advancement?"

Ben rolled his eyes and got out of the car, beckoning Aaron to follow. They walked into the large cluttered store. Mrs. Eggers was at the front counter finishing up with a customer, but she exclaimed at the sight of Aaron, and Ben waited patiently as they hugged and chatted excitedly with each other. When after a few minutes another customer walked up to the register carrying a ghastly bronze lamp, Ben took his opportunity and pulled Aaron away from his former boss and through the warrenlike aisles of the store, stopping at last in a little tucked-away section filled with overflowing shelves of antique jars, bottles, and glassware of every imaginable size and color. He stopped and gazed at Aaron expectantly, but Aaron still looked clueless.

"Babe, this is where we met!" Ben exclaimed. "Remember? I came into the store to get out of the rain, and I had no intention of buying anything, but then here you were unpacking a box of old medicine jars, and you had a smudge of dust on your nose and cobwebs in your hair and those bent wire-rim glasses, and I about died from how sexy you were."

"But we met at that club," Aaron said with a puzzled look. "I was staring at you for hours and trying to work up the balls to talk to you when you finally put me out of my misery and came over."

"Yeah," Ben said, "but my opening line was '*You sold me a hundred dollars' worth of glass balls I don't need, so I think you need to come over to my place and tell me what to do with them.*' Meaning we'd met already."

"That was a good line." Aaron smiled but then shook his head and admitted, "I didn't remember you, though. Glass fishing floats are popular."

"But you said, '*Oh yeah, of course I remember you*'!" Ben frowned.

Aaron flushed. "I thought it would be rude to say I didn't. And you were so gorgeous, I have no idea *why* I couldn't. I guess I get into a work zone and not much registers other than what I'm doing."

Ben sighed. This wasn't quite what he had envisioned for the beginning of their walk down memory lane, since Aaron seemed to be walking down some other lane entirely. But Ben was nothing if not adaptable, so he formulated a quick plan B and led Aaron out of the store.

"Where to now?" Aaron asked once they were in the car again.

"The club where we met, of course," Ben put air quotes on the word "met" but winked at Aaron amicably as he started the car. It took a while to get there through weekend city traffic, but they finally found the street, and Ben slowed, looking for the entrance.

"It was right between a Laundromat and a Thai place," he murmured, scanning the storefronts. "Right there. Or maybe not." Because the Laundromat and the Thai restaurant were there, but the space that had once been a slightly seedy but still happening nightclub had been transformed, with a new large plate-glass window revealing an interior very pink and very frilly and very unclublike.

"Mimi's Cupcake Boutique," Aaron read from the sign. "Huh. Well, cupcakes are big, I guess."

"Honey, cupcakes are so over," Ben said. "It's all about petits fours now. I hope Mimi has a contingency plan." He frowned and stared at the store as if he could will it to change back to what it had been. "And she's not even open, so we can't go in and reenact how we got together. *Your* version of it, anyway." He couldn't quite hide a note of reproach in his words.

"I'm really sorry, Ben," Aaron said.

"Nah, it's okay." Ben tried to regroup. "How about we head out? I've got us reservations for lunch at a place I know you'll remember." Aaron's quiet "I hope so" in response didn't sound very confident, but Ben ignored that and navigated them out of the city and northwestward. By the time they reached the coast, they were both in good spirits again. It was impossible not to be in good spirits on such a beautiful day—the kind of early-spring afternoon that felt almost like summer—brilliant blue cloudless sky and sparkling water like liquid diamonds stretching across the horizon. That is, until they pulled into the parking lot of the Bistro by the Waves.

"Hey, it's the cute little restaurant we've been meaning to get back to!" Aaron said happily. "And, uh, it looks like the entire staff is coming out to greet us."

"And all the customers too," Ben said. "Fire drill?"

As if on cue, they heard the sound of approaching sirens, and by the time they got out of the car, three fire trucks had roared up to the restaurant.

"This doesn't look good," Aaron said, and Ben had to agree as the firefighters dashed out of their vehicles and into the restaurant. A few minutes later, the owner came out looking frazzled and explained to the gathered crowd that something had gone wrong with the ventilation system, and he needed to close until it could be repaired. The boyfriends looked at each other as the couple dozen or so customers closed in around the owner, some commiserating, some griping, and by unspoken agreement hurried to their car and headed back onto the road ahead of the pack. Since the next destination Ben had planned was not too far from the restaurant, their lunch options were limited to the handful of clam shacks and fish-and-chip shops on this stretch of coast. Again, not quite what Ben had imagined when he was planning this day. But Aaron refused to be drawn into griping about plans gone awry, and it was impossible for Ben to stay annoyed when his boyfriend seemed as happy as a child on vacation.

A little while later, they were sitting on a weather-beaten deck in the warm sun, eating clam chowder and watching seagulls watch them in hopes of handouts. Ben was so used to seeing his boyfriend stressed out about school that he could barely remember a time when it wasn't Aaron's default setting. Now he smiled as he watched Aaron spoon the last of his chowder out of a Styrofoam bowl and then settle back with a contented sigh.

"You look like you don't have a care in the world," Ben told him. "It looks good on you."

"I'm as happy as a clam," Aaron said, eyes closed.

"Those clams just got eaten, you know."

"Good point," Aaron said with a mischievous grin. "So they're ahead of me. But the day is young, and I have high hopes."

It was tempting to linger, but Ben had an agenda, so after a few more minutes lounging in the sun, he announced it was time for the next stop on the itinerary and drove them a few miles farther up the coast. He pulled into the parking lot of a popular coastal trailhead, and they clambered out of the car.

"Fancy a bit of a stroll, love?" Ben asked in his best upper-class British accent.

"Aye, mate, that suits me fine," Aaron replied with an accent of his own, causing Ben to roll his eyes. "What?"

"That sounds Aussie, not British," Ben explained. "I was trying to sound like an English schoolboy seducing his sexy classmate away from his books."

"Oh," Aaron said. "I was going for Cockney."

"Close enough, I guess," Ben smirked. "Since I was going for cock."

They laughed and set off on the trail that led southward. For the first quarter mile or so, they encountered quite a few strolling tourists, but after that they had the path mostly to themselves as it narrowed and meandered through rough grass and low shrubs. They chatted as they walked, stopping often to peer over the cliffside onto rocky, driftwood-strewn beaches far below. The sea was sparkling and brilliant blue, and the air was warm with just a light salty breeze. Aaron reached for Ben's hand and held on to it even when the path occasionally narrowed so much they had to walk single file, even when a boisterous group of young men passed them from the other direction. They'd been walking for about twenty minutes when Ben finally stopped.

"Here we are," he said excitedly, leading Aaron off the path and onto a small grassy plateau that jutted out from the cliff. Near the edge was a rough wooden bench, and from its vantage point they could look down at the tiny isolated beaches on both sides as well as the breadth of the ocean as far as the eye could see. Aaron sat next to Ben and grinned.

"Beautiful," he said. "I love this place."

"Me too," Ben agreed. "And…? Do you remember why it's special?"

A bit of anxiety crept back into Aaron's eyes. "Other than that it's beautiful?" he asked.

"Yes, other than that," Ben encouraged. "I'll give you a hint. We did something for the first time here."

Aaron looked around as if hoping one of the wheeling seagulls might have the answer, but finally turned back to Ben with an apologetic shrug. "I don't know. What did we do here?"

Ben fought a twinge of disappointment but persisted. "This is where we kissed for the first time," he explained. "It was a couple of weeks after we met, and we'd been texting and talking on the phone, but my schedule was crazy, and it was hard to get together. So finally it worked out, and we had an early dinner at the bistro, and then you said there was a gorgeous place nearby where we could walk for a while. I'd never been here before, and I was thinking '*Oh my God, please don't tell me this guy I have a crush on is one of those rabid outdoorsy types who's gonna want to go hiking in the wilderness and hunting elk and fuck knows what else.*' But then you brought me here, and the sun was almost setting, and you kissed me, and I was a goner. Remember?"

Ben was relieved to see Aaron's eyes turn warm with recognition before he was pulled into one of those kisses that always stole both his breath and his senses. It was only the sound of voices from people nearing them as they walked up the trail that compelled Ben to reluctantly pull away.

"I do remember," Aaron said and then sheepishly added, "*now*. But in my defense, all our kisses are amazing, so each one is like the first time." Ben couldn't help laughing.

"Nice save," Ben said. He reminded himself of the rest of his itinerary and pulled Aaron to his feet and headed them back the way they'd come. By the time they returned to the car, the sun was setting, and the last of the light faded as Ben drove them inland.

As much as he didn't want to be disappointed, Ben found his mood sinking along with the sun as he realized the day he had planned so carefully hadn't gone anything like he had hoped. Sure, it had been nice, but he couldn't help feeling frustrated that Aaron hadn't remembered any of their relationship milestones so far. Surely Aaron would remember this next one, though.

"One last stop," Ben said as they neared the destination.

"Another test question?" Aaron asked, and Ben's hands clenched on the steering wheel.

"You know, I'm not doing this to torture you," Ben said tightly. "It's our anniversary, and I thought it would be nice to go back to some places that were meaningful, that's all. Sorry if it's been a chore for you."

Aaron sighed. "That's not what I meant."

"Then what did you mean exactly?" Ben asked.

"Never mind," Aaron said. "Let's not argue, okay? I want to see this next milestone. I love that you planned this." He reached across the console and stroked Ben's thigh consolingly, gently scratching the faded denim. Ben drove on in silence, regretting his outburst and trying to get back into a good frame of mind. By the time he pulled up at their last destination, a roadside ice-cream stand, he was able to muster a smile, which Aaron met in kind.

"Our favorite ice-cream place!" Aaron said, getting out of the car and leading the way to the order window. There were only a couple of other customers, and they drove off after they had bought their ice creams, so Ben and Aaron had the little picnic area all to themselves. They sat at one of the well-worn tables under pine trees that whispered in the cool evening breeze and savored their treats in silence for a few minutes—Ben his rocky road on a cone and Aaron his bowl of strawberry.

"You had strawberry ice cream on that day too," Ben finally said, giving Aaron a meaningful look.

"What day?" Aaron asked, and then, "Oh, the milestone day. Okay, give me a minute."

A minute went by, and then another, and Ben felt his heart sink. He thought for sure Aaron would remember this one, but he looked completely at a loss.

"Is it something about ice cream?" Aaron asked. Ben sighed and stood up, tossing the rest of his unfinished cone into the wastebasket nearby.

"Never mind," Ben said. "Come on, let's go home. I'm cold and tired."

Aaron caught up to Ben as he walked briskly to the car and put his hand on the door before Ben could open it.

"I know you're mad, but at least tell me what happened here," Aaron insisted. Ben shrugged dismissively but told him anyway.

"First time we said *I love you* to each other. June seventeenth, five years ago. Now can we go?"

Aaron dropped his hand and nodded. The drive home was silent.

"It's cold as a witch's tit in here," griped Ben as he walked into the apartment, dropping his keys on the table by the door and toeing off his shoes before making a beeline to the thermostat. "Fuck, you had to turn it all the way down to zero? It'll take forever to warm up."

"Pretty sure I only turned it to sixty-five," Aaron replied calmly, and Ben rolled his eyes as Aaron walked past him into the bedroom with his book bag. The only thing on his mind was getting warm and zoning out for a few hours. And trying not to think about how this day had turned into an unmitigated disaster. Well, maybe that was a bit overdramatic, but still. There was champagne in the refrigerator Ben had bought for the occasion, but he wasn't feeling very bubbly, and he pulled out a half-empty bottle of white wine instead. He poured himself a glass, drank half of it all at once, and took the rest of it to the living room, where he turned on the TV and curled up onto the sofa with an afghan. Ben flipped the channels listlessly, barely registering what was on the screen, not looking up when Aaron joined him on the sofa a few minutes later to interrupt his one-man pity party.

"I'll start dinner in a few. There's more wine," Ben said coolly, finding a cooking show and pausing to study the chef's onion-chopping technique.

"I'm good," Aaron replied. "But you're obviously not," he said a moment later, looking at Ben.

Ben shrugged and changed the channel again because onion guy was seriously boring. Fucking infomercials. *Click, click, click.* Nothing worth watching.

"Ben," Aaron said, "can you talk to me, please? And don't say nothing is wrong, because I've never heard you go twelve minutes without talking, but we just spent an hour in the car driving back home, and you didn't say one word."

Ben shrugged again, but Aaron was right. There were pent-up words inside him, and there was no point holding them back. He hit Mute and took a deep breath.

"I don't know what to think, Aaron. I'm confused, okay? I have all these great memories in my head of you and me, of our life for the past five years, all the things we've done together, talked about, places we've gone, great sex we've had, all of it, you know? And then we go out today, and it's like, fuck—all these memories that are important to me, that I thought were important to you—you don't even remember them."

Ben swirled the pale wine around in his glass and bit his lip. He could feel Aaron's gaze on him, but now that he was talking, he wanted to get it all out before looking at him. "And now I'm wondering, are we even on the same page? Does this"—he gestured vaguely between them—"mean as much to you as it does to me?"

When Ben finally looked at Aaron, his heart sank, because instead of responding, his boyfriend stared at him with an unreadable expression and then stood and left the room. Fuck. Was he being an idiot? Overreacting? Ben frowned. *But why shouldn't he feel like shit that the love of his life basically could barely remember the major moments in their relationship?* he thought defensively. But then Aaron was awesome in pretty much every other way, so why did it matter? Before Ben could figure this out, Aaron came back into the room and sat down again, setting a round tin container on the sofa between them. Ben looked at him, confused.

"Um, I appreciate the gesture, but I don't see how my Gramma's fruitcake is applicable to this conversation, not to mention it doesn't go that well with chardonnay," Ben remarked, trying to lighten the mood a little.

"Sorry, no fruitcake in there anymore." Aaron smiled. "It's just what I use to put some important stuff in, and I thought...." He paused, and Ben could see the effort it was taking Aaron to talk, and despite his own confused feelings, he reached out and touched Aaron's wrist.

"Thought what?"

Aaron opened his mouth, closed it again, shook his head, and glanced at Ben apologetically before taking the tin and prying off its lid.

"I'll just show you," he said, reaching in and pulling out what lay uppermost inside. It was a piece of folded paper, and Aaron handed it to Ben.

"What is this?" Ben asked, opening and smoothing it out on his lap. "Oh wait, a page from your GRE study manual?" He scanned the words and smirked. "Oh my God, analogies. How many fucking hours did we spend?" Ben read from the paper. "'Attentive is to officious as....'" He trailed off, making a face. He looked at Aaron questioningly. "I don't get it. I thought you burned this study guide after you got accepted into grad school."

"I did. But I kept a page just as a reminder," said Aaron.

"A reminder that you aced a test you were so worried about?"

"No." Aaron smiled. "That was definitely nice, but I kept it because it reminds me of how amazing you were during that time. The day after I decided to apply to grad school, you bought that book for me. And every single night, whether I wanted to or not, you'd help me study. Vocabulary words, math problems, the stupid analogies. You never for a minute let me doubt that I'd ace that exam, even though I've always been scared to death of tests. You believed in me so much that I started believing in myself."

Aaron took the page out of Ben's unresisting hand and folded it again carefully. From the tin he next removed a crayon and held it out.

"Cornflower," Ben read and waited for Aaron to explain.

"So about a month after we started seeing each other, we were talking about when we were kids, and I told you that I'd never had a sixty-four-pack of crayons. You were so horrified!" Aaron chuckled at the memory. "Right then and there, even though it was almost midnight, you got me in the car, and we drove around to three different all-night drugstores until we found one that sold the sixty-four-pack. And then we went back to your place and made art. At least, it felt like art. Probably the weed helped." He grinned wryly and then turned serious again. "But that night I realized how much you really listened to me, and how you wanted me to experience things I'd never had before. You told me that it wasn't too late to have a happy childhood. That's the night I realized what a kind person you were."

"And why cornflower?" Ben managed to ask after a moment.

Aaron took back the crayon and set it beside the folded paper. "It's the one I used for your eyes."

Ben swallowed past the sudden burn in his throat. "Aaron," he started, pushing away the afghan.

"Hold on," Aaron said. "There's a few more things." He pushed the tin toward Ben, and Ben took it and lifted out the objects one by one, holding them up so Aaron could explain.

"From that Japanese restaurant," Aaron said about a fancy paper napkin with an embossed oriental design. "The first time I tried sushi. Or should I say, the time you *made* me try sushi for the first time. And I loved it! Except for the unagi, I loved it." He grimaced. "I mean, eel? Come on. But other than that, it was great. And I loved that you pushed me out of my comfort zone and that you made me try new things. And I loved even more that you were okay even if I didn't like everything about it. It made me feel brave and safe all at the same time. I'd never felt that way before."

Ben studied the other things in the box. The key to the apartment Ben had been living in when they met, which Ben had given to Aaron even before he'd moved in. ("You trusted me, and you believed in where we were going together, even though I was so scared.") The plastic identity bracelet from the time Ben had insisted on taking Aaron to the hospital after he'd almost passed out, dehydrated and half-delirious from the flu. ("I'd never let anyone take care of me before," Aaron admitted). Five years' worth of cards from Ben—Valentine's Days, birthdays, Christmases, anniversaries. Dozens of scribbled sticky notes Ben had put inside Aaron's lunches, stuck on his laptop, tucked into his schoolbooks.

Good luck on the test.
You can do it!
Stay strong, baby.
I love you.
Love you.
I love you!!!

And finally at the bottom of the tin, a couple of crumpled boarding passes.

"From when we flew to Idaho and you met my family for the first time," Aaron said, and Ben sighed, remembering how difficult that trip had been. The uncomfortable dinners, the strained silences, the awkward introductions ("Uncle Joe, this is my boyfriend, Ben...." and watching Uncle Joe blink in confusion and walk away without a word). Ben had been so worried about Aaron, scared that the man he loved would be hurt again. He knew Aaron's family had never really accepted the fact that he was gay, and his father had been especially cruel, telling his son once that Aaron was the biggest disappointment in his life. There were no transformations during the trip: no one had a major change of heart, and there were no tearful apologies or declarations of unconditional acceptance. Each day was a quiet test of endurance, and each night Ben had left his sofa bed in the den and quietly crept into Aaron's childhood bedroom and held his boyfriend tight in his arms, telling him he was perfect and beautiful, until Aaron fell into exhausted sleep, and Ben kissed his forehead and returned to the den.

Now Aaron smoothed the boarding passes and spoke quietly.

"I needed you to see where I came from. I knew before we went on that trip that you loved me, but after… well, I knew that you totally accepted me, even though my family was a mess, and I was sort of a recovering mess. And I realized I could forgive and move on, because even though my past wasn't perfect, I had an amazing future ahead. With you."

Ben gently tugged the passes out of Aaron's hand, put them into the tin along with all the other objects, and set it on the coffee table. He moved into Aaron's space and wrapped himself around his boyfriend as tightly as he could, stroking his back, running fingers through his soft curls, feeling Aaron's body start to relax as Ben held on to him.

"I know I have a shitty memory for some things," Aaron said.

"Yeah, you really do," Ben said. "That's okay. Between me and Google alerts, we'll keep you on track. And obviously you remember the most important things."

It was nice to remember birthdays and anniversaries and first kisses. But Ben realized it was even better to be with someone who knew and treasured the best parts of him, someone who remembered what their love was all about. It was a while before Aaron spoke again, his voice muffled against Ben's neck as they held each other.

"Still, I'm sorry about the way it worked out today," he started, but Ben pulled away and shook him a little.

"Shut up," Ben said, fighting back tears. "Just shut up, okay? I've been a shitheel, and you're amazing, and I need you to kiss me right the fuck now."

And Aaron did, pulling Ben even closer and licking into his mouth, gentle at first and then building in heat, sending sparks along Ben's spine and scattering his thoughts. He gave himself over to the deliciously heady feeling of Aaron's mouth possessing his own, Aaron's hand slipping beneath his shirt and over his belly and up his chest, his thumb stroking Ben's nipple, making Ben twitch and gasp, making his bones turn liquid. Ben loved that just beneath Aaron's quiet, somewhat nerdy exterior was all this passion and heat and that Ben was lucky enough to have it all for himself.

"Tell me what you want," Aaron breathed, his lips brushing Ben's cheek, his temple, warm against his ear. Ben held on to Aaron tighter, squirming on Aaron's lap and against hardening heat, making Aaron gasp in turn.

"Surprise me," Ben said. "You know what I like."

"I do," Aaron said, unbuttoning Ben's shirt and pressing kisses along his collarbone. "For some things I have a *very* good memory."

"Mmm, you do," Ben murmured, shifting just enough to let Aaron unzip his jeans. "Gives me an idea for an anniversary theme for next year."

"I think I'll pass that one with flying colors. A year's a long time away, though...."

"Nah, just gives us time to make some more good memories," Ben said, sliding off his pants and pulling Aaron down beside him on the couch.

"Okay, I can get behind that," Aaron said.

"Well, get behind me now"—Ben smirked—"and let's get started."

LATER they opened the champagne and curled up together under the afghan.

"To five years," Aaron toasted.

"To fifty more," Ben said, clinking his glass to Aaron's.

"Wow, can you imagine how bad my memory will be in fifty years?" Aaron said.

"Yup. And I'll be right here to tell you just how terrible it is," Ben replied.

"Looking forward to it." Aaron smiled. "Cheers!"

RIVER CLAIR has been dreaming up stories her whole life and writing them down for almost as long. When she's not writing, she loves to read and travel and make up stories about the unsuspecting people she encounters. She's lived all over the US and now makes her home in the beautiful North Bay area near San Francisco.

River loves the possibility of happy endings, true love, and things that are meant to be. She is occasionally prone to bouts of cynicism, which she figures makes her nicely balanced.

River believes in the power of words, both written and spoken, to change the world. Or at least make it more enjoyable.

Twitter: @RiverClair

How to Date Your Husband

AC Valentine

HAS *your marriage fallen into the quagmire of routine? Do you make time for each other, or is your daily interaction reduced to a peck on the cheek in passing? Is your lovemaking spicy or bland? Do you wonder whatever happened to romance? We'll tell you how to bring back the magic in five easy dates.*

"You are nuts." Ryan looked at his husband in disbelief.

"No. Just hear me out." Mike's hands made a placating gesture. He wanted to calm the barrage he could hear coming. While he found Ryan ridiculously hot when he was on a tear, it was hard to get a word in edgewise.

"No, of all the crackbrained, batty, loony…." Ryan continued.

"It's just an idea," Mike protested. He watched his husband pick up the knife he had been using to chop broccoli and start waving it around. He prayed that Ryan wouldn't accidentally sever something that would require an emergency room visit. He still hadn't recovered emotionally from the big toe debacle of 2011.

"I'm not done yet…. Non compos mentis, loco and meshuggeneh…." Ryan's normally deep bass voice was starting to get comically high. His blond crew cut fairly bristled with indignation. Mike looked on in awe as his husband's fair skin, normally the color of porcelain, turned a deep, dark beet-red.

"Finished?" Mike tried to keep the laughter out of his voice. No sense in waving a red cape at two hundred pounds of compact muscle. Especially since Ryan could bench-press Mike's own slim frame easily and once in a while demonstrated that fact. That display of strength always turned Mike on, ending in some very satisfying orgasms for both of them. It was a constant source of bemusement for Mike that his bookish professor of a husband was regularly mistaken for a marine.

"Nope. Certifiable, daft and pixilated." Ryan punctuated each word with a sharp chop of the knife through the tough broccoli stems. "Now I'm finished. You may proceed," he said magnanimously.

"I'm not sure I can. Pixilated?" Mike started laughing. Ryan's tendency toward fairly florid vocabulary was one of the things that had first drawn Mike to his husband. Mike had only registered for Prose and Poetry 102 because it covered the freshman English lit requirement. He had considered dropping it, though, when he found another student staring at him during every class. The other student looked like a typical frat boy jock. Mike loathed jocks. They gave him flashbacks to the locker room taunting he experienced in high school. His father had made him try out for every team despite his protests. Once the coaches had determined why he was being bullied, they left him off the team rosters. Mike thought it was more out of worry of what putting the only openly gay student on a team would do to team cohesion than any worry about his safety or athletic ability. The distrust of athletes had lingered to the point that he got tense even passing a group of them on the quad.

So Mike had made it a point to sit as far away as possible from the muscle-bound guy in the tight T-shirts until the day Ryan had embroiled the aged professor in an argument on whether or not the poet they were discussing had been referring to male genitalia in a particular purple phrase. Ryan had been pro-penis, and the professor had been anti-penis. Mike had needed to look up the some of the words used to figure out half of what they had been saying. The next day he had made it a point to sit a seat away from Ryan and forget a pen.

"I've been dying to use pixilated." Ryan smirked. His color was slowly fading back to normal.

"You've been watching Frank Capra movies again," Mike surmised.

"Yeah, I forgot to tell you I finally got permission to teach Frank Capra and the American Ideal."

Mike rolled his eyes. Ryan often complimented them when he was in a good mood. Dark blue and surrounded by long dark-gold lashes, they were deep pools of the soul when Ryan was drunk and the devil's marbles when Ryan was pissed off. Ryan had never gotten over his affinity for poetry. It was one of the ways they were complete opposites. Mike happily geeked out over comics and worshipped at the altar of Joss Whedon, while Ryan muttered stanzas from Burns under his breath and watched obscure directors like Hal Hartley and Jim Jarmusch. Mike was pretty sure Ryan was the only one in the university's history who had gotten PhDs in both film theory and poetry.

"Yeah, I'm pretty sure Jones was not referring to Gary Cooper's face when he said you could teach that." Gary Cooper was on Ryan's list of celebrities he had Mike's permission to sleep with if the chance ever came up. Well, Gary Cooper's ghost was, anyway. The permission to sleep with celebrities on the list did not extend to necrophilia. "Anyway, as our anniversary is coming up, I thought it would be fun," he pressed.

"Fun? Following a ten-year-old advice column is fun? That column was written for women looking to beef up their relationship with the tired frat boys they married." Ryan leaned against the kitchen island. Mike appreciated the view of his husband's chest but preferred looking at his husband's backside. It seemed he didn't get to see it very often these days, as their work schedules were getting increasingly incompatible. Despite being in professions that theoretically provided for maximum schedule flexibility, they frequently could go for days without more than a grunt hello or good-bye and a quick kiss. Ryan had been on the tenure track for the last couple of years, so he had been churning out papers and going to conferences constantly. Mike had managed to find work that didn't involve actually talking to people but did involve nonstop requests for last-minute translations into the four languages he could read and write in. Once in a while they managed a morning fumble or routine blowjob, as long as neither one was stressed over a deadline.

"Hey, it was eleven years old. And it was from the year and month we met. I thought it was serendipity, meant to be, destiny." Mike was starting to feel defensive. He crossed his arms over his chest, obscuring the latest inappropriate T-shirt Ryan had bought him. It was a good thing he worked from home. He wasn't sure he was willing to be seen in public in a shirt with unicorns humping.

"First of all, no self-respecting gay man should use the word 'serendipity', especially when he's using it incorrectly." Ryan proceeded to clean up the dinner prep mess, scraping vegetable scraps into the trash.

"Don't go all college professor on me." Mike decided to try a different tack. He ducked into the pantry to grab Ryan's favorite wine and two glasses.

"Well, don't misuse words. Serendipity means a happy or fortunate accident. Kismet means fate." Ryan threw the broccoli into the roasting pan and shoved it in the oven.

"Yeah, but could you say it in German?" Mike muttered as he poured Ryan a large glass of cabernet and passed it to him. Hopefully once Ryan was a little tipsy, he'd be more open to the suggestion. Ryan took a long sip.

"So it was kismet, then," Mike finally offered, pouring himself a large glass as well. He actually didn't like cabernet, but he figured he could use the fortification.

"It's kismet that you found an advice column on spicing up a dead love life in some women's magazine that had been in the dentist's office for *eleven* years so that you could apply it to our love life?"

"Okay, fine. I just thought it would be nice to pep things up a bit." Mike pulled the salad fixings out of the fridge while Ryan started mixing up the vinaigrette.

"Pep things up? Things aren't peppy enough for you? Things looked pretty peppy when I was on my knees blowing you in the shower this morning." Ryan waved his whisk menacingly at Mike.

"It was Thursday morning," Mike pointed out.

"Your point being?" Ryan raised his right eyebrow. Mike hated that Ryan could do that and he couldn't. He had major eyebrow envy.

"You always blow me on Thursday mornings." Ryan did too. Almost every Thursday morning they had scrambled eggs, and then Ryan blew Mike in the shower before he headed out to a nine a.m. class, and Mike settled in to translate the latest content the publishing house sent him.

"Not always," Ryan objected as he carefully poured the oil into the vinegar he was whisking rapidly.

"You do when your favorite show has been on the night before," Mike pointed out.

"What does that have to do with it?" Ryan had the defensive look on his face he got every time he felt guilty about something.

"I'm getting that actor's leftover lust. Don't tell me it's me you blow every Thursday morning. Now don't get me wrong." Mike walked behind Ryan once the dressing had been safely emulsified and wrapped his arms around him. He lowered his voice to a husky growl. "I'm grateful to anything that puts you on your knees, because your mouth was made to suck cock. I'm surprised you don't have an additional PhD in cocksucking, but I'm merely pointing out we could use a little reconnection to each other in our love life." He gave Ryan a gentle squeeze before stealing a pecan from the salad.

Ryan deflated at that. "It *is* you I blow every Thursday morning," he insisted as he turned his head to look at Mike. "But okay. I have no idea how we're going to find the time for it, but okay."

"Okay?" Mike really wanted them to do this. They had fallen into a rut, whether Ryan wanted to acknowledge it or not. He wanted to feel the same flutter in his stomach he had the first time he'd realized the real reason Ryan had kept looking at him across the English classroom.

"Okay. What do you want me to do? Make a blood oath? We can date. But for the record, one of the best things about having a relationship instead of just dating is being over the awkward getting-to-know-you phase and the clumsy sex and so on."

"Okay, I don't think we have to worry about clumsy sex anymore. If it *was* ever clumsy, it was only out of inexperience. We've had lots and lots of practice since we got together, and how can we possibly be awkward with each other after all these years? C'mon, you know it'll be fun."

"You know you just jinxed us," Ryan muttered. The only reply from his husband was a snort and a wet kitchen towel thrown at his head.

THE First Date: Plan a surprise date. Pick something you have never done together. It could be fabulous or a disaster. Either you'll have a great time or a new memory to bond over.

"A revival of Puppetry of the Penis?" Ryan hissed. "Are you touched in the head? How was that not going to be awkward? We live in a university town. I work at the university. Jesus! It was a freaking fundraiser for a fraternity's charity! How on earth did you think this was a good idea?"

"Come on! I thought it would be funny!" Mike protested. "It was funny! And to be fair, I didn't realize that they used their own penises. I thought it was some sort of puppet show with fake penises or something."

"It wasn't funny. It was painful. And I'm not just talking about what we saw on stage. Do you realize that was one of my thesis students up there? I'm never going to be able to discuss film theory with him without remembering what his penis looked like." Ryan groaned.

"Really? Which one?" Both the guys had been fairly attractive. Mike wasn't sure how he felt about his husband having cute thesis students. He thought he would've gotten used to the niggling feeling that Ryan had settled for him, but he still feared Ryan would go racing off toward younger and butcher pastures if he got half a chance.

"The redhead."

"Wow. How does he even fit that snake in his pants? That boy is hung." Mike kept his voice light.

"I know. And now I will feel like a pervert because every time I see him, I'll be wondering how he fits in his pants, and how on earth did he manage to contort his frank and beans into 'The Hamburger' shape?" Ryan whined.

"I imagine a lot of stretching is involved. They were selling a guidebook on the way out. Something about the 'Art of Genital Origami'." Mike looked at the book in his hand and opened it.

"You didn't." Ryan tried to grab the book.

"I did. I can look up how he did it if you can't remember." He held the book out of Ryan's reach. It was one of the few advantages to being an inch taller than Ryan. That and being able to hide his chocolate stash more effectively.

"Why? Why would you buy that book? I'm pretty sure that even I'm not that bent. Pun intended." Ryan tried another halfhearted grab at the book.

Mike shrugged. "Souvenir. I wanted to remember this."

"Why? I think I'm mentally scarred for life!"

"Because I was with you, and we had fun, even if you were hiding behind the playbill for eighty percent of it, pretending to hate it." He tucked the book under his left arm and grabbed Ryan's hand.

"Ninety percent of it, and who was pretending?" Ryan grumbled. "Did you see 'The Bulldog'?"

Mike leaned in and gave Ryan a calming kiss on the lips. "Yes, I did. Now let's go home, and I'll comfort your penis by petting it and stroking it until it calms down from all the excitement. Either that or until it throws up." Mike sniggered.

"It's going to need a lot of petting. I swear it climbed up inside my pelvic cavity in fear." Ryan shuddered. He gripped Mike's hand tighter as they strolled home toward faculty housing.

THE *Second Date: Buy each other some new underwear. You've seen it all in this point in your relationship, so there is nothing wrong in dressing it up with something new! If he balks, remember turnaround is fair play. He gets to dress you up in what he wants to see you in, and you get to do the same to him!*

"What the hell kind of name is Ginch Gonch?" Ryan held up the package in puzzlement.

"It's a brand name. They are funny and sexy at the same time," Mike explained.

"What are you, a commercial? I need sunglasses to even look at these." Ryan peered into the package.

"Fine, then try these on." Mike passed him the next box.

"Who is Andrew Christian, and what did he do with the rest of this underwear? There is nothing to these. They're see-through. A jockstrap would provide more coverage."

"Speaking of which...." Mike tossed him the black jock he had found at the local sporting-goods store while Ryan had been picking up a new baseball bat for when he used the batting cage at the university's sports center. He could just picture Ryan's tight, muscular ass perfectly framed by the black straps.

"*No!* Just no!" Ryan caught the jock automatically and then dropped it like it was on fire.

"What's the problem? You wear one all the time when you work out," Mike pointed out.

"Jocks are not sexy. They are sweaty and gross," Ryan argued.

"According to whom? This one is nice and clean. You have three different gifts to choose from. Whichever one you choose, I'll take them off with my teeth."

"Promise?"

"Cross my heart and hope to make you come." Mike traced an X across his chest, laughing.

"Fine. Which one do you want me to wear?" Ryan said with a pout Mike couldn't wait to remove with a kiss.

"Whichever you want me to take off with my mouth first."

Ryan grabbed the obnoxiously colored Ginch Gonch pair.

"Fine. I can deal with loud and obnoxious for the sake of coverage." He noticed the print on the briefs was of a hand holding a banana over his crotch as he pulled them on. "Visual puns. You got me the underwear equivalent of your T-shirts. That's… fair," he said as Mike peered into his gift bag.

"Really? Another T-shirt?" Mike pulled out the black shirt.

"Technically, T-shirts count as underwear."

"But that's all that's in the bag. No boxers, briefs, boxer briefs, or jocks?"

"Exactly."

"You want me to wear a T-shirt? Just a T-shirt?"

"Yes. I love seeing the curve of your butt peeking out from under your shirt. I can't resist you when you look goofy and sexy at the same time. Plus easy access to your tallywacker."

"Tallywacker?"

"Bait and tackle? Twig and berries? Skin flute?" Ryan offered as alternatives.

"Sex with you is so educational." Mike laughed and finally looked at the T-shirt in his hands. "'I would bottom you so hard'?" He snorted.

"What's wrong with that? It's accurate."

"True." Mike slipped off his clothes and put on the black shirt. The hem fell just halfway down his ass. He glanced sideways at Ryan to see his reaction. Ryan looked like he was resisting the temptation to lean over and take a bite.

"How does it look?" Mike asked, slowly turning around. From the look in Ryan's eyes the swaying of Mike's cut penis hanging out from under the shirt was having a hypnotic effect on his husband.

"Like you should never leave the house again." Ryan growled.

"Like I can leave it now. Half my wardrobe consists of shirts I can't wear around anybody but you."

"My evil plan is working, then." Ryan grabbed Mike's wrist and yanked him into his lap.

"What evil plan?" Mike turned around in Ryan's lap until he was straddling him.

"The one where I give you embarrassing T-shirts and you are forced to stay home." Ryan grabbed Mike's hips.

"Your evil and diabolical plan is to keep me prisoner in my own home through the use of tasteless T-shirts?" Mike trailed his finger down Ryan's chest.

"That's step one of my plan." Ryan moved his hands to clutch the globes of Mike's ass.

"What's step two?" Mike mumbled as he mouthed at Ryan's neck.

"I make you a very happy man, so that you want to be my prisoner," Ryan whispered.

"Oh yeah? And how are you going to accomplish that?" Mike rubbed his now hard cock against Ryan's abs.

"By wearing anything you want me to. Even ridiculous see-through underwear." Ryan kissed Mike deeply in a way he hadn't in a very long time. When had Mike forgotten how good making out felt? They should do this every day and twice on Sunday.

"Promise?" Mike whispered the question before chasing Ryan's lips again.

"Promise." Ryan touched his forehead against Mike's.

"I think I could live with that."

THE Third Date: Sit down with drinks (trust me, it helps!) and write out those fantasies. All the crazy things you've wanted to do and were afraid to ask you partner to indulge. Chances are your partner will be up for some spice; whether it's cool cinnamon or habañero hot is up to you.

Mike poured them both ridiculously large glasses of wine, an almost sweet pinot gris for him and a nice rioja for Ryan, and set them on the coffee table.

"We're really going to do this?" Ryan groaned. He pulled the overly large hoodie he was wearing over his hands as he grasped the wineglass. Mike doubted it was because he was cold. It was unreasonably warm in the room thanks to their perpetually faulty thermostat.

"Yes. We are really going to do this. Are you going to be shy about it? We've been together forever. Do you really think you're going to surprise me or that I'm going to judge? We share a porn collection." Mike pulled out the notebook he always scribbled in when he was planning a project. Maybe he should have gotten another notebook for this. It would be embarrassing to pull it out at the hardware store for dimensions and have it fall open to their fantasies, which would definitely not include Marla, the seventyish woman in charge of paint.

"Hell yes, I'm going to be shy about it. Secret fantasies are supposed to be secret for a reason! I really don't want to know who you're thinking about when you're trying to get off with me or on your own unless it's me!" Ryan was now gnawing on a thumbnail, something Mike hadn't seen him do in years.

"Are you kidding?" Mike hadn't seen evidence of Ryan's jealous side like this in a very long time.

"No! Why? Do you want to picture me picturing someone else?" he asked.

"But I don't. I mean, we have the list. But I don't actually picture myself with any of them. So I don't think of Liev Schreiber doing kinky things to me in bed when I'm with you or by myself. I think of doing kinky things with you. If I'm exhausted and I need an extra boost to get over the orgasm hump, I don't go 'Oh Ryan… Gosling' and come. I think of you bending me over the bed spanking me, and I get there just fine." Mike chewed his lip, uncertain all of sudden. "Why? Do you picture someone else when you're with me? Say, an actor from a certain Wednesday night show?"

"No." Ryan paused. "No. Even when I get turned on by someone else, like when we're watching porn or something, I'm always picturing you in the moment," Ryan insisted.

"So what's the harm in swapping fantasies?" Mike tried to still his hand from tapping his pen against his notebook nervously.

"Okay. Fine—you go first."

"Will that make you feel better?" Mike asked.

"It'll give me a chance to get enough wine down so I can get through this entire conversation." Ryan gulped from his glass. Mike shoved a plate of crackers and cheese at him. Relaxed was one thing. He didn't want to be nursing Ryan through a hangover tomorrow.

"Are you blushing? The guy who had a twenty-five-minute debate over representations of male genitalia in eighteenth-century literature with Professor Finklerose?" Mike snorted.

"Yeah, well, I wasn't talking about my kinks with the love of my life."

"I should hope not. Finklerose was pushing eighty, and I'm pretty sure he was straight from all the harping he did on representations of female attributes in the same literature." Mike ignored his own wine in favor of teasing Ryan and watching that blush turn darker.

"As I said before, you first," Ryan gritted out between his teeth.

"Fine." Mike took a calming breath. "Spanking."

"Excuse me?" Ryan choked on his wine.

"I know it's relatively tame, but I wasn't being rhetorical when I mentioned it earlier. I. Want. You. To. Spank. Me."

"That's it? That's your deepest, darkest fantasy? A little light S and M?"

"Light, yes. I'm not ready to go visit a dungeon or something. However, I want to be punished for something." Mike grinned at Ryan's muffled groan. "I take it that's a yes?"

Ryan swallowed. "I think I can work with that. In fact, it might dovetail rather nicely with my own… um… fantasy."

"Which is…?"

Ryan took another gulp of the wine. "I want you to be my naughty TA who needs a big favor from me," he muttered.

"Say that again."

"You heard me the first time. And this *cannot* get out. So don't even think of gossiping about it with the other spouses at the next faculty dinner."

"I wouldn't," Mike objected.

"You would. I couldn't look Melanie's husband in the face for months after you guys compared notes on sexual positions."

"I mean I wouldn't gossip about *that*. I mean, thank God your teaching assistants tend to be women, since yeah, I guess that wouldn't do your reputation much good, at least not with the staff. Also, I'm not sure I want you to have a line of cute film grad students hoping you request them as your assistant next year."

Ryan's look turned speculative as he gazed at Mike. His voice got harsh.

"I think I might use you as my TA for next year again. But I'll need some convincing first. Especially since you haven't finished grading those papers for the freshman class yet." Ryan looked stern and forbidding.

Mike could feel his skin flush hotly. In a flash he schooled his face to look contrite and sheepish.

"I'm sorry, Professor Ivers. It won't happen again. I'll finish them first thing in the morning," he apologized.

"That's not good enough. I think you need to show me how sorry you actually are." Ryan's voice was quiet but threatening.

"How can I do that... sir?" Mike came over and knelt by Ryan's side and tentatively placed his hand on the loose sweats covering the other man's muscled thigh. They weren't really dressed for this scenario, but being in comfortable yet easily removed clothing did have its benefits.

"Use that mouth for something other than excuses. I need something hard to punish you with," Ryan demanded.

"But Professor—"

"I said no excuses." Ryan's voice came out as a raspy whisper. He grasped Mike's face with one hand. The bruising grip made Mike's breath hitch and his cock start to thicken. "Unless you want everyone to know what an incompetent excuse for an assistant you are, you will not say a word. Do you understand?" Mike nodded. "Use your mouth properly." Mike shuffled on his knees until he was between Ryan's legs. He reached up to pull down the waistband of Ryan's sweats. "I said use your mouth!" Ryan swatted away Mike's hands. Mike clasped his hands behind him so he wouldn't be tempted to use them. He gripped one end of the drawstring tie with his mouth and pulled slowly until the bow unraveled. He then gripped the remaining slack tie in his mouth and pulled until nothing held up the pants except Ryan's hip bones. Mike licked at the sparse treasure trail with his tongue until he reached the top of the pants and bit down on them and pulled. Ryan sucked in his breath as his husband's cheek brushed against his burgeoning cock. He raised his hips to make Mike's task easier, and the pants fell to Ryan's knees.

"Keep going," Ryan urged.

Mike buried his head in the crease of Ryan's thigh. He loved the smell. Just a whiff of musky maleness worked better than an hour of porn to spike his arousal. He tilted his head and rested it on a trembling thigh that indicated that Ryan was just as turned on. He took a tentative lap at the slowly engorging muscle in front of him, wondering if he should act reluctant or enthusiastic. He pretended to hesitate, only to have Ryan egg him on.

"You can do better than that."

Mike licked the underside before surrounding the head with his mouth. God, he loved Ryan's salty-bitter taste. He sucked at the end before taking a deep breath and plunging down on Ryan's length as far as he could without choking on it. He sucked hard as he withdrew before doing it again, encouraged by Ryan's stifled groans. He could feel his own cock getting painfully hard. He loved sucking Ryan. He had never done this with anyone before Ryan, so he didn't know if he would have enjoyed it as much with other men. But the smell and taste of Ryan made him hard and leaking faster than he thought was possible. Mike could feel Ryan tensing up and pulled off. He didn't want the game to end prematurely. He looked up at "Professor Ivers" and very deliberately licked his swollen lips.

"Pull down your jeans and bend over the desk." Ryan's hands were gripping the couch cushions so hard his knuckles were white. Mike hurried to comply. He yanked down his jeans and bent over the desk, placing his elbows square on the surface.

"Pick up that pen and check those papers for grammatical mistakes. You obviously can't be trusted to grade them," Ryan instructed him.

Mike looked down at the stack of papers on the desk. Oh, this was either going to be very good, or very bad for the students if he actually tried to correct them. "I'm going to punish you for being so slow to finish your work. If you take your punishment satisfactorily. I will let you come... back next year. Now, what do you think would be an appropriate number?"

"Number, sir?"

"Number of smacks to demonstrate your contrition. Think carefully. Too few, and you won't convince me that you are truly sorry."

Mike swallowed. His breath was getting shallow from his arousal. Why hadn't they tried this before? He gulped for air before requesting, "Ten, sir." He paused. "Please." The plea in his voice was obvious even to his ears.

"All right. If you don't take your punishment, you won't get the TA position, and you will fail to get a recommendation. If at any point you feel that the task is too great for you, all you have to say is 'fail', and I'll stop immediately. However, I'm not entirely unsympathetic to the challenge facing you. If you need a minute to collect yourself, just put the pen down, and we will pause. Do you understand?"

Mike had dreamed of Ryan putting him over the desk like this but had been too embarrassed to ask. He had been so inexperienced when they had gotten together, and this fantasy, while relatively harmless, had seemed too dirty to suggest. He had to bite down on the inside of his lip to stop from coming at the mere thought that Ryan was actually dominating him.

"Yes, professor."

"Pull down your underwear. I won't be able to tell if you've been adequately punished if I can't see how your skin reacts."

Mike placed his cheek against the pile of papers and reached back to hook his thumbs in the waistband of his boxer briefs to pull them down. The action exposed his golden skin to Ryan's avid gaze.

Ryan ran his hand reverently across the soft globes before raising his hand quickly and smacking it abruptly across the right cheek.

"One," he counted. "Now start marking those papers," he demanded.

Mike picked up the red pen and desperately tried to focus on the task instead of the jolt of lust he felt at the afterburn of the strike flooding across his ass. He wasn't at all confident he could even start the task he was given when his cock was drooling precome at an alarming rate. He tried to read the title of the top paper. "Slashing the Superhero: Homoerotic Subtext in Comic Book Cinema." Mike was supposed to grammar-check a paper on homoerotic imagery in the Avenger films? This had to be the seventh circle of hell. He could tell because his body was on fire.

"Two." Smack. This time it was the other cheek. "If you don't finish at least one paper, I won't be able to show you how much you pleased me."

Mike frantically started to look for typos. The student with a gender-neutral name had obviously used Internet fan sites for most of his or her research. They had misspelled Asgard in at least three places to amusing if unfortunate results. He couldn't help giggling, momentarily distracted by the inadvertent pun.

"Focus!" Ryan demanded. "Three. Four. Five." Mike gasped at the flare of pain. "I think you need to work on how to act properly contrite."

"Yes, Professor Ivers. Sorry, Professor Ivers." Mike quickly corrected the typos.

"We can stop this anytime. Just say the word 'fail'." Ryan rubbed his hand over Mike's ass in a soothing manner.

"Please, sir. I will do anything to get another year assisting you," Mike pleaded, his mind firmly back on the scenario.

"Six." All the blood left Mike's brain in a frantic effort to get to his lower regions, and his handwriting's legibility dramatically decreased.

"Seven." Ryan's breath sounded rough and uneven. "Your ass looks good with my handprints on it."

"More, please...." Mike's voice cracked.

"Eight, nine, ten." Ryan quickly smacked Mike's globes three more times before he lunged for the desk drawer where they kept lube in case they ever decided to have sex in the living room. He struggled with the cap; they had never even broken the safety seal. He frantically slathered lube on himself.

"Will you prove to me that you will assist me in anything I ask?" Ryan asked.

"God. Yes. Whatever you need. I swear." Mike tried to focus on anything that would prevent himself from coming.

"Even if I need someone to see to my *every* need." Ryan ran his lubed finger around the edge of Mike's ring before pushing in.

"Use me as you see fit. I will do anything you require," Mike begged.

"Anything?" Ryan's voice was rough as he quickly thrust another finger inside the first. Mike started gibbering nonsense.

"Please, fuck me, Professor. Use me. Anything."

Ryan couldn't wait any longer. He thrust into Mike in one long push. Mike didn't stop pleading. "More. Harder. Come on. Punish me." Ryan pistoned his hips, slamming against Mike's body even as it thrust back to meet his.

"Oh fuck!" Mike groaned.

Mike looked down in amazement to see spurts of creamy white spunk hit the front of the desk and the floor despite the fact he hadn't touched his cock. In the next moment, Ryan hurtled over the edge too.

"I didn't even touch you!" He panted against Mike's back.

"Did I get the job?" Mike asked as he laughed. His arms trembled with the weight of holding them both up.

"Um… yes?" Ryan's laughter joined Mike as he pulled him up off the desk and turned Mike's head sideways for a kiss. "The pay's lousy, but the benefits are pretty good." He paused as he ran his hand up and under Mike's shirt. "And I'll write you one hell of a recommendation."

THE Fourth Date: Have a game night. Make sure there are forfeits. Clothing? Kisses? That way no one loses and everyone wins.

"Monopoly?" Mike held up the board game.

"Too long, and you always win," Ryan complained.

"So? Is it my fault that I'm good with money?"

"So this is supposed to be an everyone-wins scenario. Trivial Pursuit," Ryan countered.

"*You* always win."

"I don't."

"You do, and if you don't, you grouch about it for the rest of the day. I never thought of Trivial Pursuit as a blood sport until I met you." Mike ducked to avoid the pillow Ryan tossed at his head.

"Well, it could be fun. For every question you get wrong, you have to remove an item of clothing or perform a sexual act." Ryan pondered.

"That has potential, even if I'll be completely naked or on my knees in about five rounds," Mike said, "but I want to play Truth or Dare."

"Really? Don't you think we're a little too old for that?" Ryan rolled his eyes before flopping back on the couch.

"And we're not too old for board games?" Mike sat on the other end of the couch and pulled Ryan's feet into his lap. He absentmindedly started massaging them.

"Board games require skill and strategy. Truth or Dare is what kids play at high school parties along with Spin the Bottle and Seven Minutes in Heaven."

"Both excellent suggestions, but there are only the two of us, and we have issues if it only takes us seven minutes." Mike waggled his eyebrows. He might have single-eyebrow envy, but he could do the Groucho Marx waggle with the best of them.

"Why Truth or Dare?"

"It's a getting-to-know-you game."

"We know each other. Biblically, even." Ryan laughed.

"Ha! Until a couple of days ago, you didn't know I got off on being spanked, and I didn't know that you got off on dominating. So I think we have new areas to explore. Consider it a getting-to-know-each-other-*better* game." Mike moved on to massage Ryan's calves. Ryan gave an appreciative grunt.

"Can you even play just with two people?" Mike shot Ryan an irritated look. "Fine. I'll be good."

"Being good is not the point of the game. Being honest is." Mike dropped Ryan's legs and angled himself so he could look Ryan square in the face.

"Fine. I'll be honest, then. But I think you're missing out. 'When I'm good, I'm very good.'" Ryan leered at Mike.

"Don't quote Mae West to me. I audited your Sex and Sexuality in Early Twentieth Century Film class. I know you left off the rest of that quote."

"'But when I'm bad, I'm better'? You know that's true." He teased. "Okay. I'll play." He added almost sullenly, "As long as you go first. Truth or dare?"

"Truth," Mike said unhesitatingly.

"Damn, I was hoping you'd say dare. I've got a long list of requests, now that we've discovered your hidden propensity toward kink."

"Too bad. This is supposed to be about us reconnecting more than just our dicks. Truth."

Ryan got very quiet. "Why did you pick me?"

"Pick you for what?" Mike asked, honestly confused.

"Pick me to be your first. You could have had anyone. Seriously." Ryan nudged Mike's leg with his foot.

"What are you talking about? I couldn't get a date to save my life. I couldn't even start a conversation," Mike protested.

"Only because you didn't try. I could name six people in our class, including me, who would have gone out with you in a heartbeat. But nobody could get a read on you. It's like they weren't even there."

"That's not true."

"Yes it is," Ryan insisted. "And if you truly were that clueless, why did you choose me? Is it because you thought I was your only option? Did you choose me out of some misguided and idiotic belief that I was the only one who would have you?"

"No, I chose you because I fell in love with you. You realize you quoted me poetry? You were the biggest nerd on the planet, and I loved it. I felt like you saw me. I felt invisible all the time. I wanted to be invisible. In my life I had learned that being invisible was essential to my survival, and then you came along and saw me despite my best efforts. You were this big, strong dork who quoted poetry and looked at me like I hung the moon, and you didn't give a crap that I was about as sexually experienced as a starfish."

"A starfish?"

"They don't need to have sex to reproduce," Mike explained.

"But they can," Ryan tried to clarify.

"What? Have sex?"

"Yes."

"Yes, sort of, to reproduce. I don't actually look at nature porn. Aren't we off the topic?" Mike wouldn't put it past Ryan to try to derail the dating assignment.

"You were the one who brought up the sex life of the starfish. And aren't they called sea stars now?"

"See? You are the biggest dork ever."

"Hey, you're the one who knows the sexual habits of sea stars."

"Your turn. Truth or dare?"

"Truth," Ryan said cautiously.

"What did you first notice about me?" Mike had always wondered why Ryan had hit on him in the first place.

"Your T-shirt."

"My T-shirt?" Mike hadn't expected that response.

"Why do you always repeat my answers? Yes, I noticed your T-shirt. It was red and said 'Have you hugged my T-shirt today?' And I thought to myself, I haven't hugged that T-shirt, and I really, really want to. Plus it was so at odds with *you*."

"What do you mean?" Mike asked, not sure he really wanted to know.

"I watched you after that first day. You were so quiet. You didn't speak up in class, but I could tell just by watching your facial expressions when you agreed with a point and when you thought the person speaking was a complete idiot. I spent half the class watching you."

"I noticed. I thought you were plotting to beat the crap out of me. You had this permanently pissed-off look on your face."

"I was plotting how to ask you out. I wasn't even sure if you batted for my team, and I was upset that the semester was halfway over and I couldn't even find someone in the class who knew you enough to tell me if you were straight or not. I kept trying to get your attention, and then one day out of the blue, you sat next to me and asked me for a pen."

"Smooth, huh?"

"You forget, I had been watching you for half a semester. You always had, like, ten pens tucked in the front pocket of your messenger bag. I was the smooth one," Ryan claimed.

"Saying 'Here, let me test it out first' and writing your name and phone number on my notebook was smooth?"

"You know it was." Ryan grinned. "Your turn. Truth or dare."

"Dare." Mike smirked.

"What happened to getting to know each other better?"

"I want to know more about this kinky request list. Can I add to it?"

"Sure." Ryan pulled out a piece of paper from the back pocket of his jeans.

"You actually have a list? Give that to me." Mike grabbed it from Ryan and started to scan it. "Role-playing? A certain blond vampire? Yes, please. Playing doctor. Wait.... A real doctor or, like, Doctor Who?" Mike asked, his nose crinkling in confusion.

"You are such a geek. I love you." Ryan shifted position so he could crawl over to Mike and steal a kiss.

"Hmmph. I love you too. Now can we talk about the role-playing?"

THE Final Date: Go on your first date again. If you followed our plan, you've reignited the fire in the bedroom. But recreating your first date can remind you why you fell in love with this person in the first place, and isn't the fire in your heart the reason you married them?

Mike thought a lot about the final assignment to recreate the first date. He remembered the amount of angst he had suffered over the thought of asking out Ryan the first time around. Back then, he may even have downed more than his prescribed dosage of antianxiety meds that week trying to decide whether to call Ryan or not. Was he really the focus of some hot jock's attention? Ryan *had* been hitting on him, right? He'd never even been on a date before. He was socially incompetent. He had come out of the closet in the fifth grade, not out of any bravery or social statement, but out of a lack of social filter. Apparently when asked who you thought was cute at your first boy/girl party, you were not supposed to actually be truthful and blurt out the same name all the girls had said. He had spent the next seven years actively keeping his mouth shut in any social situation so he wouldn't inadvertently blurt out something else that would cause any attention to be drawn to him.

He had never told Ryan, even after all these years, the reason he had worn funny T-shirts that first semester. They were his lame attempt to initiate some sort of conversation with people that didn't involve him actually opening his mouth first. And it worked. People came up to him and tried to make conversation, but he usually blurted out the first thing that came to mind, and their faces would freeze in polite grimaces, and they'd find somewhere else to sit the next class. When Ryan started the conversation about the stanza he thought was blatantly referring to the "male member," Mike had been silently cheering him on. He agreed with Ryan but would never have the balls to say so to a teacher who so staunchly maintained the interpretation wasn't valid. When Ryan then pointed out that if you did think the interpretation was valid, the poem took on homoerotic overtones, Mike's stomach got queasy with fear for Ryan and shame at his own silence. He agreed with Ryan, and nobody else in the classroom weighed in on the argument, either through not caring or for fear of ticking off the teacher and jeopardizing their grade. He always felt he should have spoken up to defend Ryan's interpretation. Mike had also been struck by the homoeroticism of the poem. It made him want someone to see him in that light instead of the awkward, lanky mess of fey geekiness he was. It was an odd feeling of hope that made him take the leap to actually make the first move to get to know Ryan. The fact that his first lame volley was so easily and effortlessly batted back into his court left him at a loss for a next move.

Mike made it to Friday without knowing how to proceed. After three days of internal debate, Mike made the momentous decision just to drown the fuck out of the voices in his head in with a Xanax chased by neon-colored cocktails at Hart's End, the only gay club in the nearest city. He flailed around the dance floor, heading back to the bar every time he felt self-conscious. On the third trip back, he stumbled into a very broad chest and felt hands steadying him. He looked down to see the guy from his English class looking up at him.

"You!" he accused.

"Me," Ryan agreed.

"You—you go to MIU!" Mike was pissed off. He had gone out tonight to forget this guy.

"Yes, I do."

"You're in my poetry class."

"Yes." Ryan smiled.

"You're gay."

"Yes. And apparently so are you." Ryan's smile got even broader.

"Will you go out with me?" Mike managed to say without slurring a single word. There, that would show him. He had given him his number, after all.

"You're asking me now?" Ryan shouted to be heard over the music.

"Yes, now. Tomorrow I'll be sober and won't have the guts to call you. Because you have muscles." Mike drew his hand down the side of Ryan's biceps. Yep. Those were definitely muscles.

"You like my muscles," Ryan said confidently. "Don't you?"

Mike shook his head. "I like your brains. You were right!" he shouted while managing to spill the last of his cocktail.

"Right about what?" Ryan looked puzzled.

"The poem. In class. About the penis." Mike ignored the startled stare of the bartender who was cleaning up the remains of Mike's drink. "The poet totally wanted to do his friend. So, will you?"

"What? Go out with you?"

"Yes. Because I really, really like your brain. And you know… your face. I would really, really like to kiss your face." Mike leaned in before he realized they were still standing in the bar. "There are too many people in here. I'm shy."

"I can tell. Want to come back to my place?" Ryan offered.

"Are you going to take advantage of me?" Mike purred.

"Not until you sober up some," Ryan said gently.

"Bad idea."

"Taking advantage of you?"

"Probably. Don't have much experience. But it's kind of like a job," Mike said gloomily.

"I don't follow."

"Can't get a job without experience. But can't get experience without a job. It's the same with sex. Nobody wants anyone who doesn't know anything about sex. But can't get sex without…. What was I saying?" He stumbled a little.

Ryan put his arm around Mike's waist. Mike thought he had never felt anything so good. People didn't touch him. He really liked being touched.

"C'mon. Let me get you back to my place. Your virtue is safe with me," Ryan promised.

"Damn. I was really, really hoping to get laid before I died," Mike confessed.

"Do you have a disease that will suddenly kill you in the next twenty-four hours?" Ryan asked as he steadied Mike to lead him out of the bar.

"No."

"Then don't worry about it."

"I could have an aneurysm. Or you could be a vampire. You're not a vampire, are you?" Mike stopped short at that thought.

"How much have you had to drink?"

"Lots," Mike said abashedly.

They walked back to Ryan's place, where Ryan gave him two Tylenol and kept feeding him water. They talked for hours about random things in their lives. Mike's nonexistent filter combined with alcohol led to several embarrassing confessions. Much to his relief, Ryan didn't seem fazed by any of them and even offered some of his own.

Ryan suggested they curl up in bed with clothes on once he noticed Mike was starting to doze off. As they lay there, drifting to sleep, Ryan whispered to him while stroking his face.

"I'm nobody! Who are you? Are you nobody too?"

"That's sweet. Who wrote that?" Mike murmured the question back.

"Emily Dickinson. The second stanza is cool too. But it involves frogs." Ryan sighed. Mike tried to answer, but he couldn't, as he was sliding into sleep.

The next morning Mike awoke to a brush of lips across his forehead.

"Hey, wake up." Ryan gently shook him.

Mike groaned.

"Hangover?"

"No. Just embarrassed."

"Why?"

"Did I confess to both my virginity and the fact that I first masturbated to covers of old Doc Savage novels last night?" Mike mumbled into the pillow.

"Yep." Ryan smiled.

"Yeah. I'm going to just… go." Mike rolled to get off the bed.

"No. Nope. Not going anywhere." Ryan grasped his arm and rolled him back.

"Why not?"

"Because I promised to do this when you were finally sober." Ryan grasped Mike's head in his two hands and kissed him. Mike finally realized what all the fuss was about two seconds before he realized he hadn't brushed his teeth, and it felt like two cotton balls had bred six more in his mouth overnight.

"Stop." He gasped when they came up for air.

"Why?"

"I need to brush my teeth." He started to get up.

"Later." Ryan hauled him back to the bed.

"But."

"Later…."

They wound up slotted against each other, still in the clothes they had worn the night before. Mike relished the feel of Ryan on top of him grinding down as they exchanged kisses until morning breath wasn't a problem and the wet spots leaking through their pants were.

Mike got up to remove his pants and brushed his teeth while Ryan looked for a pair of pants that would fit him. When he came out, he saw Ryan staring at him.

"What? Do I have toothpaste on my face?" He wiped at his mouth with the back of his hand.

"No. It's nothing. Here." Ryan handed him a pair of black sweatpants. "So what do you want to do this afternoon?"

"You want to see me again?"

"Yes, I want to see you again. Did you think I just wanted sex?" Ryan looked hurt.

"Holy shit. That counted as sex?" Mike said wonderingly. Did that mean he was finally devirginized?

"Yes, it counted. Is that all you wanted? You said you liked my brain last night.... I thought...." Ryan sounded uncertain.

"Yes, I do. I definitely like your brain. And the sex. So, afternoon. Yes." Mike pulled on Ryan's sweatpants, which were a little short but otherwise covered him. "What would you like to do?" he asked.

"Take a hike," Ryan said.

"Okay. I'm confused, but okay." Mike started to look for his wallet so he could leave.

"No, I mean go for a hike. With you," Ryan explained patiently.

"Are you sure? I'm not particularly athletic." Mike flexed his nonexistent muscles and was rewarded with laughter from Ryan.

"It's an easy hike. It's just around the lake."

"Wait. How many times?"

"Does it matter?"

"Yes it matters." Mike exhaled impatiently.

"Why? It's not a particularly long hike. It's like half a mile or something."

"Don't you know? It's campus legend that if you walk three times around the lake, it means you're going to get married to the person you're walking around the lake with." Mike hoped the panic in his voice wasn't as obvious as it sounded to him. Ryan came up to him and petted the sides of his waist. He kissed Mike before answering.

"Stop panicking. Gay marriage isn't legal. I mean, I guess we could move to Vermont. They have civil unions."

"That's the part you're focusing on?" He had the sneaking suspicion that dating Ryan was going to kill him.

"Yes. C'mon. Let me feed you, and then we'll go for a hike." Ryan reached out and grabbed Mike's shirt and pulled him in for another kiss.

ELEVEN years later, Mike wasn't sure how the hell to recreate their first date or even what counted as their first date. He finally consulted Ryan, who was sitting at the desk. He still couldn't look at the desk without getting partially aroused.

"We didn't have a first date." Ryan looked up at him, surprise written all over his face.

"What do you mean, we didn't have a first date?" He thought they were done with Ryan not cooperating with the dating project. He had found Ryan quite enjoyed… cooperating.

"I mean, we didn't have a first date. I ran into you at the bar, and I took you home. We never called anything a date. I mean, you technically asked me out the first night, but we never really did the dating thing. We just were," Ryan said steadily.

"Were what?"

"We were us. We were just together. Even before we could actually legally get married, we acted married. You moved in a week later, remember? So we can't recreate the first date, because we never went on one." Ryan sighed and tossed his pen onto the desk. Mike processed this.

"Ryan?" he asked tentatively, "will you go out on a date with me?"

"I'd thought you'd never ask…." Ryan's face lit up as he added, "Again."

AC VALENTINE is a New Yorker who recently traded her quiet bohemian life in the Village for the wild metropolis of Vermont. She dragged with her a tattooed corporate husband, a small child, a neurotic dog, and several libraries worth of books. She can't clean or cook but can throw a mean party. She can always be found bemoaning the lack of a day job while happily reading or writing m/m fiction or fiddling around with some craft project to add to the pile that is threatening to take over the dining room. She believes in true love, marriage equality, and happily-ever-afters. She'll continue to write about them until someone pulls her laptop away from her cold dead hands.

She would love to hear from readers and can be contacted at acvalentineauthor@gmail.com.

More romantic anthologies from DREAMSPINNER PRESS

http://www.dreamspinnerpress.com

Coming in October 2013 from
DREAMSPINNER PRESS

http://www.dreamspinnerpress.com

CPSIA information can be obtained at www.ICGtesting.com
Printed in the USA
LVOW13s1147070813

346331LV00003B/9/P